Ambrose, Prince of Wessex; Trader of Kiev.

By Bruce Corbett

ISBN: 978-0-9879247-9-7

DEDICATION

To the light of my life, Cynthia.

CONTENTS

Author's Note	VII
1 The Vikings!	1
2 Phillip Carries Ambrose, and They Reach the Ships.	8
3 The Ship!	13
4 Ambrose and Phillip Help to Fight the Savage Storm.	18
5 A Frisian Port is Reached.	22
6 Polonius and the Land of the Danes.	28
7 Ambrose Works Hard, and Learns to Make Love.	43
8 Phillip has Cruel Masters.	56
9 The Flight.	64
10 They Sail North and East.	72
11 They Reach Land.	77
12 Gunnar of the Rus.	82
13 Gunnar Hears their Story.	93
14 They Make the Ship.	102
15 They Reach the Gathering Place.	106
16 They Arrive at Novgorod.	114
17 They Establish a Trading Post	118
18 A Rus is Killed, and Bothi Retaliates.	123
19 Bothi's Warriors Have a Victory Celebration.	129
20 Winter Sets in.	133
21 An Expedition to Kiev.	139
22 The Khazars.	149
23 The Island.	156
24 Attack!	162
25 The Expedition Reaches Kiev.	168
26 The Pechenegs Arrive!	177
27 Kiev is Besieged.	188
28 Battle!	197
29 The Varangians Fight at the Ford.	210
30 Kuralla.	218
Appendix I: Characters.	223
Appendix II: Glossary	227
Appendix III: History of Russia and Wessex in the ...	232
Appendix IV: Map of Ambrose's Travels.	245
V About the Author.	246
VI Other Fiction Books Coming from the Author.	247

AUTHOR'S NOTE

You are about to read a fictional story set in an era several centuries after the fall of the Western Roman Empire; circa 859 A.D. Ambrose, Prince of Wessex; Trader of Kiev is the first novel of a series. It is a work of fiction, and I freely admit that when I was unable to discover the true facts, or when there was a conflict of opinion between scholars, I did not hesitate to use my literary license to invent facts that would best fit my story. The truth is, however, that most of my story is based on historical facts.

The Angles, Saxons and Jutes were already involved in the first skirmishes of a quickly escalating struggle with Danish Vikings, though the major invasion of the Danish 'Great Army' was actually some five years in the future. The slave-trading port of Wyk te Duurstede did exist. The Rus, or some other Viking tribe, probably living in what is presently Sweden, really did travel the Russian rivers in their boats; even navigating as far as the Black and Caspian Sea. The trade to *Constantinople* is well documented. A Rus chief apparently was invited to *Novgorod* to help the native rulers.

There is considerable debate as to who actually founded Kiev, but it appears clear that Viking tribesmen were involved at some stage. The Khazars did control the mouths of several major rivers emptying into the Black Sea, and they fought off other marauding nomads who traveled the vast open steppes.

The Viking funeral is based on descriptions by contemporaries
of the time. Many towns along the rivers of what is now Russia
and the Ukraine were attacked by nomad raiders from the
steppes, and this, in fact, continued for several more centuries.
There was a documented attack on Kiev by the Pechenegs
some twenty years after the date the Russian Chronicles tell us
that Dir and Askold arrived in Kiev.

Ambrose clearly did not exist, nor Polonius, yet they may have.
This was a time of great turmoil and change in the world. The
travels they made in this book are at least plausible. First and
foremost, however, this is a novel. I hope you enjoy it.

**Nb. Italicized words are in the glossary
(Appendix II) at the end of the story.**

CHAPTER 1

The Vikings!

As the first rays of sun pierced the fading night, the throbbing note of a Saxon war-horn echoed through the little village. The sound swelled and then suddenly stopped. Roused by the eerie sound, several village dogs responded with a chorus of barks and yips.

Ambrose, young *atheling* of Wessex, raised his blond head from his sleeping pallet. His protector, Phillip, weapons--master to a king, was listening intently.

"Phillip, what is it? What is happening?"

"Sleep, Prince. I will investigate. It is probably nothing, but something has roused the dogs, and that worries me."

As Phillip spoke, he threw off his deerskin cover and stood naked.

Ambrose noticed the grizzled warrior did not seem to feel the cold. He reached for the broadsword that the big man had used all his life to protect three successive kings, the same one his father had wielded before him. With the famed blade in his hand, the giant warrior stumbled through the doorway of the sturdy residence. Ambrose, wrapped in a deerskin, strode close behind.

The mystery of the blaring horn was quickly solved. The sentry in the watch tower over the main gate lay crumpled over the log wall of his post. His long signal horn lay on the ground below. The distance to the gate was considerable and the light still poor, but Ambrose could see what appeared to be a javelin protruding from the man's chest.

Even as Ambrose and Phillip stared, a motley horde of raiders poured through the open gate. Almost simultaneously, Ambrose's peripheral vision caught more motion at the other end of the village. He turned his head in time to see a second group burst through the much narrower harbor gate. Ambrose realized instantly that the sturdy log walls of the village had suddenly become a potential death trap.

"Sweet merciful Jesus!' Phillip muttered. 'The pagan devils are amongst God's sheep, and the sleepy sentries did not even buy us enough time to get the villagers up and prepared."

Ambrose stared at the hut where an even dozen of the king's own

Personal Guard slept, not twenty paces away!

"Phillip, my brother's Personal Guardsmen . . ."

"Nay, back you go, Prince. If you value your life, you will return to your lodging and bar the door! He raised his voice in sudden anger.

"Aldrich! Eadward! Wake up and get the king's *thanes* out here! Satan's devils are amongst us, and it is past time to show the heathen bastards some good Saxon steel!"

The dogs' noise turned to a shriller barking, and then a frenzied yapping as they charged at the strangers. The business end of axes and spears greeted the boldest, and suddenly there was no barrier at all between the Viking attackers and the villagers.

Ambrose heard muffled noises from the huts where his escort was quartered, but he feared that it was already too late for any systematic defense. Phillip would need more men and the few he had, had had more than their fair share of mead the night before.

The attackers, now safely through both gates and aware that they had lost the element of surprise, broke forth into battle cries. Their wild cries of "*Odin*! Odin!" woke any villagers who had not already been roused by the growing din.

As the mob of cloaked warriors fanned out in disciplined teams, Ambrose knew with a sinking certainty that the worst nightmares of Christian Wessex were being realized. These pirate raiders, the dreaded sea-Vikings, scourge of all civilized Europe, must have slipped past the shepherd sentries on the lower Meon River. The bastards had somehow managed a secret landing!

Moving efficiently in multiple pairs, the raiders swiftly moved to each hut, charged in, and cut down anyone who was armed or dared resist. Phillip spoke quietly to his young charge.

"Now, Prince! Inside and shut the God-cursed door!"

Ambrose retreated to the residence, but kept the door open a crack and watched his protector standing before an even dozen pair of barbarians moving toward him at a run.

Phillip yelled again for his men. Even Ambrose could see that they had only seconds left to form a defensive line. "Get out here, you lazy bastards! I have work for you!"

The running line of pagan warriors closed the distance quickly, however, even as the first of Phillip's men stumbled out into the soft morning light. The befuddled warriors stepped into the light, only to be struck down by a fusillade of javelins. The three nearest Vikings, having already thrown their spears at the groggy guardsmen, drew swords or axes and slowly sidled towards Phillip.

The attackers saw Phillip's giant sword and realized that few men living could effectively use such a massive weapon. The naked man holding it, however, twirled it with contemptuous ease while he awaited their arrival.

Buckler held high, the first Viking came within reach and swung his axe at Phillip. The Saxon warrior parried the blow skillfully and retaliated with a fast low swing of his long sword. Not expecting anyone to be able to swing such a huge weapon with such speed, the warrior was unable to lower his shield in time. The massive blade of polished iron hit the lower corner of the attacker's buckler with tremendous force and glanced off it on to the man's legs.

The powerful stroke, even slowed, almost cut entirely through the man's right leg. With a look of stunned disbelief, the Viking crumpled to the ground.

Ambrose watched Phillip turn toward the other two. They seemed to show a sudden respect for their Saxon foe. Calling a companion to join them, they formed a loose line and spread out, hoping to trap Phillip against the hut wall. Without their spears, they would have to close on him if they wanted to get him.

Two axes and a sword rose in unison, and Ambrose bit his knuckle in fear for the giant protector. Sighing, Phillip started his huge sword swinging in glittering arcs that threatened death or mutilation to anyone foolish enough to enter its reach. The defense was effective against any single foe, but it could not provide adequate protection on three exposed sides indefinitely. With precision born of obvious experience, the Viking directly in front of Phillip tentatively engaged him, while the other two edged in on either side.

Phillip's powerful vertical stroke split the front man's wooden shield in two. Before the surprised warrior could recover, the thane thrust right through the man's chain-mail. The hard-driven blade penetrated right through to the man's heart.

The Viking fell beside his own crippled comrade. As soon as Phillip thrust, however, Ambrose knew that it would take a few precious seconds for the weapons-master to withdraw the blade. In using the point of his weapon, he had left himself vulnerable on both sides. The Viking warriors, too, were veterans, and they had been patiently waiting for any opening they could exploit. While the fur-clad barbarian on his left aimed a cut at Phillip's shoulder, the man's partner on the right swung his own weapon. Even as Phillip parried the heavy axe cut, the second flashing sword begin its descent. The big man collapsed.

ᚠ

Suddenly frightened, Ambrose quickly closed the wooden door, but and then realized that there was no bar to secure it shut. He ran to his bed to get his own sword when he felt the renewed chill of the cool morning air. He turned back toward the door he had so recently closed. The door was open again, and the early morning light silhouetted two strange men!

Ambrose was momentarily paralyzed with sudden fear. Though not the giants of Anglo-Saxon imagination, the northern strangers were nevertheless strong and fearsome looking men.

Hastily Ambrose remembered the catechism so well known to all civilized Britons. He repeated it silently. "Oh Lord, deliver us from the fury of the Northmen!"

Ambrose's brief prayer was interrupted as Dael, his tutor and a frail and old man of over sixty winters, rose stiffly up out of his own nearby bed to protest the intrusion. The old man's hearing was going, and he was near-sighted, which only increased his natural garrulousness.

The scholar stumbled towards the door to confront the intruders. "Just who are you that you dare to come in here and disturb my lord's sleep!? Get you gone before I have you thrashed!"

A quick swing of an axe ended Dael's protestations. The look of indignation never left the old man's face as he toppled backward with his throat crushed.

Ambrose, splashed with his tutor's blood, was suddenly trembling. He drew his own sword from its scabbard. The second Viking swordsman noted both the movement and spotted the shiny blade. He stepped forward and swung his own weapon. At the last second the sword was twisted sideways, and the powerful blow slammed into Ambrose's arm and numbed it. The sword fell onto the fresh rushes that covered the earthen floor.

Unable to understand the words thrown at him, Ambrose stood, irresolute, while cradling his injured arm with his other hand. Finally a *sax* point conveyed clearly that they wanted him outside. Still nursing his numbed arm and unmindful of his nudity, he stumbled outside of the hut that the villagers had so recently erected in honor of the young atheling's visit.

Outside, a scene of horror and debauchery greeted the young prince. The prince's mind struggled to accept what he saw. His entire

Personal Guard lay butchered in front of their sleeping quarters. Phillip, his mentor and guardian, lay unmoving on the ground. The entire town was some hundred odd paces in each direction, and was surrounded by a dry moat and palisade. The village was bathed in the reddish light from the sun just rising above the horizon. Under its gentle light, numerous victims were being driven towards the central square. Where men had fought in defense of their families or treasures, bodies lay still and blood-stained. Several more men were cut down even as Ambrose watched.

Nearby, young children were being callously butchered, along with old men and women. Perhaps, felt Ambrose in a momentary flash of pity, they were the lucky ones. The older girls and the women, most still naked from their beds, were driven, with much prodding and laughter, towards the central square.

Already some of the huts, having been stripped of their meager treasures, were going up in flames. A painful touch of a Viking spear point encouraged Ambrose to keep moving. In shock, he shambled towards the fast-growing group of boys and women in the square.

The Viking warriors both fought and pillaged with grim efficiency. They were, in short order, through with the last Saxon home.

The blood-spattered Viking warriors gathered in the village square, along with their captives and the loot. For the first time, Ambrose saw that the 'great savage horde' in reality consisted of perhaps a hundred men; barely two small ship-crews.

The captives were allowed to cover their nakedness with rags from the piles of belongings that just the night before had been theirs. They were then tied with rope looped from neck to neck. Ambrose's mind, curiously detached from the terrible scenes he had just witnessed, idly compared the human pack train, now being secured and loaded down with the villagers' own goods, to the mule trains of the London traders.

The traders heralded spring when they arrived at the royal court on their yearly journey around the island. Faithful as the seasons, the trade caravans had visited his father's lands annually since beyond the memory of even the very oldest living men.

Ambrose suddenly remembered that the time for the yearly visit was soon. If he didn't return to his brother's court soon, he would miss the excitement of seeing the laid-out treasures, gleaned from a huge and mysterious world. He would also miss the festivities that would continue unabated for two full days and nights. It had even been his hope to celebrate by lying with a willing wench for the first time; an event he had recently been dreaming about a lot.

Suddenly the state of passivity and shock lifted, and Ambrose felt the keenness of fresh loss and grief. It cut into him like a sharp knife. His own men were lying butchered nearby. Phillip, friend and mentor, had died defending him. His tutor had his throat slashed, and around him men, women and children were still dying. These were his brother's subjects! These people had sworn allegiance to the crown of Wessex, sacrificing a measure of their personal freedom in exchange for guaranteed protection from the pagan hosts. In God's own time, they would have sworn allegiance to a nephew, to another of his brothers, or even to him, if the *Witan* so willed it.

Brought back to reality by the dawning implications of what was happening, the adrenaline coursed through his arteries. For the first time since he awoke, he was both fully alert and not disoriented. He saw that he was soon to be added to the coffle. The knotted rope would effectively end any chance of escape.

Darting between two Vikings who were more than a little distracted by the glimpses of soft curves on a pretty girl stooping to pick up a load of goods, Ambrose raced madly for a pile of logs stacked against the palisade. Using them as steps, he quickly scrambled up to within a few feet of the tops of the sharpened stakes. From that height, he was easily able to vault over the top.

With the expectation of a spear in his back at each step he took, Ambrose had leapt without hesitation or estimation. He landed hard, but exultantly, twelve feet below.

Remembering the Weapons-Master's training, he let his body absorb the shock by collapsing and rolling. Scrambling to his feet, he quickly climbed the embankment of the dry moat and raced across the budding fields. Less than a thousand foot-lengths away lay the dense forest and freedom. Lithe of body and unencumbered by any sort of clothing, Ambrose felt sure he would now be able, since he was out of spear-range, to give the sea-pirates a good run for their gold.

Lungs heaving and heart pounding, he ran with a last desperate burst of speed. Ambrose safely reached the forest's edge. He hoped its cover would make his recapture impossible.

The prince knew that the Vikings had to move quickly, for within hours the alarm fires would have been lit both up and down the coast, and, for a day's journey in every direction, the thanes would gather their sworn men and march to the smoke.

In his eye's mind Ambrose could envision the Saxon *fyrd* now, as he had seen it so many times; the thanes and wealthy *churls* that made up the core of the force, heavily armed and mounted. And behind the fyrdmen of the king, who held land in exchange for their military services, would come their retainers and the landless churls. Many of these would march on foot. Some would carry bows and axes, while others carried mattocks or spears. All, however, would be armed and ready to fight the heathen invader.

Ambrose knew that these assorted weapons could be used to deadly effect in support of the better-armed fyrdmen, as long as the force was leavened with enough well-armed veterans. The Saxons of Wessex, when they managed to gather enough forces quickly enough, had turned the table on the Viking invaders more than once. Even as the image of brave Saxon warriors filled Ambrose's mind, his eyes caught a flash of movement to the left. From behind a giant oak, an evil-looking warrior stepped forth. For the second time that day a sword blade hit Ambrose flat-side on, and this time he toppled heavily to the ground, like a poleaxed ox.

CHAPTER 2.

Phillip Carries Ambrose, and They Reach the Ships.

As Ambrose regained consciousness, he felt a terrible throbbing in his temples. As long as he didn't attempt to move any part of his body, the pulsing thunder remained bearable.

Gradually the prince regained control of his senses. Very slowly, as if his mind was returning from a very long nightmare, he searched through his memories. As he reconstructed the confusing events, anger, mixed with self-pity and fear, pushed aside his previous preoccupation with the pain.

Abruptly Ambrose realized that the constant jarring he felt was his bruised body moving. He opened his eyes and forced his pupils to focus. The prince shifted his weight, and instantly a gruff voice responded.

"Lie still, Prince. You're safe enough for now," it said.

Ambrose slowly forced his thoughts to go past the pain. He ran through the catalogue of voices he knew. The voice was one he had never expected to hear again . . . Phillip! Fearless warrior; long-time member of the king's Personal Guard, and Weapons-master to royal princes!

The gruff familiar voice brought tears to Ambrose's eyes. Once again he felt the cocoon of security this brave warrior and faithful friend represented. The feeling was only momentary, however, as Ambrose's vision also followed the loose rope from Phillip's neck to that of the several peasant girls following. In the periphery of his vision, he saw one of the cloaked and armored raiders stalking along, his naked and blood-stained sword poised to punish disobedience.

Ambrose, with his head pounding and his stomach churning, managed to croak a few words. "Phillip, put me down. I think I can walk."

Phillip responded quietly. "Nay Prince, for if you are on your feet and unable to keep the pace, they will kill you where you stand. Lie still and let me carry you until you have regained some more of your strength."

Secure over Phillip's shoulder, Ambrose was about to let himself succumb to his weakness, until he saw the upper extremity of a terrible gash that was on the back of Phillip's lower neck. He spoke more easily now.

"By the good God, Phillip! You're injured!"

"The pagan twisted his blade as he struck me so that it is nothing more than a surface cut. 'Tis nothing, Prince, except that it stopped me from being at your side when they took you. I am so sorry that I failed you!"

Touched by the eloquence of this man of few words, Ambrose started to demand that Phillip put him down at once. As he was trying to organize the words, however, he slipped back into unconsciousness.

⮧

When next the blackness lifted from Ambrose's mind, he found himself lying on soft, yielding moss. As he opened his eyes he had an ant's view of Phillip looming above, sitting cross-legged beside him.

Not more than fifty feet away lay the gentle ripples of the Meon River. The tide being out, an expanse of wet sand and gravel was exposed that stretched almost all the way between the beach and two *long-ships* that lay close offshore.

Ambrose noted with sudden surprise that the Vikings seemed totally unprepared for any hostile action. An attack from an avenging Saxon force could cut the Vikings to pieces! Instead of being in a military formation that could quickly transform into a defensive posture, the enemy warriors were strung out along the entire length of the slave coffle. Equally important, the Danish ships seem to have been stranded by a retreating tide.

Ambrose felt a surge of sudden hope. Saxon horsemen charging along the wet beach could separate the Viking marauders from their ships, and archers and spearmen from the near-by woods could easily finish off any cores of resistance.

Where was his brother's fyrd? The smoke from the burning village should have alerted the fyrdmen for miles in all directions. Why weren't his brother's brave warriors charging the disorganized and stranded enemy? Instead of brave Saxon fyrdmen charging across the tidal flats, he saw only a human chain of captives ripple and struggle to its feet. Shouts and prodding spears made it very clear that the prisoners' break was over.

Phillip spoke warningly to Ambrose. "Stand now, Prince, if ever you could. Now that they have seen you conscious, they will kill you out-of-hand if you do not seem capable of keeping up."

Doggedly, and calling on sources of energy he didn't know he had, Ambrose struggled to his feet. "Except for a splitting headache and some nausea, I think I'm all right, Phillip."

Being unfettered, he was able to stand at Phillip's side. The coffle of captives in front of Phillip were now in motion, and Phillip was forced to walk across the wet sand towards the beached long-ships.

Ambrose continued to walk at Phillip's side. He saw that, as he started to move, a gaunt Viking clasping a wicked-looking spear moved silently along, paralleling his route. Ambrose spoke quietly to his giant companion.

"Phillip, I'm confused. I thought that you were killed when the second bastard struck you. I ran to get my sword when two Vikings burst through the door. One killed old Dael and the other disarmed me. When I didn't see you in the square, I leapt the palisade and ran for the safety of the forest. That's about all I remember. I was just entering the woods when I caught a glimpse of a warrior and then darkness closed over me."

Phillip's gruff voice was music to Ambrose's ears. "There's little enough to tell, Prince. I was struck a glancing blow from the side, but it didn't crack my thick skull. When they saw I wasn't mortally wounded, they dragged me to the square. I only awoke after you made your run for freedom. I'm told that you had the bad luck to run into the arms of one of their outer sentries."

As they spoke, the human baggage train neared the closer of the two *long-ships*. Ambrose, a keen sailor, studied the two ships critically. He could see that they were clinker-built of overlapped planks, and he could even see the rust spots where iron rivets held the hull together.

Sailors at his brother's royal court had told him that the swift Viking vessels could withstand even the most violent pounding of the North Sea. Relatively shallow of draft, the ships could sail with impunity through shallow and treacherous water. Above each ship towered the dread symbol of these pagan Northerners; an intricately carved dragon's head. The heads were exceeded in height only by the single masts, which towered overhead. By their sheer size, they looked easily capable of supporting the weight of a single huge square sail.

A Viking strode purposely towards the middle of the coffle. He drew his sax, and Ambrose wondered momentarily if he was going to kill someone. The warrior, however, only sliced the rope between two women. The captives were now in two separate groups.

Ambrose and Phillip were part of the second group. They were herded out into knee-deep water and then forced to climb aboard the nearer ship. Once again, Ambrose's mind was stimulated by the novel situation, even as he obeyed the threatening gestures and obediently moved amidships, towards the base of the bare mast. Once seated, the prince inspected the ship from his new vantage point. Though he saw the hull was decked, Ambrose knew that relatively little room lay below, except for some limited storage space. In the stern, there was a small but gaily striped canvas tent.

The loot stolen from the village was carefully wrapped and then stored under the planking, and the captives all sat just aft of the great mast. Surrounded by the fierce sea-raiders, exhausted by their ordeal of the last few hours, and again mindful of their terrible vulnerability, several of the younger women began to wail. Finally a short, swarthy crew-member, who had been with the commander in the stern, was sent forward to where the wailing women were. His accent was abominable, but his Anglish was comprehensible.

"We not able to sail for another little time, until tide come higher. Any noise until then, you sorry!"

Matching his gestures to his words, he uncoiled a stout length of rope. One woman, the grief of having both her baby and husband killed in front of her fresh in her mind, was still unable to stifle her wails. The rope lashed out with a vicious whistle, struck her back, and curled around to tear at her breasts.

The woman responded with a scream and then a renewed wail of horror and pain. When the Viking next drew his sax, one of the other women, sensing his intentions, placed her hand firmly over the wailing woman's mouth. Although the distraught woman bit the hand until it bled, the neighbor would not let go, and her cries were effectively stifled.

Satisfied, the swarthy sailor resheathed his weapon and continued his speech. "Some of you will be chained. No chains for all, so some must be tied with rope. You touch knot, you die - understand?"

Even as he spoke, he beckoned to a group of waiting sailors. The crewmen stepped forward with a long chain and an armload of massive iron collars. With less than twenty metal collars, and over thirty captives, they collared only the most mature of the captives. One by one the chosen were led to a massive oak stump that lay amidships. There, a brawny man, presumably the ship's smith, placed a rivet through a hole in the neck collars, and, with the captive laying his neck on the stump, hammered each rivet open.

Within minutes all of the men, and a few of the most intransigent women, were connected together by iron links going from collar to collar. One end was fastened to itself through the last person's collar. The other end was permanently fastened to a large iron bolt set into the mast mounting. Ambrose was mortified to be tied by rope with the beardless youths and the girls, until he realized that his own sparse beard and small statue had caused the Vikings to misjudge his age.

Again the swarthy sailor approached them from his post in the stern. "The ship, soon she float again. You give us no trouble, we no hurt you. Any trouble - you die. No one to move without you ask him." At that he pointed to a young sailor, little older than Ambrose himself, who was sitting idly on the deck just behind them. At his shipmate's gesture, the young man smiled slightly, exposing bad teeth, and hefted an axe.

CHAPTER 3.

The Ship.

The ship lifted free of the sand with a sucking sound. As each warrior was sitting on his storage chest and had his oar pushed out and ready, the ship rapidly got underway. Ambrose was surprised to see how many empty chests there were. The vacant seats seemed to indicate that the crew had somewhere suffered severe casualties. To the tune of some chant unknown to Ambrose, the warriors stroked rhythmically. Noise was obviously no longer a concern. The sea pirates were again free of the land.

With some twenty long oars to a side, the craft was soon turned about and heading towards the open sea. Almost immediately Ambrose was able to spot, on one of the headlands, a large party of horsemen. The armor of many men glinted in the sunlight. Because of the distance, they looked like children's' carved wooden toys.

Anger filled the young prince. In spite of the fact that the Saxons should have been able to muster almost 500 men with a few hours notice, they had chosen to let the pirates just sail away! Where was the courage that had brought the ancestors of his brother's people over the water in ships, and, along with the tribes of the Jutes and Angles, allowed them to conquer this land from a formidable enemy? Where were the glorious warriors of song and legend who had successfully defeated entire British armies almost single-handedly? He turned to Phillip and pointed.

"Look, Phillip! The fyrdmen have gathered, and they knew where we were.'

A single tear rolled down the prince's cheek. 'Why? Why did they not come to our rescue?"

Phillip stared hard for long moments before he answered. "I count enough warriors to be a match for two ship crews. That leaves only treachery or cowardice."

Ambrose glared at the mounted fyrdmen. "Who would betray us, Phillip?"

"There are many royal Athelings, Prince, and few enough shires to go around. I do not know if you were betrayed, but I do know there are many jealousies in the royal household. Your own father promised your mother on her deathbed that he would someday give you Dorset to rule."

"But Phillip, my mother's British ancestors once ruled it as sovereign kings."

The burly thane shrugged "That fact does not make it yours, Atheling. A major province of Wessex's heartland was promised you, and that is enough to cause jealousy."

"But of who?"

"Well, Ethelbert is new to the throne, and he does not much love you. Unlike Ethelbald, he intends to keep the various subject kingdoms united under his crown."

"True, Phillip, but Dorset is not going to make a difference to Ethelbert's power, even if he did choose to honor my father's request."

"Ethelbert is ambitious, Prince. One less atheling around would simplify matters."

"But Ethelbert has not even agreed to give me Dorset!"

"With you gone, there is no need to even consider honoring your father's promise."

Ambrose sat silently for a long time. At last he spoke. "Do you really think Ethelbert could have done this to us, Phillip?"

"I do not know, Prince, but it is at least possible. Someone kept the sentries on the river-bank from sounding the alarm, and perhaps held the fyrdmen back from riding to our rescue."

A new resolution grew in Ambrose. Just let me return safely to my brother's court, and I will hunt down my betrayer! If only . . . Ambrose knew he dreamed the thoughts of adolescents. Reality was that he was a captive of a cruel and pagan people. His fate might yet be to be castrated so he could safely serve in the boudoirs of noble women in the East, or perhaps he would be hitched to an iron plough; to live out his life as a human beast-of-burden.

The ship started to rock more violently and Ambrose feared that soon they would be on the open sea. The faint sound of a ram's horn wafted to his ear, and Ambrose knew that the shepherd sentries had finally decided to announce the movement of the sinister ships now nosing their way towards the open sea.

Within what seemed like only a few hundred heartbeats, the two ships cleared the last headland, and *Angleland* had been left behind. The rest of the prisoners sat as quietly and glumly as Ambrose. Until the land had been left behind, there had been hope for some kind of rescue. Now, it was clear that there would be no miracle.

Casting aside his despairing thoughts with a great effort, Ambrose spoke to Phillip, who had pulled on the chain until he could sit near his charge.

"Phillip, do the Vikings coast the shores, as do our ships, or do they really venture beyond sight of shore and sail directly across the great Northern Sea?"

Phillip answered quietly. "Of that I know little, my prince, but I suspect that they will coast east to the white cliffs. From there they can see across to land friendly to their kind. From the Narrows, south to the mouth of the Seine, lie settlements of Danes. The Frankish king is too busy elsewhere, and the Danes too powerful, for him to drive the heathen pirates from his shores."

"But if', Ambrose mused, 'the raiders sail east, they might pass the mouth of the Thames, where even now my brother's continental courier fleet sits idle. Is it not possible that our vessels would give chase to two pirate ships?"

Phillip spoke glumly. "I wish I could give you hope, Prince, but it's been many years since the Saxon fleet tried to clear the waters of pirates. These ships are under-manned, but they are very impressive to the watchers-on-the-shore. I think your brother's captains count themselves lucky if they can successfully escort ambassadors and official royal messengers to safe territory on the Frankish coast."

"Phillip, old Dael told me many times how our ancestors broke the back of massive Roman fleets. We still sing the ballads!"

"Truth be told, they broke the backs of a few local ships long after the main Roman fleet was withdrawn. We have become land-people, farmers, and the Vikings are now the daring sailors. Each year now they come south again. The islands to the north of Briton no longer swear allegiance to us. Instead, they have become bases for the pirates. The northern Saxon lands are all facing raids from the Danes, and the *Norse* are sweeping down the Irish coast. There are few island kingdoms left which have not suffered the calamity of having the pagan Vikings raid their shores. And finally, Prince, if it is your brother who is the culprit, then there is little chance his ships will dash out after two Viking long-ships. Even if it is not him, there is little likelihood that news of your abduction has yet reached your brother's ears, let alone the commanders of the fleet in far-away Kent."

As they talked quietly, the two ships moved parallel with the coast. Ambrose realized that they were moving steadily towards the Thames, but he had lost all hope.

Whenever the fickle breeze gave evidence of blowing from their rear quarter, ten or eleven sailors would eagerly haul up the great square sail. This done, the oars would be shipped and all the sailors would relax on deck. When the breeze shifted back, however, as it often did, since they were still near the coast, the sail would come crashing down and the oars would be pushed out again. The Vikings were clearly in a hurry to leave the area.

Further, Ambrose noticed a strange transformation of the warrior-sailors. Although when not on duty they tended to cluster about the captives and ogle the younger women, they did not lay a hand on them. Rude comments and obscene gestures were the worst things that befell the captives. The women, already more humiliated than they had ever been in their lives, took the visual inspection of their bodies mutely, or broke into sobs of mortification and despair.

Ambrose cast about for an explanation of this in his mind. Finally, he ventured to ask his faithful weapons tutor. "Phillip, why don't they take our women? They seem to ache to pleasure them."

"Prince, I can only guess. I would like to think it is because they think of their own women and children at home, but I doubt it. The Vikings are known as brutal masters."

"Then why?"

"Most like, they are forbidden by the captain. At sea is not the time to fight over women. It doesn't lend itself to ship-board discipline."

Ambrose sat quietly for a few minutes, digesting the comment. His mind, normally very active, sped on, questioning the events of the last day, as well as the reason why they occurred.

"Phillip, I had heard that on Viking ships all men are free companions. Why then, do the men man oars like galley-slaves, and obey their leader as if he were a god?"

"Prince, Galley slaves require extra food and water, and must be constantly watched to prevent rebellion. By replacing the slaves with warriors, you more than double your ship force and, at the same time, need to carry less food and water.

I understand that each pledges obedience to the commander for the duration of the voyage. It seems to me to be the only way any expedition can work effectively. I expect no less from my fyrdmen when I lead them into battle. It also occurs to me, Prince, that we must soon learn their heathen tongue if we are to survive."

It was as the royal Weapons-Master talked that Ambrose for the first time became aware of the fact that none of the other prisoners were talking. Instead, they all seemed to be looking at him and Phillip with pleading eyes. They seemed pathetically hopeful that the captive prince and his mighty warrior guardian could somehow strike off their chains and these two noblemen could somehow solve their problems.

The looks of desperation cut Ambrose deeply. Once again he remembered that, to these villagers, he was the king's representative. As an atheling, he was so far above their status that they were normally afraid to even talk to him. Shame for his ineffectiveness and humiliation for his own plight filled him. He bowed his head forward until it was resting on his knees, and there he sat, mute with despair.

Phillip, seeing the disinclination of his young charge to talk further, slipped into a state of apathy himself.

CHAPTER 4.

Ambrose and Phillip Help to Fight the Savage Storm.

Ambrose's head slipped from his knees, and the sudden motion jerked him awake. He realized that he had been dozing and was disoriented for a moment. The hard deck and the rope around his neck quickly reminded him, however, just where he was.

He looked for the shoreline of his beloved island. No land was visible! Ambrose cast frightened glances in all directions, and finally noted, far to the stern, a tiny touch of purple-haze that separated the dark waters of the sea from the vast vault of blue sky. His heart started hammering in his chest. Although near to sunset, the prince realized that the insane pagans were heading out directly onto the unknown sea!

Never in his life out of sight of land, Ambrose was terrified by this new event. The route the Angles, Saxons and Jutes had used from time immemorial was to sail east or south, until Europe and Angleland were both visible. At this point, crossings were customarily made. Starting early in the day ensured that the far shore was reached before darkness. Further, all vessels were beached or anchored for the night. No sane captain traveled the dangerous island waters after sunset.

The rumor then, that these people sailed directly across great stretches of water, seemed to really be true! In Ambrose's mind he had always known this, for how else did these pagans attack the islands far to the north even of the Scots and Picts? How else did they arrive unseen on the Angle, Saxon and Jute shores, in spite of thousands of watchful sentries and signal fires prepared all along the coast?

Although intellectually it was a concept simple to grasp, the sheer bravado of it struck Ambrose hard. From the Meon river valley, it might be several days journey to the Continent.

Even as the momentary panic sent adrenaline coursing through his body, however, Ambrose's mind flicked along a checklist of potential consequences. The list started with fear of unknown terrestrial creatures and lands, and ended with sudden visions of the Viking vessel being attacked by a ravenous sea-monster. A great gaping mouth was poised just below the ship, while great tentacles held the ship high above the water. One by one, the crew slid into the gaping maw, while the chain of captives dangled from the ship like a broken necklace.

A great fire roared in his bed-chamber, and Ambrose felt relaxed and secure in his father's palace. The sheets were of silk, and he lay buried under a pile of the finest wool blankets. A sudden lurch of the vessel forced Ambrose's brain to cease its random associative chains of thought. His mind returned reluctantly to reality.

The ship had heeled over when the breeze mischievously changed its angle of pressure on the sail. Behind the ship's stern, a great fiery orb of molten gold was sliding into the sea. The clouds above reflected some of the glory, and the celestial colors varied from a somber grey to gorgeous reds and orange. Directly astern of the ship, a long simmering trail of gold was visible in the water, stretching back to the sun. Surely, thought Ambrose, that trail will link me with my homeland, now so far away. He prayed that the intangible connection would one day lead him home again.

With a minimum of shouted orders, the crew shipped their oars for the last time that night, and the ship's travels became dependent upon the massive square sail and the steering-crew who patiently held the massive steering-oar that was attached to the ship near the stern.

Spent, the rest of the crew lay where they had worked for much of the day; on the open deck. Soon only the sleeping crew and one lad, who had spent most of the day staring at the captives, remained awake. The boy continued to faithfully watch over his charges.

Once it was dark, Ambrose carefully felt the ropes with his fingers. He could easily loose the slip knot. But if he did, what could he do? Not more than a few body-lengths away, on all sides, dozed a score or more of work and battle-hardened warrior-sailors. While their swords and axes were secured in their oak chests, yet all wore knives on their belt. Any one of them, so armed, was capable of easily killing an unarmed boy. Ambrose decided to follow the lead of both the sailors and the other captives, and lay back in the hope that sleep would reclaim him.

With the sea calm, there was little seasickness among the prisoners. The only sounds, other than the occasional creaking of ropes and wood rubbing against wood, was some snoring, and the occasional whispering or gentle sobs of his fellow captives.

Ambrose lay on his back and idly looked skyward. There, a vast array of glittering gems were encased in deepest black. Ever so gently, the myriad stars shifted, first to one side, then to the other. A few hid momentarily behind the towering mast. Ambrose idly wondered if the day's events were enough to rouse the heavens to such movement, but he knew all the time that the vessel simply never ceased rocking. Gradually the black velvet of the heavens closed in around his mind, and he escaped again into temporary oblivion.

Two days passed thus, relatively uneventfully. On the third day, however, strong winds arose. The large square-sail was lowered, and a small storm sail was hoisted in its place. Again and again Ambrose marveled at the carpentry skills that had made the long-ships so sturdy. The clinker construction meant that a severe pounding of the hull merely meant a great groaning as one oaken board slipped slightly over another. Instead of being unable to give, and therefore breaking, the boards of the ship were thin enough that they could flex. The worst that a terrible pounding did was to force out some caulking and allow sea-water to penetrate into the hull.

At the worst of the storm, several of the captives had the loops removed from their necks and were ordered by curt gestures to bail out the ship's bilges. Ambrose was handed a wooden bucket, and he hurried to join the others already dumping water over the side.

The wind increased steadily until even the storm sail split under the pressure. The rowers were all sent to the oars in a desperate attempt to keep the ship from turning broadside to the waves. Their companion ship was long gone from sight, and now all the freed captives, ill as they were from repeated bouts of sea-sickness, worked feverishly to bail out the bilges with the wooden buckets.

Even as Ambrose scuttled to the side of the ship to dump a pail of sea-water back into the ocean, a freak wave rose suddenly and smote one of the oar-banks unexpectedly. While one rower was lifted bodily and thrown overboard, another received the full force of the transferred energy on his jaw. Although the sound of the striking oar-handle couldn't be heard over the banshee howling of the wind, Ambrose saw the rower sail high and then fall back onto his rowing chest. By the unnatural angle of his neck, it was clear that he would never again see his loved ones or tread the paths to his home village.

Without thinking, Ambrose slipped from his neck-rope and raced to the oar. He strained mightily and was finally able to draw it in before its frantic thrashing could entangle the oars of the other rowers and break the rhythm of the strokes. Ambrose did not need to be told that the oars alone kept the ship from turning broadside to the waves and instantly turning turtle. He had seen already that even three strong men leaning on the steering-oar could not singlehandedly control the direction of the wildly heaving ship.

Ambrose had the presence of mind, once he pulled the long oar in and laid it on the deck, to grab a coiled rope from a cache on deck and race to the stern with it. The man, however, had been swept far astern of the ship within seconds. In the short time it took Ambrose to subdue the oar, the man had been lost to sight. Clearly, there was no hope for a rescue.

With a sudden, almost contemptuous gesture, the sea hurled another rogue wave down the length of the entire ship. One man misstroked, and the entire starboard oar bank became tangled.

An intolerable weight of water struck the mess, and massive oars shattered like campfire kindling in a giant's hand. Several more sailors suffered terrible blows from the flailing oars, and a couple of them fell unconscious onto the deck.

Inexorably, the bow of the ship began to turn broadside to the waves. No ship, of whatever construction, could long survive a broadside position.

Ambrose desperately crawled back to where he had pulled in the oar and thrust it back out. He heaved on the heavy oar, trying to match his puny strength against that of the elemental forces.

With a roar that could be heard over even the wind and waves, Phillip struggled to his side. Near the free end of the coffle, he had nevertheless to drag with him two terrified men and a woman. They slid helplessly across the deck in his wake. Ignoring the protests and panic-stricken pummeling of the three people in front, he reached the oar, and the two Saxons started rowing desperately.

Several Vikings recovered. They and the officers raced to unlash spare oars and push them out to replace the broken and lost ones. From the other side of the vessel came several more crewmen, and slowly, grudgingly, the ship turned away from the wind until it was once again running cleanly before the storm.

All that day, and well into the night, Phillip and Ambrose, occasionally spelled by Phillip's coffle mates, rowed steadily and desperately. They rowed until their hands were raw and their muscles screamed for mercy from the unaccustomed labor.

After an eternity, the wind dropped. As suddenly as it had come, the wind left them and the sea gradually calmed.

Everyone aboard ship dropped to the decks and slept as though drugged. For several turns of an hourglass, there were no slaves or masters aboard ship; only survivors.

CHAPTER 5.

A Frisian Port is Reached.

"Land ho!"

The cry woke both captors and captives. Ambrose, still physically exhausted, yet raised his head in curiosity. The ship floated serenely off a low and sandy shore. Immediately the ship's crew sighted the land, they manned their oars. Under the captain's direction, the ship turned to the north and paralleled the coast.

Within hours the comatose captives saw the first signs of civilization. The crew started to cheer up as occasional tufts of smoke indicated small hamlets on the shore. The ship, still without its companion vessel, coursed smoothly between the many islands. Several times they passed large vessels. Some had much higher sides and no provision for oars; obviously true merchantmen. While the long-ship's crew ignored the great clumsy vessels, yet they posted lookouts high up the mast, with instructions to look for both their missing companion ship and also for any hostile craft.

When the first ship had passed, Ambrose turned to his faithful companion. "Phillip, what strange land is this we have come to?"

A portly man, next to Phillip on the chain, took it upon himself to reply.

"My łud, 'tis the land o' the Frisians. See them little islands?' At that he pointed a dirt-encrusted finger at the low sandy isles past which the ship was sailing.

"Tis the land of the folk who used to come to our village to trade for the wool of our sheep. 'Tis the same kind of ships I see tied up, and they told us of their sandy and flat lands. But, my lud, 'tis many years since they last landed on our shores."

Ambrose nodded thanks for this information. He looked around at his fellow captives. He felt a new and curious kinship with these simple people of the plough. After all, his own mother, for all her royal ancestry, had been a British slave who had been taken and used by a Saxon king. Ambrose had been born to a slave and a king.

Ambrose's curiosity was completely satisfied when, towards dark, the ship rounded a headland. There, spread out before them in all directions, lay one of the trading emporiums of Europe. Even Ambrose, young as he was, had heard of the great trading center of the Frisians, *Wyk te Duurstede*, and he had no doubt that this was it. He had heard that this town of wooden buildings, some of which soared to four stories above the ground, was the nexus of a great commercial empire.

To Ambrose, however, the town also had a more sinister connotation. This was one of the cities that traded any goods gathered from mystical Byzantium to the Northern lands of perpetual snow. Ambrose shivered. He knew also that Wyk te Duurstede specialized in a single commodity - slaves!

The battered long-ship slid past the breakwater and into the harbor proper. The ship found a haven near a small covey of similar vessels; all Viking pirates by the long and lean shape of the ships. Ambrose stared at the lines of gaily colored shields that hung along the relatively low waists of each vessel. Although it was no surprise to Ambrose after the terrible storm, he noted that their companion ship was not amongst the anchored vessels. Ambrose idly wondered if they would ever see it again.

Nearby, three Frisian merchantmen swung at anchor, and a large number of Frankish galleys were moored near the breakwater. Even more interesting, a group of frail-looking ships in the inner harbor were manned by turbaned men who wore hugely baggy pants. The crew were all of a swarthy complexion, but a few seemed to have been burned black by exposure to some giant sun.

Ambrose, in spite of his predicament, was fascinated by this great metropolis where men of so many lands seemed to meet in peace and for trade. His only concern was that his captors might decide that he should be some of the merchandise they haggled over.

For some reason the sight of the strange craft appeared to cheer the captain greatly. He was a tall man, with his long blond hair tied in two pig-tails. The man emerged from his re-installed deck-shelter dressed in splendid finery. He ordered several crewmen to unlash the skiff, a double-ended shell of some eighteen foot-lengths. Willing hands lowered it into the calm water, and, with its three pairs of oars, it fairly skipped across the ripples towards the quays where many other ship's boats were tied. Once again the young armed Viking appeared at the captives' side, and the ropes were carefully replaced around their necks.

The crew, except for waves at the brash women on the quay, lay in the warm sun, and relaxed as sailors do, splicing ropes and swapping tales of bravery and treachery. Ambrose already was vaguely able to follow some of what was being said. His learned tutor had told him once that Ambrose's father's ancestors had come from Germany, and that they, though good and true Christians, were kin to both the Danes and the Frisians. Indeed, the language did seem to have many similarities and Ambrose's quick mind and good memory was able to fill in many of the gaps in understanding the sailors' conversations.

Ambrose glanced at Phillip. The giant Saxon warrior lay mute and glum on the deck near Ambrose. Ambrose was concerned. "Old friend, you do not wish to look at the great city?"

Phillip touched his metal slave collar. "I have visions of my beloved Matilda and my precious daughters. They are far away and I wear this damned thing around my neck! Prince, we may soon be parceled out, and that could mean we will be separated forever. My king entrusted me with you, and I have failed in my task."

Ambrose spoke. "We are alive, Weapons-master, and where there is life, there is hope."

Phillip slipped back into his despondency, and Ambrose just continued to watch all the activity. Shortly before sunset, Ambrose noticed the tall figure of the captain, towering even in this land of tall and blond people, stroll to the wharf-side. With him walked a darker figure. At the distance, even Ambrose's keen eyes couldn't make out subtle distinctions. He could see, however, that the man was swarthy and wore a green turban. As the captain's boat scuttled back towards the long-ship, the other man's boat moved towards one of the strange and seemingly fragile vessels, which Ambrose had earlier thought looked out of place amongst the sturdy ships of the Northern seas.

The crew proceeded to change into fresh clothes. Several, to the prisoners' surprise, dove overboard naked into the freezing waters before dressing. Finally dressed to their own satisfaction, and carrying coins metered out carefully by their captain, they were ferried ashore group by group. At last only eight crewmen and an officer, well armed and alert, remained on board. With the sounds and smells of gaiety so close at hand, the bonds of slavery never chaffed Ambrose as much as they did that *night*.

The remaining crewmen assigned to stay on board were now aloof and short-tempered. They grudgingly fed the prisoners dried fish and biscuits; monotonous fare for everyone. The crew themselves took great pains to buy several plucked chickens from a passing boat vendor. They set up a cooking fire in the sand-pit amidships; a dangerous practice that the captain had forbidden during their voyaging upon the open sea.

The aromas of this repast struck Ambrose, and wafted his mind back to the great house where he was a prince; a master amongst many minions and servants, his every wish a command. Now, he thought, looking down at his torn and grimy rags, he felt the part of a farm animal, less than human, and certainly of less value than a good horse. His own father's many estates had been partly maintained by *thralls*, and Ambrose had never before considered how they had felt. Hard work had merited a curt nod, and slackness had merited painful punishment.

Of course, he reminded himself, his father's slaves had all been heathen, for Mother Church did not condone a traffic in Christians. Nevertheless, Ambrose began to develop a distinct aversion to the whole idea of one man owning another's body.

With self-pity welling up within him, the prince reached out mutely for Phillip's arms. Embraced there, like a little child, he lay still. The gentle motion of the ship gradually relaxed him, until at last he fell asleep.

᠊᠊᠊᠊᠊᠊᠊᠊᠊᠊᠊᠊᠊᠊᠊᠊᠊᠊᠊᠊᠊᠊᠊᠊᠊᠊

Dawn found the crewmen awake. They roused the prisoners with dispatch. After the captives were shoved into a relatively neat line, the captain deigned to march along in front of them, casually pointing his stick of authority at several of the more comely women. To Ambrose's surprise, the captain pointed at both Phillip and him. He desperately tried to comprehend the captain's terse comments. Unable to translate it all, he did understand something about a gift and loyalty.

The chosen captives were quickly and efficiently released and then re-shackled. They were then lowered into the waiting skiff and, one group at a time, rowed to the quay. After the last group was loaded into the boat, the captain himself climbed in and ordered the crew to shove off.

Ambrose felt a last tie within him snap when the boat pulled away. First he had been forced to leave his brother's kingdom, then all Angleland. Now he had been forced to watch helplessly as some of his brother's subjects were taken away to an unknown fate. He felt keenly the loss of his fellow Saxons. The faintest of metallic clanking heralded the last view of the captives as they disappeared from sight along the quay.

The younger captives, like Ambrose, were now herded to the oak stump that served as anvil. With so many prisoners gone, there were enough iron collars to go around. Ambrose felt the rusty iron collar close around his neck with a terrible sense of finality. For several hours the group of remaining captives, as despondent as Phillip, sat still or moved only fitfully when nature called.

Scarcely a word was exchanged. Only the crew on board who had already had shore leave were in relatively good spirits, bitching of course about not being ashore, but fairly contentedly laying about, napping and soaking up the sun's spring warmth. As ever, the talk was of war and women. Ignoring their captives except for an occasional idle glance, the crew swapped tales of the women they had been with the night before.

Ambrose, idly incredulous, listened and tried to follow the tales of women whose skin shone of burnished gold, or who were as dark as the coal some of the Saxons dug out of the ground and used as a fuel. He listened more knowingly of the four-breasted women and the ones nine foot-lengths in height; of the ferocious battles each man had fought, single-handedly, against hundreds of savage foe. In short, the conversation was much as he had heard it scores of times before, from countless sailors and soldiers in his father's land.

The harbor was never quiet. There was a constant movement of people coming into sight on the quays; getting into or out of rowing boats, carrying strange goods, and speaking in a babble of foreign tongues that Ambrose had never heard. At any given time, several ships were arriving or preparing to slip out with the tide. Many others were being on or off-loaded by smaller, oared vessels. The long-ships, such as Ambrose was on, and their larger cousins, the *dragon ships*, appeared like swift sharks amongst great whales. On all sides, the great tubby merchantmen towered over the sleek and low Viking vessels.

As the sun prepared to dip into the great sea already cooling from molten gold to a duller orange, Ambrose saw the captain and the rest of the crew arrive at the quay without any of the captives. The crewmen split into several groups, presumably to be rowed out in relays to the anchored long-ship.

Ambrose wondered again what had ever happened to the sister ship that he had last seen when the storm struck. He thought how ironic it would be if the storm had, in one fell swoop, done what the avenging Saxon fyrd had been unable, or unwilling, to do - kill the pagan

Vikings.

In the first boat-load came the captain, resplendent in his finery. The prince watched the man's scarlet cloak spilling out behind him. Ambrose had been inordinately proud of that cloak when his father had smilingly chosen it for him from the London peddlers the year before he had died.

Second over the side came a veritable scarecrow of a man, with both his arms and legs fettered. Shoved up from below, he landed ignominiously in a bundle. Phillip, bless his gruff soul, moved over to him, and assisted him in joining the group of captives again linked to the mast-chain. The man had obviously been ill-used, as his bare back was covered with congealed blood and welts, and he was nearly incoherent. The rowers watched dispassionately as Phillip poured fresh water into the scarecrow's mouth, and then they helped their comrades aboard unload the boat, amidst much coarse jesting and leers.

CHAPTER 6.

Polonius and the Land of the Danes.

In the pre-dawn cold, Ambrose heard the clatter of the chain. Opening one eye, he watched a young girl, just barely nubile, move to the waste bucket and squat over it. She lifted her makeshift skirt to her waist and let her bladder empty with a sigh. How fast, he thought, does modesty die. Even now, after several days of bitter captivity, where each movement was by necessity shared by fellow members of the coffle, several of the women would suffer until the dark to relieve themselves. The others, more adaptive, or perhaps merely more despondent, just relieved themselves when the urge arose, with little more thought to their grace, dignity or modesty than they would have about breathing. Ambrose himself, after a day or two of discomfort and moral outrage, had seen the merits of the natural approach.

With a last rattle that echoed from both along the deck and along the length of the chain, the girl returned to her former position and lay down. Even as she did so, the sky, a dark opaque grey, started to shift towards daytime blue. Ambrose stared skyward to watch the candles of Heaven being extinguished one by one by the increasing light.

The prince could hear the stirring of the crew, as well as the start of active life both on board the neighboring vessels and from the town itself. Within a short time the crew performed their rather sketchy toilet, which generally consisted of urinating or defecating over the sides, and began to prepare the ship for sailing.

The crew-member designated as cook nursed a few coals on his sand-pit, and soon the odor of savory stew wafted to both captives and crew. With a surprising touch of largesse, the cook ladled out portions of the hot food to the prisoners. Having eaten nothing but the worst of the dried fish and meat, and stale biscuits, since their captivity, the captives ate ravenously.

Ambrose interrupted Phillip, who was intently shoveling food with his fingers from the hollowed wooden food vessel into the gaping cavity that was his mouth.

"This is better than the slop they have been throwing at us, but why this sudden change of heart, do you think?"

The Weapons-master reluctantly stopped shoveling and started to swallow to clear space for speech. Before he could answer, however, the scarecrow that had lain beside him, unmoving for most of the previous day, shifted to an elbow and made so bold as to answer in stilted, but understandable Saxon.

"I think, lord, as I can see from your bearing, whatever present circumstances be, you are; they want to fatten us for home. I heard one sailor tell another last night that we are leaving today for their homeland, and we are to be gifts.

I can understand them wanting to take the women back.' With that he leered appreciatively, 'and I, of course, a learned and valuable scribe bribed and cajoled to come and impart some wisdom to their little ones, but I am not sure why you two have had the good fortune to join the privileged group."

Ambrose smiled uncertainly. The muscles he used felt stiff. It had been a long time, a lifetime of several days, since he had last felt the inclination to smile.

"I wonder too. How did . . . How did you . . ." Ambrose saw Phillip's expression shift to silent warning. He knew Phillip would warn him against asking a slave about his past. Nevertheless, the words had started to tumble eagerly out of his mouth, only to hesitate in the completion.

The scarecrow responded, his relaxed smile indicating a lack of concern about the propriety of the question. His willingness to reply was plain. He did not seem offended. He, in fact, seemed eager to talk.

"Say no more, my lord. I know what you ask. How did a man such as myself, Polonius by name, find myself aboard this luxury craft, with chains to keep me comfort and welts to remind me of the love lavished upon me by the heathen?'

With a conspiratorial wink, he continued. 'In fact, 'tis a long story, which I will probably bore you with many a time 'ere this journey is over, but let it suffice for now for me to tell you with all brevity, as I hunger!'

Even as he spoke, he crammed his mouth full between sentences. "The son of a noble family of Thracia, I was enslaved by my own countrymen when my father's debts became burdensome . . . Several of his business enemies pressed for payment in an unreasonably short time . . . Although they drove him to bankruptcy and eventual death as a slave laborer, that was not enough for their greedy souls, and they had my mother, my sisters and me sold as slaves, in order to gain some partial compensation and, likely, much personal satisfaction.

After some adventures, I came into the hands of a new master who decided to travel to the west, to the lands of the Lombards. On that long and difficult journey I was captured by brigands and sold to some Frankish traders . . . A short scenic stroll over the mountain range the natives call the Alps, where over a third of the captives died in the snows; a brief sojourn on the coast of *Frankland* as the unhappy tutor of uncouth barbarians' children, a blow to a spoiled brat, many blows to my back, and a Frisian ship in harbor concludes my story, except that the commander of this August vessel decided that I might once again be convinced to share my knowledge with barbarian brats, and bought me as a teacher."

Having ended his story, as well as his repast, Polonius turned the tables on Ambrose. "And would it be, my lord, uncouth for me to ask why one of your station travels thus on this floating pig sty?"

The story gushed forth from the young prince. The taciturn companionship of Phillip notwithstanding, Ambrose felt the need for one who could share in his inner world of useless facts and tremendous intellectual curiosity.

Polonius absorbed the story of the raid and the subsequent events silently, but nodded sympathetically when Ambrose touched upon the utter indignity and frustration of it all.

"My lord', Polonius said, 'I think I know how you feel, as I remember like it was yesterday the day I was seized and branded a slave!"

With that, Polonius pushed up the unruly patch of dark hair that adorned his head, and exposed an ugly burn-scar that would forever brand him a slave, a toy, a plaything to be coddled or whipped, depending upon the whim of a master, any master, who had the gold to buy the human toy.

The captain suddenly shouted to the men manning the long steering-oar, and the lean vessel began to veer towards an isolated island. Ambrose turned to Phillip.

"Old friend, why do you think we are heading for the sandy shore?"

"Look ahead, Prince. The island has an easy approach, and is isolated. It will be dark soon, and the crew is exhausted. I think they intend to sleep on solid ground tonight. See to the right? There are shelters there, and you can see fire pits along the shore. I think this must be one of the regular landing sites for sailors coasting these shores."

Phillip's prediction was accurate, for the ship ran as close to the shore as possible, and then selected crewmen splashed ashore with thick ropes. The ropes were tied to trees, and, once the vessel was secured, the rest of the crew leapt overboard and ran ashore, splashing each other and laughing all the way.

Several guards, heavily armed, remained to keep an eye on the captives and the open water. Most of the other men eventually returned and then loaded up with their weapons and food. In a remarkably short time, all the supplies needed to erect shelters, defend themselves and cook a meal were deposited on the beach.

The crewmen stretched out on the beach and broached several kegs of good Anglish mead. The savory aroma of cooking mutton tortured the captives, but to their surprise, enough meat was brought back aboard ship to feed the guards and captives both.

Day slid into night into day as effortlessly as the sun slipped into the western sea. Ambrose still chaffed at his captivity, but found in Polonius a distraction from his dreary predicament. The Byzantine scholar drove both Phillip and Ambrose hard, and all three of them rapidly became proficient in the Viking tongue. Polonius, although only exposed to the Danish dialect since shortly before coming aboard the ship, learned it with the ease of a man who was already able to speak more than a dozen languages.

Polonius explained to the young prince. "When you live in a house full of slaves garnered from the four corners of the world, you soon pick up a smattering of many tongues. Your life may depend upon it. Truth be told, I learned your tongue by speaking pillow-talk with a beautiful slave, though in truth my lovely tutor was from Saxony, and not Angleland."

The ship crew, apparently no longer in fear of ambush or chase, spent each succeeding evening anchored near small and uninhabited islands. The crews, after posting a guard, trooped ashore to feast and then sleep in comfort.

The great sail of the ship, stretched across the dismounted mast and tied to the gunnels, at least provided some protection for the captives against the evening dew. By day, the craft slid ever northward along the low coast.

As the fourth sun chased the third moon since leaving Wyk te Duurstede, the captives detected a new level of excitement amongst the crew. Judging from snatches of overheard conversation, Ambrose and his two companions deduced that the sailors' home village was no more than a few hours of travel away. Already the men waved at any fishermen or travelers along the shore.

A few at a time, the captives were unchained and put to work. The vessel soon shone. Weapons and clothes were burnished or arranged for best possible display. The sleek long-ship, battered by the savage storm, again looked fit for inspection. The wind, however, refused to co-operate. The mast was stepped and locked in place, but the winds were contrary, so the great sail could not be hoisted.

With the power provided by hard-working rowers, the sleek vessel continued to labor northward. At last the ship passed a sandy spit of land upon which a signal fire burned with a greasy plume of smoke. The captain ordered the oars in and secured, and tested the wind. The crew seemed impatient, but awaited instructions.

As soon as the wind veered a few more points to the east, the captain ordered the crew to hoist the square sail into place. Amid cheers and much excitement, the ship turned into a small natural harbor. Ambrose was fascinated to see several crew members unbolt the fierce dragon-head that towered over the ship and remove it from its pre-eminent position. Polonius explained the significance to Ambrose and Phillip.

"I understand that it is because of some pagan superstition about devils, my lord. The dragon head may lead the ship into other ports and shores, but never their own."

With the wind now at the right angle, the sail filled and drove the sleek vessel hard towards the shore. The captain ordered the men on the steering-oar to head directly towards the beach upon which were drawn up a variety of small fishing vessels.

Shouts could be heard and suddenly the beach was covered with yelling and gesticulating men, women, and children. Ambrose realized that the dreaded Viking emblem on the sail told these people that their men had finally returned!

In the distance, slaves ran after startled animals. The first preparations for a feast seemed to be already under way. With impeccable timing, the sail was dropped at the last possible moment. The crew stood by their oars, but Ambrose realized that it would have caused much shame if they had to be used. The bow of the ship sliced hard onto the beach.

Once the oars were neatly shipped, the crew broke ranks and swept overboard like a tidal wave; splashing ashore into a multitude of smiling and screaming people. Temporarily abandoned, the captives alone showed no great happiness at having arrived at their destination.

Ambrose, Phillip, and Polonius took a few minutes to inspect the town which would presumably be their new home. Phillip turned to his two companions.

"Well, the houses look somewhat rudely built, but at least they seem sturdy and snug."

Ambrose scanned the village again. "Phillip, they look a far cry from my brother's favorite *royal seat at Winchester*. Polonius, you said that you had lived in *Constantinople* for some time. How do these compare with the homes of your people?"

Polonius smiled. "Not like some cities I've visited, my lord, but, for a rude hamlet, it at least looks prosperous."

The clothes worn by the villagers were of a bewildering variety, and Ambrose wondered how many of them had actually been made on the looms of the local people. Silk and other exotic clothes were as commonplace as woollen ones, but Ambrose was sure that much of the finery had been taken from victims of their raids, and donned for the benefit of the returning men.

Polonius spoke. "If you look through that barrier of trees, you can see glimpses of a network of fields further inland."

Ambrose replied. I can see no forest. Apparently little land is wasted. Most appears to be crop land."

⌐

The captives were not totally forgotten, for towards dark the captain returned to the vessel and had a burly man strike off the rivet that kept the chain attached to the mast mounting. The massive chain was pulled through the large link welded to the iron collars, and the captives were finally loose. Now mobile, the captives were herded ashore and into a storage shed near the water's edge. A rude fence surrounded the hut, affording the captives a place to walk outdoors, but making it easy for two young guards to keep an eye on them. Just before the captain left, he turned to the captives and spoke not unkindly to them, in Danish.

"You are now *thralls* of the Danes. Tomorrow you will be assigned your masters and tasks. You will obey your new masters in all things or you will suffer great pain. If you try to escape, we will organize a hunt with our dogs, and any survivors will have their tendons cut. Go now, and obey your new masters!"

Long after the captain left, Ambrose and his two comrades sat silently by themselves. Each was deep into his own thoughts. The other captives all copied their passivity. Two women, however, drew from each other that phenomenon of society - mutual and cumulative reinforcement of their anxiety. They worked themselves into a panic. Seeing that Phillip and Polonius were lost in their own private worlds, Ambrose spoke up in a voice of command; one that he had almost forgotten he owned.

"Quiet women! You are alive and unharmed! Be thankful for God's small mercies. Tomorrow we discover our fate, but we are all alive and well. Tonight we should thank God for our blessings."

Ambrose was never sure if it was the snap of a voice accustomed to command, or if it just started the womens' thought processes down another pathway, but the two subsided into little more than a few muffled sobs and snuffles.

In God's truth, Ambrose thought, looking at the women, they all have retained at least some beauty of face and figure, in spite of the tangled and matted hair and the obvious filth covering them.

Ambrose spoke softly to the Byzantine scholar. "Polonius, what will really happen to the women tomorrow?"

The lean man looked pensive for several moments. "My lord, women, especially beautiful ones, generally suffer only one fate in life, whether they be free or slave. Some are lucky enough to have their lover spread their legs, while others have a master mount them. The difference between rape and lovemaking is nothing but a nod from the woman."

Ambrose mulled over the comments. "Are you saying that they will enjoy being raped?"

"No, my lord. Not at all. But a kind master may be more gentle than a brutal husband chosen by a well-meaning father. I believe all women can learn to love the touch of a man . . . if the man is sensitive and gentle enough. And in the end, the consequence of both rape and lovemaking is the same; a small bundle that needs much loving."

"Polonius, I just pray to Almighty God that the women can find some measure of happiness here in this foreign land."

"Amen, Prince. May that be true for all of us. Much will depend on whose property we become tomorrow."

As the darkness gradually crept up the side of the hut, each of the captives remained in their private universes. They were only visited once, when an affable woman brought them fresh water and hearty food. Throughout the day, and long into the night, the noises of drunken revelry reached their ears.

When a particularly loud cacophony of noises caused Phillip, Ambrose, and Polonius to look up at the same time, the emaciated

Byzantine smiled and spoke.

"I suppose, my lord, that it be only just and fitting to give the returning heroes a great party. I have no doubt but that there's many a pirate-raider that never returns to his family and children, and many a bed only half-full in such a nation of adventurers. The wind, the waves, even the peasants' scythes and arrows must have taken their toll, on beaches from Frisia to Hannibal's home.'

Noting Ambrose's puzzled expression, Polonius hurried on. 'Which was, as you no doubt remember, young scholar, on the northern coast of Africa, south of Italy. There are even persistent rumors of these Viking scavengers sailing the Asian steppes and interrupting the flow of furs and slaves from the northern lands to my own homeland."

Ambrose interrupted. His interest was piqued. "How, Polonius, great sailors as they may be, could these sailors travel the great plains of Asia in boats?"

"Well, in plain fact, 'tis true, my lord, that there is a chain of mighty rivers that extend from the *Pontus Euxinus*, far to the north. Legends say they extend even to the great northern frozen sea. A daring sailor, could, perhaps, sail a smaller vessel along these rivers, for it is these rivers that are used to bring goods across the Asian steppes. It is God's truth that I have seen fur-clad Viking barbarian traders walking the streets of Constantinople."

"What interest does Byzantium have in this vast area you speak of?" asked Ambrose.

"Oh, many,' Polonius responded, 'since many of the towns along the shores of the Pontus Euxinus have been partners with Byzantium in trade for centuries, and a major portion of the shore itself is an integral part of the Empire. It is through this area that many barbarian slaves come. The fair Circassian maidens of the Caucasus mountains are legendary for their beauty, as are their horses for speed. From the far north comes furs, ambergris, and ivory from giant sea-animals.

Equally important, Byzantium hires some of the horsemen from the mounted nomad tribes that migrate across the open grasslands. The Empire has a large mercenary cavalry force, made up of Magyars, *Khazars*, and many other barbarian nations. Byzantium throws these wild horsemen against the inroads of other barbarian nomads, and, especially, against the fierce Arab horsemen riding out of the South."

Ambrose was puzzled. "But why should the Byzantines want to pay others to fight their battles? Are not war games the most important lessons taught to all noble citizens?"

In the dark, Ambrose could barely see the smile on Polonius' face.

"My lord, I know not exactly how to answer. The life of most of the Byzantine citizens, or at least those of the capital of Constantinople, is tied up with affairs of commerce and culture. The risk of one's life, at least to a Byzantine, is a foolish thing. One only fights a savage and implacable enemy host if one is unable to hire others, more brave or foolish, to do the job for you. Although there is a very well-trained and strong Byzantine army, it is composed of professional soldiers. Some of the soldiers have even come from as far away as the northern Viking lands in order to enlist.

The Empire, you see, is surrounded on all sides by many fierce people, any one of whom is far stronger than the Danes, or, begging your pardon, the Angles, Saxons and Jutes of Angleland. Each of these new tribes that arrive on the frontier either want to settle on the Empire's most fertile land, or they want to loot the wealth of the great commercial cities.

The Byzantines drive them back, often into the arms of other tribes that have themselves advanced into the former tribe's territory. With their old land taken, our riches to goad them on, and their own warlike traditions, it is little wonder that each of these migrations is a potential threat to the Empire.

Worse, in the last hundred years have come wave after wave of Moslems from the south. They preach conversion by the sword to all nonbelievers. Allah is their god and his prophet is Mohammed. They are not content with tribute, bribes, or even the treasures of our cities, but fight to stamp out Holy Mother Church itself! How does one fight fanatics whose interest in gold is less than their interest in adding your name to the list of the true-believers?'

Ambrose nodded and Polonius continued. His voice was the only sound heard in the compound. All the captives were either listening to his comments, or had lost themselves in reverie.

'My lord, with the blood of both the ancient Romans and Greeks running in their veins and surrounded by millions of barbarians, how could the Byzantines not be expert at war? They, however, prefer not to bloody their swords unless it becomes necessary. What better approach can you think of than to hire mercenary barbarians to fight off other barbarians? In the killing, both barbarian nations are weakened."

There was a long silence. At last, Ambrose replied.

"All the same, it somehow does not seem right to hire others to fight when you are able to do it yourself."

"My lord, does a prince sweep dirt from his doorway, or does his bondsman not do it for him?"

With no ready answer, and as yet only a nebulous set of feelings that something in Polonius's statements did not add up, Ambrose sat silently in the dark. Intruding into the darkness were the continuing sounds of wild revelry.

Each person sank deeper into his or her own personal and intimate thoughts, and no one else ventured to break the silence that descended upon the group. High above, the glorious canopy of velvet black, studded with twinkling sparks of light, wheeled in slow motion.

The night seemed to last forever. One by one, however, each of the captives eventually managed to fall asleep. Only after the sun had risen at least two hands above the horizon did a group of armed warriors enter the little hut and awaken the captives.

"Outside! Out! All to go out!"

The sailor who had acted as interpreter before was with the men, and it was he who shouted at the frightened captives. The prisoners obeyed with alacrity. The village warriors looked much the worse for wear. They carried bared weapons, and their tempers were vile.

Once the captives were blinking in the early morning light, they were unceremoniously herded along. "You! Go to man there!"

One by one, the prisoners were sent over to the burly man standing by a massive tree stump. There, the man, with a single skillful blow each, knocked out the rivet that held their collars shut. Then, one at a time, they were directed outside of the palisade.

At last the entire group of prisoners was gathered in the open, in a kind of village green surrounded by the Viking homes on all sides. The sun shone brightly, the day was glorious, and Ambrose waited to hear his fate.

Ambrose's eyes again roamed over the sturdy timber houses, with their earth berms along the sides, and thatched or sod roofs. Various groups of villagers arrived and gradually merged into a continuous circle of curious onlookers. Each of the captives felt the eyes of the people upon them, and the women blushed when the men stared hungrily at them.

Ambrose watched the apprehension and embarrassment play across the women's' faces. He knew they feared that the dreaded moment had finally come when they would be forced to submit to their captors. The men were no less apprehensive. Each man wondered if he would receive a relatively easy assignment, or be brutally worked to death. The answer would mean life or death to each of them.

Oddly enough, however, the crowd was not intentionally cruel. A barrier of language existed, as of culture, but Ambrose realized that, so far, except during the attack on the village, there had been no evidence of wanton cruelty. It was obvious to the young prince that horns did not grow out of the Viking heads, nor were they all seven foot-lengths tall. Ambrose had been surprised to note that not even the Viking helmets sprouted horns. The prince wondered if Mother Church was also wrong about their diabolical natures, for he had heard terrible tales of the Vikings when he had sat at the feet of visitors to his father's court. He did remember their ferocious fighting manner, however, and their utter ruthlessness with the slow or disobedient.

When most of the villagers had arrived, the captain, wearing Ambrose's flowing scarlet cloak and breeches of fine wool climbed upon a suitable parked cart. From there he started to address the gathered throng. Ambrose was able to follow, at least haltingly, what was said, but Polonius, with his gift for languages, was faster, and he whispered a translation to Ambrose and Phillip.

"My people, I, Lief Olafson, and my faithful crew, have successfully returned from a long and arduous voyage."

With that the people let out great cheers and pummeled the crewmen on their backs. After allowing a minute of pandemonium, Lief raised his hand and continued.

"After a bitter and unsuccessful fight with the Moors of southern Spain, our long-ship crew sailed north again. Some of our finest young men had died in battle, yet the crew had little to show for it.

At last our vessel separated from the main fleet, and the combined crews of it and another ship coasted the shores of southern Angleland. Then an odd thing happened. A small ship came out from shore and intercepted us. We were ready to put the reckless fools in chains, until one, in quite good Danish, told us his master waited for us on the shore, under a flag of truce. The brash fellow held up several gold coins, so we decided to humor him.

We rowed close to the shore, and some nobleman waded out to parley with us. Before stepping into the surf he lined the shore with a shield-wall of spearmen protecting archers, so we could not try any tricks."

The audience stared enraptured. Several of them could stand it no longer and called out.

"What did he want?!"

"The Saxon wanted to pay us to attack a village further down the coast! He handed us several more gold coins, and promised to take care of the sentries if we struck that night."

A heavy-set woman spoke on behalf of the crowd. "And what

happened?"

Lief shrugged his shoulders. "The river-side sentries really were withdrawn. That night we attacked the town. We achieved total surprise. Besides the booty, which you all saw displayed last evening, we returned with these captives who you see before you now."

Many of the Vikings broke into loud discussion, until Lief raised his hand for silence. "It has been decided at the *Thing*, and with the consent of all the crew, that every family who lost a man on the voyage may choose a male or female slave to help in that man's place. Any crew member may choose a maiden and deduct the value from his share of the booty. After they have chosen, each village widower of the last two years will be given first choice of a maiden for his bed, though he must pay fair recompense into the expedition treasury. The rest will be put to auction; the money to be split equally amongst the crew and the bereaved families.

I believe this to be a just and fair distribution of the booty. As is our custom, a tithe will be sent to our *Jarl*, that we may continue to be in his favor. If all this is satisfactory, we will now have the selection of the captives, that we may sooner return to our homes and celebrate the town's good fortune."

The roar of the crowd indicated that they agreed happily to these proposals. The captives huddled more closely together as the circle of citizens started to close tighter around them. Polonius looked sharply at Ambrose. He whispered. "Did you hear that, Lord?"

"Aye, I understood enough! Phillip, what did you make of what he said?"

"We knew it was either treachery or bad luck, Prince. Now we know. By God's beard, we now know that you were betrayed by a Saxon!"

Ambrose looked at Phillip with horror on his face. "Surely even Ethelbert would not dare to sell us to the heathen?!"

"It appears that someone did."

"But for what purpose?"

Phillip shrugged. "As I said before, it makes for one less atheling to choose from if anything happens to your brother, King Ethelbald, and Dorset does not necessarily go to an *ealdorman* who is fanatically loyal to the king."

"But Phillip, we have already discussed this. Ethelbert is already Under-King. He is the logical successor if something happens to Ethelbald."

"That is the choice of the Witan, boy. Their choice is never known in advance, but you are not now in a position to oppose him should Ethelbert make a bid for the crown."

"Then I pray that Ethelbald lives to be a very old man."

A crewman, the one who had twice before translated for the captives, stepped forward and held up his hand for silence. When the crowd had muffled their good-humored good-humored noise, he spoke to the captives in bad Anglish.

"The . . . village of Fornsgaard welcomes you . . . The terribly Viking decide not to eat you . . . You will be divided, and must . . . work at what you told to do . . . Any one who tries run away will be hunted and crippled so.'

As he spoke he chopped with his hand at his Achilles tendon, and the meaning was clear, for it was not uncommon to see slaves even in Angleland with their tendons cut, effectively preventing their running away a second time. He then smiled with anticipation of the fun about to begin.

'Now, each person to remove ALL clothes for to show bodies. All clothes!"

In a fit of good natured humor, the villagers aided the shyest in pulling off what remained of their garments. Within seconds, and to the accompaniment of gales of laughter, the captives stood naked and exposed to view. Most of the women vainly attempted to cover their genitals. They felt little concern for their breasts, as it was common for most women in Angleland to suckle their young openly and without shame. Ambrose took his cue from Phillip and Polonius, and they all stood as still as resting herons, making no attempt to hide that which gave them claim to manhood.

The villagers circulated freely, and had much merriment pointing at the exposed parts of the captives, pinching fat breasts, or examining teeth. One by one the captives were chosen and taken before the chief's scribe. The scribe recorded who had taken a captive, and who agreed to pay what.

Ambrose and Polonius, however, were waved to the side of the ship's captain. The commander, still dressed in Ambrose's cloak, was talking to an old man dressed in somber garb. Both prisoners were able to follow the gist of the conversation, and carefully did so.

"I suggest, honored father, this boy here. He is young and small, but he has the heart of a Viking! When the ship was in danger because of a storm and a broken oar, it was he who leapt to the oar and helped to save us all. Although not yet fully a man, or as strong as he will be, he is of like age to your son when he died, and would mayhap be useful to you. It be further true that he is of noble blood. His hulking guard there,' And with that he gestured to a couple who were leading a naked Phillip away, 'Killed two men in order to keep us from him, and the other captives all listen to and obey this young one.

In truth, I can recommend none better if you want more than a dumb work-beast. Take this one without cost, if he pleases you, for the death of your son lies heavily upon me, and I want you to have some of the help you will need in your old age that your son could have accorded you."

Thus was Ambrose's fate secured, and he was led off with a captive Saxon maiden, so young that her breasts were still high, pointed and firm.

Even as they were being led away, Ambrose overheard the captain speaking to the scribe about Polonius, and he listened as long as he was able.". . . and I want him kept aside. It may be that we will have to cripple or castrate him, but he is a scholar and I want our boys to learn more of the world than just our northern lands."

"Lief, do you plan to fill our young warriors with Christian prattle?"

"Make no mistake, scribe, the power of the Christians is great, and their truth is contained in the scribbles they call writing. I want our warriors to know the secrets of our enemies, and, to do that, some of us must learn to read their sacred writings. This one will teach our children the secrets of writing, and even how to converse in other languages. I want . . . "

The conversation faded as Ambrose was led through the crowd and taken towards a large timber house. As they walked, their new master spoke to them in Danish.

"Do either of you speak Danish? No . . . of course not! What would German barbarians be doing speaking a civilized tongue? Well, come along and I'll teach you your tasks soon enough."

Ambrose spoke up in Danish, haltingly. "Your pardon, Master . . . I speak . . . a little of . . . your language. If it pleases you, I will teach it . . . you woman slave, who speaks only Anglish."

The old man smiled at, presumably, the sound of Ambrose butchering his language. "Well spoken, my boy. What is your name, and that of the young woman?"

"Ambrose, sir, if it pleases you." Ambrose then turned to the girl and asked her in Anglish what she was called. She responded timidly.

"Anna, Sire."

Ambrose passed on the information to the old man, who asked a series of questions about their home, their interests, and their likes. Before they reached the house, they were quite at ease with him, and quite forgot the ludicrous spectacle of two naked youngsters following an ancient man of over sixty seasons.

They arrived at the old man's home, and Anna seemed intimidated at the size of it. The compound consisted of several outbuildings and one large building. Inside, Ambrose and Anna were surprised to see that the building was divided into two separate rooms, with hide curtains providing privacy.

Ambrose, used to his brother's eight room *burh* at Winchester, was not overly impressed, except for the fact that the house was extremely snug, and would provide good shelter from the raging storms that would surely sweep along the coast come winter. Anna, however, stood in awe at the size of the building.

Seeing them hesitate, the old man introduced himself to them and then explained the domestic arrangements.

"My name is Canute. Sit, barbarians, and I will tell you more about myself. You see before you my house, built by Jorn, my son, and myself, for my dear wife. She passed away last winter, always mourning for our dear son. Somewhere in Frankland, some years ago, a barbarian spitted him. His body now lies moldering on some riverbank, and I will never be able to give him the honor of a Viking funeral."

Canute paused. His eyes, even in the limited light, appeared misty to Ambrose. Ambrose did his best to translate for Anna, who desperately wanted to know what the old man was saying. At length the old man continued.

"But I stray from my subject - my quarters are beyond the curtain. It is the way my wife wanted it."

With that he pointed at the far end of the room, and then turned again to look at Ambrose and Anna. Suddenly he clapped his hand to his mouth.

"My dear little savages, I had quite forgotten your state of undress. Ambrose, go you to that wooden trunk over there, and look for clothes that will fit - they were my son's.

Anna, come you with me. I will try to find something to match your barbarian beauty."

Anna hesitated, and then, after Ambrose's translation, followed Canute into the old man's personal quarters.

CHAPTER 7.

Ambrose Works Hard, Trains, and Learns to Make Love.

Thus Ambrose settled into his new home. Canute was a kind and gentle man, if somewhat given to shouting great oaths when he dipped into his mead. He took good care of both of his thralls, however. It was not long before a strong bond of friendship grew between the strange trio. Anna was called but seldom to sleep with her master. She spent most of her time tending the field of crops that belonged to Canute, or grinding meal and cooking for the three of them.

Ambrose, slight of build, helped her when he could, but he was often also instructed to help Polonius in the hut of learning the village chief had set up within his own compound. Of all the inhabitants of the entire village, only the two of them could write or read any southern languages, and even Ambrose's skills were rudimentary compared to the Byzantine's.

In a matter of weeks, Ambrose's Danish was more than adequate, while Polonius' was as smooth and polished as anyone in the village. Daily, Polonius and he drilled away at an odd assortment of lads. The two foreigners attempted to teach them the basics of math and how to read in Latin, although here Polonius was handicapped by not knowing the Danish runes. He had been surprised to learn that most adult Vikings could read runes, as well as write them. Thus he threw himself into mastering the Viking runes.

Life in the village wasn't terribly onerous, though all, Danes and slaves together, worked hard. The thralls saw much of each other in the evenings, after the chores were done for the day. Of them all, only a few had brutal masters. One girl, ill-used by her master and several of his drunken guests, went insane and ran naked through the village, screaming and foaming at the mouth. Even the thralls were thankful when an accurately thrown boar-spear ended her torment.

On one particularly fine summer morning, when Ambrose was free of any duties, he eagerly sought out Phillip. More than once, when sent on some errand, Ambrose had seen the massive thane working the fields of his new master.

Ambrose's old friend and tutor wore a heavy thrall's collar and was harnessed to a plough. Only his great strength and endurance allowed the Weapons-master to survive, as his master was generous with a whip and frugal with food. Village thralls told Ambrose that Phillip's master was a drunkard who believed in the theory that it was cheaper to overwork and underfeed a thrall to death, rather than wastefully feed him the amount of food that the strenuous work required.

Worrying about Phillip alone kept Ambrose from settling into a rut of contentment, for he himself had considerate treatment, good food, companionship, and fresh air. His muscles hardened and skin bronzed in the summer sun.

Although still small for his age, the prince put on weight and grew some two hand-heights in height. Polonius went to great efforts to push the young man's mind hard on the mastery of several tongues and the many mysteries of the universe.

Ambrose was splitting firewood when Anna approached and called his name. The prince turned to see Anna silhouetted against the sun. Her blond hair glowed with the reflected light, and Ambrose could clearly see that she had nothing on under the thin gown. He looked away from her lithe body, but he could feel a flush spreading across his face.

She too, seemed to blush as she spoke to him. He had often noted the blush when she said something to him. Although he wanted to say something about her blond beauty, he just spoke tersely.

"Yes, Anna?"

"Master Canute asked me to send you to him right away."

"Then I am on my way.' He blushed again. 'Will you walk with me?"

Anna looked down at her feet, and Ambrose loved the way strands of blond hair slid over her face. "I would be honored, Atheling."

Ambrose thrust aside the hide covering that acted as door in the summer heat. He stepped into Canute's home and looked around in the semi-darkness for his master. At last, as his eyes adjusted, he saw the old Viking warrior standing by his weapons chest.

"You wanted me, Master?"

"Aye, Ambrose. Come stand beside me."

"Of course, Master."

When Ambrose had joined him, Canute reached into the open weapons chest and withdrew a sword made in the Viking manner. Stripping the oiled protective cloth from it, he held it high in the air.

"Ambrose, I fear that this is not as fine a weapon as a prince might have, yet it is a good and serviceable blade. My own son wielded it in battle. Its name is Deep-biter."

"It looks to be a fine blade, Master."

"Do you know how to use such a blade, Ambrose?"

"Until I was captured, I spent several hours a day practicing martial arts, Master."

"Were you good with a sword?"

"I lacked strength, Master, but Phillip, my instructor, said that I had a good eye and fast reflexes.' Ambrose spoke with sudden pride. 'Phillip said that when I got a man's strength, I would be a formidable fighter."

"Well, Ambrose, I have watched you at work for some time now. I think you have now developed that strength."

"I know I have grown a lot since I first arrived, Master, and the physical labor has hardened my muscles beyond anything I ever knew. I fear, however, I will never grow to the height of most Viking men. The lack of height is from my mother's side of the family."

"Ambrose, you have never told me about your mother. Was she a small woman and of Saxon blood?"

"Master, she was of royal British blood. In her veins ran both the blood of the ancient Romans and of the tribal chiefs who ruled my homeland even before the coming of the Romans."

"And that made you a prince, Ambrose?"

"No, Master. Our family long ago fell into hard times. When the Saxons came, my ancestors were defeated in battle. My mother's people became tenants in their own lands."

"But your people call you a prince, young Ambrose."

"My mother was of British royal blood, Master, but my father was king of the empire of Wessex."

"Ah, then he saw your mother and made her a queen."

Ambrose smiled. "Not quite, Master. She was a slave, but he did fall in love with her and made a royal mistress of her. And he recognized my birth. It is this kindness that made me a prince, Master."

"Until the terrible Vikings captured you, young prince."

"True, Master. That is how we see your people. But you have been very kind to me, and I am grateful."

"I do not think that you will always be a thrall, Ambrose. I want you to take that sword and clean it well. There is a wooden scabbard in there somewhere.

Starting tomorrow, the village lads will be training for war. I want you to join them."

Ambrose looked shocked. "Master, I cannot! I could lose my right hand or even my life if I raised a weapon against a free man of the village!"

"I spoke in the last meeting of the Thing. Thralls and *freedmen* are allowed to train with the sons of the village. You are only punished if you raise a weapon against a Viking in anger or disobedience."

"Then I will do as you command, Master. I will strive to make you proud of me."

Canute smiled. "Tomorrow at noon, Ambrose. Go and learn the Viking art of war."

౼

Lars, the youngest son of Lief the Drunkard, owner of Phillip, laughed as the diminutive Ambrose joined the little group. "Go back to your dung heap, slave! You have no business here amongst men."

"What you say may be true, Master Lars, but my Master Canute bade me come and learn the Viking way of fighting. I must obey."

"Ha. Then strap on your shield, and I will show you how a man fights!"

Without even waiting for Ambrose to unsheathe his sword, the bully attacked. Ambrose desperately swung up his shield. It saved his head, but he was driven to the ground with the force of several blows. Kiarr, the eldest of the unblooded youths, called out in alarm.

"Lars, we are supposed to train with the wooden swords! Ambrose is wearing neither protective padding nor helmet! If he had not been able to throw up his shield in time, he would be dead!"

"Then my father would pay the blood-price. This thrall thinks he is good enough to train with us. I intend to teach him otherwise."

Kiarr yelled in anger. "Amongst his own people he is a prince! And he only does what he is told by Canute. Your own father agreed to let him train with us."

"He didn't. He was outvoted. And no one asked my permission. If this Saxon from the dung pile is to pretend that he is a man, he will have to learn to fight like one!"

As Lars spoke, he started forward again. Ambrose rolled several times across the grass, and then climbed to his feet. **Deep-biter** slid from the scabbard.

"Master Lars, let me get a wooden practice sword. **Deep-biter** is sharp, and I have no wish to harm you!"

Lars started his own glittering blade swirling through the air. "Then throw down your weapon, slave, and return to the dung pile from whence you came!"

He stepped forward steadily, until he was within reach again of Ambrose. Keeping his light wooden shield high, he swung his sword again and again at Ambrose. The prince backed and shifted from side to side. Most of Lars' swings missed him completely, or grazed harmlessly off Ambrose's own shield.

Ambrose, afraid to harm the boy, protected himself from the hammering blows without attacking. Lars became furious when he realized that Ambrose's quick reflexes and skill prevented him from landing any telling blows.

"Stand still, you dancing fairy. Come here and fight like a man!"

"Master Lars, I am here to practice, not to fight a real duel with you!"

Lars turned in triumph to his friends. "You see? All slaves are cowards! A real man would die in battle before he is taken. Only cowards live to feel a thrall collar around their neck!"

With no place left to retreat, Ambrose was again forced to his knees.

"Lars!"

The mob of boys looked up to see old Uigbiorn approaching. Dressed in a fine shirt of chain-mail, the grizzled veteran of a hundred battles strode angrily into their midst. He had been responsible for training the village boys for more than a dozen years, and he was known as a fierce taskmaster. Amongst the unblooded youths, his word was law.

"You are attacking a thrall who is afraid he will be punished if he hurts you, boy! Only a coward would do such a thing. Both of you put down your weapons and pick up the wooden practice swords!"

Lars burned in embarrassment. "Why is this piece of Saxon shit amongst us? He is thrall and we are free men. He has no business here!"

"And do you wish to be old Canute's right arm and eyes? The Thing approved Ambrose's training, and you will obey your elders or find yourself exiled for life! Do I make myself clear?"

"Yes, Warrior."

"Good. Then strap on some protective clothing, get a practice sword, and then you can have at him. You, Ambrose, will do the same. You will then be able to defend yourself properly from this blowhard . . . No, Lars. You two are to use the weighted swords. Well, go to it, lads. You will fight until one of you cannot stand."

The two young men circled each other warily. Assured by both the weapons and the padding that he could not accidentally seriously hurt Lars, Ambrose attacked with a vengeance. The stocky and much heavier boy found himself driven back by the sheer fury of Ambrose's attack.

Pitting shield against sword and sword against shield, Ambrose pressed Lars to the edge of the crowd. At last, however, the sheer weight of the heavily weighted practice sword wore down the last reserves of Ambrose's strength. He faltered, and Lars, though sore and bruised from Ambrose's many successful hits, was finally able to return to the attack.

A powerful stroke from Lar's blade drove Ambrose's wooden sword from his nerveless fingers. Lars grinned and carefully stepped over Ambrose's blade. Triumph glinted in his eyes and Ambrose was sure that he intended to beat him half to death.

Ambrose's eyes flicked to his sword. Lars had positioned himself so that Ambrose had no chance to retrieve it. The prince saw Lars' sword descending. He deflected the blade with his shield, and then unexpectedly threw his shield at Lars' unprotected legs. Even while the shield struck Lars hard, Ambrose tried to roll into the attacker. Lars shrieked in sudden pain, but his sword struck hard against the padding Ambrose wore.

The blade fell again and again, until Uigbiorn called out. "Enough! That's enough, Lars. You have won. You, Ambrose! Can you get to your feet?"

Ambrose struggled to rise. His arm and shoulder were on fire. In spite of the thick padding, the blows had been very painful. "I think so, Warrior."

"Good. Lars, you are training to be a warrior, not a butcher. If that is the best you can do, then you have a long way to go before you can call yourself a warrior. This man has far faster reflexes than you. In a real fight and with a real sword, Ambrose would have cut you to pieces.

And you, Ambrose. You will have to work hard on developing your arm muscles. A Viking sword seems to be too heavy for you. And why did you throw away your only protection?"

"I'm sorry, Warrior. I hoped to close before he could use the sword on me. In real combat I would have attacked with my sax."

"And did it work?"

Ambrose hung his head. "No, Warrior."

"Then what would you do next time?"

"Go for the head, Warrior."

The old warrior and trainer threw back his head and laughed. "You will yet be a great fighter, little one. You have the spirit and the drive."

Lars was furious. "He is but a slave, Warrior! He should lose his right hand for even lifting a blade to me."

The old warrior turned to face the brash young man. "He did not, boy! Knowing that he could not defend himself properly against you, you chose to try and beat him to death. Only a coward would take on a man forbidden to fight back!"

Lars paled. "Are you saying that I am a coward, Warrior?"

"I do not yet know, Lars, son of Lief. If I find that you are, you will never go *a-viking* with these young men! There is no place amongst a warrior band for a coward."

⚑

Ambrose dejectedly slid around the deerhide that kept the insects from Canute's home. Canute was sitting in his seat-of-honor, and called out to the young man.

"The warrior returns! How went the training, boy?"

"I was able to batter Master Lars with the heavy wooden sword, but in the end I tired and lost my weapon. He beat me until I could not rise."

Canute's eyebrows lifted. "Oh ho! And is he as stiff as you?"

Ambrose suddenly smiled. "I think so, Master. If we had been using real swords, I would have killed him several times over before he was able to strike me."

"Then you have nothing to be ashamed of, young Ambrose. Strip off your shirt and let me see the damage."

Both Canute and Anna stared at the many marks criss-crossing Ambrose's arms and chest. Showing red now, Ambrose knew they would soon show as purple welts."

Canute looked concerned. "Anna! Go and fetch my healing unguents. We will rub it into Ambrose's muscles, and he will be a little less stiff tomorrow morning. Boy, what is that bruise by your left nipple?"

Ambrose's finger went to the mark Canute's old eyes had spotted. "Do you mean this, Master?"

"Aye, that one."

"It is but a birthmark, Master. My mother had the same mark on her left breast, and she told me her mother and her mother's mother had the same mark, down through many generations."

"My eyes do not focus as well as they used to, but from here it looks to be in the shape of a leaf."

"It is in the shape of an oak leaf. My mother told me the leaf was sacred to the ancient Druids, and the birthmark was proof of our claim to royalty. All the kings of our ancient lands had such a mark."

Canute looked thoughtful. "Your own Christ-priests have eradicated most of the Druids, but I have landed on islands in the Irish Sea which the Christ-priests have not yet conquered and the Druids still rule. The old-ones had powerful magic."

"My father's priests said that my mark was a sign of family sin and a brand to forever mark me with shame. They said that I should always keep it covered."

"And did you believe them?"

"It was what I was taught, Master."

"Then they were fools. Never be ashamed of what your ancestors were, Ambrose. They are who made you. They gave you life, and for this they must be always revered.

Ah, I see the beautiful Anna has returned. My dear, would you be so kind as to rub some of that liniment on our young warrior here. We want him to be able to move in the morning.

Ambrose, what did Warrior Uigbiorn say about your prowess?"

"Master, he said I had quick reflexes, but had to work on developing the strength of my arms. We were using heavily weighted wooden swords, and my arms eventually grew numb from fatigue."

"Anna, leave off rubbing the unguent on him for a moment. Come, Ambrose, I have an idea. Follow me."

Canute climbed stiffly from his seat and walked quickly back to the arms chest. Throwing open the chest's lid, he reached deep and withdrew another weapon well wrapped in oiled cloth. He tore off the covering, and then held the weapon out for inspection.

"This magnificent sword is called **Victory-Maker**. Have you ever seen such a weapon, Ambrose?"

"No, Master. My father the king had a vast collection of swords. Many came as gifts from foreign lands, but I have never seen such a one as this."

"What do you think of **Victory-Maker**?"

"It is beautiful. By the intricate work I would say that it may have belonged to a great nobleman or king, but it is thin, Master. Can it stand up to a heavy Viking blade?"

"Better than you think, young warrior. Our smiths often add a little carbon to the molten iron when they forge our swords. A lot of carbon makes the weapons much more able to hold a sharp edge, but it also makes them brittle. Our warriors prefer a blade that will bend rather than break. But the soft iron means that we do not attack with the point, nor can we achieve a razor sharpness on the edges.

Victory-Maker is different. It will cut nicks in the best Viking sword, yet it will not shatter. Here, hold it in your hand. Swing it, gently. What does it feel like?"

"Light as a feather, Master. I could swing this all day without tiring."

"Anna!"

Anna ran to approach old Canute.

"Yes, Master?"

"Fetch a small square of silk from my wife's chest, please."

"Which color would you like, Master?"

"The color does not matter. I want one a little larger than my hand."

Anna quickly returned with a small piece of bright red silk. "Here you are, Master."

"Good. Come, you two. Let us step outside. I need sunlight to show you my next trick."

The three stood side by side near the doorway. Canute smiled.

"Step well back. I don't want to hurt either of you. Watch carefully now."

Canute wadded the delicate material and threw it as high as he could. As it opened and floated gently earthwards, the old man swung the sword at it. To both Ambrose's and Anna's great surprise, the slim blade neatly sliced right through the material. Two separate pieces of silk landed on the ground.

Canute now grinned. "Have either of you ever seen a blade that can do that?"

Anna fingered the torn cloth. "No, Master."

Ambrose picked up the other piece and stared at it. "I have seen a razor once that could do it, but never a sword capable of such magic."

"Nay, Ambrose it is not magic. Some smith added unknown metals to the iron. See here? You can see by the ripples in the blade that the metal was heated, beaten, folded, and then beaten again. Whoever made this blade was truly an expert smith. He possessed skills and knowledge that our best smiths simply do not have. Even the best blades we import from Frankland cannot do this."

"Master, where did the blade come from?"

"Long ago when I was young and daring, we sailed through the passage we call *Narvesund*. We landed on the shores of a desert and surprised a caravan following the coastal road, killed the few guards who did not run and looted what pack-animals we could catch.

The animals themselves were very strange. They were much taller than a horse, and had a single large hump on their back. They had an evil temperament, and spat at us, yet they died quickly enough when we slit their throats. That sword was in the first pack that I opened."

Both Ambrose and Anna were enthralled. Ambrose spoke.

"Master, what happened after that?"

"It was as if we had disturbed an anthill. Within minutes, line after line of fierce mounted warriors attacked us. Whatever it was that we had attacked; it was not an ordinary caravan. We did, however, teach them proper respect for our *skjaldborg*.

"Skjaldborg?"

"The Viking shield-wall formation. We held off cavalry charge after cavalry charge. They were brave men and the bodies piled high in front of us. Finally the commanders realized that horsemen could not break our skjaldborg, so they changed their tactics and used their mounts to pass quickly by and loose a torrent of arrows at us. They were master archers and we would have died to a man if we had not managed to retreat to our boats.

"And so you did not learn anything about the sword, Master?"

"Only that I stole it from someone in Africa, and it was part of a treasure being taken somewhere. No, I learned one more thing, Ambrose."

"What is that, Master?"

"Look at the end of the blade, Ambrose. What do you see?"

"It is pointed and as sharp as the rest of the blade."

"Good, Ambrose. Unlike **Deep-biter**, the point is as deadly as the edge. Have you ever trained with a stabbing sword?"

"I have tried a stabbing sword based on the ancient Roman legionary model, Master, and Phillip, my weapons tutor in Wessex, taught me how to use my sax - my long knife, to slip through a crack in the shield-wall when I was in the Saxon shield-wall formation."

"Excellent. Then you know the power of a sharp point. This blade can give you an insurmountable edge over a Viking warrior armed with a traditional blade, if you but learn to use it properly."

"Master, I can not use **Victory-Maker**! It is worth a king's ransom."

"Ambrose, you are in training to protect me in my old age. I expect you to use the best weapons available. Is that clear?"

Ambrose noted the twinkle in Canute's eyes, and he grinned. "Yes, Master!"

Returning **Deep-biter** to the weapons chest, Ambrose spent the next few weeks concentrating on developing his skills with the fine and gently curved sword that Canute owned and insisted Ambrose learn to use. Of an unknown alloy of steel, and light as a feather, Ambrose could twirl it far more dexterously than the Danes swung their own clumsy swords.

The supple blade even bent two or three far thicker weapons. With his speed with Canute's sword and rapidly improving accuracy with the bow, Ambrose found himself becoming one of the more formidable of the village boys; although in sheer brawn they continued to well outmatch him.

Only once did Lief, father of Lars, watching his own son's sword swept out of his hand by Ambrose's fast-moving blade, argue again that a thrall should not be training with free-born Danes. When the matter went a second time to the village Thing, Canute merely spoke quietly.

"If Ambrose is not to learn the skills necessary to protect me, will you volunteer to sleep by my front entrance and guard my person? Will you, Lief, be my eyes and launch the arrow that will bring down the deer?"

Lief looked hard at the ground by his feet. "Well, I could hardly do that."

Canute called out. "I cannot hear you, Lief. Are you saying you will?"

"Uh, I cannot do that."

"Then perhaps you will lend me Lars."

"He has his duties. What you are asking is not reasonable."

"If you or your son are not able to protect me and hunt for me, then who is? Our laws are quite clear. A thrall may fight in his master's defense, and in time of war he wins his freedom by doing so.

Lief, am I to have an untrained thrall to protect me against brigands and bears and such, or one who has learned the military arts? Or, perhaps, you are angry because Ambrose has the skill to defeat Lars? Ambrose was given to me to replace my own boy. I expect

Ambrose to have the same training my own son got. Is this, neighbors and friends, such an unreasonable request?"

With the pattern of sleep, eating, school work, armed practice, and field work becoming a constant, Ambrose slipped from day to day, until several months were painlessly devoured. Polonius' pattern was a little different, as he worked at the school most of the time, and slept there, but the time slipped by as effortlessly.

One night during that first summer, Ambrose sensed Anna approaching naked from the master's room and bending over him. She whispered softly into his ear. "My lord, may I lie beside you?"

Taken aback, Ambrose didn't know what to say. He had never lain with a girl, and the hormones in his young body often caused an ache in his genitals that he only managed to assuage through hard work and violent exercise.

As Anna lay down, a beam of moon light from the uncovered window lit up her body, showing it to be lustrous and smooth. She lay beside him, and he felt her sweet breasts rub softly against his bare skin. His loins ached as he briefly saw the soft patch of downy fuzz that hid her maidenhood.

Anna lay shyly beside Ambrose, making no movement to touch his inflamed body, nor preventing him when at length he reached out one trembling hand to caressingly and shyly explore her female wondrousness. His hands slid over her cheek and mouth, sliding to her neck and exploring gradually lower. He cupped a warm breast in his hand, and could feel her heart throbbing almost wildly in her bosom.

Here he lingered, afraid of going any further in this madness. Well he knew that capture at this time could mean castration, a painful and lingering death at the hands of his master, or, worse yet, as a plaything for the women of the village.

As he struggled with his thoughts and emotions, Anna whispered softly into his ear, in a voice at once so gentle and shy that Ambrose trembled uncontrollably at the sound of it.

"My lord, unworthy as I am, I am yours to take as you will."

Ambrose responded, putting some of his anxiety into words. "Anna, you belong no more to me or any Saxon! You are the property of old Canute, who has the right to do with you as he pleases. Although I long for your body more than anything else on this mortal world, I fear for you if he discovers us!"

Anna bent her head in submission to Ambrose. "My lord, Master Canute specifically bade me leave his side. He said he has never been so tired, and he strictly enjoined me to make sure that you were comfortable. Thus I am here."

Ambrose's tortured body couldn't stand it any longer, and his hand, almost with a will of its own, plunged down her smooth belly to the ultimate secret place of womanhood. There, he explored clumsily. He felt Anna become clammy and then wet within desire for him.

Emboldened, he mounted her, and his penis, with an instinct as old as man, found its thrusting way into her. A gasp of pain proved to Ambrose that Anna, too, was new at this, and then she began to convulse in his arms.

Frightened at first by her response, Ambrose soon found his own body coming closer and closer to release. While her grasping vaginal muscles squeezed the head of his penis, he fought his way to the precipice. Both moaned and clung tightly to the other. They became oblivious to all else in their universe.

At last it was over, and both lay panting and quiet on Ambrose's bed of pine boughs. Anna spoke softly.

"My lord, I have long hoped for, and feared, this night. I prayed when I was taken captive that it would be someone like you who would relieve me of my virginity, and not some filthy pirate. I am grateful that you could find it in you to sleep with such a one as I."

Muffled sobs attested to the depths of her feelings, and Ambrose held her long into the night, caring little for the ache in his arms caused by the cramped position. A boy no longer, he felt shamed that he had taken her virginity, but wondered, too, that Canute had not done so long before.

CHAPTER 8.

Phillip Has Cruel Masters.

The months followed each other as one goose follows another in their twice yearly migrations. Winter came, and Ambrose's rhythm of life slowed a little. All was well at Canute's household, and Anna began to grow plump in her belly.

Canute smiled and told the two young slaves that he was terribly pleased that he had this uncontested proof of his sexual prowess. For Polonius, little changed. The classes with the village youths continued whenever they could be spared from work. When the weather allowed it, military practice continued.

Ambrose grew adept at snaring animals in the nearby woods. Polonius continued to stuff his head with what the scholar considered to be many important and interesting facts, and Phillip was at least no longer harnessed to a plough. With the food surreptitiously given him by Ambrose, taken with Canute's blessing, Phillip grew stronger than he had been for months. Often set to gather firewood, he and Ambrose spent some relatively carefree days in the woods, pairing up to chop wind-fallen timber.

A man of few words, Phillip was able to mutely express his devotion to his young former master. For his own part, Ambrose felt deep love for this giant thane who had long been his arms trainer, and had acted as his bodyguard and mentor. Anger at the angry welts that now crossed Phillip's back smouldered within the young prince.

Although Phillip never spoke of it, the stories of the family's cruelty was told to Ambrose by various Saxon thralls. Phillip dwelt in the house of Lief the Drunkard with several other slaves, the wife, and two sons. The offspring were great greasy louts who had few brains and a mean temperament. Lars, the youngest, avoided more contests with Ambrose, but continued to bully anyone he could.

Generally idle, and often drunk, both father and sons terrorized the thralls. Lars was accused of raping a neighbor's woman-servant, but he was allowed to pay *wergeld* to the woman's master, and the matter was forgotten. When angry with each other, or when feuding with their neighbors, they took out their anger on their own servants, for, like many drunkards, they were cowards, and knew their thralls to be defenseless before their wrath.

ᚦ

Spring arrived, and soon the entire village was busy with the spring planting. The sandy soil was reasonably fertile, and, with great care, bounteous. Once Ambrose asked Canute why his people had taken to such a dangerous pastime as raiding other lands. Canute thought long before he answered.

"My boy, the land of the Danes is fertile, and we make good use of all of it, but it is small, and our population constantly grows. To the south, there are the Franks and the Frisians. To the north, the east and the west, there is only water. We have stolen some of the Frisian lands, but now we face the Franks. After Charlemagne's death they became divided and soft, but they are still as many as the spawning salmon.'

Canute shrugged. 'They have built fortifications against us along our southern border that we cannot easily broach, so we just slip past their walls by ship and sail to other, weaker parts of the land of the Franks. We have managed to raid considerable coastal stretches of Frankland, but we do not have enough young men to do more than raid the Frankish coast. We have countered with a wall of our own across the southern end of the isthmus, but I pray to the gods every night that the sons and grandsons of Charlemagne never manage to re-unite the old empire.

To the north and the east, over the waters, lie our cousins the Norse and the Swedes. We do occasionally fight with them, but their land is much less fertile than ours, and the climate is more extreme. The Swedes rule much of the inland sea that laps on our eastern islands, and they guard their trade routes jealously. They, too, have been forced to turn to their boats and sail in search of plunder, trade, and land for their children to farm. Thus, in Angleland, Irishland, Frankland, and the northern islands, our ships and armies are familiar sights. The Christ-believers there have grown weak, and we need their land for our children.

You must understand, Ambrose, that only the young and foolhardy sail to rape and burn. Far more important is the silver and gold to buy food and weapons; and land to settle. It is our people who are settling now in the north of your island, and they want mainly to live in peace and settle. The Picts and your tribesmen, of course, hate all Danes as demons, and strive mightily to push us back into the sea. It is not so much greed that teaches us to be savage warriors and fearless sailors, but sheer need."

Ambrose nodded. "And you told me once that your religion teaches you that the only way to Valhalla is for a warrior to fall fighting bravely in battle."

"That is true, Ambrose. Our men are not suicidal, but most do not fear death. It makes for brave warriors. In time, when I become infirm, I would have asked my son to stand me up in battle with a sword in my hand. Perhaps that will be your task, young Ambrose."

"And only thus could you join the gods at Valhalla?"

"Only thus."

"May that time be far in the future, Master."

"There are days I feel ready to join my son at Odin's feasting hall, young Ambrose, but, no, I do not think that the *Norns* have woven my fate to end quite yet."

"The Norns, Master?"

Canute smiled. "I do not know what the Christ-priests have filled your head with, Ambrose. The Norns are three maidens who live under the tree of life and weave every man's future."

Ambrose smiled in return. "I thank you, Master. You have explained much."

↦

Ambrose spent some days mulling over what Canute had said, as well as discussing it with Polonius. In truth, it seemed to explain much which had previously been to him inexplicable. Now that he lived amongst the Danes, he had wondered how such simple people of the plough and sea had become famous as the cruelest marauders that existed on the face of the earth.

↦

In May of that year, which Canute explained was called the month of Harpa, an important local Jarl's army passed through the little village. For the first time Ambrose and Polonius saw some of the regular Danish tribal levies. The expedition which had captured Ambrose and Phillip had been but a private venture, independent of the tribal raids that had started years before in northern Angleland.

For years the Danes had limited themselves to brief forays on the Saxon coast; lightning quick assaults on villages and abbeys. But Ambrose knew that even in his brother's empire of Wessex the Danes had several times landed in force.

The far north of the island, as Canute had pointed out, was already partly settled by Danes. Larger and larger armies wintered in the parts of Frankland that were weak, and, in recent years, they had started to build permanent settlements.

When Ambrose heard the drums of an approaching force, he ran to the hut that served as the village's school. Polonius and the few students suffering numerical sums willingly stepped outside in response to the noise and excitement. Ambrose watched with a critical eye as the force of over eight hundred warriors marched along the coastal road and through the village itself.

Ambrose spoke to the thin Byzantine standing by his side. "Look, Polonius! They seem well armed. Each man carries both spear and sword or battle axe. And look! Each man has an identical metal cap to protect his head, and all wear a chain-mail shirt."

The eight hundred soldiers marched by in neat columns; stepping in unison and singing bawdy songs. Even Polonius seemed reasonably impressed.

"Aye, lord. They are well armed, and at least seem to have trained enough to march in formation. I see no cavalry, however. Not since the days of the ancient Romans has an army consisted only of infantry."

"But Polonius, their ships are their steeds. They but march to join their fleet south of here."

The troops were followed by a vast column of ox-carts and military camp followers. There were the supplies and spare weapons, wives and children, prostitutes and traders, of the powerful army. There were more than enough soldiers to fill the Jarl's fleet that waited at anchor.

Polonius watched the column march by for a full minute before he spoke. "How would your Saxons handle these invaders, Prince?"

"The sheer numbers are not a problem, Polonius. My brother has raised several times this number at short notice, and, given time, he can call upon his sworn men from Cornwall all the way to the Kentish coast. These Danes appear to be professional warriors, however, and that is a matter of great concern."

"Oh, how so?"

"Against such disciplined ranks would be thrown a horde of churls, leavened with some thanes, ealdormen and athelings; each armed in his own manner, and each fighting as he chose. Of all the Saxon forces, only the veteran fyrdmen, all mounted and well armed, could match this force man for man. My brother, however, has less than two thousand sworn fyrdmen spread across his entire kingdom, including even the subject provinces. Most of the forces that march to battle in Wessex when the call to arms is sent out are the retainers of the fyrdmen, and any other peasants who are able to carry a mattock or axe."

Polonius spoke quietly, but it seemed as if he was reading the prince's mind. "It would take more than mattocks and sickles to halt such a force, my lord. If your countrymen wish to throw such into the sea, they must copy my own people, and keep a standing army of well-trained professionals. Only thus, in conjunction with your levies of village archers, slingers, and pikemen, would they stand a chance."

"Polonius, each Anglish king, even each important ealdorman, retains a personal guard, what we call a *comitatus*, at his side at all times. These men, well mounted and well armed, are the flower of the king's warriors."

"And how many does your brother keep with him?"

"It varies, Polonius, but it may be up to a hundred, or even more."

"Even a hundred of the finest warriors in the world cannot hope to meet such as we just saw march past."

"Aye, I suppose you are right, Scholar. But you well know the island of Britain is divided into small kingdoms. The Angle, Saxon and Jute tribes once fought their way across Germany, and then conquered all of Angleland from your Roman ancestors."

"But, Ambrose?"

"But brave as they are, they remain divided, and each kingdom is unable by itself to keep a strong enough army together to face a serious attack. Only a new *bretwalda* over all Angleland would stop this Danish scourge."

"Ambrose, you use a new term. What is a bretwalda?"

"My apologies, Polonius. A Bretwalda is a king who is so much more powerful than the others that all kings on the island pay tribute to him and recognize him as an over-king.' Ambrose spoke proudly. 'My own grandfather was declared Bretwalda of all Britain."

"And does your island have a Bretwalda today?"

"No. The power is too evenly split. I realize now, when I see what we are up against, that, one by one, our island nations are likely to fall victim to these fierce intruders. Yet the British kingdoms insist on fighting their petty squabbles, and waste gold and lives killing and raiding fellow Christians."

"I know, my lord,' Polonius replied. 'My people rule an empire of many million citizens. They rule as much by keeping the enemy divided as by force of arms. If ever, God granting, I have a chance to show you golden Byzantium, I will show you many nationalities held together by bonds of trade."

⚑

As the year moved towards the summer solstice, the tale of the previous summer repeated itself. Phillip was once again driven to the edge of exhaustion, and a whistling lash was his reward if he paused in his labors. Polonius continued to teach the village boys when they could be spared from the farm work and the military training, and Ambrose helped out when Canute could spare him.

When not helping Polonius, Ambrose helped Anna in the fields. Anna, in turn, began to swell until her abdomen was egg-shaped. Her breasts became fuller, and she bloomed with the loveliness that is unique to an expectant mother. She continued to tend elderly Canute, but often slept on Ambrose's pallet.

Life, although far different from what Ambrose had known in Wessex, was placid and pleasant enough. Polonius' life was also relatively easy, except for his being required to tolerate the abuse of rude peasant boys.

On the third day before the full moon of June, however, disaster struck. The villagers had worked over the winter and the past summer on a new long-ship. It was to be their donation to their jarl's fleet, and if he did not call for it, well, the young men might try another raid on their own. Yet, in order to fittingly launch the ship, the village elder, in his capacity as priest, demanded the customary tithe. He commanded that ale would be poured on the waters to placate *Aegir*, and that a slave was to be hanged as the vessel hit the water, thus buying the blessing of Odin.

Ambrose whispered to Canute. "Master, why would a slave be sacrificed when the ship is launched?"

"My boy, even as we talk, Odin looks down from his throne in Valhalla. With just his one eye he can see everything that happens in the nine worlds. He is the god of war, but also wisdom. We want him to give our young men not only strength in battle, but also to impart to them some of his hard-earned wisdom. Thus we antagonize no god, and hopefully we buy our ship good luck."

All of the villagers, including most of the thralls, had gathered two days before the official launching, in order to hear the elder's pronouncements, and to admire the vessel's clean lines and solid construction.

Lief the Drunkard, Phillip's master, staggered up to the priest, and in a slurred voice, called out to the assembled villagers.

"I wanna offer my Saxon thrall as a sacrifice to Odin. The lazy bastar' won' hardly work no more anyway. All I ask in return is that you ask Odin for a blessing for my family.' He tried to snap his fingers, but was unable to produce any sound. At last he just called out. 'Boys! Bring the lazy bastar' 'ere!"

His two older sons then dragged the Weapons-master, naked, emaciated, and covered with his own blood, forward. Throwing the beaten and bloody body onto the ground, they both exclaimed how this worthless slave was lazy, ate too much, and had actually dared to try and prevent Lars, the youngest of his boys, from seizing and raping another slave-girl belonging to their neighbors.

"Fifty lashes from my bull-roarer showed this carrion who is master in my father's house!" shouted Lars.

Ambrose felt sudden nausea. He had, when chopping firewood, heard the screams emanating from a whipping from the other end of the village. He had thought little of it, for it was not uncommon for a master to beat a thrall for some offense.

The slave-owners, however, seldom did more than administer a mild whipping, for the purpose was to encourage greater effort, not to mutilate or kill a valuable commodity. Slaves thus treated generally suffered no more than welts and stiffness for a few days. What had happened to Phillip, however, was another matter, and Ambrose could tell from the stony faces of the crowd how they felt about this kind of viciousness and wanton cruelty. Nevertheless, it was the right of the master to dispose of a slave as he pleased. A *freedman* and a *bondi* both had specific duties to their master, but also certain rights. The life of a thrall, however, was utterly dependent upon the whims of his owner.

At last the village elder, acting in his role of priest, nodded assent, and Phillip was seized by several villagers and quickly fastened to a tree near where the vessel sat upon the shore. There he would stand or hang limply by his wrists until dawn two days hence, when he would be hung while the ship slipped into the waters. Even through his filth and emaciation, all could see the great cords of his muscles when his wrists were tied around a branch of the tree. He made a superhuman effort, and his gaunt head, bloodstained and covered with matted hair and beard, stared straight into the silent crowd.

With agony, Ambrose saw Phillip's haggard eyes piercing the crowd. They finally focused on him. He could feel the eyes burning into his head. After an eternity of perhaps four seconds, Phillip's head dropped forward, and the battered thane slipped into merciful unconsciousness.

The village elder posted two sentries to guard the now sacred body of the sacrifice. He then bid all the villagers go and prepare for a great celebration feast in two days.

Quickly forgetting the sordid ugliness of the evil deed done by Lief and his sons, the villagers spilled out of the square to their homes in excitement. A summer feast was a time of great excitement, when oceans of drink and mountains of food were consumed. All celebrated, and even the thralls drank and were permitted to sleep freely with one another.

CHAPTER 9.

The Flight.

On the way back from the tribal gathering, Canute spoke to the prince. "My boy, I know that the death of your friend is a hard thing to accept, but to be sacrificed to Odin is a great honor. Of course you and Anna may attend, and if it pleases you, I will send a keg of good ale for Phillip to imbibe. If he drinks enough, he will feel little. Now let us retire. I am tired."

Ambrose, when he sensed the arrival of the early morning light, rose with heavy heart. He dressed silently and headed out to weed Canute's field. He did not even pause to break fast, but took along cheese and bread to eat later. As the sun neared its zenith, Anna suddenly appeared. "Prince, Canute has asked me to send you to him at once."

Concerned, Ambrose hastened back to his master's house, even leaving behind the now slow-moving Anna. The prince found Canute sitting in the privacy of his bed chamber.

The old man looked up and spoke. "My son, for I think of you as such, though I know you to be from another land, we must talk."

Sensing the gravity of the old man's words, Ambrose knelt at his feet. "Yes, Master." Ambrose answered humbly.

"My people . . . my people are a brave and good people, but in . . . . all tribes, there are good and evil people. I always thought that in each tribe there are greater differences between individuals then there are between tribes as a whole.'

Ambrose knew that such philosophy, worthy of some of Polonius' Greek ancestors, hinted at much thought from the habitually easy-going Canute. The old man was obviously struggling with some deep or conflicting emotions. After a pause, he stumbled on.

'In our village, it is only Lief and his family who bring dishonor to our tribe.' Canute paused again. 'But I ramble. Let me get to the point. I have an urgent errand for you. You are to take this message, written by your friend Polonius the Scribe, to a friend of mine in the tribal lands of the *Rus*. His town is on the north shore of the *Viking Sea*.

Doubtless you will wish to stay with him awhile, and in the letter I have asked him to teach you a little of trade, for the Rus are famous for their great trading houses . . . You are to go as my adopted son.'

Ambrose, shocked at the words, lifted his head and made to speak, but was silenced by a wave of Canute's hand.

'Nay! Say nothing - you have been to me as a son and more. Hear me out. You may, by coincidence, arrive with some fellow travelers . . . I have made a request that any such companions would also be cared for. Further, you will carry this purse of silvers and coppers to spend as you see fit.'

With that, he handed Ambrose a heavy leather purse.

'You are to take **Victory-Maker** to protect yourself with, and my boat, the Falcon, is moored around the point, in the bay where we went fishing last autumn. Although she is big for one sailor to handle alone, I am confident you can manage her. Anna has seen to its provisioning. Go with my blessing, my son, and that of your Christ god."

Ambrose, conscious of the gnarled old warrior's pride, detected a watery glint from Canute's eyes. He gently and lovingly kissed the foot of his master. His head low, his mind reeling, he backed out of Canute's presence, and went off to make swift arrangements.

His arrival at the hut where Polonius slept when it was not being used as a school found his friend packing food and writing utensils into a leather pouch. Anna sat nearby.

Polonius said to him. "Anna has told me that Canute feels I might be able to help you on a forthcoming journey. I would be honored if you would let me escort you to the wild lands of the north. It occurs to me, too, that perhaps you or Anna could suggest another companion for our expedition. We need someone who is as strong as an ox, though it would not hurt if he was more intelligent than one.

Ambrose couldn't help but smile. "I think I know just the one! He used to teach errant princes how to fight. But Polonius, if you come with me, you will be a fugitive. If they catch you, they will not deal kindly with you."

"Then, my prince, we had better make sure that we are not caught!"

Ambrose grinned with excitement and happiness, until his eyes fell on Anna, swollen and near ready for childbirth. His good humor vanished instantly. She saw his glance, and spoke sadly.

"Good my lord, much as it grieves me to be parted from you, I intend to stay and tend foolish old Canute. He has more need of me than you."

Even as Ambrose reached out to clasp her, she whirled and fled the room. Polonius and the Prince managed to successfully sneak their personal goods into the woods and across the sandy peninsula to where Canute's small sailing vessel lay pulled up on the shore and covered with brush.

Thanks to Anna's hard work, a good supply of food was stored aboard, and the water cask had been freshly filled. The vessel was ready to sail on the next high tide. Both Ambrose and Polonius knew, however, that they still had the dangerous job of freeing Phillip and transporting him to the boat.

"My Prince, it occurs to me that we really need that third member of our expedition. Perhaps, if we could borrow a horse to carry the great hulk, we could go collect Phillip."

Ambrose, in spite of the cramps of nervous tension that tortured his stomach, smiled at his friend. "The very man I had in mind, my Greek scholar!"

By midnight, most of the revelers, both servant and master, had fallen asleep over their mead, or had wandered off into the bush with a member of the opposite sex. The boat's launching was a major event in the life of the little village.

It took little effort for Ambrose and Polonius to crawl unseen back to behind the school hut where they had left their weapons. Feeling only slightly guilty, Ambrose buckled on the slim foreign sword which he loved so dearly, and picked up his bow and quiver. He knew the blade, with its amazing edge and suppleness, to be worth a king's ransom. Old Canute, however, had insisted that he take it for personal defense. Polonius strapped on a straight sword borrowed by Ambrose for the occasion, and followed his companion through the woods to the horse corral.

Anna had long since made sure that the horse guard had drunk his fill of mead, and more. The man lay in a drunken stupor when the two travelers arrived to conscript a horse.

Ambrose and Polonius prepared a quiet mare, and were ready to move off when one of the other horses nickered loudly. Instantly Ambrose and Polonius froze. No one came, however, and not even the cursory challenge of a sentry greeted the horse's cry.

With great care, Ambrose and Polonius crawled close to the two sentries watching over the Weapons-master. Lars and Kiarr, two of the youths taking turns guarding the sacrifice, had had the poor grace to take their sacred task seriously. They had abstained from most of the mead, and only stolen a little of Phillip's ale. They were thus relatively alert.

Ambrose stared into the darkness. Within a thousand foot-lengths lay over a hundred stalwart warriors, who, whether they condoned Lief's cruel actions or not, would protect with their lives the sacred sacrifice to their god Odin. Thus, Polonius and Ambrose reasoned, they must reach the sentries simultaneously. One single cry and the entire village would be roused.

They had few illusions about their own value to the villagers, or of the people's drunken state. Ambrose knew well that all of the men had trained for war, and would fall into order within seconds of any alarm being sounded, whether they were drunk or sober. It was something the village practiced occasionally, in case of sudden attack. Each warrior knew his place. A vigorous pursuit would take no more than a few minutes to organize.

At last Ambrose reached one hundred by slow count, as Polonius had suggested. He knew they must attack now or Phillip was a dead man.

Not more than ten foot-lengths from Ambrose stood the sentry who the prince knew to be a bully. Lars had great strength, however, and had more than once given Ambrose a good drubbing. Ambrose leapt from the bushes and raced for the youth's unprotected back.

He carried in his hands a stout branch of two elbow's length and a wrist's thickness, while Polonius had elected to use the flat of an axe blade. Their other weapons lay behind the bush that had served as a screen.

Because of the nearby surf, the sound of Ambrose's approach and rush was effectively masked. Successful in closing the distance undetected, Ambrose swung the club and then watched with satisfaction as Lars slid silently onto the sand.

Just as Ambrose hit a hundred and started forward, Polonius started and was forced to stop. His target had stepped into the faint light of a flickering torch, and was relieving himself.

The youth obviously heard something, for he called out to his companion. "What in the name of Odin's good eye are you doing, Lars?

Did you drink too much of Canute's good ale?"

The sentry had turned away from Polonius when he heard the slight sound. While his victim was thus distracted, Polonius rushed to close the distance. Kiarr only caught Polonius' movement in his peripheral vision at the last moment. While he half turned back, Polonius brought the flat of his axe down upon the unfortunate man's pate. Because he had twisted, however, the axe slipped off his head, and sliced into the sentry's arm, bringing a dark welling of blood.

Finished with his target, Ambrose ran to Phillip's side. His sharp sax sliced the rawhide thongs that had kept the thane immobilized and in a semi-standing position. As the last bonds parted, Phillip started to slide in an unconscious heap to the ground.

Even before he hit the ground, however, Polonius arrived. Between the two of them, they were able to drag Phillip, a heavy and inert burden, away from the village and to where the horse was tethered.

They lashed Phillip across the horse's back, as he was quite unable to stay mounted by himself. Quietly then, the strange caravan wended its way clear of the village and along hunting paths well-known to Ambrose and Polonius. They skirted open fields until, having crossed the neck of the little peninsula, they arrived at the boat.

After launching the little sailboat and stepping the mast, the two friends got hold of Phillip and dragged the giant through the shallows. With a last mighty effort, the two companions heaved him into the boat.

Ambrose went back to slap the mare's rump and send her off, while Polonius tried to manoeuver the boat into deeper water. Only after Ambrose had joined Polonius were they able to successfully float the vessel. They were none too early, as the tide had turned and was beginning to recede.

Polonius spoke quietly but urgently to Ambrose. "Quickly, Master! Let us hoist the sail and get under way. It might not even be remiss to bend our backs and man the oars, for the accursed wind has dropped, and in these latitudes the sun rises early!"

Once the boat was free of the shelter of the headland, the ocean breezes picked up, and the trim vessel, of almost twenty foot lengths, slid joyously through the waves. Polonius sat by the steering oar, aimed the vessel straight west, and held that course.

Puzzled by his choice of direction, Ambrose questioned the Byzantine scholar. "Polonius, why do you steer us thus? In the direction you have chosen lies only open ocean, and then the edge of the world!"

Phillip, who had been lying supine and had appeared oblivious to the events of the night, roused himself enough to croak a response to his rescuers.

"For myself, I'd as soon die by falling off the edge of the world as hanging from a bloody oak branch! But please, for your sakes, return while you can. Live! I have no wish to be the cause of both your deaths."

Polonius responded. "Good Phillip, don't worry. We are well provisioned, and we have the sun and the North Star to guide us. We will be out of sight of land before the dawning of the day.

Think, my friends. We could coast northward, but we would be spotted by every passing vessel, and probably a lot of shore sentries. Eventually we would come to the *Skagerrak*. After turning there, we would pass through a maze of islands, the inhabitants of which are all loyal to the king of the Danes. Further, the Viking long-ships, if the villagers choose to pursue us, are far more swift than us. If they did not catch us on the way, they would only have to wait at the islands until we arrive.

Alternately, we could turn south. We know there is an entire Danish fleet between us and your homeland. We saw the soldiers marching to their ships. Again we are likely to be spotted and run down long before we can reach friendly shores.

So, my friends, our choices are limited. I thought we might sail for the open sea, where even the mighty dragon ships hesitate to go. Far out of sight of land, we can cut back north, and then, once we think we have reached the Skagerrak, we can head back for the coast and, God willing, the Viking Sea."

Ambrose swallowed twice. What Polonius proposed was incredibly frightening. On the other hand, however, he knew what would happen to all three of them if the Danes caught them.

The prince spoke. "You are right, Polonius, our choices are limited. But even if we find the Skagerrak without being spotted, we must still travel through the maze of islands. As you said, it would be an excellent place for a long-ship to wait for us and catch us."

"That is where the greatest danger lies, Prince. Once we reach the islands, we will have to hide by day and travel exclusively by night."

Ambrose, leader of the expedition by right of birth, looked at the dark waters surrounding their little vessel, and then nodded assent. "What you propose scares me more than you can know, Polonius, but it is a viable plan. I can certainly propose nothing better."

Phillip, after being cleaned and having salve rubbed into his wounds, had begun to recover. Though he still slept most of the time, he remained awake and coherent for varying periods of time. After sipping some water, he spoke.

"My lords, though I be not a man of learning, yet I wonder if it would it not be wiser for us to sail as far as the west coast of the Norse tribes. From there we can cross overland to our destination. Well can I see Canute's map of the Danish islands before me, in my mind's eye, and I fear that it would be impossible to travel past so many islands without being spotted."

Polonius responded. "An interesting suggestion, Phillip. Some Danish sailors once told me that there are trails, though long and arduous, that connect the Norse homeland with the Viking Sea.

We speak the language, have money, and there is no reason for the Norse to mistrust us. I think it unlikely that the Danes will search for us along the Norse coast. In truth, I think it a wise suggestion, old friend. If our young lord agrees, we will do it!"

Ambrose looked nervously at the dark waters surrounding him, but nodded assent. The rising sun found the small vessel far from shore. Polonius kept it aimed west and north, until the contrary winds shifted enough that the sail became a liability.

Polonius spoke. "We have, Prince, another problem. The prevailing winds of this latitude are from the west to the north and east. I fear it behooves us to man the oars, as we can count no more on off-shore breezes this far from land, and it is imperative that we keep moving further out to sea."

Phillip attempted to rise, but Ambrose spoke sharply, "Phillip, you have to lie still and regain your strength for the long journey to come. We will need your mighty strength later. For now, you are to do no more than eat and sleep! Polonius, do you agree?"

"You took the very words from my mouth, my prince."

Thus, with Ambrose and Polonius each manning a pair of oars whenever the vessel was too close-hauled for the wind to fill its sail, the little ship ventured ever further to the north and west.

As Polonius pulled the lines that raised their triangular sail, he couldn't help but comment to Ambrose. "Master, it is well that the Vikings patterned their long-ship sails on the ancient Roman style, for their great square sails are only useful if they have the wind more-or-less at their back. This vessel, with its rigging, is far more useful when one wants to sail into the face of the wind. Only if they know we have taken this tack, and wish to man their oars until the blisters burst, can they overtake us."

Ambrose, in the throes of throwing the boom over and trying to get the sail to fill, close hauled as the boat was, could only once again nod assent.

CHAPTER 10.

They Sail North, and East.

Phillip, now recovered enough to move about, crawled to the stern where Polonius sat. Although his face hurt from the beatings he had taken, he smiled at the Byzantine who had risked his own life in a crazy gamble to save him. "Move aside, Greek, and I will spell you for a while."

"Rest, old friend! You should be lying down. You have been through a lot."

"Nay, my Byzantine scholar, I am tired of resting. I am alive and free, thanks to what you and Ambrose have done. I think I am recovered enough to hang onto a steering oar."

Polonius grinned in return. "In that case, Saxon, the steering oar is all yours."

Phillip was now seated facing the bow. He had been asleep or unconscious for the better part of two days, and had only recently roused enough to know what was going on around him. He questioned his friend even as his eyes scanned the horizon. "Has there been any hint of land?"

"Not a sign; not even any coastal birds, but from what I was able to glean from our former masters, there is no land if we continue northward and a little westwards. The last thing we want at this time is to be spotted by Danes coasting the shores."

On the morning of the third day, Polonius called out to Ambrose, who was taking his turn at the tiller. "I think it is about time, my lord."

"About time for what, Polonius?"

"About time to put the wind at our stern. If we have truly traveled as far as I suspect, we should be due east of the land of the Norse. If so, it is time to run for their coast."

Ambrose spoke. "And if we have not gone far enough north and hit the mouth of the Viking Sea?"

"We can try to slip unseen between the islands, but Canute said there were many, and some are garrisoned. If the townsmen have come north looking for us and have left a description, then I would guess that we would soon all be hanging from some oak tree."

"Then, Polonius, pray to God. We go east!"

The little vessel came about smartly, and Phillip, who was still weak and fallen asleep again, roused a little. "What is the matter, Prince?"

"Nothing, Weapons-master. We are turning east for the coast."

Now able to relax as the fresh wind pushed the bobbing vessel eastward, Ambrose, Phillip and Polonius took great delight in imagining what great epics were ahead of them. One point they all stressed again and again - the three of them were free of slavery, and they would do their best to remain so.

Ambrose, secure in his new military skills, and knowing Phillip's colossal strength when recovered, felt confident that they could remain free. Only the iron band that encircled the Weapons-master's neck connected them with their former servitude. Ambrose spoke to his two companions.

"Without tools to remove that cursed band of metal, Phillip, we must let on when we go ashore that you are my thrall, brought along to serve me. When we reach the land of the Rus, we will get it struck from your neck!"

Phillip responded. "My lord, with or without a collar, I am your man, and will stay by you even unto death."

Phillip's declaration touched Ambrose more deeply then he could put into words. With misted eyes, the prince scanned the far horizons, which shifted from a few feet, when a trough swallowed the craft, to several Roman miles when the boat rode the crests.

Suddenly his wandering attention was attracted by something unknown, but which had broken the unvarying expanse of blue-green waters stretching in all directions. Ambrose's voice was anguished.

"There's something out there, a few fingers off this side of the bow!"

Polonius leapt into action, and within seconds their sail was released and lowered.

Three tense faces scanned where Ambrose had pointed. As the vessel was tossed to the crest of a great roller, all three could see the mysterious object. There, a leisurely hour's row away in distance, sailed a long-ship."

Polonius spoke tersely. "At ease, my friends. A bare mast is not as easy to see as a long-ship's great square sail. With luck, she will pass in front of us, and never be the wiser. Besides, from her direction, it's likely that she is a Norse vessel, perhaps returning from Irish-land, for

I've heard that the Norse are making inroads there. That would mean that even if she spotted us, she would probably be friendly, and certainly not be scouring the seas for three simple escaped slaves."

Polonius' prophecy was valid, and the sleek long-ship, its square sail held turgid by the wind almost directly astern, skipped by on its own eastern course. Oddly, its crew must have been asleep, for the vessel closed the triangle until it seemed impossible for any watchers to not see the smaller ship bobbing on the rollers little more than a half hour's row away in distance. All three fugitives heaved a deep sigh of relief when the square sail, its brilliant red and white vertical stripes melding into pink, indicated that the vessel was past and disappearing rapidly.

"Thank the merciful God!' Polonius said, 'that the lookouts chose to sleep on their journey home. For more than a moment I thought I imagined the ship veering towards us on a ramming course. And yet, what, aside from the monsters of the deep, would a ship's watch be looking for? This sea belongs to the Vikings, and no other ship would dare sail it, even if some captain could force his crewmen to sail beyond sight of land."

Once again, within minutes, Ambrose raised the danger cry. This time, however, the several dark shapes resolved themselves into whales; leviathans of the deep and no menace to the small boat. Within the range of no more than an easy spear cast, the giant creatures surfaced and spouted. The three travelers were filled with awe at the size of the marine giants.

Ambrose was fascinated watching the huge animals break the surface, blow, and then dive, but when one broached particularly close to the sailboat, he felt very nervous. "By the sweet beard of Jesus, Polonius, each creature is the length of a long-ship, and more! Are you sure that we are safe from their attention?"

"In truth, my lord', Polonius answered, 'my experience is limited to their smaller cousins, which are often to be seen in the Roman Sea, not far from the city of Constantinople, but 'tis said by our most learned men that these huge animals are warm-blooded, like us, and eat only tiny things their teeth strain from the water."

They stared in awe as individual members of the pod of whales surfaced and then slipped beneath the waves. Ambrose was clearly puzzled by Polonius' statement.

"Surely that is an old wives' tale, Polonius. How would such leviathans survive if they ate only tiny fish and plants? If I was of that size, I would eat great pieces of meat, or quickly starve to death."

"Of that I know not, Prince, but I think I prefer to believe Polonius's tale," responded Phillip, now much recovered and taking his second turn steering the ship. Whichever theory was correct, the whales continued to ignore the puny vessel, and their superior speed soon drew the pod far ahead of the boat.

For the rest of the day, nothing broke the monotonous pattern of sea and sky, until the sun slipped low. It then cast a metallic golden sheen across the endless water. Gradually the sky turned crimson, and then the base of the fiery orb seemed to expand far beyond the width of the top as it slid into the sea. As it finally sank, it left only dilated pupils and sudden darkness.

The numbing routine of the voyage was broken after dark when the three companions paused to break their fast. They drew sparingly upon their limited supply of fresh water. Steering by the North Star, Phillip kept the vessel on course; until the star became almost totally obliterated by a thin haze. Polonius finally broke the silence.

"My friends, see you the ring of mist that infects the moon? . . . I fear that it means that we shall soon receive rough weather. I am afraid that we have a choice to make."

Polonius sensed rather than saw the two expectant faces that pivoted to stare at his faint outline.

"We can sail all night, and hope that the wind is steady and can guide us in the absence of our directional star. Yet before sunset I saw some shore birds, and I fear that they auger a shore close by. In the dark, we could easily flounder upon the coast, and I was once told that the coast we are approaching is one of the most savage and rocky in the world. Alternatively, we could lower the sail and wait for dawn to resume our progress. Doing that, however, increases the odds of us being caught out here in a major storm. What say you?"

In his youthful faith, Ambrose answered. "Old Canute would say that our fate is in the hands of the three Norns. I prefer to think, my learned friend, that we are in the hands of Almighty God. Let us continue on our journey, but slacken speed and keep an attentive ear for breakers."

Phillip, by choice and logic a steadfast landsman, made no coherent answer, except to grunt, and let a moan escape from the depth of his tortured stomach. Both Ambrose and Polonius responded with wild gales of laughter.

"At least, Polonius, 'laughed Ambrose, 'Phillip has recovered enough to once again feel the sickness of the sea!"

Thus with light hearts, and, in the case of Phillip, a sodden stomach, they pressed on through the darkness. The waves, encouraged by the gusty winds, foamed and grew ever larger, until the stout craft seemed no more than a mere walnut-shell floating upon a world of waves. The distance in height from trough to crest became enough that when the ship slipped into a trough, it was surrounded by enormous walls of water that stretched almost three body lengths above the ship.

The God of the Christians appeared more powerful than that of the sacrifice-cheated Odin, for the rains held off. Even so, it was an exhausting chore to bail the ship, as gusts of winds hitting the wave-tops seized foaming peaks and dumped them into the boat at a prodigious rate.

All through the night the three of them bailed desperately in an attempt to keep the vessel afloat. By exposing only a small portion of the sail, the ship scudded along at a great speed, but under at least a semblance of control. Several times the three of them were afraid that the boat might break up when a maverick wave smote the boat. The very boards of the hull bent and let in the sea. Nevertheless, Canute had built his fishing boat well, and the boat escaped unscathed except for a considerable amount of missing caulking.

CHAPTER 11.

They Reach Land.

Taking his turn on the steering oar in the pre-dawn darkness, Ambrose tried to stay alert while his two comrades slept the deep sleep of exhaustion. As the first almost horizontal rays of light heralded the new dawn, Ambrose called out.

"Wake up, Polonius! Look dead ahead. I think I can make out what looks to be land! Phillip, lie still and rest, old friend, but I think that we have finally found the Norse coast."

In spite of Ambrose's admonition, The weapons-master stirred and forced his battered body to sit upright. They had been caught in an almost palpable darkness for what had seemed an eternity. Invisible, the savage ocean had surged all around them, tossing their small boat about like a child's toy. Now, suddenly, the rising sun illuminated jagged peaks of a mountain range. Partly bathed in light; the appearance of the rugged land coincided with a sudden drop in the savage intensity of the waves. Coming together, the experience was almost mystical.

All three travelers drank in the beauty of the rugged coast. On either side of them were some of the many thousand rocky islands Canute had told them guarded the Norse shores.

Ambrose finally broke the awed silence. "Well, friends, do we want to land on an island to rest and dry ourselves, or do we head direct for the mainland?"

Polonius replied. "I am wet and sore, and would like nothing better than to step onto solid land, but our supply of both water and food is about finished. I vote we look for a settlement as quickly as possible."

Both looked at Phillip. He ruminated carefully, and then replied to the question.

"To the Norse we are not fugitives. I would rather we sail boldly into a harbor then be caught skulking on some island."

Ambrose smiled. Their situation was serious, but he was young and resilient, and he was sure that God was smiling on them that day.

"So be it! I will follow the coast until I see some evidence of settlement, and then I will sail for it."

Ambrose steered the little vessel parallel with the coast and northward, as in this direction they could use their sail and tack. At last, towards mid-morning, Ambrose called out again.

"Look to the right! Is that a smudge of rising smoke I see?"

Polonius, who had relieved Ambrose a little earlier, threw the steering oar over. "Watch the boom! I'm changing tack." As per Polonius' warning, the boom shot across with a loud snap when the sail alternately emptied and then re-filled in response to Polonius' course change. Even Phillip, lying on the bottom of the little ship, instinctively ducked.

Polonius turned the vessel into a narrow passageway protected by two great mountains that appeared to be standing sentinel. The inviting plume of smoke lay dead ahead.

Once within the shelter of the land, the water became relatively calm. All three thrilled to see that the narrow arm of the sea expanded into a large bay. Below, the water remained a deep green, but Ambrose began to look anxiously over the side.

Polonius smiled. "Don't worry, Ambrose. As long as the water remains that color, you will find adequate water under the keel.

Ahead lay a veritable wall of mountain peaks. They were fringed with green, and the tallest were surmounted by snowy peaks. The faint smudge of smoke that Ambrose's keen eyes had spotted was now dead ahead. It had differentiated into multiple columns that indicated that some kind of reasonably large settlement was nestled in the lap of two mountains. Around the village, and climbing the gentler slopes of the mountains, the three sailors could see the various shades of green and gold that signified agriculture.

Polonius, ever the expert sailor, adroitly used the little wind that reached this sanctuary to propel the boat towards the log wharf where were tied several fishing vessels and a single *knarr*. No larger vessels were visible.

Echoing across the water, from somewhere on the mountain slope of one of the sentinel mountains, came a mellow blast of some kind of horn. Clearly their arrival had been noted and their progress reported from a hidden sentry post.

As their ship neared the wharf, Ambrose dropped the sail. Phillip and Polonius broke out the oars and eased the vessel against the wharf. Women and armed men joined the children who awaited them. At the sound of a second long horn blast, the village men put down their spears, bows, and axes, and smiled broadly at the three companions. Ambrose knew without being told that the evident relief was because no menacing warship followed the little sailing vessel into the calm serenity of the sheltered fjord.

Phillip threw a line to a waiting boy, and their ship was made fast. The die was cast. A barrel-shaped man with a long grizzled beard and bald pate stepped forward. He boomed a hearty welcome.

"Welcome, strangers, to our humble village! Come ashore and tell us news of the world!"

As the language expert, Polonius took the responsibility, and responded in his best Danish, which seemed similar enough to the Norse tongue that each could be easily understood.

"Thank you, sir. We have come from the land of the Danes and were on our way to the land of the Rus, but a terrible the storm blew us far off course. Aegir almost took us several times, and I think that we will continue our journey on foot. We ask in friendship for food and lodging, and would be pleased to offer some silver in exchange for your hospitality."

The portly man's voice boomed again. "Nay, speak not of payment, but rather of friendship! We are friends to our cousins the Danes, and, because of our isolation here, hunger for what news you have of the world beyond our mountains. In that way you may earn your keep, strangers."

Polonius responded as gracefully as he could. "Sir, nothing would give us greater pleasure then to discuss the world's affairs with you, but first let me introduce to you my worthy companions. The young lad is Canuteson, adopted son of Canute, who is a distant relative to the Danish High Chief himself. Phillip here,' Polonius said, indicating the giant, 'is a thrall from a barbarian land, and is a faithful servant of my lord Canuteson.

I, too, as you no doubt have astutely ascertained, am from a foreign land. My name is Polonius, and I am from the New Rome, which, I am told, some of your people call *Miklagard*. I serve as guide and servant to my lord Canuteson."

"Well met!' shouted the village leader in his booming voice. 'I am Eric the Round, and, I must confess, I am getting thirsty from all this talk!"

Holding his hairy belly and laughing loudly, Eric sent his own thralls and free servants scampering off in all directions to prepare a feast for the visitors.

"It's seldom we get visitors here, and I long for an excuse to breach our supplies of mead and ale. Come!"

With surprising swiftness, Ambrose, Phillip and Polonius found themselves led to Eric's house, a sturdy timber dwelling of two rooms. There blushing and laughing servant girls helped them remove their brine-soaked clothes and put on fresh attire from the waterproof sea-bag that Canute had insisted Ambrose take, along with the weapons and money.

The servant girls were taken aback at Phillip's inflamed back, and for a moment the three companions thought their fate was sealed, but Polonius' verbal ripostes and flattery soon had them fluttering about him, as Phillip valiantly attempted to fit into a shirt that had once been Canute's.

At length they were ensconced on long benches in the central chamber that constituted most of Eric's house. The room was obviously used for meetings by the village elders and warriors. Shields and spears decorated the walls, and the smoke from the open fire pit hung in the air until it could infiltrate the thatched roof and escape.

The men of the little hamlet; many dressed in finery of by-gone years and far-away raids, arrived and joined the guests on the benches.

"As you have seen,' boomed Eric, 'we are an isolated folk, and yet even here each man goes forth at least once for a Viking. Several of our younger sons are even now with our jarl's fleet. They have sailed to harry the Irishers.'

As he spoke, he waved his horn of mead. 'Will you join us in a toast to the gods, and to the safety of all travelers? We poor folk are not without some crude refinements."

All three guests smiled, and Polonius responded. "Of course."

Eric clapped, and several more serving wenches ran out from behind a leather curtain. They brought with them gold and silver chalices which they gave to the guests.

Once again Eric the Round's voice boomed out. "In this village, we pray to Thor. May you return to your homes as surely as *Mjollnir* returns to his master's hand."

He stood and held his drinking horn high. "To Thor!"

The villagers stood as one, and the room reverberated with their reply. "To Thor!"

Ambrose looked at Polonius. He didn't want to antagonize the Villagers, yet he feared to put his immortal soul in jeopardy by praying to a false god.

Polonius whispered. "Drink, Prince, to the one true God. The father of gentle Jesus will understand."

Ambrose felt the many eyes focused on him. He said a short prayer and raised the chalice to his lips. The hall erupted in cheers when he and his two companions all emptied their chalices in one continuous motion."

Eric beamed at them. "We now drink to your gods!"

Again the horns and chalices were filled and emptied.

"Eat, drink, and be merry, my friends, for today we celebrate the safe arrival of strangers from the lands of the Danes!"

CHAPTER 12.

Gunnar of the Rus.

As they walked the shoreline where their little sailboat was beached, Polonius turned to Ambrose. "Lord, I have a favor to ask."

"We are friends, Polonius. Ask!"

"Lord, I would like to beg several silver pennies from you."

"The coins were given by Canute to the three of us. You do not need to beg, my friend. They are yours for the asking."

"Thank you. The money is important to me."

"Polonius, the coins are yours, yet I admit to being puzzled."

"Prince, for the first time in many years, I am a free man."

"We are fugitives, and far from safety yet."

"Yet for the first time in memory, my body does not belong to another man. I am free to do as I please. I do not intend to live as a slave again."

Ambrose grinned. "And a few silver pennies will prevent this?"

Polonius smiled in return. "It will help, Prince. It will help."

Polonius stood in front of Big Kell, the village blacksmith. "I would like to purchase some iron and rent your forge. Do you have any iron that I could buy?"

"Oh, aye. I have a little bog iron ore that I dug up last week. I guess I could sell you a little. If you'd like, I will make you whatever you want myself. I will only charge you for the iron I use."

"I thank you. That is very kind of you, yet what I must do I must do myself. I would be honored if you would assist me, however."

"Oh, aye. I will do that."

Polonius painstakingly laid down a level layer of charcoal. Over this he laid a layer of crushed ore. He alternated the layers until the clay furnace was full to the top. At last, satisfied, he stood back. "Well, my friends, I think I am finally ready. I will light the charcoal now, and, Phillip, when I give the word, I want you to pump the bellows as if your life depended upon it. Oh, and if you agree, Canuteson, I would like to use the iron that adorns Phillip's neck. Would you mind if I removed it and melted it down?"

"Polonius, I do not think that Phillip needs that band of iron any longer to remind him who his Danish master is. You certainly have my permission."

"Kell, can you remove the collar?"

"Oh, aye. It will take but a moment."

At last, with the thrall collar on top of the ore and with enough time for the charcoal to start burning, Polonius was ready. "Pump, Phillip! The metal must get white-hot."

Phillip's powerful muscles contracted and relaxed, contracted and relaxed. Great pulses of pure air raced from the leather bellows through the clay furnace, until the charcoal glowed a bright red. Gradually, under the ferocious heat, the iron melted and collected at the bottom of the pit.

Ambrose spoke to his friend. "Well, Polonius, as a child I always enjoyed watching my father's smiths at work, but I fail to see how this will ensure your . . .' He looked at the smith right behind him. . . 'will give you your wish."

"Well, Canuteson, I will show you before the day is over. When the furnace has cooled we will return and remove the slag. Then I will have my metal."

"I have watched this done before, old friend. What you will have will be a lot of very impure iron."

"Then we heat it again! After that . . . well you will see."

Ambrose and Phillip knew that Polonius loved mysteries. They were curious, however, and followed Polonius back to the smithy, where the charcoal had finished burning and the metal had cooled. Polonius repeated the process, and this time he was left with a misshapen hunk of relatively pure iron.

"And now we start. Phillip, hand me those tongs. Canuteson, the hammer please!"

Polonius re-heated the metal until it glowed red, and then he quickly pounded the mass of iron into rods. After each hammering he again re-heated the rods and sprinkled charcoal powder on them. He now had Ambrose and Phillip puzzled. The burly thane spoke.

"Every time you purify the iron, you contaminate it again with charcoal. What is the purpose, Polonius?"

"Phillip, iron is soft and can bend when it hits armor. The charcoal adds carbon, which gives the iron strength."

"Then why are not all swords and spears treated so?"

"Many are. If you add too much carbon, then the blade becomes brittle and will snap. Too little, and it bends. A master smith knows the exact amount to add, depending on what it is he is making."

Ambrose spoke up. "And just where did you learn the art of smithing?"

"I was once a scholar who indulged in learning for the sheer pleasure of it. But I learned this much later. A man who wishes to survive as a slave is wise to learn many things."

As he spoke, he withdrew the first of his eight rods from the roaring fire, and started to shape it on the anvil.

It was soon obvious to the three observers what the object would be. The rods were twice the length of an adult hand. Polonius started to flatten and shape one end, until the rough shape of a blade appeared.

Ambrose was excited. "Why didn't you say you needed some knives, you rascal!? We have enough silver to buy you the finest ones in all Norseland!"

Polonius didn't respond until the blade was almost complete. He dipped it into a clay pot of vegetable oil, and then replied.

"This is not an ordinary knife, Canuteson. Does it look right to you?"

"I recognize a blade, but it is not the shape of any knife I know."

"Precisely. Phillip, would you please move that chopping block over under the tree?"

Phillip's muscles bulged, but he managed to lift the massive stump for the requisite distance. Polonius passed a smooth stone over his new knife several times, and then looked satisfied.

"Canuteson, the knife is still in need of much smoothing, but let me show you its purpose." With one smooth motion, Polonius swivelled and threw the knife. The spectators turned just in time to see the blade thunk solidly into the stump.

"You see, Canuteson? It is not yet perfectly balanced, and I have not yet wrapped the handle, but it is shaped for throwing."

"It is no-doubt going to be a fine knife, Polonius, but just how does this guarantee your previously-expressed desire?"

"With eight of these in my belt, I can incapacitate or kill any warrior in the world."

"That is a powerful boast. You can kill armored warriors who carry shields, and wear chain-mail, armor and helms?"

"Unarmored is easier, but yes, with or without armor. Probably more than one. It depends on how fast they close."

"Polonius, you are a man of many unusual skills. Where did you learn this one?"

"In the east. My master at the time was amused by tricks of skill, and his lash encouraged me to learn both quickly and well. I did. I am no warrior, yet I have managed to kill several enemies in a matter of seconds."

"Polonius, my friend, would you be willing to give Phillip and me a little demonstration?"

"It would be a pleasure, Canuteson, but only after I have finished the throwing daggers. Would that be satisfactory?"

Ambrose slapped his emaciated friend on the back. "Whenever you are ready, friend, whenever you are ready . . . I do have one task for you, however, that I would like you to attempt as soon as possible."

Polonius stared at Ambrose. "Name it, lord, and it will be done."

"Since you are so good with the forge, could you make me a claymore?"

"A big claymore?' Polonius suddenly grinned. 'Would you by any chance like one so big only some overgrown oaf could handle it?"

"If that great oaf is to protect us properly, I think it only fitting that we provide him with the proper tool. He seems to have lost the last one he owned."

"If that is to be its purpose, Master, I would be proud to forge the biggest bloody sword you ever saw."

"Kell, would that be satisfactory?"

"Oh, aye, I would be happy to sell you a little more iron." He shrugged. 'tis quiet this time of year. Master Polonius is welcome to use the forge as long as you replace the charcoal you use."

"Agreed, my friend . . . and while we are at it, Kell, I need the services of a master bowyer. Do you have such a man in your village?"

"Oh, aye, sir. Me cousin Latham is a bowyer. If you would like, I will take you to him."

$$\approx$$

Ambrose picked up and put down several bows from the man's collection. "Latham, I am looking for a bow both thicker and longer. I do not see any strong enough. Could you cut us a thicker one?"

Latham looked hurt. "Canuteson, it takes years for the wood to mature before I can use it. What you ask is not possible."

"Then could you strengthen one of these with sinews?"

"Sir, the one you hold can only be used by a very strong man. If I strengthen it further, no man would be able to draw it."

"I am not thinking of just any man"

Polonius suddenly grinned." Could it be that you are thinking of some giant oaf?"

Ambrose turned and smiled in return. "The very one."

Polonius spoke. "If the bow is for Canuteson's servant, than, Latham, you can strengthen it. Fear not. Phillip will be quite able to draw it."

"If that be what you wish, I will start to strengthen my thickest bow in the morning."

ᕤ

Ambrose and his two companions stayed for several weeks in the little hamlet between the two mountains. Phillip mended quickly, except for the scars that he would carry forever on his back. He was thrilled with the giant blade that Polonius fashioned for him. At first he could only swing the massive weapon a few times before he was exhausted, but he persevered. Within a week he could swing it with effortless ease.

Polonius finished his eight throwing daggers. After patiently grinding the blades and wrapping the handles until they had the perfect balance he was looking for, he bought a scrap of leather and proceeded to stitch a sheath for the blades. Only when this, too, was completed did he agree to give Ambrose and Phillip the promised demonstration.

On the chosen day, many of the villagers joined Ambrose and Phillip. Little exciting happened in the isolated village, and Polonius' boast had been reported. Polonius asked for eight volunteers, and asked each to retrieve his shield. Once the men had returned, Polonius used a little honey to stick a piece of birch bark on each shield. He spoke to the crowd.

"Is it agreed then, that if I hit each piece of parchment fairly, we will consider that as a kill?"

Ambrose teased the thin Byzantine. "Are you saying that your blades can not penetrate chain-mail?"

"Canuteson, the key to victory is to apply sufficient force to a vulnerable place. It is vainglory to attack your enemy's strongest point and still assume that you will win. All I need to do is to hit the face, or bare leg, or find a chink in the warrior's armor."

"Polonius, you are truly good enough a thrower that you can exploit such tiny targets?"

"We shall see, Canuteson.' He turned to the eight men holding their shields. 'Warriors! Please form a semi-circle around me. When I give the signal, hold the shields in front of your face, and do not move! All right now. Shields up!"

As Polonius swivelled, he launched all eight blades. Each struck truly, and the crowd cheered the dark foreigner. While no warrior, yet he had skills that could unerringly kill from a distance. This earned him a respect from the rough Vikings that all his knowledge could not.

Phillip, not to be outdone, had an archery target moved well out-of-range of the best of the village archers. The big man then notched an over-long arrow and drew the massive bow until the string brushed his face. When he released the arrow, it arced high and fell within feet of the target. The Vikings looked at Phillip in awe. None had ever seen an archer shoot such a distance.

Phillip, however, just looked irritated. "Sorry, Canuteson. I do not yet know the bow. May I try again?"

"Of course, Phillip, shoot away!"

The second shaft struck the target truly. The audience gasped. It was now obvious that the first shot was not a fluke. The big man could hit targets far out of range of any of the village archers.

Polonius borrowed a *fidla* from a villager, and deftly put his stories into rhymes. Soon all the villagers pleaded with him to sing one of his ballads. For the thirty day span they remained, Ambrose and Polonius spent the days either hunting in the mountains or fishing in the fjord. Phillip, for his part, spent much of his time exercising or practicing with his new weapons. Evenings all three feasted with Eric.

At last, however, Phillip was well enough that they could travel. While Eric was sorry to see his interesting guests move on, yet he knew that the mountain passes would be closed for the winter in another two or three months. The village elders, keen mountaineers in their time, and still experts in the lay of the land, drew upon a sheepskin a map of how to pass through the worst of the mountains to the rolling hills and land of the Rus on the Viking Sea.

By good luck, the trio's destination was nearly opposite them, though a massive backbone of mountains. Many weary Roman miles were still between them and their destination.

Ambrose, Polonius and Phillip, in turn, each firmly hugged Eric in farewell and waved to the other villagers. The three of them mounted up.

Eric, standing in front of the assembled village, boomed out a farewell of his own. "My friends! I know not what drove you to dare the mighty ocean in your tiny boat, but my people have measured your hearts, and I want you to know that we find you worthy of our friendship.'

When he noticed Ambrose move his hand to his purse, he laughed merrily. 'Don't reach for silver, my friend! Such a base reward for hospitality would be insulting to our honor. We charged you the value of the horses, as we are not rich, and they must be replaced when next our envoys go to the place of the yearly gathering of the tribes. Food and lodging, however, is something we freely offer any way-farer. In your cases, it afforded us much pleasure to have had you here, and we, indeed, are in your debt. Fare you well, friends. Know you that our continuing friendship awaits your return."

The journey through the high mountains took the three comrades over two weeks. Although much of the trail led along green valley floors, or beside stream-beds, parts of the trail were through areas where nature had never consented to allow a pathway fit for a man. Here, generations of men had hewed, sometimes from solid rock, precarious trails. Several stretches were literally built out of the side of a cliff, so that the supporting timbers hung over the edge of precipices.

On two occasions, it was necessary to blindfold the horses, inured though they were to heights, and lead them, ever so gently, along the narrow trail. One slip at this point would have sent man or beast plummeting hundreds of foot-lengths to river beds chattering far below.

The land they passed through was magnificently wild. Tall trees stubbornly climbed the mountains until they reached the heights where even the most tenacious couldn't survive the slope and the altitude. At that elevation the vegetation grudgingly gave way to Arctic shrubs, and, sometimes, snow-capped peaks.

Evidence of settlement was almost non-existent, except in the occasional fertile valley bottoms, but they all felt unseen eyes upon them in several of the remote areas. Their reception, when they found evidence of habitation, was generally good. The fact that Eric the Round had hosted them and sold them horses seemed to put them in good stead.

It appeared from various comments of the people that this trail, if not a paved road of Imperial Rome, was at least relatively well used by messengers and local travelers. Thus, by the tradition of hospitality by which the Norse met travelers in their own land, the road was generally free of brigands and slavers.

On the thirteenth day of travel, weary, the three travelers broke out of the high mountains of the Norse. According to what they had been told by Eric and his men, they would still have a long way to go, but the worst was behind them. They understood that they would be shortly entering the land of the Rus.

The mountains gave way to hills. Here the debris of the mountains, over eons, had filled the valleys, and the land became progressively more fertile. The Rus territory was one of rolling hills and dales. The land, wherever possible, was intensely cultivated.

It was obvious to even the inexperienced Ambrose that this land would support many more people then the high mountains and stony slopes of the Norse. Nevertheless, compared to the flat land of the Danes, it remained largely a mountainous and barren territory.

After finally reaching the 'traders' highway', which paralleled the sea only a part of a day's march inland, they turned north toward their destination. Here at last they met other travelers on the road, and the local villagers, though hospitable, were much less willing to put up travelers. Unlike the Norse, the people expected payment in return for their food and lodging.

Only once, when the soldiers of a local Jarl stopped them to charge them for the use of a toll bridge, were they challenged. Polonius' glib tongue and masterful command of various dialects, however, got them safely through.

Finally, less than a day's journey from their destination, they were stopped by a troop of soldiers. At spear point, they were forced to dismount. Polonius spoke up quickly.

"Warriors, why do you stop innocent travelers?"

The leader of the troop, a gaunt man of inordinate height and blond braided hair, answered. "We look for brigands and escaped slaves. Three days ago a merchant was robbed in this very place.

Where are you going, and why are you, foreigners, in our country?"

"Good captain,' Polonius responded. 'My master and I seek the house of Gunnar, son of Carl the Brave, of the tribe of the Rus."

"What proof have you of this?"

Polonius turned to Ambrose. "Master, please give me the message, that this officer may read it for himself."

Polonius smiled smugly, for he knew well that the soldier would be unable to read the letter, especially as it had not been written Viking runes, but was in Latin. Even the runic translation he had made was indecipherable to many of the Vikings. Ambrose handed both documents to Polonius, who in turn handed it to the officer.

Holding the letter at first sideways, and then upside down, the sergeant carefully scanned the missive. "Umph!" he stated indecisively, not wishing to admit he was able to neither read a letter in a language he had not even heard of, or even read the runes of his own land. He was, however, afraid to let three foreigners slip through his cordon. At last, he was inspired.

"Umph!' he stated again. 'All appears to be in order, but because of the danger of brigands, I will detail you four men to escort you to the family you speak of. They are very rich and proud, and would doubtless expect no less of me . . . You four! Mount up and show these travelers the way!"

With that, honor salvaged, the Viking commander turned to the next group who was approaching, and imperiously gestured Ambrose's party, with its new escort, on its way.

⚐

Towards dusk the three of them, along with their escort, entered a long, wide, and obviously fertile valley. The flat bottom land was planted with a variety of crops. There was little land wasted. On the steeper or higher slopes, woods alternated with pasture land, and flocks of sheep could be seen grazing complacently. The houses looked to be made of timber, and well constructed. Several times in their several hours' journey the assorted group had passed through prosperous farming villages. Here, obviously, was a concentration of population and wealth that they had not seen since the Danish lands.

Ambrose turned to the closer of the two escorts. "A prosperous and populous place, Warrior. Is this the land of the Rus?"

"Aye, sir', came the reply 'and much of what you see belongs to Gunnar, the man you are to visit. He be a wealthy landowner and trader both. In the southern lands of the Swede tribes, there be much of such land, but our northern tribes live in a bleaker land, where there is little but for grazing livestock and hunting."

After thanking the man for his information, all five of them rode a way; each too engrossed in his own thoughts to break the silence. Suddenly, however, cresting a small knoll that was contained in the much larger valley, they saw before them the sparkling waters of the Viking Sea. All paused to admire the view, and each person's attention focused eventually on a great stone and timber dwelling that towered two stories; far above the nearby town.

"There, travelers, is your destination; the house of Jarl Gunnar, lord of this valley, and son of Carl the Brave, he of the Rus,' commented the second escort, a trifle smugly. 'Not every day do you see such a sight!"

Passed through the town gates with a wave, Ambrose and Phillip stared at their surroundings. Here was civilization at least as advanced as any they had known in Angleland. Town walls circled both Gunnar's house and much of the rest of the town. The palisades had sentry walks along the tops, and thus presented a formidable obstacle to any attackers.

The streets were laid out neatly, and the buildings were made of both stone and wood. Substantially constructed, the houses indicated a degree of wealth here that had not been evident in the interior areas of the country that the little party had traversed.

Open sewers had been carefully constructed, and the escort leader bragged that a diversion channel had been constructed so that each rain swept through the channels and removed all offal, draining it into the sea. In truth, Ambrose noted that the odor, in spite of small quantities of putrefying feces and food, was no worse than Ambrose's brother's own favorite royal burh at Winchester.

At last they arrived at the gate of the large house whose very silhouette had so attracted their attention. Ambrose, Phillip and Polonius exchanged glances. How did Canute, a humble farmer and former warrior, merit the right to call upon such an important person for help?

Two alert men, armed and dressed in like outfits, stepped up to the closed gate and asked the group its business. The escort leader responded.

"Peace, warriors! I have been sent by my commander to escort these three travelers to your gate. They carry with them some message from far away, and it is doubtless imperative that it be taken to your master at once. If you would be so good as to open the gate, we will stable our mounts and quench our thirst at your servants' table, for in truth it has been a long and hot ride, and the fame of your table has . . ."

"Enough! Enough!' shouted the first sentry. 'Give me the letter and I will take it immediately to our master. Bosk! Open the gate and let them in as far as the courtyard . . . but no more, mind, until I return."

With that the servant reached through the massive grill of the gate, and Ambrose handed him the letter. As the sentry walked off into the home with the message, Bosk, the other guard, swung open the gate. Inside, the entrance opened into a large courtyard, framed by the wall, a portion of the great house, and stone stables.

Signaling the little group to follow, Bosk, after he closed the gate, led the five travelers to a hitching post for horses. Several young stablehands ran out of the stable to take charge of the horses after everyone dismounted.

The first sentry appeared on a second-story balcony which overlooked the courtyard. "Bosk! Have the grooms rub down and stable their horses. Our esteemed guests are to be shown to the family's private quarters and there given a chance to freshen up. Have the maids heat the stones for a sauna, and make sure that we show our proper gratitude to these four stalwart soldiers by getting them each a horn of mead and something to eat!"

And thus, as honored guests, Ambrose, Phillip and Polonius were led to the luxurious quarters of the main house itself. There they were shown a sauna, where they sat happily and felt the dust of the long trip flush off their bodies.

Afterward, refreshed, they found that their clean clothes had been laid out for them, and a smirking house maid told them that her master would be pleased to have their company for the evening repast, which would be in but a few minutes.

CHAPTER 13.

Gunnar Hears Their Story.

Led by the maid, the three travelers descended a wide staircase directly into the main room of the house. They were led to a great oaken table laden with food. The man at the end of the table stood up at their approach, and smiled a broad welcome.

"Welcome to my humble house. I am Gunnar."

With that he stepped around the table and approached the trio.

Ambrose, still uncertain about his exact status, swept the stranger with his eyes. The man had long, reddish hair, expertly trimmed, and he was clean-shaven. Slightly taller than Ambrose, the man wore loose robes of the finest red wool. Around his neck and on his left wrist were ornaments of bright and beautifully worked gold.

When Gunnar reached the three of them, he hugged each in turn, and spoke to them individually. "Canuteson, is it? Adopted son of Canute, I welcome you to my home. My house is yours . . . And you must be none other than Phillip. The letter mentioned only that you were in great danger, and that you might be coming with Ambrose. Yet judging by your size, I warrant that you are not a man easily faced down . . . And you, dark as you are, must be Polonius the Scribe. The letter appears to be somewhat vague about you, as well, but I'm sure we will have time to fill in any gaps. Your writing, sir, is excellent, and if it is not too presumptuous of me to mention it here, you may have a scribe's job with me any time. But come, I speak too much and you all must be hungry after your long journey. Come! Sit you down and eat!"

Chuckling heartily, Gunnar clapped his hands, and a bevy of serving-girls came out from behind a curtain and proceeded to place both mead and wines in front of the guests, as well as adding still-steaming cuts of beef, pork, lamb, and salmon to the already overloaded table.

Silence reigned as the three travelers set to with a will. Only after much feasting did they all sit back, adopting Gunnar's relaxed manner, and sip delicious wines.

Polonius spoke. "My lord Gunnar, you keep a most excellent

larder and cellar. It has been many years since I have sampled a good wine, for, as you know, the Viking custom is to drink mead. Yet do I detect a light wine of southern Greece, or perhaps Crete?"

Gunnar laughed mightily. "Well done, Polonius. You are indeed a connoisseur of fine wines, and it will be my pleasure to hold discourse with you upon the merits of your Byzantine wines. In fact, what you are drinking is Spartan. But first, honored guests, allow an old man to indulge his curiosity. What are these mysterious insinuations that I seem to read between the lines of Canute's letter? As you know, it bids me make welcome the adopted son of Canute, and asks me to help him in his desires. Yet it refers only vaguely to some trouble of Phillip's, and only mentions Polonius as close friend and boon companion."

Ambrose looked slowly from one face to another. Neither Phillip nor Polonius nodded negatively. It was obvious that they must trust someone, and Gunnar appeared to be as good a bet as they were going to find.

Ambrose recounted their story carefully, leaving out no details, even from the day Ambrose and Phillip were captured in far-off Angleland. Gunnar easily absorbed all Ambrose said; only occasionally stopping to ask perceptive and pertinent questions.

As the tale finished, he sat back silently, pushing his two hands together repeatedly in a reflex action. At length he spoke.

"My friends, your story is safe with me. You may stay here for as long as you wish, and you have only to ask for anything that you may want. I have already so instructed the servants."

Ambrose frowned, and spoke softly. "Jarl Gunnar, we do not seek to hide here from anyone. I had hoped, as Canute told me of your vast commercial interests, that we might be of use to you in some capacity, so that we can earn our keep."

"Nobly spoken, Canuteson', responded Gunnar. 'If I was in your situation, I would feel the same way. How say you to employment in my company?"

Smiles of relief crossed the faces of all three companions, and any lingering tension in the air was released almost audibly. Ambrose nodded assent for all three.

"I always have need of young, intelligent factors and managers. How say you, Canuteson, to training in the field of commerce? Mind,' he interjected quickly, 'You will get no special treatment, but must pull your weight with the other trainees."

"Agreed, Jarl," smiled Ambrose.

"Polonius, I have urgent need of a scribe who can read and write the Byzantine tongue. Know you ought of the Latin, German, Frankish, or Slavic tongues?"

"In truth, my lord', answered Polonius, 'I read and write Greek and Latin as well as any. I can speak Frankish as a native, but can write in it only reasonably well. German I can speak somewhat, but know not the skill of writing in it. Of Slavic, I regret I know relatively little."

"Ho, you're a catch, even so, and it is a stroke of luck that I hire you now, for my tribesman, the Rus, are right now planning to strengthen trading routes down the great inland rivers as far as Byzantium itself.

Phillip, I ask only of you that you guard these two well, and insure that no harm comes to them."

"I will protect them with my life, Jarl Gunnar."

Time passed rapidly for the three of them, for each day was exceedingly busy. Much was expected. After a long day in the trading offices of Gunnar, the Rus jarl would often ask them to visit various commercial establishments of his in the town.

The first time the three of them accompanied Gunnar to the public docks, Ambrose was awed with the number of ships. The port appeared to be almost as busy as Wyk te Duurstede, which he only remembered as in a dream. Ships of all sizes and types were in the process of arriving, or leaving, or were tied securely to the docks.

The bay swarmed with fishing boats and a multitude of coasting vessels. In amongst the *knarrs* and *karves*, lean and hungry-looking long-ships floated serenely. Most impressive to Ambrose, however, was the small fleet of dragon ships. Towering over the long-ships and even the high-sided knarrs, the mighty warships personified the maritime power of the Rus.

"Jarl Gunnar,' asked Ambrose, 'how is it that the Rus lands can support so much trade?"

"An astute question, Canuteson. The answer lies in the strength of Rus and Swede sea power. Not for nothing is this sea called the Viking Sea. As the entrance is controlled by the Danish isles, foreign pirates are prevented from entering these waters. You must understand, too, the setup of our nation. Unlike Daneland, we have vast areas of land, and yet, as you have seen yourself, much of it, especially in the north, is fit for little except grazing and hunting. We do not have sufficient lands for our children to farm. Thus, we too, like our cousins to the south and west, were forced to take to the sea.

We have conquered the pagan northern lands, but there is little arable land there. It is good for little except slaving, pelts, and meat.

Opposite us, on the mainland, are both endless forests and great plains, stretching for hundreds of days' of travel. All along the barbarian coast you will find our colonies and settlements. These colonies absorb most of our excess population. Yet the barbarians who live there are far more numerous than us, and if they ever wanted, could soon push us into the sea. Thus, we act the role of trader and middleman, making ourselves indispensable to them. In this way, we control all the waters of this great sea, and our ships can travel in relative freedom wherever they choose.'

Gunnar shrugged. 'Some tribesmen attempt to go a Viking on the waters of the closed sea, but few dare to face our dragon ships.

I may add, as you probably have realized by now, that if our trade does not seem as exciting as the great ravaging conquests of our cousins the Danes and the Norsemen, yet it is many times more lucrative, and at a much lower price in terms of the blood of our sons."

One evening, when all three of the companions were able to leave Gunnar's trading factory before dusk, they wandered down towards the wharves to talk with the sailors and imbibe some mead. Looking out through the open portal of a sailor's inn, Phillip saw three long-ships, in formation, sail into the protection of the harbor.

"Master,' he said to Ambrose. 'Is that pennant flying from the mast not the ensign of Canute's own local Jarl?"

The trio moved outside the building and looked carefully. Sure enough, all three warships flew the pennant that signified allegiance to the jarl in whose province they had lived in, and subsequently fled.

Polonius, perhaps the first to recognize the possible significance, spoke first. "Holy mother of God! I pray that this is only a coincidence, but it may well be that this bodes ill for us. I would suggest we return to the sanctuary of Gunnar's house immediately, before those sailors come ashore."

Matching word to deed, the three returned directly to their rooms at Gunnar's home.

The next morning, when the trio were preparing to leave for the trading factory, Gunnar himself came to their chambers and tensely asked them to stay in the house for the day, or at least until he returned from a meeting of the town leaders.

As Hans, the German steward passed their chambers, Ambrose called him in. "Friend Hans, I have but thanks for all that this family has done for us, and yet no one has yet told us why Gunnar so respects the wishes of my adopted father Canute, who is, after all, but a poor farmer and ancient warrior. Gunnar appears unwilling to tell us, and, in my curiosity, I would appreciate knowing."

"I think I can help you there, honored sirs. The reason is not a great secret, but it is one that Gunnar finds painful, and thus avoids discussing.

Some years ago, Gunnar took his long-ship to the southern lands far beyond the Viking Sea. He participated with several Danish ships in a Viking raid on the land of the Franks. The Rus did not normally raid in that direction, and yet the crew was young, and what restrictions are ever upon young warriors intent upon adventures and treasure?

While the Danish adventurers kept their small fleet together, and made a strongly fortified camp near the mouth of a small Frankish river, the single Rus ship crew remained aloof. They beached their long-ship somewhat further up the river. When dawn broke, a strong force of Franks suddenly attacked the isolated Rus. Using their accursed bows, the Frankish soldiers picked off those Vikings who leapt overboard onto the river flats to try and launch their ship. A hastily improvised skjaldborg on the sands by the ship's side was quickly broken by a furious charge of heavily armored horsemen. At last, because of the vast difference in numbers, it became obvious that the only chance the Rus had was to flee down the river - and without their vessel. Their only hope of sanctuary was in the camp of their Danish cousins.

Gunnar was one of the few left who was able to run. They raced madly along the shore, abandoning all their weapons as they ran for their lives. Finally, the soldiers and horsemen had caught all but Gunnar, who in his youth was an excellent runner.

You must envision it so. When the Danes were woken and called to arms, it was to see a single man running swiftly towards them, with a pack of Frankish jackals yapping at his heel and trying to tear him down.

To the Danes' everlasting shame, only your adopted father and his young son dared to step forth from the Danish encampment. As they reached the runner's side, four lancers were about to run the Rus down, as Gunnar had fallen to his knees on the sand. Canute's great boar spear split one man's shield and punched him off his horse; dead.

As Canute leapt to attack the second rider, his son stepped over Gunnar's body, and raised his shield and axe in valiant defense. Two riders hurled their spears simultaneously, and the boy had a bitter choice. The shield would protect himself, or the stranger, but not both. Without hesitation, he threw his shield to the left to deflect the spear thrown at Gunnar. The other hit fairly, and penetrated his stout metal-plated jerkin as if it were soft doeskin.

In a berserk fury, Canute split the skull of his second attacker, and then turned on the remaining two. The third he bowled over by launching himself madly through the air and emptying the Frankish saddle.

The forth, seeing the futility of attacking a berserker, swung his horse about and attempted to flee. Canute's sax, thrown from a distance of almost forty foot-lengths, pierced his back and killed the man.

Gunnar, when he regained his feet, looked down at the corpse of the boy who had saved his life. Noting the resemblance of the boy to the raging berserker nearby, he broke down and cried like a woman. He lived, while this brave youth, hardly able yet to grow a beard, had died in his stead.

At that moment, Gunnar swore undying love for Canute. He would have served as body servant if Canute would but accept it. In this strange way, their great friendship developed. It has remained constant over the years in spite of separation by distance. Gunnar would willingly sacrifice his life to protect the adopted son of Canute."

Late that afternoon, Gunnar returned to the house looking very sober. Quickly he sent Hans to fetch Ambrose, Phillip and Polonius. As they assembled in the great dining hall, Gunnar waved them to seats and spoke.

"My friends, I fear I bring you only bad news. Our Rus High Chieftain has agreed to honor a Danish request for the capture and return of three escaped slaves. Regretfully, it appears that when you three escaped, one of the sentries, son of a relative of the local jarl, who is in turn distant cousin of the Danish High Chief, had an arm severely slashed.

The family will not settle for wergeld, but insists that the three slaves be returned for mutilation and death. One slave's return is also demanded as his life is sworn to Odin. Of course, my master cannot refuse such a request, and so has signed his name to the warrant.

Gunnar held up his hand for silence even as the trio, stunned, started to talk amongst themselves. "Friends, before you discuss any future actions, it behooves me to mention a plan I have been considering for some time."

Suddenly a momentary smile crossed his face. "It seems to me that you may have a renewed interest in traveling. You may thus find my offer irresistible. As I mentioned some time ago, many of our trading expeditions are along the great rivers of the vast land south and east of the Viking Sea. Our agents have actually made contact as far south as the Byzantine Empire, and we would, of course, like to develop a direct trading route from the Viking Sea all the way to the Bosporus. Furs, slaves, northern ivory, ambergris and horses are all in great demand in the south. Yet in the north, there is great demand for Byzantine glass, silver, gold coins, cotton and silk cloth, as well as such things as ostrich plumes and exotic slaves. It thus seems a simple proposition for us to sell our merchandise in the south, and use the payment to purchase trade goods for the north.

As you have no doubt learned, after your conscientious efforts in my trading factory, being a trader is an incredibly complicated business. You must obtain your goods at the lowest prices, yet get the best quality. You must have a regular source of supplies, and you must provide protection not only for your ships, but for the trading factors and their families.

Most important, you must find local businessmen and factors that you can trust; who will only skim a little off your rightful share. Now, it happens, by a great stroke of luck, that the Rus have been invited to the Slav town of Novgorod, to help the people fight off a veritable horde of raiders and to help bring peace and trade to them and their neighbors. Many families of the Rus are taking up the challenge and sending ships to help colonize, and, of course, develop trade.

The opportunity is a great one, for this town of Novgorod controls a major river, and may be the gateway to both eastern and Byzantine trade. I am too old and comfortable to traverse the great distances involved, so I need good men to represent my interests.

This then, is why I have need of your help. As you have proved yourselves both astute and conscientious, I would ask you to sail south to the great rivers. There, as special agents of mine, I want you to establish permanent bases that will make it possible for my men to safely pass trade goods from factory to factory, until my traders can make the final run south to Byzantium itself.

In particular, I want you to establish my presence as far south as you can. Mind, it is essential that you find easily fortified positions. Stay away from the open steppes, since that is the undisputed territory of nomads who hate buildings. The locations you choose must be convenient to the eastern caravan route, yet command the southern river trade.

With luck, and several years experience on the rivers, I will consider you, Canuteson, as a partner in my company. But note you well, I will offer you this not for the love of Canute, but only if you prove your worth as a trader. I had hoped to train you personally for a much longer time, but events have unfortunately been precipitated. What say you?"

All three friends exchanged glances of amazement. The offer made by Gunnar was little short of miraculous. It was an offer that most could expect only after many hard years in the service of a trading company, and yet, to reap the full benefits, they must prove themselves, so it was not an offer foolishly or rashly promised. Knowing that he spoke for the three of them, Ambrose responded.

"Jarl Gunnar, I hardly know what to say. In truth, we feared that we might have to just blindly flee, and your offer is far more generous than we deserve, and yet I must state that, tempted as I am, I am unable to avail myself of even such an incredible offer until I know that Canute is not suffering because of what I have done.

Further, I have a responsibility to my brother and the Kingdom of Wessex. My responsibility cannot be shirked, and, in God's own time, I must return to my people."

"Ho!' shouted Gunnar, 'Better and better! I think that any arrangement between us cannot but be mutually profitable. Know you then, that Canute is well. The captain of one of the three vessels was from a neighboring town, and knows him. Canute was called to report to the Thing to answer for his action. He rightfully stated that he had sent you on an errand to here. He swore by Odin and Thor that he had naught to do with your two companions' escape, and none dared brook the fierce old warrior, especially as he freely and openly told all where you had been sent. They doubt that you will reach here, because you were not spotted coasting through the Danish guardian islands, but they delivered their message anyway.

As to your king and brother, I will give you a boat any time you wish, but the islanders have been warned, and you will not make it home to the island of Angleland. Better that you try when the Danish searchers have given up and headed home. There is even a possibility that you can reach Miklagard and travel home to Angleland that way. Knowing all that, what say you to my offer?"

Once again, Ambrose spoke. "Jarl, once again we are in your debt. It is a magnificent offer, and we heartily accept, with only the provisos I mentioned earlier."

Gunnar sighed as if a big load was removed from his mind. "Good! Go then, and pack your belongings. Your ship, the Deerhound, sails in the morning with the tide. I will arrange to have you rowed out to meet her secretly."

As they departed the room, Ambrose looked quickly into the eyes of their benefactor, and smiled a thank you. Gunnar chuckled and said.

"It is with great regret that I must inform the Danish captains that they are too late, and that your ship sailed before I could stop you."

CHAPTER 14.

They Make the Ship.

Dawn found Ambrose, Phillip, and Polonius being rowed out into the open waters of the Viking Sea in a small skiff. They had set off from a small fishing village a half-hour's ride north of Gunnar's magnificent residence. This precaution had been suggested by Gunnar, who had felt that this would prevent any potential problems if the commanders of the Danish vessels became suspicious and pulled alongside the Rus vessel as it slipped out of the harbor.

Thus, it was almost an hour after dawn when the waiting boat load of people saw a low vessel round the point.

Polonius spoke quietly to his two comrades. "Well, old friends. Let's hope that this is the Deerhound. There is no way we can make it ashore if we have been betrayed or the Danes just plain found us."

Normally taciturn Phillip replied. "Look at the length of the vessel and the height of the gunnels. This is a vessel designed for inland waterways, not a Danish warship."

Ambrose smiled. "Then, my friends, let us thank merciful God. It appears that we are safe and will soon be on our way!"

In spite of the verbal assurances, all aboard the little vessel remained tense. Betrayal meant a painful death for all of them. The Vikings were not gentle with escaped slaves, and those who defiled a sacred sacrifice would be given particularly unpleasant deaths.

Both passengers and rowers all heaved a large sigh of relief when they were finally able to detect Gunnar's eagle crest on the ship's sail. As the land-sea breezes were constantly shifting, the karve crewmen were manning their oars, and the low ship quickly closed the distance.

The three fugitives all inspected the ship with a critical eye, since they were now more familiar with the various Viking ships, and their lives could depend on the worth of this one. It was clinker-built, as were most Viking ships. It seemed almost a scaled-down version of the long-ship they had traveled on, but it had a surprising beam for so small a ship.

Ambrose ruminated out loud. "Well, friends, it looks more like a small mastiff, instead of a greyhound built for speed and surprise."

Polonius nodded. "It makes sense, Master. Gunnar told me that the Deerhound is a river karve, a special design of his own. He said they must be able to sail and fight, and yet carry a large quantity of trade goods. They might be called upon to traverse hundreds of Roman miles along rivers, and pass over shallows and rocks. In short, the vessel is a compromise between a vessel built for raids and war, and one that can carry enough goods to make a profitable voyage.

Once aboard the vessel, the trio waved thanks to the oarsmen who were fast disappearing shoreward. They settled themselves down comfortably, for they were to be honored guests of the captain, traveling as they were with Gunnar's direct authority to carry out company business as they best saw fit.

As soon as the wind picked up enough that the oars could be shipped and the huge square sail was propelling the ship towards its destination without help, the captain came to see the three of them.

"Son-of-Canute, my name be Hammar. Know you of our plans?", he asked, showing increased respect for this lad when the boy's ever-present bodyguard, Phillip, uncoiled himself and stood straight, a giant amongst a race of tall men. Phillip was resplendent in his new outfit of wool and buckskin; a man truly to be reckoned with.

Ambrose responded to the captain. "I have instructions to sail with you to Novgorod, set up a trading factory, and eventually do the same thing as far south as I can. As to your instructions, however, I regret I know little. I and my companions would appreciate it greatly if you would enlighten us."

In truth, the three of them were bursting with curiosity about this mysterious mission, and even Polonius' vast storehouse of knowledge had been of little help, as, for once, he had no knowledge of the area they were sailing to, except that Byzantium acquired furs, horses and slaves from somewhere in the heart of the continent. That, and the fact that the land to the south and east was famous as the land of the steppe horsemen; where lived the fierce Scythians, Huns, and a hundred other unknown (at least to Polonius) tribes. Polonius explained to a skeptical Ambrose that these savage horsemen had helped to destroy mighty Rome itself, and they were an occasional threat even to the New Rome that had risen on the crossroads between Asia and Europe.

Hammar smiled. "Son-of Canute. Sit, and I will try to answer any questions you have. As I know not what you know, I will tell all I can think of, but I ask you to tell me if I repeat information you already possess."

So saying, the four of them settled down on the hard-wood deck, and the captain began.

"As you know, we, the Rus, have built settlements on the southern coast of the Viking Sea. We have taken our wooden steeds up many of the rivers that empty into the sea, and we have thus traded far inland.

Novgorod, along one of the interior rivers, has long been an important trading town on our river journeys. We have found it expedient, in turn, to fight at the townsmen's side when danger has threatened. Thus we have become friends. Pressure from marauders to the south and east, and bickering amongst themselves, means that the Slavs there are an easy target for the steppe barbarians. The Slavs, the people of the forest, the inland towns and the farms, fear the barbarian horsemen greatly. Thus, they have asked us, the Rus, to bring our families, settle amongst them, stand at their shoulder in time of danger, and help teach them our way of fighting.

Even now, at a colony of ours at the mouth of the Neva River, a fleet is gathering to sail to Lake Ladoga. From there we will go down= =river to the town of Novgorod. There we will settle our families and build proper defenses.

Gunnar's instructions to me are to assist you in any way I can. When Novgorod is secure and you no longer need my men, I am to take our cargoes south. It is my hope to sail as far south as I can before selling. Slavs and other Vikings who buy our goods then transport them all the way south, as far as the Black Sea, or even Miklagard itself.

Gunnar did tell me that you three would be, after establishing a trading post at Novgorod, eventually traveling the rivers south."

Ambrose replied. "Yes, Captain. Our instructions were to first establish the Novgorod post, but Gunnar seemed anxious that we eventually push south as far as we could safely go. He is hoping to eventually have a trade route directly to Miklagard."

The captain smiled, showing gleaming white teeth. "Aye, it would be a great help if we had secure posts along the entire length of the rivers, where we could stay safely and be properly supplied."

"I thank you for the information,' Polonius said. 'And yet I know little of what we will face."

"Then you do not know the problems of the steppe-lands?" asked the captain.

"No", answered Ambrose and Polonius together.

"Greek that you are, Master Polonius, no doubt you know something of the Huns and Magyars, Scythians, and of the other mounted tribes?

"I know of the might of the ancient Huns under Attila', said Polonius. 'Today I know it is mercenary Huns, together with the regular Byzantine cavalry, who protects imperial Byzantium."

Hammar smiled. "You know then, of the awesome might of the mounted bowmen of the steppe people. Their numbers, yea, even the number of their tribes, are as the sand. For in the distance of hundreds of day's marches, lives untold numbers of fierce nomads. When combined under a strong leader, they are as unstoppable as the tide. If a thousand died for every Rus, then when we all had died, there would seem to be no less nomads.

In this great flat sea of grass and sand they wander eternally, foraging for greener grass, and frowning when, driving before them their vast flocks of sheep, horses, camels, or cattle, a city blocks their passage.

It is these people who are the scourge of the steppes. It is a simple matter for us to rule the Slav townspeople, for they are not by nature warlike, and want only to farm or trade. In order to hold our new lands against the steppe raiders, we bring families, and build forts as well as trading factories. There we will live, and there we will fight off all attackers. The days of just trading on the rivers are finished. Make no mistake. Novgorod is just a start. We intend to rule the Slav river lands!"

CHAPTER 15.

They Reach the Gathering Place.

Several days' journey, making use of the square-sail when possible, and otherwise using the oars, found the Deerhound approaching the rendezvous. The captain kept the trading vessel near the coast for most of the journey, and the crew and passengers spent the nights ashore or on off-shore islands.

On several different occasions Captain Hammar put in at villages for fresh water and food, and Ambrose noted that in each village visited there were at least some Viking settlers. It was obvious that the forested shores of the Viking Sea were well colonized by the far-trading Swede tribesmen.

In many settlements, apparently, the Swedes controlled the town, its immediate environs, and the local trade. By setting themselves up with or over the local chiefs, they controlled large areas of these forest-lands. Most important, the captain explained to Ambrose and his friends, the towns acted as bases for further forays up the various rivers.

At last, after sailing up a small river and into a huge lake, they found their fleet anchored off another small town. Here, at the mouth of one of the great rivers that led into the interior, floated a large fleet of Viking vessels.

Ambrose and his companions watched their destination near from the comfort of the little tent set up in the bow of their ship. The prince spoke to the captain who stood beside him.

"Hammar, the ships of the fleet seem to be heavily laden with women and children. From the insignias on the shields and banners, it appears that the Rus make up the vast majority of the complement. If my count is right, then this expedition seems to be little short of a tribal migration. I do see other tribal banners as we pass, but the overwhelming majority seem to be Rus."

"Aye, Canuteson. What you say is true. We have traded south for many years. Constantinople is so well known to our traders that we generally just refer to it as Miklagard, or, in our language - the big city.

We have never before been offered the opportunity to settle so far south, however. That several Slav leaders have invited us to settle at Novgorod is a great opportunity for us. My people intend to take full advantage of it.

Think, Canuteson, what it would mean if we can establish ourselves firmly in the river valleys. In a few years we will have a stranglehold on the trade both to Byzantium and on the northern route to Asia."

"I notice, too, Captain that there are few long-ships and no dragon ships amongst the fleet."

"You are right, Canuteson. The ships have all been chosen so that they are able to traverse the sometimes shallow rivers. And look there. Those ships are towing even smaller vessels. Those little boats are for portage or navigation on the headwaters of the smaller rivers. The few long-ships you see will return north from here once they have unloaded their cargoes."

All in all, Ambrose thought it was a brave sight. The many vessels were decked with pennants. The many dragonhead bows bobbed to the waves' motion. Ashore, crowds of women and children milled about.

Ambrose turned again to the ship commander. "Captain, why are so many of your tribesmen not only willing to face the dangers of unknown lands, but willing to bring their wives and children?"

"Canuteson, ambition and overcrowding in our own lands have always persuaded large numbers of our tribesmen to migrate. There is little left for them if they stay in their homelands, but there may be that shining new future we talked about somewhere down these rivers. The leaders of Novgorod have asked not just for warriors, but for settlers who will live with them, raise many strong children, stand shoulder to shoulder with them, and be prepared to face the steppe invaders with naked steel. The city elders are not stupid. Men who bring their families are committed to stay and fight. The women and children ensure my tribesmen will not run."

Ambrose had a look of puzzlement on his face. "But surely the Slav leaders know that by so doing they are sacrificing control of their own lands? You yourself said that your tribesmen meant to rule as much of the river lands as you could."

The captain nodded. "Aye. I suppose so. Yet their own rivalries have caused endless bloodshed for generations. And the steppe hordes. Ah, the steppe hordes. Canuteson, I have been at a cataract on the Dnieper hauling our ship through the rough water when a detachment of the Pecheneg horde struck. They are terrible fierce fighters, my young friend."

"But you are here, Hammar."

"Aye, naked from the water, we stood shield to shield and stopped their charge cold. Their archers, however, would have soon made short work of us."

"But you survived. You must have beaten them."

"That is the story no doubt told in many halls on a winter night, but the truth is that a Khazar patrol heard the sounds of battle and rode to our rescue. The Khazars take a ten percent toll of our trade goods, but without their help the lower Dnieper would be closed to both the Slavs and us too. The Khazars exact a stiff tribute, but they earn it with the lives of their young men."

"Are you saying, then, that the Slav leaders are willing to give up control of their own town in return for protection?"

"Canuteson, I think that is the long and the short of it. Better to have half of a loaf and hold it securely, than to hold a whole loaf, but to have it all stolen. I think they know who will rule their lands, but at least they will be partners with us, in a strong confederation where the lives of their wives and children are not threatened every year."

"Thank you for your words, Hammar. What you say makes sense. My own ancestors back in Britain faced a similar decision when Imperial Rome withdrew its protection from our shores. They invited German tribesmen in to help them hold their lands."

"And what happened, Canuteson?"

"Amongst others, they invited a tribe called the Angles to help them."

"And?"

Ambrose smiled. "The island of Britain is now generally called Angleland."

Hammar grinned in return. "I like your story, Canuteson. It is my hope that the lands south of us may soon be known as Rusland, the new lands of the Rus."

With precision strokes, the trading vessel slid smoothly past the many beached and anchored ships of the Viking fleet. The captain turned momentarily away from his guests, and spoke a single quiet instruction. Instantly the oars were raised, then smartly dipped. A strong forward push of each rower brought the stubby vessel to a sudden halt, and a second signal caused the crewmen of the port side to stroke while their companions lifted their oars from the water. The ship turned shoreward and gently slid between two other Rus karves.

With the ceremonious arrival completed, the sailors shipped their oars. The crew abandoned their seats and eagerly shouted to people in the other vessels and on shore. Several young men ran to the bow and leapt into the water. Ambrose watched them wade ashore and join the other bachelors broaching kegs of ale and mead. From the many conversations Ambrose had overheard while aboard ship, he knew they were also eager to see if they could catch the eye of any nubile and single young women traveling on one of the other ships.

Within minutes the vessel was all but abandoned. Old comrades hunted for each other ashore, and extended families were reunited.

Hammar spoke again to his three passengers. "Canuteson, Phillip, and Polonius, please feel free to join the crew ashore. In a day or two I will be summoned, along with all the other fleet captains, to a conference with Rurik, the expedition leader. Then I will find out when we sail. Until then, you are free to do as you wish. Just check with me each morning."

ቈ

Once ashore, the three companions wandered around the massive temporary encampment that had grown up all around the small town. What surprised Ambrose and Phillip, in particular, was the large number of dark townspeople. Their humble clothing indicated that they were largely slaves or thralls. It was plain that the original owners of this land, the Finns, had bowed to the superior prowess of Swedish military might, and had become vassals in their own land. They, in turn, captured and ruled the dark people; the people of the primeval forest and taiga.

ቈ

At dusk the people of the large encampment gathered around their campfires to sing and drink. Ambrose, Phillip and Polonius continued to wander about aimlessly, absorbing random comments and boasts, and meeting many of the warriors.

As they passed a tent, they saw a drunken group of young men, unblooded and bachelors by the look of them, standing about. One great lout was tugging the pigtail of an old Finn servant and was unsheathing his sax with the apparent intent to slice it off. The servant, stoically enduring the fierce upward tug of her hair, cried out when she saw the knife appear in her tormentor's hand. The group of drunken friends clapped happily and egged the lout on.

Ambrose and his two companions stood mutely for a moment, and then turned to sidle past. Unhappy about the treatment as they were, they were well aware that it was the right of a master to do as he chose with a slave. If a master went too far, then it became a matter for the Thing to deal with, and not foreigners accepted only on sufferance. As Ambrose stepped to the side, however, the woman struggled, and the lout was pushed into Ambrose. Furious, the man turned with a snarl.

"Pig, you dare to hit Bjourn?"

Realizing that the man was drunk, Ambrose spoke humbly. "Your pardon, warrior. I was but attempting to pass you by when your struggle with this woman moved you backwards into me."

Noting the diminutive size of Ambrose, as well as the fact that the woman had scurried away the second he had let her pig-tail go, Bjourn felt that Ambrose would be as much fun to play with.

"On your knees, pig swill, if you expect to escape my presence with your skin intact!"

A second warrior, even more drunk than the first, lurched over and reached for a spear stuck into the ground.

"Bjourn, allow me to spit this beardless calf, and perhaps then we can remove his manhood from him. It's obvious that he has no need of his balls!' The man smirked. 'Maybe he ain't got any to cut off!"

So saying, he drew the spear from the soft ground and started to level it. Polonius, silent until now, spoke quietly, but in a hissing voice that carried far.

"Raise that spear another finger length, and you're a dead man!"

The entire group was startled by his voice, and even the warrior who was raising the spear hesitated. He looked at Polonius and then pointed with his other hand.

"Look! A simpering foreigner! Scarecrow, you dare threaten me? Your blond friend can wait his turn. I'll spit you first!"

At that he turned the spear to aim it at Polonius, whose own hand leapt to his belt. Almost instantaneously, two slim throwing knives left Polonius' hand. The first thudded into the shaft of the spear, and the second nicked the man's hand. With a scream of surprise, the man dropped the spear.

Polonius allowed his gaze to wander over the rest of the group. Each of his hands held another blade poised for throwing.

His voice rang out in the sudden silence.

"Does anyone else wish to interfere with my master's business?"

At the same time, Phillip, who had until now been standing in the shadows, stepped into the firelight, his hands on the hilt of his giant sword. With one look at Polonius' poised daggers, and another at the armored giant, the drunken group subsided. They had been, after all, only out for a little entertainment. No one wanted to start a blood-feud.

Polonius retrieved the first blade from the spear which now lay on the ground, and the second from where the man had thrown it when he wrenched it loose. When the three made to turn away, however, Bjourn swore a dreadful oath and yelled out at Ambrose.

"By the balls of Odin, you little piece of dung, you need protectors, do you? Leave your sword here, and join the women in the cooking tent, unless it be true that you have balls and are a man! If so, I challenge you to blood-combat!"

Ambrose knew with a sinking feeling that he could not well refuse. These were the men he must live and work with, and if he was not able to gain respect, then they would be unable to work with the Vikings.

"Once again, I am sorry that we bumped, and I would be pleased to teach you some manners, but I cannot involve my employer in a blood feud."

The dark warrior grinned. "This will not be a blood feud. Boy. I will spread my cape and that walking oak tree behind you can plant the hazel twigs. I declare a *Holmgang*!"

Ambrose looked at the burley warrior. He knew that to refuse a holmgang challenge was to admit cowardice, and there was no room for cowards in Viking society. A man who was unwilling to stand up for his rights was considered only fit to be a slave.

The prince spoke. "Then spread your cloak, big-mouth. It seems I will get a chance to teach you some manners after all."

"Ho!' cried Bjourn, 'someone find this rooster two more shields and a real sword, instead of that tiny thing he carries. Plant the twigs and stand aside! I'll carve this boy into little pieces with my left hand!"

The crowd, sensing excitement and entertainment, grew quickly. Two of the man's companions stripped his cloak off his back and spread it on the ground while several others gathered branches and shoved them in the ground all around the cloak.

Bjourn grinned. "You have three shields and one sword, boy. Now all you need are some balls. We fight until one of us is forced to stop. Are we agreed, boy?"

Ambrose looked grim. "Save your breath, blowhard. You are going to need it!"

With his peripheral vision, Ambrose saw Polonius holding Phillip back. He knew the old warrior wanted to rescue him, but he knew that only his sword would earn him the respect he needed.

Bjourn hefted a long sword and a heavy round shield. Ambrose, across the circle, held his prized foreign sword and a smaller buckler.

"Boy!', shouted Bjourn. 'I don't butcher unarmed geldings. Get yourself a weapon!"

"Come, blowhard!', responded Ambrose, 'And taste my steel!"

"Then may *Ull* guide my blade. Today is the day I carve you like a roast!" At last, surrounded by armed and neutral men who would ensure fair-play, and with reflected firelight lighting their respective enemies, the two closed for combat. Bjourn attacked first, swinging his sword in an all but irresistible arc at Ambrose's head.

Stepping nimbly back, and taking only a little of the force obliquely on his shield, Ambrose calmly awaited the next attack. He knew that it was Viking style to swing a sword so. Since the soft metal would not hold an edge long, it was the custom to parry blows with the shield rather than the sword. Bjourn, in turn, realized that the stripling was not a complete novice, and he became a little more cautious.

Thus it was Ambrose who attacked next. Keeping his shield ever-ready for a savage swing of the long sword, he moved in warily, feinting and swinging in the Viking manner. Bjourn, with considerable alcohol in him, and a much heavier shield and sword, rapidly tired. The firelight was soon reflecting off the beads of perspiration that crept down his face. He attempted to use the advantage of his long sword by keeping Ambrose at a distance, where the shorter foreign blade was at a disadvantage.

Though his sword's attack-range was shorter, Ambrose, to the surprise of all, began a series of chopping sweeps. Again and again he put his light sword directly against his opponent's more massive blade. To everyone's amazement, the great iron sword of Bjourn's showed large nicks, while Ambrose's looked as sharp as before he started.

Disconcerted by Ambrose's approach and rapidly reaching exhaustion, Bjourn charged in, meaning to use his superior strength to quickly end the contest. In spite of all he could do, however, Ambrose's sword; equally effective in slicing and jabbing, was able time after time to slip past his shield. Though the force of the blows were almost completely spent, they managed to slice Bjourn's leather to pieces, and only Bjourn's chain-mail shirt prevented serious damage. Try as he would, Bjourn's much longer sword simply could not sneak past the small shield and flashing sword. While Bjourn was rapidly being drained of blood from the numerous small cuts, Ambrose was untouched, and was scarcely breathing heavily.

Ambrose watched Bjourn closely. He could see the fatigue building and he knew that Bjourn must soon make a last desperate attempt or collapse. The big Viking suddenly threw aside his shield and grasped his sword two-handed. While Ambrose stood still, Bjourn raised his sword high and brought it down in a great irresistible sweep. If he missed, he would be helpless, but he obviously hoped even this dancing fairy would not be able to get away from or parry such a blow. Ambrose, calculating the reach of the opposing blade, realized the futility of attempting to dance back. He could do little more than throw up his own blade for defense. With a great clang and a shower of sparks, the two blades met in the air. Incredibly, Bjourn's blade, in spite of its size and weight, bent Ambrose, although forced to his knees by the terrific force, was quite unharmed. Bjourn suddenly held a useless weapon.

By the rules of the combat, Ambrose was now free to finish it, but instead he got back to his feet. Bjourn, covered in blood, exhausted, and with only a severely bent sword for defense, slid suddenly to his knees, and then fell unconscious to the ground.

Ambrose saluted his fallen foe with his sword. "Warriors, I salute a brave and noble warrior. Is there any other here who feels he has just cause to challenge me? If so, speak now!"

A roar went up from the gathered men, who respected and appreciated a good fighter. "Nay! Nay!", roared the warriors who made up the crowd. After many back poundings and cheers, Ambrose, Polonius, and Phillip were invited to drink mead and celebrate the victory. Even Bjourn, when he recovered, drank to Ambrose's health. It was only after a few hours that Ambrose and his two comrades were able to extricate themselves from the hard-drinking Rus fighting men, and when they left, they left behind new friends.

As he left, Ambrose realized that he had truly fought for the first time in his life, and he knew he could easily have killed his first warrior foe.

CHAPTER 16.

They Arrive at Novgorod.

It was the time of the third full moon past the spring equinox when all was ready. Several more large ships arrived and deposited supplies at the village, after which they turned around to return to the Viking Sea and home. Most of the vessels, however, were to make the voyage south, and the vessel of Rurik, who was the leader of the expedition, led the brave flotilla down river.

Ambrose and his two companions watched the endless forest slide by on either bank of the river. At last Ambrose approached Hammar, who had traded on the river before.

"Captain, where are the great treeless steppes you spoke of?"

Hammar chuckled slightly. "I am afraid, Canuteson, that we will have to travel down several rivers and spend another week or two sliding past forests before ever you will see the mighty steppes. In fact, our immediate destination, *Holmgard*, is still in the forest, except, of course, where the peasants have made clearings to make room for crops.

But fear not! If you go far enough, you will find the steppes right enough. And once on them, if you keep the North Star on your left, you can travel for hundreds of days without ever seeing a forest again. There are more grasslands and deserts than you can imagine. For myself, I prefer the forest. It keeps the terrible nomad hordes at bay, and, besides, it is more like our homeland."

After several more days' journey, when all the crewmen, spelled occasionally by the passengers, pulled at an oar until their hands were raw, the flotilla arrived at its destination. On the bank was a considerable town, with fields stretching away from the river.

Rurik directed the entire fleet to a large, wooded island in the middle of the river. Within minutes the efficient crewmen had beached or tied up all the ships. Rurik himself, along with several leaders, was rowed over to meet the village officials.

Ambrose, as a representative of Gunnar's powerful trading house, was invited to join them. Phillip and Polonius had to remain behind, and they headed ashore to cut branches for lean-to's and to set up leather tents that had been brought as temporary dwellings.

Before the sun set, Ambrose returned to the island and sought out his companions.

Polonius looked up and smiled in greeting. "Welcome to our little camp, Prince. Tell us what transpired when you met the Slavic leaders!"

"We met a delegation of Slav leaders, and after the customary greetings, Rurik got down to the business at hand. He is a shrewd man and drove a hard bargain."

Polonius looked impatient. "What arrangements did he make, Master?"

"He demanded an equal voice on the ruling council in exchange for Rus protection."

"And the Slav rulers accepted this?"

Ambrose nodded. "Rurik reminded them that they had invited the Rus because one of the nomad tribes had threatened the town just the year before and the town urgently needed allies urgently."

Polonius looked puzzled. "But why would the Slavs choose the Rus as allies?"

"I wondered that, too, but I soon learned that two years previously a force of Pechenegs had indeed been beaten back by a group of Rus trader-warriors. Their defensive shield-wall managed to hold a wild cavalry charge - something the Slav traders had never seen before.

A naked berserker had apparently, in a fit of frenzy, singlehandedly killed six horsemen with bow, spear, and axe, before he was cut down. Shocked by the ferocity of a single Viking, the nomads had then moved off in pursuit of easier game. Thus, the area rulers, who were also tired of the incessant raids from their neighbors, listened to good sense and decided to ask the Rus to settle as partners. In return, they asked only that the Vikings would train levies of villagers in military tactics, provide help in constructing forts, and be themselves willing to form a nucleus of a defensive force.

Each captain, or Rus leader, is to take an area, and, with his men, provide security there. I was amused to discover that most of the areas the Slavs intend to assign to the Rus are not yet under local control, but belonged to rival settlements. The present leaders, of course, insisted on retaining the areas they already controlled.

Rurik had laughed when his lieutenant pointed this fact out to him. I will try to remember his exact word. I believe he said. 'Of course they will give us the domains they don't control! But the secret to success is the rivers. We have mobility with a fleet of wooden steeds. We have over a thousand battle-hardened warriors, and our friends here will no doubt be happy to loan us a few hundred good Slav men.'

Ambrose continued. 'On balance, the arrangement does not seem completely uneven. The townspeople have the responsibility to feed and house some two thousand dependents while the thousand-odd well-armed warriors march out to conquer their new domains. The Vikings have a secure base-of-operations to work from. The Slavs have fierce protectors, and their young men are expected to fight alongside the Rus warriors and learn their fighting methods. Further, there are great prospects for loot, slaves, and glory."

Within days the process of colonization began in earnest. While Rurik and his followers remained and settled on the island opposite the town, many Rus tribesmen abandoned their ships, requisitioned horses, and rode out to scout out or conquer their new domains. On other days, small fleets of karves, heavily loaded with armed warriors, sailed up and down-river to harry those who were slow in swearing allegiance to the new power centered in Novgorod.

All who remained on the island were put to work, for the simultaneous tasks of building for trade, colonization, and defense were a priority. A stockade, adequate for storage of goods, as well as defense, was built within a week.

Ambrose and Phillip both spent many long hours with axe in hand, and their muscles, softened by their stay in Gunnar's home, hardened and became like strong ropes. Polonius, to his delight, became an advisor on military defense.

With his not inconsiderable knowledge gleaned from his early studies, and life spent in countries from Asia to Scandinavia, Polonius knew more than any of the *Varangians* about the science of combat, although he was the first to admit that he was no fan of war, nor even very personally proficient in its practice. Amongst many other things, he was able to describe a marching camp as built by the ancient Romans; one which, with a minimum of time, was all but impervious even to siege weapons.

"Jarl Rurik, in the days of the Caesars of Rome, it was the practice for each soldier to carry a stake and shovel. When the site was chosen at the end of each day's march, each legionary would go to his assigned position, and, before nightfall, they would throw up an earthen palisade, surrounded, of course, by the dry moat which is where they got the dirt. Logs would be collected to help support the structure, but each soldier was responsible for transporting and placing a sharpened stake at the summit of the palisade. Within this square, tents, or, if longer term, cabins, would be set up. When well constructed, the walls were proof against battering rams, fire darts, and catapults. The fort itself was cheap, effective, and absolutely proof against cavalry attacks. For your purposes, my jarl, can there be a more effective fortification?"

Polonius spent many more hours discussing the merits of various military tactics against mounted horsemen. The Rus relied on their impenetrable skjaldborg to break any charge or defend against archers. How to train the rapidly growing bodies of native Slav levies was the big problem, though each Rus overlord applied his favorite idea. As massed spearmen or swordsmen the Slavs were a disaster, for the Vikings were trained from childhood for the skjaldborg. At the sight of a massed cavalry charge, the native levies would never stand true, not because of a lack of bravery, but because it simply seemed to them inconceivable that they could stand against the thundering tons of horseflesh. Also, they had a deep-seated fear of the savage horsemen that the Vikings lacked.

Polonius explained the use of the ancient military phalanx, where even relatively raw recruits could, with their twenty-foot lances, hold fast against anything that moved. He explained how Alexander the Great's phalanxes had conquered most of the known world, and he also explained their fatal flaw; the discovery of which had caused the Roman star to rise and the Macedonian one to wane.

Of more promise appeared to be the bow, sling and pike; the last a weapon which was unfamiliar to the Rus, but one which Polonius had seen put to effective use on his travels.

The sling was rapidly discarded, as it was obvious when they tried some that the fantastic skill Polonius had seen demonstrated by Byzantine auxiliaries was due to many years of constant practice. The hunting bow, however, was something the native tribes knew, and they were reasonably adept at using it.

After Polonius had a blacksmith make up some pikes, and demonstrated their use on cavalry. Rurik waxed enthusiastic. He ordered many more to be made. Their hooks allowed warriors to reach out from the safety of their ranks and pull a mounted rider off his horse. They made the match between infantry and cavalry a little bit more even.

CHAPTER 17.

They Establish a Trading Factory.

While the three companions were anxious to press on further into such a vast and mysterious land, they realized that the first priority now was a solid base. A strong Rus colony on the river would provide both a refuge and a base for operations. It would go a long way to help ensure control of the river trade. Polonius swallowed his eagerness to see his homeland again, and contented himself with regaling Phillip and Ambrose with the glories of the Byzantine civilization.

They labored hard on setting up first joint defenses for the entire town, and then a trading factory for the House of Gunnar. Although the Deerhound and several smaller vessels belonging to Gunnar traveled both up and downriver, scouting out trading prospects and buying and selling goods, the three companions remained at Novgorod.

Almost before the colonists were aware of it, brilliant foliage heralded a change in seasons. The short, hot summer ended suddenly, and frost could be found on the ground at dawn. Secure in their new log home, with a massive stone fireplace and a copious supply of wood, Ambrose, Phillip, and Polonius yet appeared to be trapped for the winter. Forced idleness, now that the post and warehouse was established and a factor appointed, encouraged the three of them to leave the isolated island settlement and ride forth into the valley-lands that had so recently become Varangian fiefs.

Near the time of the autumn equinox, the three of them left Novgorod on a journey to the domain of Bothi; distant relative of Gunnar, whom Ambrose had had dealings with and found most friendly. Son of a petty jarl, he had been elected as one of the ship captains at the start of the expedition. He and his crew were now ensconced on river-side territory about a day's journey south of Novgorod, in an agricultural settlement which had formerly belonged to Slav tribesmen hostile to Novgorod.

The land was largely forest, with a fair number of small hamlets and fields carved out of the wilderness. The primitive settlements provided subsistence living for the Slav inhabitants. The peasants had grudgingly surrendered to the giant blond warriors who had so suddenly arrived simultaneously by both land and water. Those who had refused to swear allegiance were savagely cut down while their families were captured for export to the Byzantine slave market.

The trio followed the river as best they could, as they knew that Bothi's holdings were near the great river. For all three of them, it was a pleasant treat to ride horses again, for they were landsmen, and preferred the horse to the wooden steeds of the Vikings.

As Phillip turned a bend in the narrow forest trail, an arrow struck him, hitting him obliquely in his chest. Although his chain-mail jerkin broke the main thrust of the shaft, the long narrow point was able to force itself part-way into his chest.

Almost simultaneously, Ambrose and Polonius ducked low, lifted their shields, and spurred their horses forward at a gallop. Passing Phillip on either side and stampeding through the undergrowth, they suddenly realized that no foe stood on the trail to challenge them. While the two hesitated, a second shaft struck against Polonius' shield, embedding itself firmly.

This time Polonius' eye caught a flash of movement. In a single smooth motion, his hand slid to his belt and launched one of his throwing knives into the leaves overhead. With a cry of pain, a dark-visaged Slav, clad in ragged animal hide, tumbled to the ground. The knife was embedded in his leg. Even so, and battered from the fall, he scrabbled for his belt, where hung a woodsman's axe. He attempted to draw it as he staggered to his feet. Polonius called out in Slavic, even as the steel point of Ambrose's boar spear pinned the man against a tree.

"Ho, stranger! Who are you, to attack three innocent travelers who mean no harm to you?"

Held helpless by the tip of the spear against his throat, and aware that Polonius' next knife was poised, the Slav nevertheless spat at the three of them before speaking.

"Paugh! Viking pigs! I need no excuse to kill you except for your accursed birth!"

Ambrose was puzzled. "Why do you feel so ill about the Varangians? We are but peaceful traders, looking for the homestead of Bothi, of the Rus."

Once again the swarthy Slav spat his disgust at the three of them. "Know you then, that I was chief of a village an hour's ride from here. It was yer friend Bothi who seized my son for hostage and raped my daughter when I protested we were free men! When my tribesmen rose to fight the strangers who claimed we were their slaves, my entire family was slaughtered. I alone was able to escape to the safety of the forests. I have vowed revenge on all Vikings!"

Hearing these words, Ambrose gradually allowed his spear-point to sag to the earth. Polonius looked questioningly at Ambrose, awaiting the signal for life or death. Ambrose signaled Roman style, thumb up, and Polonius slipped his knife into his belt. Ambrose spoke softly.

"Go friend, and know that not all Vikings are cruel. I can only wish it had been otherwise for you and your family."

Without a backward glance, the Slav turned and limped towards the cover of the brush. As the stranger slipped from sight, both Ambrose and Polonius turned to Phillip. Polonius skillfully withdrew the arrow and cleansed the wound. Looking at the blood still flowing freely from the wound, Polonius spoke to the Saxon prince.

"Ambrose, would you please give Phillip all of our mead, and start a fire while I get Phillip comfortable. While the wound does not appear to be too deep, it is one of the mysteries of almighty God that some wounds fester and kill a strong man, while another, far more severe, will heal cleanly and neatly. I do not wish to take a chance here. I want to cauterize the wound with a red-hot knife."

At length Phillip had consumed all of their supply of mead, and the knife blade glowed a dull orange. Polonius, after carefully wrapping the handle with strips of rags, seized the knife and thrust the hot metal on the wound until both Ambrose and he could smell cooking meat. Phillip, a stoic and stalwart man, clenched his teeth mightily, and only a deep groan escaped his tortured body. When the job was done, he collapsed against the tree, and Ambrose assisted Polonius in wrapping a cloth around the Weapons-master's chest.

Surprisingly, within an hour Phillip wished to ride on, and the three companions, remembering the outlaw Slav, agreed that it would be safer if they didn't delay any longer. Phillip needed some help in mounting, but he was able to sit his horse well, and the trio soon started off at a slow pace.

Following the river trail for another hour or two, they finally found the place that they had been seeking. Before them, in a large forest clearing, were fifteen or so homes, surrounded by a stout timber palisade.

To the right of the settlement wandered a river that they knew flowed into the Volkhov River not far downstream. On the river floated two smaller karves, both anchored within easy bow-shot from the palisades. A watchtower stood within the palisade, near the main gate. The appearance of the three riders caused the sentry to call out to other, unseen people.

With Ambrose leading Phillip's horse, and Polonius bringing up the rear, the two of them walked their horses towards the gate. From the fields they moved past, sullen-looking Slavic peasants measured their progress. Their expressions bespoke much for their love of their new masters, and Polonius felt a chill for the first time since he had arrived in this land. The chill slid up his backbone, augmented perhaps by the earlier words of the Slavic outlaw, as well as their long journey through the dark and seemingly endless forest. The crimson and gold forest, which had previously been something of exquisite color and beauty, had, with the meeting of that outlaw, become somehow more sinister and vaguely confining.

Thus it was with some relief that they passed through the gate and discovered Bothi advancing, followed by many smiling subordinates. Ambrose lifted his hand in greeting and spoke to the throng and its master.

"It is with great pleasure, Bothi, that we have found your homestead, and see our old companions smiling and offering us welcome! Yet we have here an injured man, and we have need of your medicines and help."

None were strangers to wounds, as warriors often proudly exhibited various scars when, around the fires at night, each got his opportunity to tell of old battles and raids. There, at least in the memory of the teller, each was as brave as a bull, and at least as strong.

Several warriors immediately ran to Phillip's horse and helped him dismount. Clucking at the dried blood which still stained what was left of his woollen under-garment, they helped him to the main lodge while one of their number ran to get him more mead; the one medicine which they knew could kill all pain if taken in sufficient quantities.

"Come you in', stated Bothi to Ambrose and Polonius, once Phillip had been helped over to the lodge. 'Tell us what happened to our friend Phillip here, and then perhaps you could tell us of the news from Holmgard, for we are eager to know how goes the settlement!"

Inside, comfortably seated on bear and wolf-skins, they talked of all that had transpired in the new Varangian realms. Ambrose and Polonius told of the captains who had sent word back to Rurik and the Novgorod settlement of how their conquests were advancing. They told of the occasional resistance of villages, but how most had succumbed peacefully enough to the new rulers when they had seen the Viking skjaldborg approach their villages; backed by Slav allies and karves cruising the waterways. They told of their own interests; of how agents had been sent south to other Varangian trading forts, spreading the news about the new Rus holdings being carved out in the midst of the vast northern forests. Polonius informed them that many of the bachelors were marrying native maidens, thus tying the Slavs and their new rulers together with bonds of matrimony.

Most important, they told of the development of Holmgard, and the defenses that, when complete, would render it immune from either Slav or nomad raiders.

Ambrose spoke to the assembled warriors. "To that effect, Bothi, Rurik has asked for you to send a report of how your own military preparedness is coming along. The jarl wants to know how many Slavs you have trained, and with what weapons. When the raiders ride this way again, Rurik wants to be able to counter with both fixed defenses and also a strong and mobile military force capable of quick movement by ship.

Never again, he has sworn, shall an attacker find defenseless villages abandoned while the peasants hide in the woods. Never again, if Rurik has his way, will long lines of Slav captives from this territory wend their way south, to fill slave bazaars from Samarkand to Miklagard. This is the dream of Rurik."

CHAPTER 18.

A Rus Is Killed, and Bothi Retaliates.

With Phillip recuperating from his wound, Ambrose and Polonius joined Bothi and his comrades on various hunting expeditions into the surrounding forests. The hunters rode in large groups, and the hunting was excellent. Within days Ambrose and Polonius had killed their share of wild boar, deer, and even a bear. Once, indeed, Bothi ordered the hunting of a slave woman who had fled the settlement. Bothi gave the girl's bedclothes to his two giant dogs to sniff.

Originally bred to be capable of catching and pulling down wolves, they whined in their eagerness to run. The handlers released them, and Bothi and a mounted escort thundered off on her trail. Ambrose and Polonius, while understanding the pragmatic need for discipline to be enforced when the Viking masters were so vastly outnumbered, yet felt the hunt was needlessly cruel, and declined to ride on that particular hunt. While mother Church taught that each person had his or her place in God's hierarchy and should accept it with humility, yet Ambrose vividly remembered his own personal experience with slavery.

The hunters returned within less than an hour. A Slav led the two dogs on leashes. Bothi saw Ambrose, and grinned down at him from his horse.

"You missed the excitement, Canute's son! The dogs treed the girl, and then jumped almost twice the height of a man! They were able to drag her right out of the tree! We managed to catch up just before they reached her. By Odin's beard, there was never a prettier sight than that wench's face when the dogs reached her high in the tree!"

Thus time passed while Phillip recuperated. One full moon waned and was replaced by a new one. On the very next day, one of Bothi's lieutenants rode in, leading a horse with a body tied across it. He drew his mount to a halt directly in front of Bothi's house and called out angrily for his master.

"Bothi, it is I, Ragnar! Come and see the answer from the southern village! They sent you an iron dagger as tribute, Bothi! They put it in your messenger!"

Bothi led an avalanche of men out from his great hall. When his emissary had been cut down and laid out on the ground, the warriors circled about the body and stared in silence. The man, one of their companion Rus, had had his right hand cut off, and his beard had been singed.

A terrible look crossed Bothi's face, making his savagely handsome face distorted and evil looking. "By the teeth of mighty Odin,' he shouted, 'they will pay for this!"

All around him his men growled fierce assent. Ambrose asked what had happened, and Bothi angrily replied.

"We sent this man, Canuteson, to a village a few hours south of here, along the tributary river. He went carrying a white shield, as my emissary. His instructions were to demand tribute and women, as the village falls within my domain. You see my answer!"

Ambrose listened to the furious Bothi. It was clear that the Varangian leader did not like the answer he had got.

↬

All night long the warriors sang and drank, and were entertained by dancing girls. By dawn their anger had worked itself into a fever pitch. At Bothi's slurred command, all of the forty-odd warriors seized their weapons and ordered their horses saddled. Each warrior's Slav protégé ran to get their own weapons and armor. In total, the two groups made a formidable array of almost seventy men, including Ambrose and Polonius. This was a debt of honor, and all tribesmen were bound to ride to avenge the terrible deed. Ambrose well knew that even the most barbaric of the Northmen generally respected the sanctity of an emissary, for it may well be that they themselves would have need of such a one. Ambrose knew too, that Bothi would pay wergeld to the family of the dead man, but that the Slav village would supply it, and much more, for their reckless deed.

Riding single file, the war party made a large loop that was intended to bring them out on the other side of the village. Two of Bothi's Slav scouts led the band by little frequented trails. The few people who saw them go by stood silent and bowed submissively, or ran to the cover of the deep forest.

None, however, ran to warn the village. The farmers and forest dwellers were not of the same clan as the inhabitants of the southern village, and therefore felt they owed its people no special loyalty. Most of all, none wished to endure the wrath of these blond giants, about whom terrible rumors had filtered down even to those deep in the forest.

After several hour's ride, the scouts signaled with hand signs that all were to dismount and leave their horses. The men, slowly sobering, slipped into military discipline. They quickly obeyed the silent signals. The men didn't seem to be at all unhappy about leaving their mounts behind, for, as Ambrose had discovered some time before, like his own people, the Vikings preferred to fight on foot, and used horses mainly for quick transportation to a battle site.

All weapons that might clank together were carefully wrapped, for these trader-warriors were no strangers to raiding and war. The horses were left in the small dell where the men had dismounted. Several of the oldest men remained to act as guards. The rest split into two combat groups. The scouts explained, in whispers, the location of the village, and suggested that they could lead half of the men to the other side.

Like a pack of wolves closing for the kill, the men followed the scouts through forest and dense brush, until the Varangians were spaced out around the village and its fields. Because all crops had been harvested, there were few peasants out in the fields. The exception was a few wood-gatherers. Like giant lynxes, Varangian hunters crept up and dispatched the unlucky Slavs. Bothi had ordered that no warning was to be given until he ordered his signaler to blow two long notes on the hunting horn. Then the cordon would tighten; until all of the villagers were forced into the village center.

As the mournful notes of the horn sounded, the men broke cover and charged madly for the flimsy palisades. Taken totally by surprise, the villagers ran for their homes rather than to the defensive positions that would have given them some chance against the onrushing foe. Only a brave few made a stand at the open gates, and within seconds the only barrier that could have prevented Viking success had fallen. The Varangians flowed through the gates like a rising tide.

When the gates were secured, the warriors fanned out along the palisade walls, and then moved inward, driving the helpless villagers before them towards the central square. Like cattle, the people cringed before the snapping of whips and the flashing of swords. They struggled with one another to be first to the central square. Only in isolated instances were men armed and willing to fight. In ones and twos, they provided no serious obstacle, and the brave were quickly cut down.

At last, when all the surviving villagers were gathered in a dense knot, and a circle of Viking steel kept them all captive, Bothi's interpreter broke the ominous silence of the Varangians. His words echoed through the crowd.

"Let your leader and his family stand before my master!"

After a moment's hesitation, a man, tall for a Slav, and dark, stepped forth. He was followed by a woman of similar age, a young man whose facial hair was just starting to sprout, a boy, and a young maiden. Once again Bothi's voice, and then its meaning was heard by the captive crowd.

"You Slav barbarians have broken the immutable laws of diplomacy by savagely killing a man carrying a white shield of peace. Learn now, the terrible wrath of the Vikings!"

With that, Bothi had the head man trussed securely to a post; his hands tied above his head. At a signal from Bothi, four grinning warriors grabbed his wife, flung her to the ground and held her down directly in front of her husband. Bothi stepped forth and slowly drew his bright jewel-encrusted sax. He placed it at the woman's throat until a moan came from her. Her eyes, totally dilated, darted about like a trapped doe's. Then, reversing the blade, Bothi slowly sliced the clothing from the woman's body. At last she lay naked on the ground. Her breasts were flattened by gravity, but they had enough mass that they jutted slightly upwards. The men grinned again as Bothi, on his knees, began a slow caressing movement, starting from her neck, and gradually working down her body, until she was squirming helplessly. Slowly, gently, he let his hands slide, until they had slid down her belly and were between her legs. She writhed, and her husband looked away, helpless in his shame and anger. Finally, Bothi snapped. "Enough! Spread her legs!"

With that, the two men who were pinning her feet pulled them apart, leaving her helpless and fully exposed. Calmly, Bothi dropped his trousers to expose an erection, and then he slipped between her legs. As the urge came stronger upon him, he began to thrust at her more and more strongly. At last, he was finished with her, and he looked down at her lying helpless and in pain. Hitching up his trousers and climbing to his feet, Bothi spoke again.

"Tie her next to her husband. She will be used again tonight."

At that he dramatically pointed his finger at the young man. The Varangian warriors dragged him forward. "Strip him', ordered Bothi. When the young man was naked and helpless, Bothi walked over and gently fingered the young man's testicles.

'I think he would make a good gelding for some Byzantine who can't trust his concubines," laughed Bothi. As he made as to cut the unfortunate youth's genitals, the father cried out. "Mercy, lord! Let it be me!"

Bothi laughed horribly. "Your turn is yet to come, old man!"

At once the laughter left his voice, and his voice thundered. 'This youth will be sold at auction to the highest bidder in Holmgard, if he survives the castration. The younger boy will remain with me as hostage for the future obedience of your village! His blood will answer for any further disobedience on your part!"

Once again his mood vacillated. He grinned again. "Now bring to me the flower of the family, that we may inspect her petals!"

The girl was roughly seized and dragged forth. She looked imploringly from her father to her mother, but their eyes dropped. They could offer her no silent reassurance.

"Strip!" ordered Bothi, echoed by his interpreter. When she hesitated, Bothi signaled a warrior near the two parents, and a whip cracked loudly, leaving a streak across the stomach of her now securely trussed mother. The stroke drew an anguished cry from the mother.

"Strip!" roared Bothi again.

Slowly, with what grace and dignity she could muster, the girl stripped off her clothes. The villagers looked at the ground, but the Varangian and Slav warriors leered appreciatively. Shamed beyond anything she had ever known, the girl blushed and attempted to hide as much of herself from view as she could. Laughing loudly, Bothi strode up to her, and drew her hands behind her. He forced her to slowly rotate, so that all could see her lovely small breasts, and the darkish triangle of pubic hair that hid her genitals.

Suddenly tiring of the game, Bothi let her go. "Tie her with her parents, and use her tonight!"

At this Ambrose could stand it no longer. He stepped forward from the circle of warriors.

"Bothi, I would buy this girl from you. What would you ask for her?"

Surprised, Bothi seemed thoughtful for awhile. "What would you offer me, Canuteson?"

Ambrose retorted hotly. "A one-twentieth share of my year's profits."

"Nay. She's a virgin, and worth much more.' Laughing, he reached over and caressed one of her small, pearl-white breasts. 'She'd bring a fancy price in the Miklagard slave market! . . . Still, make it one-fifth and we will call it a deal!"

"Bothi, you treat a friend poorly. I will offer you one--tenth."

Bothi laughed. "Done, Canuteson! I will trust you to send me the exact amount, but you make me question your skill as a trader. I suspect that you would have been able to buy a dozen girls for that big a share of your profits!"

Ambrose gestured to Polonius, who stepped up to the girl and threw his cloak over her naked body. Polonius then led her away to a vacant hut, where he stood guard at the only entrance.

Even as the frightened girl was being led away, Bothi ordered his men to strip the headman and turn him so that his back was exposed. The Varangians laughed. They guessed that Bothi would order that the man be given a 'Blood Eagle'.

While the man hung helpless, his ribs were broken in the back, and his lungs were pulled backwards, so that they lay outside of the body cavity. The lungs quivered obscenely, until, at last, the man mercifully succumbed to his brutal treatment and breathed his last.

CHAPTER 19.

Bothi's Warriors Have a Victory Celebration.

One by one, a representative of each family was released to find, and bring back, their valuables. Slowly the pile of copper, silver and furs grew in front of Bothi. No one ran for the forest, for all knew the lives of their families and friends were being held hostage. While they waited for the representatives to return with the family treasures, the men amused themselves by inspecting the women. The prettier ones were forced to strip for inspection. The husbands and parents of the women were forced to watch. They hung their heads in an agony of hatred and shame. Only once did a man attempt to interfere when two laughing Varangians stripped his wife. He was stabbed quickly with a spear, and left to bleed to death where he fell.

Finally, when all had returned to the captives' ring, Bothi addressed the throng through his interpreter.

"The piddling treasures you have laid before me are as nothing before the life of the man you so wantonly slew. Hear then the judgement of your master. Your chief, who led you in this rash deed, has already tasted Varangian vengeance! No more shall he affront me! No more shall he breed such as himself. The woman may live, if she survives the amorous advances of my warriors tonight. The young man will be sold in Novgorod as a castrati. The boy will be held by me as a hostage for your future good behavior. Yet also will my warriors do as they wish with your women tonight. You will also donate one half of your stored crops to me and my men. Because it is my policy to live in peace with you, I will not sell you all into slavery, as you justly deserve, but I will take ten maidens when I leave tomorrow. This then, is the judgement of your jarl. Hear, and obey!"

With that, Bothi allowed the inhabitants to break from the circle. Each of Bothi's warriors retained the woman of his fancy, and their men were allowed to flee weaponless into the woods.

By the light of huge bonfires, the soldiers spent the night reveling. The women were forced to pour mead and wine, and roast and serve the village's own butchered animals. As the men drank more and more heavily, the women were reduced to dancing naked for them, and then amusing the men when led to more private places.

Ambrose said he still felt strange without Phillip at his side. He and Polonius tentatively joined in the festivities. Polonius soon found an older woman who was not in terrible fear and loathing of him, and the two went off together into the dark.

Ambrose, left alone and somewhat drunk, returned to the hut Bothi had assigned him. There, in the farthest corner, crouched the girl that he had bought at such great cost. With the firelight coming through the doorway, Ambrose could see her clearly. She grasped the cloak tightly around her as best she could, but the soft tones of bare flesh could still be seen shining gently in the feeble light.

Ambrose, fired by the liquor he had drunk, the excitement of the other soldiers, and, most of all, by the masculine sense of mastery he had over this barely clothed young girl, spoke harshly in his halting Slavic. "Come here, girl, and serve me!"

He settled on some furs, and handed her the flagon of mead and haunch of mutton he had taken from one of the cooking fires. Shyly, slowly, she crept forth. She took the mutton and sliced the meat into more manageable hunks for Ambrose. Then she found a horn mug and poured the mead into it for her new master.

Ambrose, very much the lord, suddenly felt renewed compassion for the terrified girl. He smiled at her and spoke in his best Slavic. "What is your name, girl?"

"Kuralla, Lord."

"Come and eat and drink with me, Kuralla."

"It is not our custom, Lord."

"It is not my people's either, Kuralla. But I wish it."

"Then it shall be so, Master."

Even as they both ate; she at his feet, and casting frightened glances at him, Ambrose became aroused by the soft curves that were tantalizingly exposed as the cloak gaped open. The dancing firelight filtering through the door made deep shadows play upon her body; leaving much hidden, but momentarily illuminating portions of her breasts and thighs.

The drink went to Ambrose's head, and before he was quite aware of what he was doing, he seized Kuralla and pinned her to the furs. She struggled silently. A headstrong colt, she knew only panic when it was obvious what the stranger intended. Her soft, light body arced and writhed to escape the attentions Ambrose forced upon her. At last, exhausted, she lay still while he fondled her. Deep within her she began to feel a stirring in response to his ministrations, but she feared it, ignored it, and began again to struggle. At last, excited beyond control, Ambrose thrust hard between her thighs. Harder and harder he thrust, seeking warm entrance, but she groaned and twisted the more. His battering ram tore cruelly at her tender tissue.

After a last gasp, Ambrose lay still. Once again in control of his senses, he looked down at the innocent girl who lay moaning and crying under him. It was, Ambrose felt with remorse, a poor victory over an innocent child. He, in his virility and ignorance, had obtained scant relief except from his tumescence, and she had obviously gained a great deal of hurt and fear towards him and his gender.

For a gentle soul like Ambrose, this was a sad thought, for he well knew that to many of his fellows, forcing a young and virgin woman was considered a most exciting pastime; far better than sleeping with some older woman who craved a man to fill her. He felt, however, only shame and remorse for what he had done.

Dawn found the warriors exhausted. Only by dint of terrible threats had Bothi been able to keep any sentries at their posts guarding the palisade and the corralled horses. At length the men awakened, many with terrible headaches, and gradually formed up around the surviving cooking fires. The village was without men, but women moved quietly about, some still naked. Occasionally one would smile at a warrior who passed, but most appeared to harbor a deep hatred for their conquerors. Ambrose watched Bothi systematically inspect the women, and he chose ten of the youngest and prettiest. The Rus jarl spoke to his two lieutenants. "They have many fine women here! I think I am sorry I said I would only take ten maidens.'

He smirked suddenly. 'Still, they need some women here to help work my new fields for me. I think I will demand a yearly tribute in maidens."

The column formed up in full battle formation; scouts out front to ensure that the Slav tribesmen didn't try to retaliate against their new Varangian overlords. The captive maidens were double-mounted with the lighter warriors, who would be responsible for them until they reached Bothi's village. Seized horses bearing food and looted treasures brought up the rear of the cavalcade.

At a signal from Bothi, the column surged through the gate and followed the path that would lead back to the security of his own strong point.

Ambrose rode alongside Polonius when the trail permitted, but they had traveled some hours before he ventured to put his thoughts into words. Grimly he remembered his deed of the night before. He still heard, every time he looked in her direction, the words they had exchanged that very morning. When he, in a fit of remorse, offered her freedom and the right to stay within the village. Kuralla had, surprisingly, refused. She had looked slowly down at herself, her body ill concealed in her salvaged clothing, with an intensity that signified deep thought. She had answered demurely enough.

"I thank you, my master, but I am no longer able to stay here. After the shame of my exposure and the loss of my virginity, I am no longer of value to my tribe. No tribe would marry a chief's son to a used woman; no illustrious alliance will be sealed by my body. I must go with you, or die here. I care not much which!"

Ambrose, shocked by her reaction, had only nodded stolidly, and arranged that she have a horse.

Breaking the silence at last, Ambrose turned searching eyes on Polonius. "My friend, I did a terrible thing last night, and I am neither proud nor happy with myself."

Polonius looked concerned. "Just what terrible deed did you do last night, my prince?"

With that the story poured out, and Polonius listened sympathetically. At last, seeing Ambrose's stricken face, he responded.

"My lord, what you have done is no more or less than your right as her master. It is not the right of slaves to question their masters' deeds. And yet, I fear that your Christian soul is burdened with the guilt of your deed. Know you then, that, although most of our companions would feel that you did no more than is your due, in my own meekness, I invariably seek an older, and willing, woman for my manly pursuits. The result is great pleasure, rather than pain. Believe it or not, an experienced woman can teach the more young and shapely women many tricks, learned through years of experience. And yet, lord, this is only my humble manner of deriving pleasure, and I would not impose it upon another who has different taste. Whether you enjoy the softness and expertise of an older woman, or the bones and fears of barely nubile girls is a matter of taste."

Ambrose lapsed again into deep thought. He mulled over Polonius' comments and rode on in silence. With the scouts flushing nothing more than birds and a snorting boar, the column made its way back to Bothi's headquarters without mishap.

CHAPTER 20.

Winter Sets in.

Winter closed on Novgorod. From the far north, frigid masses of cold air swept across the land, bringing severe frosts and much snow. Thanks to Polonius' medicinal skills and Kuralla's nursing, Phillip's wound healed cleanly. It did not take long before his strength returned.

While Ambrose, Phillip and Polonius at first felt constrained by the weather, the severity of which surprised and awed them, they soon realized that the Slavs and the Varangians were no stranger to such bitter cold. The three friends soon learned how to use cunningly carved wooden staves on their feet that the Rus settlers used as a means of moving through deep snow.

At length, wrapped securely in fur-lined coats and boots, the three companions learned the pleasures and dangers of a continental winter. They spent many carefree days hunting wild game and trapping in the nearby forest, until the three of them became expert with the forest lore of their new frozen land.

Surprisingly, the wooden staves allowed the hunters to set a pace that would be difficult to match in summer. To their delight, they found themselves able to skim over swamps that were all but impassable in summer. The animals became easy prey for hunters capable of sliding across the top of the snow.

Ambrose was fascinated to learn that the great northern winter, in a place unprotected by an embracing ocean, was not a scourge that stopped all trade and movement. Although on the worst days the cold was sometimes enough to kill an exposed man in minutes, yet by ski or in horse-drawn sleighs, men were able to easily travel great distances along snow-packed trails.

Once again Ambrose, Phillip, and Polonius traveled away from mother river. They visited the far-flung outposts of the little Slavic-Rus nation. Here, in the farthest *marches*, Ambrose traded for furs, and met many of the wild forest-people who bartered their catch for weapons and food.

They were particularly interested to see how the newly-ordered military training progressed. Each Slav villager, while familiar with the rudiments of fighting, was required by edict from Novgorod to study war maneuvers and drill. For armor, most Slav men made a leather jerkin and sewed metal rings and plates to it. Only the wealthiest villagers could afford the chain-mail shirts most Rus warriors wore.

Most important, on the milder days of winter, the men were required to practice archery and spear throwing. The villagers learned how to form a skjaldborg, a shield-wall in the Viking fashion. Few possessed swords, but most had axes or long knives, and the blacksmiths churned out enough spear heads that all were soon armed with a spear.

As the three companions watched a demonstration in one river-side village, Polonius turned to Ambrose. "What do you think about the Slav warriors, Master?"

Ambrose thought for a moment. "Well, I doubt that they are ready to face a serious charge, yet, in their own way, they could be a formidable force."

Polonius responded. "How so?"

"Well, in winter, armed with bows, and wearing their staves, or skis, these people would be formidable. They can travel faster than even mounted men. They are good with spear and bow, and they know the secret paths. They can set man-traps and kill from ambush. With their knowledge of the forests, they would be all but impossible to catch."

Polonius smiled. "You are saying that they would be ideal for hit and run attacks against infantry or horsemen?"

Ambrose smiled in return. "As long as the snow was deep enough to impede riders. And they would be even more effective against infantry."

Polonius turned to Phillip. The giant spoke little, but he was a master soldier. As a long-time member of the Wessex king's Personal Guard, he had been honored with the task of training the athelings of the royal court in the ways of battle.

"And what do you think, old soldier?"

"It is obvious that the local folk will never be honed into a great all-conquering force, for they are farmers first and soldiers only by necessity. They are brave enough, especially when fighting for their own homes and families, but they don't have the mentality of men who have worshiped war as a way of life and whose greatest hope is to die in heroic battle against a brave foe.'

He shrugged. 'Leavened with enough veteran Viking warriors,

they might stand against a determined attack, but you would multiply their effectiveness by putting them behind sturdy walls. They would probably be quite effective in hit and run attacks, but I suspect that it will be hard to persuade them to travel far from their wives and children. It is the same with the Saxon fyrdmen back home."

Rurik and his senior commanders seemed to conclude something similar. They decided that the major defense against further onslaughts would be a static one. To this end, both Varangians and Slavs were enjoined to live in fortified villages and walk to their fields daily.

Each village was palisaded, and the larger ones held a strongly built and easily defensible center; usually where the Varangian or Slav chieftain lived. The palisades were of green wood, and each component log was carved to a sharp point. Platforms were built along the insides of the walls, so that archers and spearmen could shoot down on any advancing foe.

As Ambrose and Polonius approached a small village just down river from Novgorod, the prince gestured towards the almost completed palisade.

"What do you think, Scholar? It is what you proposed."

"The truth? It seems very primitive compared to the defenses my people throw up. Yet against the horseman of the steppes, who abhor walls and are impatient with sieges, it should at least slow the raiders down and give Rurik's boat forces time to deploy.

Still, I have to admit, my Saxon prince, that Rurik is probably right in his assessment of the situation. It is many days ride from the open steppe to the northern forest lands, and while I am told that far-ranging raiders hit the settlements sporadically, it is not likely that an entire army, complete with siege weapons, would ride so far through forests that blot out the sun. Most important, the endless forest denies to the horsemen their most effective weapons; a furious massed charge and fluid mobility."

Ambrose turned to Polonius. "Then you have witnessed nomad cavalry in action, Polonius?"

"Scythian horse-archers are one of the mainstays of the Byzantine army, young prince. The hordes of invaders from the steppes forced the Eastern Romans to long ago abandon the infantry formations of ancient Rome. Master, did I never tell you the tale of Crassus and the Parthians?"

Ambrose winked to Phillip. "I don't think so, Scholar."

"Then your education is still severely lacking, Prince-of-the-Saxons. Well, let's see . . . Marcus Licinius Crassus was a very rich man who joined with Julius Caesar and Gnaeus Pompey to form the First Triumvirate."

Ambrose interrupted. "You were telling me about the Parthian horsemen, Polonius."

"Yes, Of course, I was just coming to that. You see, as military governor of Syria, Crassus took seven legions and invaded Parthia. Foolishly, he neglected to take adequate cavalry. It was his undoing. He left the river and headed overland through open country. The Parthians, master bowmen, refused to close. They had brought a thousand camel loads of arrows and ten thousand archers. They filled the air with the shafts. The Romans retreated into their turtle formation, but the Parthians had a thousand heavily armed knights who kept threatening the Romans. In battle formation, the Romans were safe against the cavalry, but vulnerable to the Parthian archers. In turtle formation, the archers were less of a threat, but the cavalry was a serious danger."

"So what could the Romans do, Polonius?"

"Die. They could not reach the fast-riding Parthians to fight them. In every battle between the two, the Romans had been victorious, but this time the Parthians refused to close. The Romans could not stop the hail of arrows. Less than ten thousand legionaries made it back to the river and their fleet. Over 34,000 died on the sun baked plains.

And now, young prince, what lessons should be drawn from the debacle of Carrhae?"

"Hmm. Unsupported infantry should never venture into open territory if they may face cavalry. Never neglect your archers or your own cavalry. Some kind of defensive position or fortification is likely to be helpful against cavalry."

Polonius smiled. "Well thought through, Master. In truth, I have watched several regiments of Byzantine mercenary cavalry practice. When the archers have sufficiently softened up a formation, then the cavalryman switch to the lance. By preference the riders ride knee to knee. Tons of horseflesh and men irresistibly surge over the land and sweep aside opposition as the tide sweeps aside the walls of a child's sand castle. It seems it is that mounted charge that has always broken the Slavs. Many have told me it is what they fear most in life."

"Then what can Rurik and his tribesmen do about it?"

"What the Romans did. Just a few years ago, somewhere south of here, on a Slav river bank, a Viking skjaldborg held fast against a full nomad charge. To the dismay of the nomads and the joy of the local Slavs, the Vikings stopped a seemingly irresistible mounted force cold.

The nomad riders, savage raiders from somewhere far to the south and east, attempted time and again to break the Varangian skjaldborg. When the raiders launched missile attacks, the Vikings flowed into a *shieldburg*, and as soon as the horsemen prepared to charge, the well-trained Varangians slid back into their skjaldborg formation.

The cavalry charges merely brought the riders close enough for the Vikings to tear down and chop to pieces. A simple chore; the destruction of a small body of traders and guards, caused the fierce nomads to leave the flower of their horde dead on the riverbank. Indeed, I am told that it was that battle that caused the people of the area to ask the Rus traders to bring their families and settle. Ceding sovereignty to the Vikings is less painful than being decimated by the fierce nomads."

Rurik has ordered, starting immediately, the training of all able-bodied men, Varangian and Slav both, in the techniques of the skjaldborg and such simple formations as the shieldburg. He intends that his scattered forces will be prepared when the savage pagan riders come again.

As spring neared, Polonius was called to meet with Rurik and his council. He returned late at night, and Ambrose woke and started questioning the Byzantine scholar.

"Well, Polonius, what did Rurik want from you?"

"Mostly to pick my brain, Master."

"Well?

"Word will go out within the week. The Rus and Slav allies have come up with a comprehensive plan for defense."

Ambrose was impatient. "And it is?"

"Nothing radically new, Master. According to the plan, any raiders will face a series of armed and protected villages that should be capable of providing a static defense for at least a few days. The foresters, and those of the farmers who had learned the ways of the forest, are to harry the enemy columns with archers and man-traps in the forest.

At express order of Rurik, many of the trails leading to the south and east are to be prepared with booby traps. Great wooden spikes, using the power of a bent tree and capable of sending a spike right through a horse, are to be constructed, along with covered traps, dug deep and lined with sharpened stakes.

Each village is assigned the task of guiding friendly travelers to the next village. Strangers who travel without a guide stand a very real chance of being maimed or killed.

Finally, Rurik plans that while the invaders halt to attack the individual fortified villages, warriors of Novgorod itself, traveling by boat or horse, would be moving in strength to attack the foe. Rurik boasted that the north, with its endless forests, defensible villages, connecting waterways, and a formidable fighting force, should be capable of stopping anything but a major invasion."

CHAPTER 21.

An Expedition to *Kiev*.

It was with some surprise that the three friends learned that a group of newly arrived Rus, led by the jarls Askold and Dir, was eager to head south with the spring breakup of the ice. Dir and Askold had called a meeting, and it seemed that most of the still-landless men still in Novgorod intended to show up.

Dir was an older man, big and burly. When he raised both hands above his head, the assembly quieted.

"Friends! My partner and I have recently received word of a great opportunity in the south for the bold and the strong amongst you. We are determined to take advantage of this wonderful opportunity, and we are recruiting brave men to join us!"

One warrior, almost as emaciated looking as Polonius, called out. "Speak, Dir. Tell us of the opportunity!"

"My friends, those of you who have dared the *Seven Cataracts* and traveled as far as the empire of Byzantium have sailed past the town of *Kiev*."

A warrior shaped like a tree trunk called out. "Aye, Dir, and it is high on a bluff and ably ruled. I have landed there. There is no opportunity there, old soldier!"

"But think of its location! It is much nearer the steppes. Caravan trails from the Far East end just across the river, and it is in a perfect position to control all trade south to Miklagard.

My friends. All three of the brothers who have ruled Kiev so ably have fallen victim to a plague. The town is now both vulnerable and leaderless!"

Another man called out from the crowd. "They have a formidable fortification and are still likely well organized, Dir. If they have not asked for our help, what is your point?"

Askold replied for his partner. "Think, man! Even more than the citizens of Novgorod, the people there fear the steppe nomads. They must. It is only a short ride from the open steppes to Kiev.

The citizens of Novgorod have accepted us because we offer them something that they could not obtain without us - security. Before their wives and children go south in chains, invaders will have to cut down several thousand of the bravest warriors the world has ever seen!'

A consummate speaker, Askold waited until the cheers died down. 'The Slavs of Novgorod know that with our families here we will not abandon them, and they have seen our fighting prowess. Dir and I propose that we make the same offer to the good citizens of Kiev!"

"And if they refuse us, Askold, what will we do?"

Both Askold and Dir grinned. "We will be sitting on their doorstep with anywhere up to a thousand fighting men! What do you think?"

Rurik, ruler of Novgorod, unexpectedly spoke. "I count perhaps four hundred warriors who are free to go with you. Our position here is still too fragile for me to send you my sworn men. That leaves you a long way from a thousand, cousin."

Dir turned to him. "I anticipate more than eight hundred traders arriving on the river within the next month, Rurik."

"They are not going to Kiev to fight; they are going south to the Black Sea to trade."

Askold grinned again. "The good citizens of Kiev won't know that, my friends! Most of Kiev's young men will have sailed south on their own trading expeditions long before we arrive, and the remaining ones will count over a thousand warriors when we arrive.

For any man who sails with me I promise land. For any traders who are willing to tarry at Kiev for no more than a week, I promise both gratitude and free supplies whenever they sail by the Varangian town of Kiev."

Rurik smiled. "Aye, it is a bold gamble, but it just might work, at that."

⊱

Even during the winter a trickle of Rus and other Viking tribesmen arrived from the north. Many were adventurers, eager to carve out territory for families that would follow on the spring flood. Others were the traders who had long made annual trips south. They, plus many of the warriors who had not been assigned land in the Novgorod region, eventually signed their mark for the expedition to Kiev.

Rurik was losing some of the warriors he had been counting on in case of trouble, but he knew that the spring thaw would bring a new flood of Rus from their homeland. His success in Novgorod was enticing thousands more to flock to his banner. He knew that he would be able to easily replace those who sailed with Dir and Askold. Further, a major Viking town to the south would both be a magnet to the steppe invaders, and, between the two cities, they would firmly control the river trade south.

On the way back to their home, Ambrose walked silently as he mulled over what Dir and Askold had said. He realized that proximity to the golden domes of Constantinople was a tremendous attraction to the Viking trader warriors. He had already learned that much of the wealth and trade of the world passed through, or were controlled by, the wily Greeks of New Rome.

In the fabled land of Polonius' birth was concentrated vast quantities of precious stones and metals, silk and luxuries. Also to the south, however, were the fertile grasslands, and no impediments to the fierce nomad nations such as the Bulgars, Magyars, Pechenegs, and the Khazars. Polonius had explained to him that these nomad hordes had little liking for farmers who attempted to sow crops on their ancestral pasture lands. In their arrogance, they destroyed any agricultural communities they came across.

The Byzantine scholar did say that occasional riverside trading posts were allowed to survive on sufferance, as even the nomads realized they needed some place to sell loot and captives, and obtain goods in return. But even if the trading settlements managed to live in a precarious peace with one nomad tribe, the settlements were still subject to raids by other, more hostile tribes.

All told, it appeared far safer to settle in the north, and Ambrose was surprised that so many Varangians were willing to risk their lives and that of their families by agreeing to sail south. For the three of them, however, it was a different matter. Gunnar the trader, of the Rus, had said he wanted to have agents and posts stretching all the way from the frozen northern seas to golden Constantinople itself. Kiev, long known as the southern spring staging center for the trading run south to the Byzantine Empire, would be an ideal location for a trading post.

After they returned to their snug cabin, Ambrose turned to his companions. "Well, old friends, what say you? Do we dare the journey south?"

Polonius looked serious. "As you two know, I do not love hardship and danger. For colonists it appears to be a foolhardy move, but for traders, as long as we can keep our heads attached to our shoulders, it seems to be a unique opportunity. With Dir and Askold as rulers there, we have the chance to make the House of Gunnar one of the premier trading houses on the entire river system. I guess I would vote that we go."

Ambrose looked at Phillip. The giant thane thought for a few moments, and then replied. "It seems a risk worth taking. If we take men under contract to Gunnar, and our own boats, we can always leave if Dir and Askold's plan fails. As Polonius says, if they succeed, then we have a foothold. And at the least, we will have traveled the southern rivers."

Ambrose turned to Kuralla, who was sitting by the door and listening attentively.

"Kuralla, how do you feel about leaving Novgorod?"

"I go where my lord wills it."

"Kuralla, I told you that you are a free woman. You may do as you please."

"My lord will allow me to stay in Novgorod?"

"I just told you that you may do as you please."

"Then it pleases me to go with you three."

Ambrose smiled. "Then it's settled! I will tell Dir and Askold in the morning."

⚑

So it was that as water began to flow over the ice on mild days, and the sun hung in the sky for a longer time each day, Ambrose, Phillip, and Polonius began to prepare for another journey. Askold and Dir drew up meticulous plans, and Rurik willingly gave up several smaller ships to provide transportation for any who wanted to join the brave band of adventurers, on the condition that they carried at least some of his cargo.

It was agreed that the followers of Dir and Askold would sail south when the river became completely ice-free and the river had crested. They promised to send back most of the vessels in the autumn. If all went well, many of the ships would be able to actually make the journey all the way to the Byzantine Empire. These would return loaded with the precious goods coveted in the north.

The friends made their personal preparations as well. Ambrose set Polonius to writing letters of explanation to Gunnar, and between them they made the final arrangements for the trading factory that they had set up on the island. A competent merchant was already in charge of the daily routines, and Ambrose felt that he would not try to cheat Gunnar of more than a small percentage of the profits.

On the third day of the new moon; in the Rus month of Harpa and after the ice had left the river, the Rus adventurers launched their fleet. Although the ships had been floating for over a week, the oak boards leaked abominably. In the larger boats the floor boards were lifted out, and a steady procession of buckets had to be maintained in order to keep the hulls from filling with water and ruining the foodstuffs and cargo of the colonists.

The signal was given and the oars dipped into the cold water. Made up mainly of small Karves and large dugouts, the Varangian river fleet was on its way south.

Ambrose, Phillip, Polonius and Kuralla stood at the rail with a feeling of exhilaration and excitement as they watched the land slip past. Already, much of the snow had melted under the strong sun. Soon the land would be again a verdant green. All about them could be heard the yells and screams of excited children; those of the convoy who would settle with their parents in yet another new land.

Ironically, the first breaking up of the ice on the rivers had ended communications with the south, and neither Ambrose nor, indeed, Dir and Askold, the expedition leaders, knew what events were transpiring further south. Ambrose knew only that they were headed for a town on another, even greater river; the Dnieper.

As the fleet made its way upriver, Ambrose found out that one of Dir's cousins had a small trading factory in Kiev. It had been this man who had sent word north in early winter, brought by a messenger who had been able to walk or ski right over the swamps, shallows and rivers.

To help their case even further, wily Askold had sent, during the winter, a trusted courier with a paper south to the nearest garrison town of the Khazars, ostensible overlords of the Dnieper river-valley and thus, Kiev. He had sent a promissory note for some immediate gold, to be drawn from any large-city Jewish Khazar banker upon demand. Further, Askold and Dir promised quick yearly payment of tribute, and a percent of the profits from the river trade. After all, they had explained in an accompanying letter, it was now plain that the Rus and their Viking cousins controlled the northern rivers. Their agents in the south would ensure a steady flow of trade, and of course a fair portion of these profits would find its way into the hands of the Khazars.

With characteristic Viking swiftness, Dir and Askold did not wait to see if their offer had been accepted. Askold had argued that if they did not move quickly, another strong faction might rise to dominate the excellent trading site, and so the Varangians moved south, hoping to perhaps meet the messenger returning northward along the river highway.

Dir laughed as he strode the decks of the lead vessel. "If the Khazars do not agree to accept Rus gold, then we can always offer tribute in the form of cold steel."

Brave men, and sons of brave men for untold generations, the trader-warriors sailed south, daring the Norns to challenge their raw courage.

In truth, Ambrose thought, as his eyes roamed over the flotilla that stretched both before and astern of his own vessel, such a people, shrewd in trade, and fanatical in battle, made a terrible foe. With some foreboding, he wondered again what was transpiring in the very distant west, where he had left his own beleaguered countrymen facing ever more and larger bands of Viking marauders.

Polonius stood beside Ambrose. "Master, you look very serious for such a fine day. Surely you are not trying to do my job of worrying?"

Ambrose smiled. Polonius was a man of many surprising talents, but he sometimes made himself sick with worry.

"I suppose I am worrying, Scholar. In the time of my father's youth, I am told, Viking attacks on my homeland was made only by a single, or just a few, skulking long-ships. The raids were isolated, and the pirates seldom dared to venture far inland.

In the very summer I was kidnaped, the Danes mustered dozens of ships, and my brother was hard pressed to drive them from our shores with the full strength of his army. Even then, they burned his favorite royal burh of Winchester.

It seems to me that in the last few years the isolated raiding parties of the Vikings have started to evolve into ravaging armies. The pirates take longer and longer to retreat to their ships. In my own lifetime, the Danes have seized, and settled, the Celtic islands north of Britain.

Aye, I am worried. I wonder what has become of my family and my homeland. How many more Viking armies have landed on the island, and who are they fighting? Every day I ask myself these questions, yet every day we sail further from Angleland."

Polonius put his arm across Ambrose's shoulders in silent support.

At last he spoke.

"Prince, I will not pretend that you have no cause to worry. The Vikings are a worthy opponent for anyone. Yet may I remind you that I once made the journey from Byzantium to Frankland? With luck, it can actually be a quick way home for you."

"I guess that you are right, my Greek scholar. I just feel a little guilty that my homeland may be in danger while I travel the length and breadth of far-away lands; helping the cousins of my country's foe.

I keep wondering if we had made the right decision when we obeyed Canute's injunction to sail north and not west. Still, we are here, and, for the time being, I will just tell myself that I am Canuteson, trader for the Rus, and a man on an adventure that does promise much excitement."

⚑

The fleet had several days of hard rowing, as the winds were often contrary, and, in any case, the rapidly narrowing river left little scope for even such limited tacking as the square-rigged ships were capable of. Hammar, the captain of Gunnar's largest karve, called out to the crew that they approached the headwaters of the river. Ambrose had wondered himself how much farther they would be able to move the ship upriver.

Already the crew were starting to use poles rather than the oars, and many times a day Ambrose could hear the sound of a sandbar scrapping the bottom of the vessel. Fortunately, the thin overlapping planks simply flexed, and little damage was done.

By day the expedition passed through wild forest, interspersed only by occasional settlements and cultivated fields. At some villages Dir and Askold signaled the fleet to land. In these villages they were received cordially, generally by a Rus or Slav who was a trader.

Ambrose was quite amazed that so many towns openly welcomed strangers, although when he had asked Askold about it, he was told that the Vikings sailed these rivers for trade and most towns had honey, furs, or foodstuffs that they wanted to sell. Nevertheless, there were a few villages where their appearance caused fear rather than joy. Some gates were locked tight, and other villages were abandoned entirely.

Ambrose stared as they traveled past one such abandoned village. "Here, it seems, the Varangians are not welcome."

Hammar overheard the comment, and smilingly joined Ambrose and Polonius at the rail. "What you say is true, Canuteson. Some

Varangian traders will, if they think they can get away with it, raid a native Slav village and sell all its inhabitants into slavery. Perhaps understandably, many Slavs thus do not welcome our arrival.

While such raids are understandable, considering the profits, it is severely frowned upon by most traders. We ostracize the culprits, as it destroys the trust built up over many long years, that have branded us as fair, if hard traders. Besides, there is no end of slaves to buy legitimately, as there are continual border raids, where enemy soldiers or villagers are seized and enslaved. So too, are any criminals, for in this manner they not only learn to repent of any deeds, but also earn a good profit for the town where they are sold. Finally, the Varangians and our Slav allies regularly raid within or beyond their spheres of influence; enslaving or seizing villagers for non-payment of dues, tithes or taxes."

As the captain had said, many slaves were offered to the ship's crew at the villages where they paused. Indeed, several were bought, although as space aboard the vessels was at a premium, relatively few could be brought aboard.

ʌ

When the ship floated in a channel no wider than two beam's length, Ambrose went to the captain's side.

"Surely it's not possible for us to continue for much longer on this river. How are we to continue?"

"Canuteson', said the captain, 'I have a surprise for you right soon. Thanks to Viking ingenuity, our ships sail will on through the forest and onto the grass steppes!"

Ambrose stared at Hammar with puzzlement. "Captain, how is that possible? Are you telling me that this river, narrow as it is, can take us all the way to Kiev?"

The captain grinned at the young trader. "Nay, Canuteson, you will get your explanation tomorrow. You will just have to wait to discover the Viking secret!"

As the sun drew closer to the horizon, Askold, leader of the expedition, ordered the boats to head for shore. The vessels were quickly beached, and even before the sentries were able to fan out into the forest, the children and women leapt ashore, eager to stretch and then to prepare food for their families.

Ambrose marveled again at the expanse of the continuing forest of mixed birch and evergreens. He turned to the Byzantine who rested against the rail beside him. "Polonius, have you noticed that some of the tree species that had predominated at Novgorod are making up a smaller and smaller portion of the forest?"

Polonius scanned the nearby shore for some moments before he replied. "You are right, Prince. I see far less birch and pine trees than before."

Dawn found the travelers refreshed and ready to move on. The boats, never unloaded nor left unattended, were launched again as they were every morning. They had traveled for no more than an hour, however, when Ambrose noticed that the forest had given way to open fields. Further, it was now obvious that the boats were unable to travel much further up the river. The river had dwindled to not much more than the width of the largest ship, and was, in fact, now little more than a stream.

At last the fleet reached a settlement, and all the passengers stood at the rails to gape at the captain's surprise. There, directly in front of the first ship, was a massive set of rollers that stretched across a field and out of sight into the forest!

"There,' yelled Hammar, 'lies our stream to the Dnieper!"

The ships put ashore to loud welcomes from the mainly Slavic people who populated the village. Although it was probable that they had no especially great love for the blonde pagan giants who came from the north, they had long lived in peace with the Varangian traders, and, indeed, it was the Viking ship owners who provided most of their income.

Rapidly, for it was a common occurrence to them, several groups of villagers helped strip the boats of heavy cargo, while another hitched several teams of oxen to the first boat. With some anxiety, the crew watched the Varangian ship, scourge of so many lands, dragged with many a protesting groan onto dry land and into the "V" of rollers that facilitated the transport of river vessels over land.

For those who were not experienced traders on these rivers, the journey of their vessels was fascinating. One by one the many teams of oxen and men hauled the ships overland, until they could be launched on the other side of the watershed, into a river that directly fed into the Dnieper.

Several days had seen the flotilla; one at a time, sail the wooden rollers. After much laborious effort, the ships were reloaded and ready to move on downstream to the town of Kiev. Already the spring sun was beginning to dry muddy ground, although the numerous swamps and bogs were full to the brim. The river itself still had the high crest characteristic of the spring season.

CHAPTER 22.

The Khazars.

Within a few days, aided by wind, current, and brawn, the small fleet had covered a good distance. Already the ships had slipped past Smolensk, a major fortified town on the upper reaches of the Dnieper. There the flotilla had halted and re-provisioned.

Askold and Dir had hoped to meet an official Khazar messenger there, or at least receive more news from the south, but the only information they were able to glean was a confirmation that some plague had indeed killed Kiy, Shchek, & Khoriv, the rulers of Kiev. There were rumors that there were several important factions jockeying for power, but no other news.

During the late afternoon, however, as the ships were preparing to move south again, a troop of riders was seen following the river trail. For the first time, Ambrose and the other passengers met Khazar cavalry. The small detachment had ridden all the way up the Dnieper river valley.

Since the Khazars held little more than titular authority so far north of the steppes that were their homeland, the local inhabitants paid scant attention to them except for politeness. For the new travelers such as Ambrose, Phillip and Polonius, however, these dark men were a source of much curiosity.

Dir and Askold were thrilled to see them, and held a long private conference with them. The two Varangian commanders came away smiling.

As soon as the dark warriors left the Varangian encampment, Dir and Askold ordered a meeting of all free men. Askold raised his voice, and there was instant silence. The adventurers were eager to know if the strange horsemen were with or against them.

"My friends! It is with great pleasure that I tell you the *Khagan* of all the Khazars has stated that he would not be opposed to Rus rule in Kiev, as long as the new rulers swear not to impede the river trade and continue to pay the traditional tribute to the Khazar nation."

Although Dir and Askold knew the Khazar hold on the Dnieper

River valley north of the steppes was at best tenuous, they cheerfully made great promises, knowing that any support they could get at this time could be instrumental in their forthcoming struggle.

If, in fact, the Khazar power waned, and they lost effective control of the Dnieper River mouth, then they could always renege on their promises. If they continued to patrol the river banks and effectively control the mouth of the river, then the Varangians could only travel south and trade with Khazar permission.

With written proof of Khazar support in Dir's hand, and with the promise of hot weather coming, the expedition's members had left Smolensk confident and happy. Only the rumor that bands of Magyar warriors were raiding to the south served to dampen their enthusiasm and that only slightly.

The vessel carrying Ambrose, Phillip and Polonius was third in line in the flotilla. As it passed under the shadow of a bluff, Phillip, the ever vigilant warrior, suddenly pointed to the crest. There, framed by trees, stood a mounted party of strangers. The riders sat still on their horses, apparently just watching the fleet's progress.

Polonius turned swiftly towards where the ship officers stood at the bow. "Captain! Look up at the bluff on the right. Do you see the men!?"

Even as he spoke, the mounted party turned and faded into the trees.

The captain spoke with quiet authority. "Signaler! Blow two blasts on the ox horn. On the double!"

As the mournful sound echoed up and down the river, all of the steersmen threw over their steering oars and made for the center of the river. Perplexed by the signal, but obedient, the lead ship, which held Askold and Dir, waited for the Deerhound to close with it in mid-river.

Both Dir and Askold stood at the stern of the command ship as the vessels neared. Crewmen with stout ropes tossed them to sailors on the Deerhound, so that the two vessels were temporarily attached.

Askold called out. "Captain, why did you signal us to head for mid-river?"

"Jarl, there was a party of riders on the bluff above, over there!' As he spoke, he pointed to where he last saw the mysterious watchers. 'They disappeared into the trees just as soon as they realized we could see them."

"Could you identify their tribe?"

"No, Jarl. It was too far to identify them by their clothes, and they flew no banners."

The ship captain and Ambrose, Phillip, and Polonius stood respectfully silent while command decisions were made. Dir turned to Askold. "Well, cousin, what does it mean?"

Askold replied. "Maybe nothing, but I don't think so. If they were Slav or Varangian, they would more likely have just waved to us. I do not remember any settlements on this stretch of river, so I am assuming that it had to be a scouting party for nomad raiders. What say you?"

Dir looked grim. "It's far from the steppes, but I would tend to agree. If they are on horseback, and we stick to the middle of the river, however, I don't see that it matters who they are."

"Then it's settled. We will push on, but we will stay clear of the shore until we find out who the horsemen are."

"There are two other matters we must think about."

"Such as?"

"One. We have always landed for the night."

"Paugh! So we spend a few days sleeping on wooden decks, or we find islands safely away from the shore. That's not a problem."

"Two. Are there any rapids or shallows coming up where we have to portage?"

"By Thor's thunderbolts, I don't know! If there is, then we could be in deep shit."

Dir turned back to the captain who had brought the warning. "Hammar, I have a task for you. I want you to visit each ship of the fleet in turn. Tell the captains we will go forward, but until told otherwise, no ship is to go near the shore. The width of the river is our ally. I want the men sent to the oars. We will see how far from here we can be by sundown.

And tell our navigator to check his runes. We need to know exactly how many day's sailing we have before we reach any obstacles."

The crewmen released the ropes that bound the two ships and the current quickly separated them. The commander's vessel surged forward under the impetus of the rowers, and the Deerhound slipped back towards the next vessel.

Gentle back-strokes held the Deerhound still while, one by one, the karves and dugouts of the fleet drew alongside. Captain Hammar repeated their commanders' instructions again and again as Ambrose leaned against the ship's rail and idly gazed at the large and ever-widening river. It was already larger than any Ambrose had known in Britain. He turned to the Byzantine scholar at his side.

"Polonius, if we stay out of bow range of the shore, what do we have to fear? It may be uncomfortable to sleep on the wooden decks for a few days, but it's safer than having our throats cut as we sleep."

"Prince, the Dnieper is many times larger, and longer, than any river you would have known in your own homeland. The length is the problem, and the drop."

"How so?"

A rushing mountain river is generally not a navigable. One as broad and long as the Dnieper, however, must inevitably have narrows, rapids and bluffs. These points are presumably a key concern, for you're right, little can harm the ships as long as we have room to manoeuver. The Varangians are superb sailors, and their ships are justly feared across Europe.

These people need have little fear of an attack on open water. A narrows or shallows, however, especially if allied with bluffs, could mean real danger, for archers and catapults could wreck havoc on boats unable to move out of range. And when we are forced ashore to portage our cargoes, we are sitting ducks to any attackers."

While no more signs of observation were apparent, lookouts remained vigilant. Thus it was that when the first ship rounded a bend that led to both narrows and a slight bluff on one side, a lookout shouted a warning that was instantly repeated by braying horns. Moments later, from the heights along the shore rose great flocks of arrows, which showered down around and upon each vessel.

Several warriors, as well as a few women and children, were struck. The rest scurried to hide under the partial decking or behind the wall of shields that hung along both sides of the vessel. Fortunately the enemy archers were only able to get a good angle from one bank, and thus only one bank of rowers was really exposed. The vessels moved hastily towards the other bank.

Finally the Deerhound, in its turn, made the bend. Ambrose and his companions could suddenly see the arrows flying, and, more, they could see what had caused the alarm to be sounded. Stretched across the river at its narrowest point was a continuous line of rafts. Made of stout logs, and tied securely one to the other, they made a formidable barrier.

Worse, the rafts were also loaded with large numbers of archers. Like their companions on shore, they sent shaft after shaft arcing towards the oncoming ships, until the vessels looked like porcupines.

Inevitably, more and more rowers were struck.

Fortunately for the Varangians, the raiders were mounted nomads, and although in disturbingly large numbers, they were really prepared only for fast and mobile land warfare. Thus, only a few small portable catapults lobbed stones down at the passing vessels from the bluffs above.

The light portable catapults were meant for village gates, not strong forts. This meant that they were unable to hurl the kind of stones that would have been able to sink a vessel with a single hit. Nevertheless, the stones they could shoot were capable of breaking through thin decking and wreaking havoc on any victims who were close to where they landed.

At a second braying signal from the lead vessel, the various ships back-watered. Within seconds the entire flotilla came to a complete halt, reversed, and then gathered speed upriver. Pulling the steering-oars from the water, and relying on the skill of the experienced crewmen to control the ships by rowing alone, the larger ships of the fleet changed direction in moments. The many small ships and dugouts quickly spun around the larger vessels and followed suit.

Even as the boats reversed direction, however, a large flotilla of small boats broke cover from the lower bank and swarmed out towards the Viking vessels. Cunningly placed, most of the boats broke cover towards the rear of the Varangian fleet. Ambrose realized that the Vikings were trapped between the raft-boom and the small craft.

The prince turned to his Byzantine friend. "Polonius! We can't go forward, and we can't go back! What can we do!?"

"Prince, the most dangerous decision is not to decide immediately upon a course of action. They heavily outnumber us, and they have caught us by surprise, but we are still safe on the water. Indecision on Dir and Askold's part now, however, could be fatal, but we are hardly beaten yet. If I had to make the decision, I would choose to attack the small boats. The men there can't both row and shoot, and we have the protection of our higher sides against them. We should be able to actually harvest them quite nicely."

Even as the friends watched, archers on the nearer bank broke cover, and they too, started a hail of arrows against the ships that had moved too far from the other bank. Several more rowers gasped and fell. The lead ship's signal horn blared again, ordering the vessels to keep moving back up river. The die had been cast. They would fight their way through the swarm of small boats.

Even over the massed chanting of the enemy warriors, Polonius and Ambrose could hear many of the Varangian warriors working themselves into a frenzy and calling upon Odin. In truth, a fighting rage was not difficult to achieve. More and more rowers were wounded by the great flocks of missiles that still arced at them from the shore, the little boats, and the rafts.

At last the rival fleets neared. Jubilant Varangians were finally able to strike back. The small vessels sheltered behind the high-sided karves, and the bigger vessels closed. No mean archers, although it was not their most favored mode of battle, the Varangian warriors launched arrows, and, when close, ballast stones and spears at the overloaded small boats.

Secure behind their higher sides, now that the archers on the shore had to cease shooting or risk hitting their own men, the Rus emptied boat after boat of steppe warriors. The karves themselves were used as battering rams; crushing many more boats and dumping their occupants into the dark waters.

The dugouts followed the larger boats, and the warrior-traders in them speared any luckless swimming nomads they could reach. Finally however, in spite of the fearsome toll being taken of them, an appreciable number of enemy boats reached the line of karves. The fierce steppe warriors swarmed aboard.

With glee and hate, the Varangian defenders savagely counter-attacked. Companion karves and dugouts pulled alongside long enough for the swiftest warriors to leap aboard. Reinforced with the extra Viking fighting men, the Varangians were in their element. The decks were soon awash with blood.

The cries of fear from the women and children, crammed below the partial decking, mingled with the battle cries and death rattles of the warriors of both nations. Gradually the ships lost headway, as the majority of Varangian rowers were either required to seize their arms and defend their ships, or the crews transferred to vessels in trouble.

Able only to carry light weapons in the small boats, and not as familiar with maritime warfare as were the Varangians, the Asiatic warriors fell back before concerted rushes of the giant blond warriors. The northerners stood shoulder to shoulder, carried small shields, and swung large swords and battle axes with extraordinary strength. If the Asiatic archers had the space to shoot effectively, the Varangians might have died to a man, but as it was, boat after boat of nomads lost their crews, and the corpses and overturned boats floated serenely towards their own river barrier. At last, several terse blasts on a horn recalled the nomad raiders, and the Viking vessels were once again free to move upriver unimpeded.

As the rowers returned to their duties, the women appeared on deck to bind the wounded and help throw enemy dead overboard. Phillip and Polonius watched in considerable surprise as Ambrose himself crawled under the sheltering decking where some of the wounded women lay. Not having seen his captive, Kuralla, emerge, he crawled over children and through blood to check on her safety.

Ambrose found Kuralla safe, and gently helped her back to the open deck. Yet while Ambrose was considerate and helpful, Kuralla responded coldly; obeying his will but allowing no warmth to creep into her words or actions.

Ambrose wanted once again to apologize for what he had done to the girl, as he had wanted to a thousand times, yet he just could not speak the words. Finally he just turned away. Kuralla walked to the other side of the deck. Ambrose's eye briefly caught her profile as she moved between him and the sun. She looked to him like one of the angels he had been told about by the good Abbott, his religious tutor. As a child, he had often attempted to visualize an angel. Today, for the first time, he felt he knew what they must have looked like back when they had walked on earth. Kuralla seemed impervious to his longing gaze, however.

Eventually she moved across to Polonius, sat, and engaged him in animated conversation. For the first time in his life, Ambrose felt a pang of jealousy. He watched the womanly figure glide across the deck with a sense of bitter loss. That night he had been drunk, and he had listened to the urgent demands of his young body. While Kuralla still chose to follow him, he felt in his heart that in reality he had lost her. He wondered if wearing a hair-shirt as penance would be any less painful.

Ambrose was impressed with the cool efficiency of the Rus women, who, although racked by grief at the death or mangling of a loved one, yet moved purposefully and effectively at their duties.

On either side of the river, shouting great oaths and imprecations, rode a cloud of the nomad riders. Worsted in the battle, they yet blocked the river to the south, and they spoiled for a fight on level ground, where they knew themselves to be the unsurpassed masters.

CHAPTER 23.

The Island.

Though they had to fight the current all the way, an hour's hard rowing brought the fleet to a small wooded island in the middle of the river. Here, on the instructions of Askold and Dir, the battered fleet halted. Orders went out that they would stay the night, allowing the women to more carefully attend to the injured, and the men to repair what damage they could.

With three ships manned only by bachelor warriors set to coursing around the island, the rest of the fleet was beached or moored. All other crews and passengers went ashore to rest.

Polonius, with his considerable medical skills, went to help bind up arrow and sword wounds. Ambrose and Phillip were set to work collecting arrows and attempting to patch the holes in the vessels caused by the catapults.

When all the dead and mortally wounded were finally taken ashore, the Varangians discovered that the number of dead or wounded constituted almost an entire ship's crew. There was a great outpouring of grief and mourning for the many casualties.

Askold ordered that in the morning the smallest karve would be beached, stripped of any useful cargo, and made ready for a funeral pyre; a custom generally reserved for powerful chiefs. The ship would be burned with the bodies of the dead warriors lying aboard in state. The women of the slain were at least proud that their men would be given such a signal honor.

By dusk the wounded had all been treated, and the travelers settled in for desperately needed sleep. However, to insure no surprise, all able bodied men were broken into four shifts, and, at all times, the three vessels continued to move silently through the dark waters surrounding the island.

The rest, crew and passengers, slept with their armor on and their weapons at hand. Although Dir and Askold were reasonably sure that the barbarians would not be so foolish as to try another contest on the water, yet the joint commanders wanted to be sure that there would be no more surprises.

A few campfires on the mainland indicated that the enemy scouts were still in position, and the only question was in what numbers. Early the next morning, Askold and Dir called an assembly of the warriors, as was the custom, for the men were free warriors who had a say in their own fate. Willing to obey without question in time of mortal danger, yet the Varangians expected to have full say in any longer-term arrangements.

The morning was spent in much wrangling. Several warriors wanted to take their families and return to Smolensk. There, they argued, they would be secure behind strong walls and could simply wait for the enemy hordes to move on, or until superior Khazar forces moved north and defeated them. Dir, a veteran of several trips south to the Black Sea, explained what he knew of the raiders.

"As you know, the Khazars hold the lands of the Volga and the Don Rivers in a firm grip. They hold the mouth of the Dnieper too, but north of that, their hold becomes tenuous, and only the agricultural Slavs pay them tribute. The Magyars have long raided the more northerly portions of the river, but do not try to control it. It has been reported to our southern traders, however, that the Khazars and the Ghuz, far to the east, have formed an alliance and are slowly driving the Pechenegs, a Turkish tribe near the Volga, to the west.

Because of the large size of the horde which attacked us, I would guess that these attackers might be part of the mass movement of this tribe. They have been seen more and more often in the vicinity of the Dnieper, though generally south of Kiev. I think then, that this could be our enemy."

Consternation was the reaction to Dir's speech. To fight a fast-moving raider band of Magyars was one thing, but an entire nation that might be settling between them and the Black Sea was quite another. Against the slightly more than eight hundred warriors the fleet could muster, they could face as many as 20,000 or even 30,000 horsemen; each and every one of them well armed and mounted.

Dir stood in the place-of-honor at the front of the assembly. Warriors willingly quieted when it was obvious that he wanted to speak.

"Warriors! Before you vote on the direction our expedition is to take, I wish to make two points.'

He paused dramatically, and the crowd became silent. 'First of all, I think it vital that whatever we choose, we do it together. Split into two weaker forces, we both become terribly vulnerable. Some of you are here to settle in Kiev, and others amongst you have agreed only to stay there for a few days. But if you turn around now, you will have neither the opportunity to settle in Kiev, nor to trade with the Byzantines. I will accept the majority decision, but I ask that whatever we decide, we all stay together.

Second, I would like to remind you all that between us and Smolensk are many sandbanks and one set of rapids where our ships would be particularly vulnerable while we pulled the ships through the rapids or across the sandbars. Our women and children would be especially vulnerable there since it would be necessary to disembark them, along with most of the cargo.

The passage south has been difficult enough, even with the high spring waters and the current in our favor. At any of these locations the mounted bowmen could wreak havoc with their lightning attacks and their clouds of arrows. Worse, our warriors, even if we could abandon the vessels that need to be pulled along the shore in order to fight, would be unable to mass in large numbers without abandoning either cargo or some of the ships.

At best we would be limited to a series of small defensive rings, while the enemy could call in more and more units of their horde; until a veritable avalanche of manpower would eventually overwhelm us. Better that we fight from the ships,' yelled Askold, 'where the superiority clearly lies with us!"

It was at this point that Polonius, a guest at the assembly, put forth the plan that Ambrose, Phillip and he had discussed the night before. "Jarls and warriors, if we cannot retreat without greater risk then go forward, it only remains to think of the most effective means of advancing. It came to us last night that the nomad's most revered possession is his horse, as it allows him to cross both plains and deserts, and to keep his flocks moving to fresh pastures.

It would seem appropriate then, to send a detachment of our best foresters to attempt to stampede their herd. They will not be expecting us to attack their horses, as they are of no use to us. If we can stampede them, however, we can at least distract them and buy ourselves time to break through their blockade. It is my understanding that a nomad without his horse is as helpless as a man with his breeches about his ankles."

A burly Varangian yelled out from across the assembly of warriors. "Whoa, little Greek. Just how do you intend to accomplish this stampede when they will have many alert sentries around the herds? The horses are not likely to be upset by a few yelling strangers. These are horses trained for war, and the steppe people train their horses not to fear sudden movement or noise. Further . . ."

"You asked a good question, my friend, and I will answer.' Polonius responded, 'Have you ever waved the hide of a lion, bear, or even wolf in the face of a horse or a cow? They know intuitively the smell of their mortal enemies, and will defend themselves in the way they know best - by running in the opposite direction!

It is true that a few of us alone could not precipitate a stampede, but if a large number of these animals, or at least their skins, taken from your very beds, cannot, then I would be very surprised. Further, while a band of us makes this attack, some of our dugouts could float down-river silently, under cover of dark and using only the current. If we reach the raft-boom and cut it before they can man it with archers, then we have won! The women, manning the oars only at the last moment, could bring our fleet down-river and pass through the break in the boom that we will have made."

"Can our women row our ships?" Shouted one stocky man.

"Hold!' shouted Askold. 'It is an interesting plan, and may be the best chance we have. Let us put it to the vote. First of all, would those who wish to go south to Kiev raise their hand?"

The number of hands raised constituted a large majority, and Askold smiled. He spoke again.

"Then let the commanders meet with Polonius now, and we will present the complete plan to you tomorrow morning for you to vote on. Is this agreeable to all here? . . . Good. Then return to your shelters and prepare your dead for the funeral."

The smallest vessel, badly battered, was pulled from the water by the combined strength of over one hundred warriors. It was propped on both sides with logs so that it would remain upright on the sandy beach. As dusk descended, the last few casualties were loaded aboard the funeral ship. Time was of the essence if the nomad raiders were not to be allowed to move up both boats and their main force. Their arrival would allow the enemy to consider attacking the island in full battle strength.

Askold, in his capacity of high priest, decreed that the customary ten days of mourning would be waived. He told the mourners that he thought that the fleet would have to leave its island haven before the sun rose more than one more time.

The women were unable to spend adequate time making the customary clothes for the Journey of the Dead, but each family donated finery to allow the corpses to travel in appropriate magnificence. Two slave women volunteered to serve the warriors on their last journey. They were given unlimited access to the supplies of mead.

The men collected armloads of dry wood and built a pyre for the entire ship and its cargo. The women, meantime, loaded the vessel with some of their precious foodstuffs. Two valuable dogs were butchered and loaded onto the ship. Finally, an old woman was chosen to be the 'Angel of Death'.

As the sun rose, the old woman climbed aboard the ship. The warriors beat their shields with their swords, making a mighty din. The screams of the volunteer slave women were cut off by a tightening garrotte and hidden by the thundering noise. Ambrose, when he saw the slave women being helped aboard earlier, realized that they were so stupefied from the alcohol that they probably knew little of what happened to them.

The old woman soon appeared from under the canopy raised on deck with a bloody knife in her hand. The thundering stopped as if it had never been. The crowd waited silently until she reached the ground.

At last all was in readiness. Even as the sun, now a disk of blood red, eased its way into the sky, Askold stood alone in front of the gathered throng. His voice thundered through the now silent crowd.

"It is a sad time when we say goodbye to our beloved comrades. We pray, Odin, that you were watching the nine worlds with your good eye when our warriors fought and died so bravely. Send the Valkyries to escort our slain companions to your hall of Valhalla. We know them to be worthy of Asgard. Take them, o' mighty Odin! We celebrate that they may fight and carouse until *Ragnarok*!"

As he spoke, Askold slowly raised his arms over his head, until his hands pointed to the sky. Ambrose felt a shiver and unobtrusively crossed himself. He listened in awe as the pagan gods were invoked. He knew that, in the distant past, his own people had invoked the same gods, and he felt the power of their presence. Without thinking, he touched the birth mark on his chest that his mother had told him was a mark of much older, Celtic gods.

At last Askold was through with the speech. The Jarl signaled a group of warriors, kin of the slain, to step forward. The men first stepped out of the crowd, and then stripped naked where they stood.

Grimly, one at a time, they stepped forward to receive a flaming brand from Dir. At Askold's final signal, they stepped forward as one and lit the brush piled under the ship.

One by one, the widows and the rest of the warriors followed them. Each threw a piece of wood onto the rapidly growing fire. Thus, each paid tribute to the precious cargo of bodies whose souls were soon to be on their way to Valhalla.

The flames hungrily climbed the sides of the ship until they leapt high into the sky. Askold, standing on the edge of the beach, turned to the assembled throng and shouted out to them.

"Be merry, my companions! Our comrades died bravely and in the manner most blessed by the gods. Go now, and continue the feasting!"

When the fire died down, Dir and Askold called the warriors to the promised assembly. After reviewing and revising Polonius' original plan, it was passed unanimously, but on the understanding that the rest of the day would be spent training the women in the basic rudiments of controlling the wooden steeds. In the meantime, a picked detachment of warriors, used to running and adept in the ways of the forest, would be formed to make the raid upon the herd that would be grazing somewhere near the raft-barrier.

Although the woods alternated with small tracts of more open land, yet it was anticipated that the forest cover should provide adequate protection from the spying eyes of the scouts and the herd sentries.

CHAPTER 24.

Attack!

For most of the day, the women rowed the graceful vessels around and around the island. The instructors' throats were hoarse from yelling at them to stroke in time with the drum beat, but towards evening the women, whose hands were now raw from contact with the pine oars, were able to at least row in time, and even move the vessels upriver against the strongest current.

Meantime Ambrose and Phillip, who were to go with the horse-raiders, assembled such furs of bear, wolf, and lion as they could. Before dusk came, the karves and dugouts were loaded in full view of the Pecheneg scouts on the shore. Then all the fleet, except for the chosen foresters who were hiding in the island's undergrowth, began to make their way upriver towards Smolensk.

Although the Varangians could not understand what was shouted on shore, the orders shouted to riders were audible, and a troop of horsemen galloped south, presumably to gather forces and move them upriver to the rapids. Ambrose and the rest of the small band watched in some satisfaction from their hiding place on the island.

The Varangian group waited until full dark before uncovering their small boats, sliding them into the water and rowing for shore. They pulled hard, knowing that their time was limited. Within a short time the dugouts and small boats of the warriors attacking the log boom would be drifting back down-river, past their location.

Not far behind the dugouts would come the main fleet; the larger dugouts and the karves manned by the women and the warriors not chosen for the other two forays. Ambrose had felt strange when Polonius had been assigned to help the women sail the vessels.

Luck was with the Varangians, for the slender crescent of the moon was not to rise for several more hours. Thus, only the faintest light of the stars exposed their movements.

Once ashore, the small band of foresters, carrying the heavy pelts of predators, slipped into the woods. From here on they should be safe, except when forced to cross one of the clearings. They started south at a distance-eating trot; towards where they hoped to find the Pecheneg horse herds.

While passing near the abandoned camp of the nomad scouts across from their island, Ambrose's group realized that the first of the ruses had worked. The scouts' nomad camp was abandoned. The raiders had either attempted to follow the ships northwards, or raced south to join the main camp and presumably arrange with their *khan* to send a strong force north with the dawn.

Within two hours the foresters had located both the horse herd and the main encampment. Luck and following the shoreline had brought them directly to the animals. Their scouts had found the animals in a small valley hard by the camp. Only a small herd of hobbled horses, kept in camp in case of emergency, were not in a position to be driven off.

With great care, the exhausted runners moved more upwind of the herds and then unwrapped the cow hides that had been placed over the predator pelts. The foresters could very quickly sense an unease in the herd, as the mild breeze carried the tell-tale scent of lion, bear, and wolf to the horse herd. The outriders began to circle more quickly, trying to keep the horses bunched, but unable to determine the reason for the animals' unease.

At last, feeling sure that enough time had elapsed that their best warriors, tied to logs so they could not be spotted by any sentries, should be nearing the boom. Just behind them, crammed into the fleet's dugouts and small rowing boats, would be the main attack force of warriors.

Ambrose gave the signal, and the men leapt from concealment, waving their skins madly and imitating the cries of the great carnivores that the horses instinctively feared.

With the stink of mortal enemy now strong in their nostrils, the horses had already started to retreat nervously. The sudden movement and sound panicked them, and they broke into instinctive flight. The animals instantly transformed themselves into an irresistible wall of galloping horseflesh. Outriders who were in their path were totally unable to stop the stampede, and only saved their lives by turning the heads of their own horses and allowing them to run freely with the herd.

A couple of outriders, closest to the wildly growling and yelling Varangians, realized what had happened and managed to force their way towards the strangers who had emerged from the forest. They yelled their battle cries and waved their swords, clearly hoping to repay the strangers with cold steel. As they approached the dimly moving shadows, however, volleys of spears from the nearby woods toppled many from their mounts. Charging them in turn, the Varangians quickly emptied most of the Pecheneg saddles. Between these and the hobbled horses, the Vikings had soon caught enough horses to mount their own group.

The Vikings rode southward, even as the first warriors from the Pecheneg camp streamed into the little valley. The newcomers looked about wildly to find the cause of all the yelling and for the reason for the herd to be stampeding. Screaming in rage, they turned upon any of their own outriders they could find, but most already lay dead, crushed by horseflesh or pierced by cold Viking iron.

The war horns echoed across the encampment and the Pechenegs rapidly formed into their ranks. They were fighting men, and well disciplined. Without their mounts, however, they knew that they would eventually become easy prey for any bands of Khazars or Magyars who might come across them. Using the relatively few horses that had been kept hobbled for messengers and scouting use, and a large force of runners, the khan sent out his men on a desperate horse-hunt.

Bumbling and cursing in the dark, many Pechenegs saw a hard-riding band of riders gallop south, but thought them merely to be a mounted squad of their own horde.

Shortly thereafter, a shout arose from the raft-boom. There were only the wounded and a few guards left in camp, however, to respond. The Varangian swimmers had reached the boom unseen and killed most of the sentries, but not before one had seen the dark shapes of the many small boats approaching and yelled out a warning. Those who were still in camp and able, raced out onto the raft boom. They unlimbered their bows and clutched their swords as they ran. Against the relatively small numbers who had remained in the camp and could answer the summons, however, the Varangian forces were clearly superior. Fighting from rocking boats and on rafts was not foreign to the Viking men, and they gleefully returned many of the thousands of arrows that the Pechenegs had shot at them earlier.

The Pechenegs gradually regained numerical superiority, however, for many warriors in the woods heard the sounds of battle and returned from their horse hunt. By now the Varangian warriors held the center of the raft boom. The Varangian axes made short work of the many ropes that held the raft-boom together. Suddenly, looming out of the darkness, came the fleet of ships, tall and sinister in the dim light of the rising moon.

If enough Pechenegs returned and put their bows into action, even darkness would not protect the Varangians from slaughter, for although the nomads' bows were short and didn't have the penetrating power of the longer bows the Rus tribesmen favored, yet they were made for mounted combat, and the tribesmen were able to release an arrow every few seconds with remarkable accuracy.

The ropes were finally severed and the linked rafts began to drift apart. The Varangians leapt for their ships as they came through the gap, or untied their dugouts and rowed. This time, with the women manning the oars, the men stood at the shield-walls along the sides of the ships and loosed swarms of arrows at the shores and at anyone who was not of Varangian size. In this manner, most of the crew returned to their vessels and the ships managed to finally slip past the barrier.

Just as the battle on the rafts was reaching its peak, Phillip and Ambrose looped back and took their cavalcade galloping through the encampment. After stopping to light torches at an isolated campfire, they charged through the encampment's tent area, throwing the flaming torches at tents and piles of supplies. At the entrance of the area where a large black tent stood, pennants flying from all four corners, a single line of armed guards materialized.

The riders rode hard at them, and the nomad line broke into small groups while the horsemen thundered past. While the nomads separated, they were ready to empty the saddles of anyone foolish enough to leave his guard open. Ambrose himself almost made it through them, but a fast slice of an enemy sword cut the tendons of his mount and the horse collapsed beneath him.

Rolling to his feet, Ambrose felt the Pecheneg guards pressing about him. The cooking fires about the camp cast some light, and Ambrose could see several Pechenegs closing on him. Moving quickly to place his back against a tent, he called out in Saxon at the advancing group.

"Come, you scum, and taste cold steel! Come and die at my feet!"

Without a shield, Ambrose drew his sax, or long dagger, as well as **Victory-Maker**. The Pechenegs started to close cautiously. They moved forward in unison. Once, twice, Ambrose's blade flickered out, and each time a man yelped. Pushing their shields forward to catch any blows, the nomad warriors began swinging their blades at the stranger. Several powerful blows were absorbed by the sax, and Ambrose's left wrist ached from the impacts. His sword however, formed an arc of glittering death that the Asian warriors were unable to pierce. Ambrose knew, however, that time was against him. Someone would break from their blind anger, grab a bow or spear, and finish the contest from a distance.

Several tents had burst into flames. Ambrose could hear the wild gallop of horsemen coming toward him. Preparing to sell himself dearly now that more enemy tribesmen had arrived, he flicked his eyes briefly in the direction of the noise. The riders were upon him. Suddenly he realized that the riders were using captured lances to spear his attackers!

Ever faithful Phillip, mounted on a large steed that still seemed barely able to hold his bulk, reached down and scooped Ambrose from the ground as if he were once again a four year-old toddler. All mounted again, the party fled south.

They followed the river, for they knew a vessel was supposed to await them a few minutes ride down-river. Once well-away from the encampment and free of any immediate pursuit, the little group slowed their horses to a trot and searched anxiously amongst the shadows for the shape of the ship looming out of the darkness.

At last they saw a darker shadow slightly offshore, and one of the warriors called out, imitating the cry of an arctic owl. A similar reply was heard and the shape began to drift shoreward. They heard a shouted command, in the Norse tongue.

"Step into the water, with your hands empty! Remember, there be bowmen covering you!"

The men dismounted, waded out, and then stood still until their identity could be confirmed. Once aboard, they got a rousing welcome from the jubilant crew, excitedly shouting out the results of the night's events.

Polonius, who had insisted on being aboard the pickup boat, hugged both the young prince and the giant Saxon thane.

Ambrose grinned. "Well, how did it go?"

"Better than we could have expected, Master! All of the ships made it through safely and wait for us a little down-river."

"And the casualties?"

Polonius thought for a moment. "Only two or three killed, but a score wounded."

"And you?"

Ambrose replied. "We burned part of their camp and, with a little luck, the horses are still running."

"Excellent. It seems a fitting revenge on the Pecheneg warriors who had dared to attack the Varangian fleet."

Once the fleet formed up again, the men took to the oars. They alternately rowed and drifted ever south, with no pause, until many hours of horse travel were between them and the Pecheneg horde. With no more rapids until beyond Kiev, they were free to sail to their destination!

CHAPTER 25.

The Expedition Reaches Kiev.

During the next five days, Dir and Askold only allowed the ships to touch shore when they found islands a safe distance from the river bank. As tributaries joined the mother river, the Dnieper had widened, until, with its spring flow, it filled a flood plain almost five Roman miles across. Ambrose had never seen such a mighty river before. The men, women, and children of the fleet were only forced to spend two nights on the wooden deck as they gently floated southward.

At no time in this journey did they see any further sign of the Pecheneg marauders, although mute evidence of their passing was occasionally visible in the form of scorched villages. Once they found a Varangian vessel, burned and grounded on the shore.

Several of the crew of Ambrose's vessel cried out in anger and grief when they saw the hulk. Its captain had been impatient to head south, and the ship had left Novgorod only a few days before their own fleet had set sail.

Soon after midday on the fifth day after the fight, the flotilla sighted the wharves of Kiev itself. At last the lead ship gave the signal to turn, and the ships all swung towards the shore. High on a bluff above stood the fortified town of Kiev; trading center of this section of the Dnieper.

Curious townspeople came down to the docks to stare at the new arrivals as they beached their ships. The northern trading fleet was expected. Kiev's own traders had already sailed south a week earlier. The first traders to reach the southern markets stood to make the greatest profit. But such a large fleet, carrying women and children, was still a surprise.

Dir and Askold had ordered that the crews and passengers were to set up camp in a pasture near the docks, for the town was obviously unable to hold the over one thousand men, women and children that walked off the docks or waded ashore. Besides, the Varangians weren't sure of their welcome. Unlike at Novgorod, they were not invited guests here.

Amongst the curious townspeople, there were a few Varangians visible. Some spotted old friends and rushed over to greet them. Dir and Askold, flanked by a few friends and lieutenants, were carefully dressed in their finest armor, and this group marched up to the fortified town to demand admission.

As the town gates swung ponderously open, it was not lost upon the townspeople lining the battlements that all of the newcomers were wearing full armor, and they carried all their weapons with them. Even the men in the meadow who were helping their families settle were armed and alert. More, they had thrown up a skirmisher line between their camp and the town.

Dir and Askold were escorted directly to the town assembly building, which served both as a headquarters and hall of justice, as well as assembly hall. Here the Varangian party was met by the grinning Rus trader who had sent the original summons, as well as over a dozen Slavs, who looked far less happy about the arrival of the strangers.

One of these Slavs, a portly man, bald and bearded, spoke with a rasping voice. Surprisingly, he spoke fluently in the Nordic tongue. "Traders going south are always welcome to stop and provision in Kiev. Less than a day's journey south, you will find the last staging point before you hit the steppes and the First Cataract. A fleet of trading vessels is gathering there now even as we speak. But you . . . you have brought your women and your children with you, and you have your men armored and standing in formation below our very gates! I think, Vikings, that you owe us an explanation."

Askold, ever the more talkative of the two cousins, stood and faced the assembled throng of town leaders. "My lords, friends . . . we have come in peace to your town. You are quite right, however, in determining that we are not just another group of traders heading south on the river. It is our desire to settle here, amongst you, and become good citizens of Kiev. With us as allies, the trade from the north is assured, for, as you probably know, our brethren now control the upper reaches of not only this river, but also the Volga, and others. In return for this alliance that I propose to you, we will strengthen the trade ties northward with our sister settlements, and insure peace with the Varangian traders and warriors who pass through your town. Further, we will defend these lands faithfully, and our women and children will be hostage to our commitment to you."

"And what', rasped the same Slav who had spoken before, 'Is the price of this great beneficence on your part?"

The group of Rus adventurers looked the man over carefully, for he was obviously a powerful figure amongst the local hierarchy, and no doubt had designs on the rulership of Kiev himself. The joint commanders had told Ambrose that they were sure that a vacuum had been left by the death of the previous town leaders. Certainly the chains of gold and jewels that the man wore indicated that he was at the least a wealthy man. The many nods of agreement that followed his comments indicated that he also had a powerful following amongst the Slav leaders.

Askold spoke again. "Gentlemen, let me be blunt, for I am a soldier, not a political man. I have at your front gate over a thousand armed and trained warriors. My expedition is fully supported by the other Varangian settlements to the north. I have a letter here from influential merchants in this town requesting me to come and settle here. Last, but far from least, the Khagan of all the Khazars has personally accepted my overlordship over Kiev! Consider, therefore, that I speak with the authority of 40,000 Khazar warriors at my back."

With that, Askold held up for a brief inspection two documents. One was unmistakably stamped with the seal of the Khazar Khagan. Askold allowed no one to read the letters, and instead swiftly thrust them back into the leather case hanging on his belt. He continued.

"We have no wish to displace any Slavic rulers. On the contrary, we would like to ally ourselves with you. I will swear to you now that my people will only take land that is freely given them, or is presently beyond your effective control. What have you got to lose? Together, we can expand Kiev's control both up and down-river. Kiev will become a major trade city!

Without your agreement or help, we will settle anyway, but we may be required to fight you. Your settlement will burst into civil war, with faction against faction. With your willing co-operation, however, we can together forge a single strong nation, ruled jointly by you and us! Are we to be friends, or enemies?"

The group of Slavs were obviously struck by this proposal. While in fact it meant a diminishing of their own authority, the offer could also mean that they would retain a portion of control over a much larger state. They knew of the battle prowess of these blond Northmen, and were well aware that such raw levies as they could gather from the town itself would be no match for the foe camped outside their gates. Already, a Varangian 'fifth-column' resided within their walls, and the Khazars were definitely a force to be reckoned with.

Further, it was a time of unrest in their lands, with the Pecheneg nation being driven inexorably in their direction. Such allies as the warlike Varangians could be a potent asset.

Heads swung again to the portly Slav. It was obvious that the others expected him to make the decision; whether to grant concessions or declare war. The Slav paused for a few moments, and then spoke again in his rasping voice.

"If, and I say IF, leaders of the Rus, we were to agree to such an alliance, how would you envision the control of Kiev?"

The others all nodded sagely. This was, in fact the crux of the entire question, for all feared a diminution of their own power. If they could feel secure in this, their anxiety would be largely alleviated.

Dir, a powerful figure, stepped up beside his cousin. All eyes focused on him, minutely inspecting his long braided hair, his conical steel cap, and the excellent steel-mesh jerkin that dropped to below his thighs. Even its glittering links could not hide the rippling muscles of his torso and arms when he moved. In truth, with his great moustache and piercing blue eyes, he was a formidable looking warrior. He spoke quietly, as was his wont, but his words filled the hall.

"We Rus commanders propose a town council to be composed of an equal number of Varangian and Kievian officials. It is our way that all property owners and warriors have an equal say in the Thing, or assembly. All, either Varangian or Slav, will have the right to be heard. The Thing, in turn, will appoint a leader from amongst the council, in free vote. If a Slav is elected, we pledge ourselves to follow his command as if it were Askold or myself. We ask no more from you than that."

The portly leader, whose name was Olaf, stroked absently at his beard, and then spoke. "I must admit, what you say bears some merit. We ask you to return to your camp. We will send you the final decision of this council before the setting of the sun."

Askold, at his winningest best, smiled broadly, showing white and even teeth, a rarity amongst mature warriors. He signaled his escort to withdraw.

"We can ask no more. We part as friends, and I hope we will soon be partners and allies."

With that, all the Rus withdrew to their camp, leaving the town leaders struggling with the proposal. Askold and Dir had, however, ordered selected crewmen to make sure that their epic struggle upriver had been fully recounted in the marketplace. The men had been instructed to neglect neither the great size of the roving horde, nor the humiliating defeat the small Varangian fleet had been able to inflict upon them.

۴

When they returned to their camp, Dir and Askold were pleased to see that much of the preliminary work had been completed. Tents and shelters had been erected for the women and children, and the warriors were digging a trench and erecting a palisade in the ancient Roman style. Polonius had explained its effectiveness as a military encampment to Dir and Askold, and the Rus commanders had ordered the men to set it up.

All of the men were armed and prepared for a sudden rush from Kiev itself. Below the bluffs, the ships of the fleet rode at anchor; each manned with a skeleton crew and safely within the perimeter of the armed camp.

Askold ordered those who had attended the conference in the town with him to separate and spread the news of the negotiations to the others of the band, along with instructions to all to keep up their guard. If treachery was to be attempted by the Slavs, it would be soon. Once the newcomers had time to dig in, they would be a much harder nut to crack.

The biggest problem for the townspeople, and one which the Rus commanders were fully aware of, was that most of Kiev's military strength resided in Slavic levies from the surrounding countryside. The Varangian force would be slaughtering in the streets of Kiev long before these levies could be gathered from the scattered settlements and shaped into a viable force. The Slavs, in, turn, had no idea that almost half of the powerful Viking force intended to sail south within days.

Indeed, Dir and Askold had considered an immediate attack on Kiev, unprovoked, from the beginning; killing the town leaders and supplementing them with themselves. They had rejected it as a first choice, however, as it would cause no end of hostility with the Slavic population, and they would thereafter be required to rule through naked force.

As Rurik and his followers had found out previously, it was far more effective to rule through the local leaders, who enjoyed the respect and obedience of the populace. Perhaps even more important, the traders who had agreed to sit on the shore for a few days in exchange for supplies to be delivered later, were not prepared to throw themselves against the very solid walls of Kiev. The power of the expeditionary force was partly illusionary.

Others, such as Bothi, attempted to rule by naked force, but he had soon found his domains unruly. Polonius had pointed out to Ambrose that even peaceful farmers could be pushed too far, and aggrieved outlaws would strike back from their forest dens.

"With luck and determination, Prince, the joint forces of the Slavs, the Rus, and what Varangian allies they can attract, should be able to rapidly expand their domains to the north and south along the river valley. With a strong fleet and army, centered at Kiev, many isolated villages should be willing to trade a nominal overlordship for the iron protection that Kiev can offer them."

Dir and Askold had felt justice and fair-treatment would do more to further their cause than a thousand more Varangian warriors. Besides, the townspeople were acutely aware of the Magyars who lived to the west, but liked to raid as far as the Dnieper valley. And there was the still-powerful Pechenegs, who were being driven westward towards the river by the Khazars and the Ghuz. No single town or village could stand alone against such nation-tribes without help.

At last, near dusk, the gates of the town opened and a delegation of a dozen men strode forth. Each appeared dressed in his best finery. Ambrose breathed a sigh of relief when he noticed that no large armed body of troops followed, nor were there archers to be seen on the town wall. Olaf, dressed in rich furs of ermine, led the group.

The delegation paused at the entrance of the Varangian camp. Askold himself, flanked by Dir, and their personal bodyguard, strode forth to do them honor.

"Gentlemen! Welcome to our humble camp! Please, come and join us in our command tent."

The dozen delegates exchanged uneasy glances, but obediently followed the Rus commanders.

Ambrose, Phillip and Polonius, traveling as traders with the expedition, had not been assigned a position in the Varangian military formation. Thus he and Polonius were free to stand at the rough gate and watch the delegation arrive.

Ambrose caught the glances, and whispered to Polonius. "They have come here with no military escort. Why then should they be so nervous about accompanying Dir and Askold to their tent?"

"Prince, we do not know what they have decided. Yet if I was refusing the offer of partnership, I would not come personally to the enemy camp to tell them."

"Agreed, Polonius. So the answer has to be yes. Then why are they so nervous?"

"The Varangians have a strong sense of honor, but it is not as you and I know it. They would rather die than break their word to a valued companion."

"Then, Polonius, the town elders should be at their ease. You have just said that the Varangians can be trusted to keep their word at all costs."

"Aye . . . To a valued companion."

"What are you saying, Polonius?"

"Lord, the sense of honor is very strong amongst the Vikings in general, but it depends on who you give your word to."

"I still do not understand."

"Let me put it this way. If Dir gave his word to a Rus warrior, I would expect that he would keep it even if it meant his death. But if he gave it to a foreigner, especially one who does not worship the northern gods, then he would probably consider the oath to be meaningless."

"Then we could never trust a Viking promise?"

"I think we probably could, Sire."

"But you just said that an oath to a foreigner was meaningless, and we are both foreigner and pagan to these people."

"Ah, it gets more interesting. The oath to us might be respected for the sake of Canute or Gunnar, who is not a foreigner, and is, not incidentally, a very powerful man in the Rus lands. There would be real risk of a blood feud if an oath to us were broken. It might also be honored because of us personally. If we have been tested and are now considered to be worthy of respect, then I would expect the oath to be binding."

"Just what earns us this respect?"

"Amongst the Vikings, lord, I would think that the single most important major criteria is physical courage. If you are not prepared to defend yourself or your honor, to the death, then you are not worthy of being called a man. An oath given to such a man would be nothing but a convenience; something that could be easily broken if it was expedient."

"Then, my friend, you are saying that the town leaders are nervous because they do not know if Dir and Askold have given them a worthless oath designed to get them into a vulnerable situation, or really mean what they said."

"Well put, Prince.' The Byzantine smiled indulgently at the young man. 'If you put your mind to it, you could be a serious scholar . . . But if you want to know the fate of this expedition today, we had better follow those delegates!"

The dozen Slav leaders strode into the camp and past the honor guard of warriors. If Dir and Askold planned treachery, then it would be soon. The Slavs were now effectively captives of the Rus leaders, and the entire Slavic leadership of Kiev could be wiped out in seconds.

Dir and Askold led the Slav delegation to the largest tent in the camp, their command tent. After all the Slav leaders were comfortably seated on the many furs scattered across the floor, Olaf spoke up.

"Askold, Dir, and you other Rus leaders! Be it known that we accept your terms of an alliance between us, on the strict understanding that we will have equal control over Kiev and its subservient domains. Neither we to you, nor you to us, will be overlords. Instead, we will be equal partners, forming a new and great nation!"

A cry of joy from the Rus leaders escaped their lips at the announcement. Hugging the Slavs, and clapping them on the back, the Vikings greeted them as brothers and allies.

Askold shouted for his son, Askoldson, to be brought to him. Within moments, a lithe and blonde boy, perhaps of eleven summers, entered the command tent. Askold seized him and propelled him to in front of Olaf.

"Askoldson, you will be my pledge of friendship and faith to our Slavic brothers. You will stay with this lord, Olaf, and serve him faithfully. It is my wish that your dear life will pay for any treachery upon my part!"

Olaf, moved deeply by this display of faith, shouted out in return. "This day my own son will be brought, to serve as our pledge of friendship to you. May his life be forfeit if we deceive you!"

So saying, both Olaf and Askold hugged one another again, and then sat down to drink. The women, at Dir's command, began to carry in large flagons of mead and amphorae of wine.

The gates of Kiev were thrown open and Dir ordered the partly constructed ramparts and palisade between the Varangian camp and the town to be leveled.

Fires burned late both in the town and in the temporary camp, and the people mingled freely in friendship. Veritable rivers of mead and wine sealed their bargain, and both Rus and Slavs drank until they fell into a drunken stupor, one on top of the other.

Within days, many of the fine details of the alliance had been worked out. Several good tracts of nearby land were ceded to the Rus lieutenants; that Rus leaders would be near the town in case of sudden attack. The displaced Slav land-owners were, in turn, promised larger grants of land further away. Some of these tracts, however, would only become theirs when the combined forces were able to seize the settlements from the other lordlings who had refused allegiance to Kiev. Most of the Varangian holdings, however, were to be in the frontier areas, or marches, where Slavic peasants would join the Varangian overlords to do battle against marauding strangers and encroaching forest.

The Slav noblemen were surprised to see a major portion of the fleet heading south on a fine sunny day. It did not take them long to realize that part of the Varangian army had been, in fact, made up of traders who had only agreed to lend their numbers temporarily to the expeditionary force. Then the Slav leaders laughed. Enough Viking ships and men remained that they knew they had a potent striking force against both neighbors and enemies.

In fact, many of the villages, both up and down river, sent notice of submission, for the local Slav landowners had no wish to be dispossessed of their own land, and the presence of the Rus, their Varangian allies, and their fleet, was already well known on the river. Furthermore, enemy scouts had been detected towards the south, and it was rumored that a new horde of Pechenegs were being driven across the lower Dnieper by combined forces of the Ghuz and Khazars.

CHAPTER 26.

The Pechenegs Arrive!

As they had done once before in Novgorod, Ambrose, and Phillip, aided by their friend and learned scribe, Polonius, worked to set up a trading factory. Surprisingly, most of the Varangians who had joined the Rus banners turned to colonizing with a great will.

Roving ship-crews of Varangians and Slavs, under Rus commanders, pushed the frontiers of Kiev's influence steadily north and south along the mighty river. The others settled in, built homes for their families, and traveled their new domains. The new rulers visited the local villages and met with the Slav peasants who had sworn loyalty to them.

The Rus leaders were adamant about military training. All able-bodied men, Rus or Slav, trader or farmer, were ordered to spend some time weekly in the practice of military formations, archery, and sword play.

The Slavs, who were not without courage and ability, soon built up confidence in themselves. The main problem of the Slav infantry; a lack of discipline in real battle, was worked on with constant drilling, until the men appeared more willing to face the wrath of thundering cavalry than the Varangian lieutenants when they were dissatisfied.

The fire threw up sparks and a flickering light. Polonius looked in turn at Dir, Askold, and Olaf, as they sat in the Seats of Authority. Ambrose stood behind the scholar. The Byzantine spoke.

"Jarls, you sent for me?"

Dir replied. "Polonius, I remember one night, on our journey south from Novgorod, when we talked of military matters."

"Aye, Jarl. If I remember correctly, we talked of the tactics of the ancient Romans and Greeks."

"Polonius, with no offense to Olaf, the Slavs will fight fiercely against other Slavs, but they seem to fear cavalry, and generally run like rabbits when the nomad horsemen attack."

Olaf smiled. "I am not offended, Dir. It is the sad truth. I would be foolish to deny reality."

Dir nodded to Olaf, and then continued. "Polonius, you are a military expert. Why do you think the Slavs can not stand up to the steppe nomads?"

Polonius hesitated for a few moments. "Jarls, my readings encompass the theories and history of war, not its practical applications. I do not think that this makes me a military expert. That being understood, I would be pleased to answer your question to the best of my ability."

Askold interrupted. "Please. This is a very important issue, and is, in fact, why we asked you here this evening."

"Well, I can think of several reasons. The Slavs live in small tribal units, and thus are generally vastly outnumbered when a horde of warriors rides against them. This is not likely to be the case when they face a small Slav raiding party.

The men are not born warriors, and do not glory in killing or dying bravely. My guess is that they will fight fiercely for their hearth, but, at least until now, have not had a larger entity to offer loyalty to.'

Polonius shrugged. 'And the truth is, if you gave me a three foot sword, and expected me to stand before hundreds of tons of galloping horseflesh, surmounted by wild men either trying to shoot me or stab me with a spear three times the length of my sword, I would call you crazy. I know I would die before I had a chance to strike a single blow."

Dir interrupted again. "But Polonius, you know that Varangian warriors, armed with only axes or swords, have held off entire nomad hordes."

"I know that, Jarl. The Slavs have had a very different experience. They don't know that infantry can prevail."

Dir leaned forward in his chair. "I see your point. Still, we know the nomads will return one day. We know that no matter how brave my fellow Varangians may be, we are relatively small in number. We cannot hope to defeat the nomad raiders without the help of large numbers of Slavs.

So, that being said, what can we do to stiffen the resolve of the Slav warriors?"

"You are doing it. The men need constant drill, until to obey is second nature. And they must constantly practice the basic formations."

Askold now leaned forward. "Polonius, if you were given carte blanche to arm or train a regiment of Slav warriors any way you wanted, how would you go about it?"

Polonius hesitated for several moments. "Hmm. I could think of several things. First, I would teach the men tactical maneuvering. I would drill them until they could change formations with their eyes shut. Second, I would probably train the men in the use of the Macedonian twenty-two foot ash spears. That might give them the confidence to stand firm in the face of a nomad cavalry assault."

Olaf now spoke. "The spears might hold the cavalry, but how would you protect your men from the archers? Every nomad warrior is also an expert shot, even from horseback."

"I would enlarge the size of the shields your Slavic warriors carry, and would teach them the use of the Roman Turtle formation - your shieldburg."

The three leaders looked at each other and all three smiled. Dir spoke. "Scholar, we have a very important task for you."

"Aye, Jarls?"

"Polonius, we want you to take a regiment of Slavs, and train them any way you want."

"Jarls, I am truly honored, but you know that I am no warrior! The men would never listen to me. As I said, I have studied the theory of war, not the practice."

"Polonius, we see all that as no obstacle. We have in mind two excellent officers, who can easily translate your theoretical ideas into practical instructions."

"And who might these be, Jarl?"

"One of them is standing right behind you. The other, I understand, was once the greatest warrior in far-away Wessex. There are few warriors among our own host who would willingly tangle with either one of them. Phillip's strength, and Canuteson's lightening blade, are both renowned. Canuteson, are you willing?"

"If it will help protect Kiev, Jarl, how could I say no?"

Polonius ordered that the men be armed with the twenty-two foot-length ash spears, as well as large rectangular shields. The troops, after weeks of arduous practice, appeared capable of withstanding even such dashing lancer charges as made the Pechenegs a name to be feared. On a word, a veritable hedgerow of spikes was presented forward, so impenetrable that a swallow would have trouble flying through.

To counter the deadly mounted bowmen, the shields had been made larger than normal, and each successive rank learned to hold them high enough to protect the line behind. In the face of massive superiority, Polonius taught the use of the ancient Roman Turtle, where interlocking shields provided excellent protection. Against mounted riders, and in heavily forested territory, Polonius hoped that the combination of formations would prove effective.

Finally, the allied leaders encouraged all men to fortify their towns and practice diligently with bow or sling. With several years of relative peace, the new rulers of Kiev felt that they would finally be capable of defending themselves against the hordes of savage steppe raiders that had for centuries robbed and terrorized the people of the rivers and the forest.

As the warm and dry summer gradually moved towards a golden autumn and harvest time, the Slav conscripts, both in Kiev and the vassal villages, begged for a cessation of their military work. Each able-bodied man had, with some help from Kiev's treasury, armed himself, and agreed to spend a good part of the summer training. Now, however, the harvesting required full-time attendance, or all, in both Kiev and the villages, would go hungry when the Asian winter clamped its icy fingers on the land.

A fine fall day found both Slavs and their overlords sweating in the fields. Long threatening rain had held off, and the teams worked feverishly to harvest the crops while the sun still shone. Just below the city a river karve was run aground. Its exhausted crew ran yelling towards the upper citadel.

"To the town! The Pechenegs are coming!"

Dir and Askold, when they heard the commotion, went to Kiev's open gate. Askold called down as the men stumbled up the steep hill.

"You there! What are you crying out?!"

The tallest of the men bent over for a few moments to catch his breath. At last he straightened up and replied.

"Jarl Askold . . . yesterday evening . . . we were nearing the fort at Vitchev Hill . . . We intended . . . to spend the night there. . . My cousin . . . is the garrison commander."

"And now you are here. That is a remarkably quick journey, but what exactly is the problem?"

"Jarl, the fort . . .at Vitchev . . . is gone!"

"Gone? What are you talking about?"

"The fort is . . . leveled . . . Jarl."

A deep frown covered Askold's face. "And the men? There are over twenty men stationed there."

"The men lay . . . dead on the ground . . . Their horses were gone . . . and the fort has been pulled down log by log."

"By Odin's left eye! If steppe raiders are coming north, why didn't the fools light the signal fire?"

"I know not, Askold. Most seemed to have been caught out in the open, but they all had wounds on their fronts."

"Then bloody *Loki* is up to his tricks again! Do you know who did this foul deed?"

The tall man turned to his companions, who had caught up to him, and stood panting behind him. He spoke tersely. "Show him."

Two of the men silently threw down several arrows and a broken lance. Askold first kicked at the broken weapons, and then stooped to pick up an arrow. He held it up to Dir and Olaf, who stood close behind him.

"I recognize the fletching. I should; I've had enough of the cursed things shot at me! I'm sure it's Pecheneg."

Dir looked closely. "By Odin's balls, this means the bastards are already in the forest and may have been since yesterday! Captain, how did you get here before the horde?"

"We rowed all night, Jarl. We saw that the wood in the signal pyre had been carted away. Rather than take the time to find enough for another pile, we decided to try and to beat the heathen devils here."

"Then you and your crew have done well. There will be a reward for you all once we have defeated these pigs. Go now, and rest. You have earned it.

As for the rest of you - there is no time to lose! Olaf, get the signalers on the watch towers with their horns. We must order all the people within the walls immediately, with as much food and livestock as possible. Askold, will you put together a squadron of messengers and send them on their way?"

"Aye, of course. What message would you have them carry?"

Olaf replied. "Give each a war arrow. The people will understand. And send the messengers north and south first by boat. Let them take to horse at different villages both up and down river."

Dir stared at Olaf. "What are you thinking, Olaf?"

Olaf smiled grimly. "If I were a Pecheneg, my friends, I would have sent in men in disguise, who at such a moment as this, would be waiting in ambush on all the major trails leading away from Kiev."

Askold cursed. "By Odin's bones! You are right, Olaf. There have been many Hun guards hanging around since that caravan arrived last week. I have seen none today."

Dir spoke. "I concur. If the messengers do not get out, we are in deep trouble. Let the messengers start their journey by ship. And tell them to travel the trails with a large escort."

"Consider it done! And what are you up to?"

"I will rally some men and light our signal pyre. We better be ready when the bastards get here!"

As the deep notes reverberated across the fields and river, riders galloped down to the docks and shouted for crewmen to man two sleek river vessels. The first of the great signal pyres, built at regular intervals up and down the river, was uncovered and lit. The message was unequivocal. The enemy was upon them!

Almost before the townsmen of Kiev, who were working in the fields only a short distance from the town, were able to gather the proceeds of their efforts and return to the fortress town, a band of hard-riding Pecheneg horsemen appeared from the south. They rode hard and fast on lathered mounts, obviously hoping to surprise the town's inhabitants and seize the main gate before it could be bolted shut.

Amidst screams and panic, the townspeople ran for the safety of the open gate. Within minutes the riders were mingled in with the panicked mob of running men and women. Scattering the sheep and cattle that were being driven through the entrance, the vanguard of riders rode directly at the few guards Dir had managed to assemble near the gate.

The sound of the horns woke Ambrose from his nap. He opened his eyes and stared at Phillip who stood by the open door of their trading factory. "By all that is holy, Phillip, what is all that noise about?"

"I know not, Prince, but I greatly fear that it does not bode well. There has been much shouting and running about while you slept, and the war horns are blowing recall. I think we would be wise to put on our armor and report to the main gate."

"Polonius, do you know anything else?"

"Nay, Prince, but there is very definitely something wrong."

The three friends slipped on their chain-mail shirts, grabbed their weapons, and ran to the main gate. The scene there was chaotic. Men tried to beat their way through herds and flocks of milling animals, while women clung desperately to screaming children. As Ambrose, Phillip and Polonius arrived, the first of the steppe riders burst through the open gate.

Phillip was in the lead. Facing the first of the steppe riders, he drew his giant sword, and, swinging the heavy weapon in great circles, attacked.

At the end of the arc of his swing, the sword struck a Pecheneg whose lance was aimed at another Varangian warrior. To the nomad's utter amazement, he, as well as his horse, was knocked to the ground. The nomad stared down vacantly at his lower torso where his leg had recently been attached. Matching the beatings of his heart, red jets of blood pumped out, staining the ground. With no further thought for his first victim, Phillip struck again and again at the riders who had managed to charge through the gate.

Ambrose yelled out to his companions and any sentries who remained alive. "Close the bloody gate! If many more make it in, then we are all dead!"

Phillip and a small circle of sentries who had made it to his side held the attention of the small band of mounted warriors who had entered the town. The riders rode desperately at the stubborn knot of men. Close behind them rode hundreds of seasoned warriors, and behind them rode the horde in its thousands. They were only minutes from seizing the town. All that was required was for them to keep the gate open until the reinforcements arrived.

Ambrose and Polonius, unnoticed in the excitement, slipped towards the gate. They were within several feet of the gates when Ambrose's peripheral vision detected a movement. He yelled out in warning. "Look out, Polonius!"

They both turned just in time. A single rider had spotted their movement and, lance couched, was riding hard at them. A pair of throwing knives leapt into Polonius' hands, and Ambrose threw up his shield.

The warrior chose Ambrose as the more dangerous, and aimed his lance directly at him. The warrior was heavily armored, and there was little that Polonius could aim at. Ambrose yelled out again.

"Polonius, if you can't hit him, kill the bloody horse!"

As quick as lightening, four knives spun through the air. The horse was not instantly killed, but the wounds drove it out of control. It screamed and broke its charge. Ambrose had been able to deflect the deadly point of the lance, but he had been only moments from being crushed against the wall.

The steppe warrior abandoned his lance and threw up his arms in an attempt to regain his balance. It was the opportunity Polonius had been waiting for. Two daggers flew into the man's unprotected face.

Ambrose ran the last few steps towards the gate. "Come on, Polonius! Don't just stand there. We still have to close the damned gates!"

The two leaned hard on the massive timbers of the nearest gate. Slowly, ponderously, it began to move. Renewed screams of rage and pain could be heard behind them. Ambrose cast a quick glance back, to see that Dir and Askold, with a glittering escort of heavily armored men, were wading into the fray.

Ambrose strained as pigs and sheep squealed and ran back and forth in terror. The gate was moving much too slowly. The main body of riders had to be close!

At last the gate reached the limits of its arc, but even shut, it only blocked half the entrance. Ambrose was relieved to see Phillip struggling with the other gate. Once the gates met, the Varangians and Slavs could easily take care of the Pecheneg warriors within.

At last the two gates thudded together. Phillip quickly swung the locking bar over so that the two gates were secure, and then the three turned to help finish off the now trapped warriors.

Dir and Askold, recognizing the danger of the open gates, had forced their retinue between the riders and the three men who were working so hard to close the gates. A mob of lightly armed townsmen had formed on the other side of the raiders, but they were not a disciplined force, and they broke and ran every time the riders rode at them.

Ambrose called out to his friend and old weapons tutor. "What do we do next, old friend?"

Phillip mutely pointed upward and made the motions of an archer. The three retrieved their bows and quivers and raced for the steep stairway that led to the ramparts. Soon they were loosing shaft after shaft at the milling horsemen within. Even as they started to harvest the trapped Pechenegs, howls of rage arose from without. The next large body of hard-riding warriors had arrived only moments after the gate had slammed shut!

Gradually more and more men joined Ambrose, Polonius and Phillip on the ramparts, until they were able to loose volleys that made close approach to the gate on either side all but impossible. The nomads trapped within were gradually being dispatched by the archers and the aroused townsmen. Those men of Kiev who couldn't find a place on the ramparts climbed to the roofs of their homes, and loosed arrows, slingstones, spears, and rocks, at the desperate Pechenegs below.

The very ground began to shake before the advance of the main force. Two thousand horsemen, accompanied by their herds of spare mounts, now came into view. As spectators on the ramparts, Ambrose and his companions watched in awe as the horde approached and calmly ringed the town except for the water side, where the bluff and newly-constructed ramparts leading to the river fort denied them access. Only the narrow trails and extensive marshes surrounding the town had prevented the main force of riders from arriving totally unannounced!

The prince watched the efficient warriors prepare to besiege the town, and he turned to his friend Polonius. "By all that is holy! We were almost taken without warning. How in Christ's sweet name did the bastards almost catch us with our pants down?"

Polonius shrugged. "The Pechenegs are veteran warriors. Probably the Rus and Slav sentries at Vitchev Hill were themselves working in the fields, and were caught like us. But an intelligent commander would send many scouts ahead, probably disguised as merchants. Sharp knives and darkness would be enough to silence many of our sentries. As for the rest, look at the size of their horse herd."

"I see it, Polonius, but I do not understand the implications of its size."

"Think, Master. How could the Pechenegs prevent our own sentries from reaching us before they do?"

"Well, as you say, they could leave scouts on the major trails with instructions to kill any riders."

"And?"

"And, Prince, they could then ride like hell's demons are on their tails."

"And how would they then beat our riders they didn't catch, who are prepared to kill their horses to get to us first?"

"By riding horses until they tire, and then switching to a relatively fresh mount, one that has not been carrying a rider."

"Splendid, Prince. It is actually called the Long Gallop. The nomads practice changing mounts at a full gallop from infancy. The full-tilt charge is a favorite trick of the steppe riders. If they have enough fresh horses, they can outrun the word of their coming."

A large enemy camp was set up in the meadow where the

Varangian band had camped only a few months before. Ambrose watched until darkness set in. Though riders swirled near the walls, no further serious attempt was made against the town that day.

⚐

A lone warrior, grizzled with age, and carrying his spear with its head downward as a token of peace, advanced from the main horde. He halted before the gate, and with a deep and guttural voice, he called out loudly in the Slavic tongue.

"Hear us, rulers of Kiev. We are the warriors of the Pechenegs; unconquerable in war, but merciful to those who submit to our power! It is the will of our leaders that this city opens its gates to us . . . If you will send your leaders to bend knee at our leaders feet, we will show mercy and not burn your puny town to the ground. We will make terms that leaves you with your lives, your land, and enough food to see you through the winter. If you refuse our leader's magnanimous offer, we will level your town, sell your women and children as slaves, and graze our herds upon your graves!"

Askold, resplendent in his gleaming armor, stood tall and proud in the tower above the gate. At last he spoke in a booming voice.

"Tell your leaders that I, Askold of the Rus, and joint ruler of all this land, give the Pecheneg rabble four days to cross our lands and move west. If, in five days time, you are not gone from our domains, I will order the Varangians and the Slavs to rise to a man and exterminate you!

No longer do the Pechenegs face isolated villages to bully! We are formed in an indissoluble union of many. You yourself know of the might of my men, for it was Pechenegs whom we slaughtered north of here at the time of the spring planting!"

A growl of anger escaped the lips of the envoy, who had indeed heard of the thrashing the Varangian traders had given an entire horde of his fellow tribesmen. The scowls of many of the mounted troops behind him indicated that Askold's slur had not gone unnoticed.

"You will face a hundred times the force you faced before, for the signal fires you saw on the river have called to arms all men for many days' journey. Even now our armies gather! Even now our fleet is preparing to sail south. We know you must cross the river south of here if you are to escape your enemies. In five days we will close the river crossing to your tribe. Go now, to protect your women and children. Help them across the river, before our ships sail, and our Khazar allies, arrive to destroy you."

With a wave of his gauntleted hand, he indicated the harbor, where, indeed, seventeen karves; those still in harbor and not on a trading expedition, were manned and rapidly moving into mid-river. The current would take them south to the ford that the Pechenegs favored, and where their wagons and servants, women and children, must cross before the fierce Ghuz or Khazar armies reached the eastern bank of the Dnieper.

Askold continued. "Take our hand in friendship and ride west. Hear my words! In five days, we will strike against any of you still in our territory!"

The ancient warrior threw back his head in derisive laughter. While he laughed loudly, his face gave no sign of good humor. Suddenly he snarled at the leaders assembled on the wall.

"Take heed, farmers! It is the way of the world that the Pechenegs take and you give! If you don't struggle, we allow you to live. If you defy us, we destroy you and your paltry towns! Open your gates wide, before my men tire of this game and grow angry!"

In frustration and fury, the enemy watched Askold yawn loudly and turn away from the wall. Surprised at the resistance of this oft-conquered town, with its soft farmers; the nomads felt a stab of fear. Winter was coming soon and their food stores were terribly low because of the harassing they had received in their own homeland from the god-cursed Ghuz and Khazars. They needed shelter and foodstuffs, soon, or their women and children would perish. They had to fatten their animals before winter, but knew that the best of the lands to the west were held by the Magyars, who had in any case already grazed their animals on them before they themselves moved west to fresh pastures.

Thus the two allies, fury and desperation, drove the nomads on, and they prepared to storm the town that they had so often plucked like a ripe apple. Nothing if not seasoned warriors, the battle horde prepared for a siege, setting up their portable *ballistae* and putting men to raise outer palisades and cut lumber for battering rams. It was some satisfaction to the town's people, though small, to see a large body of the horsemen ride back south, already heading back to where the lumbering wagon trains had been left; in an attempt to protect them from the ships and any Slavic bands that might really raise arms against the fierce nomad warriors.

CHAPTER 27.

Kiev Is Besieged.

In the many riverside villages and isolated forest settlements that constituted the domains of Kiev, the people gathered their animals together and turned to the safety of their walled hamlets. Many settlements were indefensible, even against horsemen, and the people fled.

The women and children hid in the forest, and the men marched to the pre-determined gathering points. There, for the first time in the memories of even their most ancient sires, farmers of different clans and tribes banded together. The new blond rulers from the north were harsh masters, and disobedience was ruthlessly punished. Petty differences were put aside.

While the Pechenegs' rapidly rising siege-works effectively cut Kiev off from the sustaining land, the citadel's tenuous connection with the river held. By boat, messengers could easily escape the tightening noose, and reports managed to reach Kiev daily. Of equal importance, fighting men and supplies were ferried in in large enough quantities that the Pechenegs were unable to cut the umbilical cord of Kiev, the twin walls that connected the river fort with the citadel on top of the cliff.

Along the western banks of the Dnieper, the smaller villages lay burnt or smouldering. Their new masters had not had enough time to build up the fortifications, and the existing primitive ones had been easily swept aside by the hordes of mounted raiders desperately foraging for food and valuables.

The Pechenegs were impotent on the rivers, however. They shouted curses at the fleets of Varangian and Slav vessels that cruised the rivers; hauling away foodstuffs and people even as the nomad raiders attacked.

The horde, which relied on its faithful horses to move from area to area, found themselves bogged down in the swamps and wetlands that surrounded the town of Kiev. Those Slavs who escaped attacks on their villages vowed vengeance, and their men, too, moved to the secret river bank gathering places to be picked up by the cruising Viking vessels.

꒡

Ambrose stared down from the bluffs at the bustling harbor fort below. He waited impatiently for Polonius to return from the strategy meeting called by the town leaders. Polonius, because of his specialized knowledge, had been specifically invited. The prince turned to Phillip.

"When does our Byzantine scholar return, Phillip?"

"Patience, Ambrose. He will come as soon as he is able."

"I know, old friend. I guess I am just nervous."

"I would be surprised if you were not, Prince. We face a nation, not just some raiding party. But look, here comes Polonius now."

Ambrose watched Polonius climb the steep steps to the ramparts, and smiled as the Byzantine scholar approached. "Well, Polonius. Out with it! What did you hear at Dir and Askold's meeting?"

"Mainly good news, Master. As reports trickle in from the scattered settlements, it becomes clear that the Varangian military training is beginning to bear fruit.

Many farmsteads and villages have been pillaged, but defensible settlements are resisting strongly, to the surprise and dismay of the Pechenegs. When they raid the larger hamlets, they find no sign of the women and children. Instead, large numbers of well armed and stubborn male defenders wait for them.

From the ramparts and holes in the palisades of dozens of settlements, archers have been able to take a heavy toll of the raiders. Already, warriors stationed aboard the river karves have seriously threatened the ford to the west bank. Though their main fighting force managed to slip across the river, we are making it both difficult and expensive for the Pechenegs to move the tribe's heavy wagons and livestock across to the western bank."

"Then the Pechenegs must be feeling desperate. I understood that Ghuz and Khazars armies were advancing on them. Their only hope is to get their women and children and their herds across the river!"

"Precisely, Master. I suspect that they anticipated a lightening raid, a large haul of foodstuffs, and a quick ride to join their families moving west."

"That's excellent news. And what other reports did you hear?"

"Well, Dir and Askold have assigned me two tasks. Tomorrow,

every carpenter and blacksmith in Kiev will be meeting with the three of us.”

“With the three of us? In the name of all that is holy, why are we meeting with carpenters and blacksmiths?”

“Because, my friends, someone foolishly told Askold that I was an expert in Byzantine siege weapons.”

Ambrose looked sheepish. “Well, Scholar, are you not?”

“It is true that I understand the scientific principles involved, and yes, I have examined the Byzantine weapons closely.”

“So is there a problem?”

“I hope not. Tomorrow we are going to find out. We are going to supervise the construction of several machines.”

“Machines?”

“Yes, Prince. It is our task to design and build Roman ballistae.”

Ambrose thought for a moment. “You mean the giant spear-throwers?”

Polonius smiled. “That’s the one!”

At this point Phillip, who had been listening quietly, spoke up. “Polonius, you said that you were assigned two tasks. You have told us of one. What is the second?”

“In less than a week I must leave Kiev.”

Ambrose looked puzzled. “Leave Kiev? Just where exactly are you planning on going?”

“Well, Dir and Askold have conceived of an audacious plan. They have stripped bare the villages north of Kiev, on the east bank. By so doing, they have managed to cobble together a force that actually outnumbers the Pecheneg forces on the eastern bank.”

“But there must still be strong enemy forces on the east bank.”

“Undoubtedly, but there is also the Ghuz and Khazar threat. The women and children, and the herds, must be protected. The Pechenegs have raided north, but dare not travel too far north in case our allies show up.”

Even now the warriors march to the assembly points. In less than a week the combined forces will march past on its way south.”

“That is wonderful news, but, with all due respect, why are they sending you?”

“Prince, as they move further south, they will seriously threaten the Pecheneg encampment on the east bank.”

Ambrose looked puzzled. “And is this something that Dir and Askold really want to do? Would we not do better to reinforce the men here? By marching south we will be threatening the tribe's women and children who have not yet made it across the river. The Pechenegs will have no choice but to attack, and in overwhelming numbers.

"All true, young prince."

"But if we meet them without the protection of walls, any force we can put together is liable to be sliced to ribbons."

"Prince, where will they get the men from to attack the approaching army?"

"Hmm. I suppose that if the force is enough of a threat, the Khan will have to recall the army that is besieging Kiev."

"Precisely. And to join their families on the eastern bank, the rest of the horde will have to march south and then try to re-cross the Dnieper."

"And?"

"The Ghuz approach from the east, and our men move south. And the men of our fleet will be waiting. The Slavs and Varangians have fortified an island just north of the ford. They wait, with bows, many arrows, and logs. Many, many, logs. Oh, and if all goes well tomorrow, I think that they may soon also have Roman ballistae to play with."

"Logs. We will fight with logs?"

Polonius smiled. "Fight? I think not. We just wait until the wagons and animals are in the deepest part of the channel and committed, and then we let the logs go. The strong current will do the rest." REREAD

* * * * * * * * * * * *

Ambrose grinned in reply. "I see. Why do I get the feeling that you just might be behind that devilishly simple plan? I hardly see why Dir and Askold want you to travel south with the fleet, however. And these ballistae are the ones we are making tomorrow?"

"Correct, my prince! You and I will be designing and making them tomorrow. And they don't expect me to sail with the fleet. I am expected to join the regiment of Slavs we trained this summer and take them south with the army along the eastern bank."

"Our regiment? Why are they going south?"

"Somewhere we will be making a stand. Dir and Askold do not fear the Varangian portion of the skjaldborg will break before even the best of the Pecheneg cavalry, but the Slav levies are another matter. Don't forget, the Varangians will constitute only a small percent of the army's numbers.

Victory or defeat will be in the hands of the Slavs. Dir and Askold feel that a phalanx formation in the front of the Slav line will help them to hold steady."

Ambrose looked thoughtful. "Hmm. It certainly can't hurt. But what is to stop the enemy from outflanking the formation?"

"Good, Prince. You remember the Roman solution to the apparently invulnerable Macedonian formation. And the answer to your question is simple."

"I regret my simple brain cannot find it, sir scholar."

"Normally the phalanx is most effective on flat and open land, where the men can hold a tight formation. We must break Alexander the Great's golden rule, however, and we never, never, fight in open country. We use the forest as a shield, and we pick the site for battle. The Pecheneg cavalry can only destroy us if we give them the opportunity. We must be very careful that we never do."

"Why do we want giant ballistae?"

"If the Pechenegs are smart, they will cover the sandbars and fill the shallows with archers. They could easily place enough bowmen to drive off the entire Varangian fleet. Remember, the nomad force on the western bank alone outnumbers the warriors of the fleet several fold."

"That will not stop the logs."

"No. It may even give us more targets. But I also had in mind a squadron of anchored karves with large ballistae that will shoot well beyond the range of the strongest bow."

"Why not *onagers*? The ammunition would be a lot easier to come by."

"I admit I thought about that. The onagers are much less accurate, however, and there is a terrible vibration when the arm hits the crossbar. The Byzantine army only dares to use the smallest onagers on Constantinople's ramparts, for fear of doing damage to the walls, and those walls are over twenty feet thick."

"Then ballistae it is. And our targets will be?"

"The warriors, if Askold and Dir will it. Personally, I would shoot for the animals pulling the wagons."

"I think I see your point. If just one animal is killed, then the entire wagon halts."

"In fairly deep and fast water. It's possible that a wagon that stops and sinks into the river bottom may not move again, and it would be certainly will be a sitting duck for the oncoming logs. Askold and Dir intend to make the crossing painfully expensive."

"You haven't mentioned yet that the regiment only obeyed your commands this summer because you had the privilege of counting amongst your officers a royal prince and the biggest, meanest drill-sergeant any of them had ever seen."

"The march south should effectively lift Kiev's siege, but I anticipate terrible danger for those foolish enough to go along. My friends, I would never ask it of you. It may well be suicidal."

"It will be if you go without us. Phillip, what say you?"

"Our Greek scholar may be a brilliant theoretical strategist, but he hasn't got the common sense God gave a toad. I don't think we have a choice. We will have to go along and nursemaid him."

Polonius smiled. "If I am to be forced to take simple barbarian officers along with me, well, I must admit, there is no one I would rather take than you two!"

Ambrose playfully threw a punch at Polonius. "Now that you have been lucky enough to recruit two of the best officers on the Dnieper, you better get to work on some ballistae plans. Your commander-in-chief will be expecting them come morning."

Polonius, Ambrose and Phillip met Dir and Askold just after dawn at the street of the blacksmiths. Slaves had risen long before sunrise, and the charcoal fires were already roaring hot. Behind the two leaders came teams of expert carpenters and metalworkers, and behind them came warriors carrying metal rods, timbers, and long lengths of rope. They had only a few days to produce the ballistae, and there was a lot of work to do.

Polonius had stayed awake most of the night, working over the plans. While the basic principles were easy, he had found the details were much more complicated. The designing of the trigger mechanism caused him particular anguish. One idea after another was tried and discarded.

Fortunately, the carpenters and blacksmiths were able to go ahead with the rest of the design. It took Polonius most of the day to design a satisfactory release. Phillip, for his part, helped Ambrose stretch the ropes that the metal arms twisted when the weapon was cranked back. Before sunset Polonius had a single rough but functional ballista completed.

Dir and Askold had come by several times during the day. They were as excited as the developers were. They came back just before sunset.

Dir grinned down at Polonius who was on his back under the weapon. "Well, Polonius, when do we get a demonstration?"

"Soon, Jarl. How goes the battle?"

Dir became sober. "Not well. Today the Pechenegs are filling in the moat on either side of the curtain wall."

"But most of that moat is within range of the Citadel. Surely rocks from on high are discouraging them. Even if they are working near the harbor fort, they should still be in range of the slingers and archers from either the Citadel or the harbor fort."

"They are."

"So why the glum expression?"

"They have managed to round up hundreds of Slav villagers. We are killing our own people."

"God's curses! Jarl, that is a terrible dilemma . . . Now that should do it. Are you ready for a demonstration of our new weapon?"

"Absolutely. If it has enough range, then maybe we can arrange a little surprise for some of the Pecheneg overseers tomorrow.' He smiled grimly. 'I would enjoy that."

Three shields were piled against the log walls of a building some two hundred feet away. Polonius carefully placed a specially-carved spear in the trough, and then jerked down on the pin that held the taut rope.

With the intense pressure removed, the twisted ropes straightened. The twin metal bars snapped forward, pulling the bowstring against the butt of the spear with brutal force. The spear leapt into the air. It wobbled a little, but struck just above the shields. The sharp tip plunged deep into the log it struck.

Polonius watched its flight carefully. "See, Jarl. I looked through these two holes. Each weapon will have to be sighted in. Once it is accurate at close range, then we can test it for distance."

Dir just stared at the shaft that was still quivering in the wall. The spear had struck with enough force to easily transfix one or even two horses.' He grinned. 'Let's try it again!"

"We could greatly increase its range by making a shorter and lighter spear. But I will try it again with a standard spear."

After a minor adjustment to his sighting device, Polonius fired the weapon again. This time the missile flew true. The steel head punched through all three shields, and still drove deep into the wall.

Dir grinned again. "That is beautiful, Polonius. How soon before I can have a dozen of these?"

"The rest is up to your carpenters and blacksmiths, Jarl. I think we can improve the accuracy of the flight by gluing some goose quills on the spears. Perhaps we could ask a fletcher to try and mount some for us. Hmm. That would necessitate a groove running down here.

Other than that, I think that it is ready for production. We can take it apart tonight, and then the artisans can each copy one individual piece. As soon as each component is duplicated eleven more times, we will assemble them, and you will have your dozen."

"Ingenious, Polonius. Absolutely ingenious. After we try a couple of them out on the Pecheneg overseers, we will start mounting them in the karves."

Polonius spoke diffidently. "Jarl, after the blacksmiths complete that task, may I ask them to do one more little job?"

Dir beamed at the scholar. "Of course, Polonius! What did you have in mind?"

The thin Byzantine carefully unwrapped a strange metal object. "I asked a blacksmith today to make this out of some scrap iron. Be careful, the points are sharp."

Dir hefted the strange object. "Is it for throwing? There are enough points that you couldn't miss."

"Toss it on the ground, Jarl."

"Interesting. A point sticks straight up."

"Toss it again."

Bemused, the Rus jarl stooped over, gingerly picked it up, and threw it down a second time. "Again a point sticks straight up. I think you are trying to tell me something, Polonius."

"It is called a *caltrop*, Jarl. Roman infantry used to scatter hundreds of these in front of their lines. They are equally dangerous to man and horse."

"Enough of these could break a full charge, Polonius!"

"The trick only works once, Jarl. Slow-moving infantry can pick them up and clear a path."

"All the better. After we have crippled hundreds of horses, our archers can pick off the men assigned to clear the paths.

Polonius, I will have a thousand of these made up, and I will send them south after the army by our swiftest ship. Would that be satisfactory?"

Polonius smiled. "Eminently, Jarl."

On the third day after the conference, word came that the mainly Slav army on the other bank was in sight. The fort became a whirlwind of activity. The laborious task of ferrying Polonius' Slav regiment across the river was begun, and Ambrose, Phillip and Polonius were ordered to be ready to cross soon after dawn of the following day.

As darkness approached, the three friends climbed to the ramparts that looked over the harbor fort and the river. They stared eastward, until Ambrose broke the silence.

"Look, here comes the last of the karves. Tomorrow, my friends, it will be our turn to cross.

I can see the fires of the encampment. They seem to stretch up and down river for miles. There are so many fires that the clouds above are reflecting the light. Is it possible that our army over there is that big?"

Polonius smiled into the dark. "Actually, each warrior was specifically instructed to make two bonfires, and to make them as close to the shoreline as possible."

Ambrose stared across the now dark waters for a few moments before he responded. "It's pretty damned impressive. If the thought of thousands of enemy warriors pouring south to where they left their loved ones doesn't scare the Pechenegs, then nothing will."

Ambrose's prediction was soon proven right. Within a day the nomads sent most of the warriors south. Enough warriors remained around Kiev to maintain the siege, but not enough for any more attacks. The town's defenses had been far from complete when the Pechenegs had arrived, and only the courage of the Slavs, the reinforcements and supplies brought by the ever-cruising ships, and the great fighting prowess of the Varangians had managed to keep the horde from several times overrunning the critical passage joining the cliff-top citadel of Kiev with its harbor fort.

The narrow passage was a critical link for the town, and the enemy had constantly menaced it. Cutting it would not have directly threatened the citadel itself, but it would have cut the defenders off from their precious river-borne supplies.

CHAPTER 28.

Battle!

Ambrose, Polonius and Phillip joined their regiment of Slav spearmen in the late afternoon, and by dawn the next morning they were marching south. Askold, who had crossed with them, marched as commander-in-chief of the eastern bank army.

The excitement and fear soon faded. Ambrose's world shrank to what he could see. It consisted of dust and sun, rain and aching muscles. Although he was in good physical shape, and had ridden across both the land of the Norse and the Rus, he had never before marched long distances, and certainly never while carrying a massive panoply of military equipment on his back.

Two days into the march a river karve caught up with them. A handsome officer in glittering armor leapt ashore and called out to Askold. "Jarl! I have news for you."

Ambrose, marching with Polonius and Phillip at the head of the Slav regiment, was close behind the commander, and Ambrose strained to hear the conversation.

"Well? Speak up, man. What is the news?"

"I have much to report, Jarl. There are still mounted Pechenegs circling Kiev, but it seems that we may only be facing a token force. All assaults have ended. We can only assume that the majority of warriors have actually gone somewhere."

"Odin be thanked! So just where have the bastards gone?"

"On our way south, we followed the west bank, Jarl. There is much evidence of a large force moving south, and two hours ago we met a courier ship heading north. They had been sent north to report."

"And what did they say?"

"They reported seeing a large force of Pechenegs riding hard for the south. By now they should be approaching the southern ford."

"Are our men there ready to block the crossing?"

"With their lives, Jarl! We have done as you commanded. Foresters have floated hundreds of logs to the island, and several shiploads of spears and arrows should have arrived by now. Dir reports a delay in mounting the spear-throwers on the karves, but he told me to tell you that they are on their way. Once completed, they will travel south non-stop. The ships should pass here either this afternoon or tonight."

Askold still looked concerned. "And do you have reports about the Pecheneg forces south of us on this side?"

"There we had good luck, Jarl.' The couriers found a present for you. The ship commander turned to the crewmen who stood respectfully behind him. 'Bring us the captive."

A dark-visaged Pecheneg warrior was casually tossed over the side of the karve, into the arms of waiting crewmen. The prisoner, still with his hand tied behind him, was frog-marched over to Askold.

The captain smiled. "Last night the courier ship anchored just off the eastern shore. They sent some men ashore to check for any potential dangers. Apparently they found four warriors drunk and camped right in the middle of the caravan road."

Askold stared thoughtfully at the captive. The Pecheneg was obviously injured, for he was caked in dried blood, but he wore expensive armor trimmed in gold.

"Where are the other three?"

"This one must have been the most drunk. In any case, he was apparently the slowest of the four. The others managed to get to their weapons before they could be subdued.' He shrugged. 'They were cut down."

"What have you learned from him so far?"

"Little, Jarl. He does not speak any Slavic tongue we know."

Askold turned around and surveyed the column. He quickly spotted Polonius. "Polonius! You speak more languages than any man I know. Come and see if you can understand this stranger's language."

"Aye, Jarl Askold."

Polonius approached, escorted by Ambrose and Phillip. The lean Byzantine took his turn staring at the battered captive, then suddenly spoke to him in Greek.

"What is your name?"

The man stared mutely at him. Polonius tried the same statement in a dozen different languages. To each the man responded with a shrug, until Polonius tried his very limited Persian. The prisoner responded immediately.

"You finally speak a human tongue. Who are you that you are so thin and dark, yet march with these barbarian scum?"

"I was once a Byzantine scholar, but I spent much of my life as a slave. My masters traveled a lot, and I learned many languages. Now I am a free man, but what I am is not important. What is important to you is what my master Askold wants. If you do not co-operate with him, he will have you killed."

The captive sneered. "I am a Pecheneg warrior. Kill me if you want. I have no fear of death. Allah Akbar!"

"What is your name?"

"Katarz."

"Katarz, I, too, believe in the One True God. I also know that you believe a warrior who falls in battle goes directly to heaven. Jarl Askold, however, will not have you killed by a warrior. The Vikings are a cruel people. You will be slowly tortured."

"I am a warrior! Allah will know the way of my death! I will say nothing."

"Katarz, the women will be allowed to have you as their plaything. First you will lose your manhood, then your sight.

If you still refuse to co-operate, they will remove more pieces of you, one at a time, which they will feed to pigs. You will be so defiled that Allah will never allow you to enter the kingdom of heaven. Are your secrets worth being damned for all eternity?"

The prisoner blanched. "If I do answer your khan's questions truly, what will happen to me?"

"I do not know, but I will bargain for your freedom, if you wish it."

"If I am promised my freedom and a small boat, I will answer your questions freely and honestly. But you must give me your personal word that there will be no tricks."

Polonius turned to Askold. "Jarl, he offers to answer your questions honestly, if you will agree to two conditions."

"I do not know what magic you spoke, Polonius. I expected that this one would hold out for hours even under torture. Truly, I am glad you are on my side. Tell him we agree, Polonius."

"But you haven't heard his conditions yet."

Askold grinned. "It doesn't matter, Polonius. We will agree to anything he wants."

"It is not that simple, Jarl. I have to swear to personally guarantee his safety if he helps you."

Askold sighed. "What are his conditions, Polonius?"

"One. We set him free after he has answered everything you want to know. Two. We let him loose in a small boat."

"Polonius, I do not see a good reason to negotiate. We can have the irons red hot in short order. Soon after that he will beg to tell us anything we want to know."

"True, Jarl, but will you be able to believe anything he tells you? I have been put-to-the-question, and at that time I would have told you anything you wanted to hear. The truth at that moment was anything that would stop the pain."

"Polonius, go ahead and tell him that we are willing to agree to his terms."

"Willingly, but I have to swear that he will be released afterwards, and I think I should say now that I cannot serve a master who would knowingly betray my sworn word."

"Polonius, you are worth ten thousand captives to me! You have already deduced that my word to him is meaningless. You, however, have my word that he will be released as promised."

Polonius turned to the prisoner. "Katarz, I give you my word that you will be released after questioning, if I believe that you are telling the truth. Is that satisfactory?"

"My life is in your hands, Greek. Ask what you will."

"What are your khan's plans for Kiev?"

The man spit on to the grass. "The army was split. A sufficient force will remain to maintain the siege, but there will be no more costly assaults launched."

"And the rest of the army?"

"Has been sent to the tents of our main encampment at the ford."

"Why did your Khan recall the force?"

Katarz shrugged. "The Ghuz are closing on us from the east. To the south the Khazars are busy defending the traders at the cataracts, but we know that eventually they, too, will ride north.

"And what are your master's new plans?"

"The Great Khan has commanded that the entire horde must gather to assist in getting our wagons across the river. We did not expect serious opposition from Kiev, either in taking the town, or in crossing the river. In this, it seems, we were wrong."

"And what of us?"

"The Great Khan had already commanded that when our families are all safely on the western bank, then the horde would push north again.' Katarz smiled tentatively. 'It is hoped that our second journey north will make you more obedient to your nomad masters, but first he intends to destroy your puny army in a lightning thrust north along the eastern bank.

Tell your master that as soon as enough warriors have re-crossed the river, the horde will close on your position. You are all dead men. You just don't know it yet."

Polonius stooped to cut the ropes around the prisoner's wrists. "Jarl Askold, this man needs a small dugout."

"Don't worry yourself, Polonius. I will have someone take care of him."

"It is no problem, Jarl. With your permission, I must take care of it personally."

Askold grinned. "Of course, Polonius, if that is your wish."

Ambrose, Polonius and Phillip continued the slow march south with the Slav regiment they had trained just a few months previously. Some reinforcements arrived by ship and the sick were evacuated, but the march south continued to be slow and tedious. Polonius was thrilled when a supply ship arrived with the caltrops.

On the next day, a small vessel was spotted moving north. It was a sleek ship, and the water around it churned. Ambrose was able to see that it was double-crewed, and both sets of rowers looked like they had been driven to exhaustion.

As soon as its lookout had spotted the column, it had nosed into the bank close to where Askold stood and waited. The commander jumped ashore and quickly made his way to Askold.

Soon shouts could be heard echoing up and down the winding column. "Officers forward! The column is to halt, and officers are to report immediately to Askold!"

In less than a quarter-hour, the army's officers had all congregated at the head of the column. They were very curious, and somewhat apprehensive. The word was that somewhere just ahead of them lay an entire horde of steppe warriors, and the Pecheneg prisoner had boasted that a reinforced force would soon be moving north at a gallop.

Askold faced his assembled officers. Each stood silent, waiting to hear their orders. The big man drew himself up to his full height.

"Slavs. Varangians. This autumn we have faced a mighty enemy, and we have fought together, as one nation. Together, we have already done the impossible. Many settlements resisted the invaders, and they survived. We have forced the enemy to reduce his forces around Kiev itself, and south of here we are doing serious damage to the Pecheneg nation as they try and cross the Dnieper River. The Pechenegs are suffering huge casualties.

One more major task remains to be done. If the Pechenegs are able to break us, then they will be free to ride south, cross again at the ford, and then move north to devastate Kiev. You, my friends, are the only barrier between our loved ones and the savage raiders soon to be riding north.

In less than two days the Pecheneg cavalry could easily be upon us. If we but stand firm, then the invasion of our homeland, and the danger to our loved ones, will be over. That's all I ask of you. You do not have to defeat the Pechenegs. All you have to do is to hold them off, in a location of our choosing. If we can do that, then we have won!

Pray tonight to *Perun* and Odin, and all the other gods . . . We will rest here for the night, and tomorrow we will begin our preparations. I want to see a secure perimeter erected before dark, including a dry ditch . . . Regimental commanders and above will remain to plan our strategy. The rest of you may return to your commands."

⚑

The great orb of the sun, rising slowly from over beyond the mighty Dnieper River, found the combined Slav-Varangian army ensconced in front of thick forest. From the south, several thousand hard-bitten nomad riders rode northward. When they found themselves facing a formation of Slav and Varangian warriors, they paused. Horns blew, and the mighty host formed up for battle.

Both armies took stock of each other. The nomads had managed to get over two thousand mounted warriors across the river to join the raiding party of a thousand, while the combined Varangian and Slav levies numbered perhaps a few hundred more. A horde of veteran steppe warriors faced Slav farmers, seasoned only by a few hundred northern barbarians.

Ambrose stood in the front ranks of the Slav wing. He watched in awe as the huge column of riders smoothly shifted into a massive wedge formation. Ambrose whispered to the faithful Phillip who stood at his side.

"By all that's holy, Phillip. I had no idea that there were so many horsemen in all the world. My knees are weak and my stomach is in knots."

The gruff giant replied as quietly. "You have killed men before, Prince. That is what you will be doing today."

"Aye, Phillip, but they came at me one at a time."

"They will today, too. All you have to do is to remember to kill them one at a time. Let the men around you take care of the rest."

"Thank you, old friend. I have never been so scared in my life."

"You have never faced a formal battle before, either. I will tell a secret to you, Prince, that I have never told another living person."

"What is that, old friend?"

Phillip's mouth showed a hint of a smile. "I've stood in a battle line over a hundred times, and my stomach still does somersaults each and every time. The fear only leaves me once I am actually fighting."

Polonius, nervously scanning the approaching force, spoke. "May God damn all pagans! Would you two look over by the copse of trees on the right?"

Ambrose stared for several moments, and then replied. "I see men, and see the trees. Just what exactly is it that I am looking for?"

Phillip replied for Polonius. "Look, Prince, at the banner. See, it is being blown by a gentle breeze."

"I see a banner of a horse."

Phillip's voice rumbled. "That is the personal standard of the Great Khan of the Pechenegs. That means the mean bastard is here personally to make sure our asses get kicked."

"Does it matter?"

Polonius sniffed. "Prince, the man's very word means life or death to his followers. Cowards today will have their herds confiscated and their entire families butchered. Heroes today will make their fortunes. In the khan's presence his men will fight like demons."

The Pecheneg heavy cavalry was selected to begin the hostilities. Five hundred heavily armored riders spurred their horses forward. Aware of both the Varangian combat prowess and their fanatical bravery, the officers planned to probe the weakest links in the allied army. They rode straight for the Slav wing.

As the horsemen thundered forward, there was clear evidence of anxiety in the Slav ranks. As the cavalry started their advance, hundreds of lightly armored Slavic bowmen retreated to their lines, scattering objects behind them as they moved. When the Pechenegs spurred to a charge, the skirmishers turned and ran for their lives.

The horsemen had probably never expected to strike home against the main force, but the sight of the running men was irresistible. The armored line swept forward like an unstoppable tidal wave.

The Pecheneg warriors were just approaching the slowest runners when the first horse screamed. Suddenly dozens of horses crashed to the ground. Many of the riders were thrown. Some of the Pechenegs died beneath the hooves of their companions' mounts.

The momentum of the charge was totally lost and the survivors wheeled to the right and left. Several dozen warriors lay dead or injured, and the two enemy forces had not yet come together.

The horns sounded anew, and this time dismounted skirmishers advanced from the Pecheneg side. Holding shields high and moving at a walk through the tall grass, the swarthy men of the steppes advanced gingerly.

Ambrose watched the steppe warriors advance and again turned to his companion. "What are they up to, now, Phillip?"

"They know that we planted something in the grass. The bastards intend to find out just what it is."

"Can we stop them from removing the caltrops?"

"No, Prince, but we can make it expensive. Just be ready to drop when Polonius gives the command."

Once the line of skirmishers reached the first injured horse, they quickly ascertained the cause of the problem. Shouting curses at the allied warriors, the men advanced slowly, checking the grass as they moved forward. Behind them, two squadrons of the heavy cavalry rode parallel to the skjaldborg, moving to threaten the Varangian wing. Two more, however, waited restlessly.

Polonius spoke to Phillip. "At all costs, the men must hold their positions."

Phillip looked up and down the rank of nervous men, and called out in his booming voice. "Spread the word! Hold your positions!"

At last Polonius could stand it no longer. "Phillip, signal the archers whenever you think it is time."

"Just a few moments more, Polonius."

The burly thane raised and dropped his arm. Immediately, the Slav war horns blew two short blasts. As one, the three front ranks of spearmen dropped. The suddenly exposed archers filled the sky with shafts.

The Pecheneg skirmisher line first halted, and then grudgingly retreated. They did so in good order, but they had not been able to clear away all the caltrops, and some two dozen of them lay dead or wounded in the grass.

The Khan signaled the light cavalry to advance. These men, lightly armed and mounted on swift steppe ponies, galloped forward. Several hundred horses were injured by the caltrops, but this time the warriors just accepted the punishment and kept coming.

A cloud of them closed on the Slav ranks, and the ranks of spearmen hastily climbed to their feet. As the horsemen neared the skjaldborg, they seemingly panicked. The riders turned and fled by the hundreds.

The ploy, however, was in vain. Askold had carefully chosen the spot by the woods and he intended his men to stand fast where they stood. His orders had been unequivocally clear. No one would budge, in spite of any repeated feints made by their old enemy. The Pecheneg riders neared a second time, shooting arrows and daring the Slavs to break formation and go after them.

Individual Slavs fell when an arrow or spear made it past their shields and armor. Phillip started the litany of battle. "Wounded men to the rear! Second rank, fill the gap!"

Finally realizing that the enemy coalition forces were not going to be fooled into breaking ranks, the Khan ordered a general softening up. Countless seasoned foes had been decimated by the excellent Pecheneg archers. Here, at last, the superb steppe cavalry could show its prowess against the stubborn river people.

The blaring war horns set the giant wheel of archers into motion. In an unending line, the warriors of the horde rode by, launched their arrows, and then passed around again. The Khan, from his vantage point, watched as the Slavs hastily formed military Turtles. Where seconds before long ranks of spearmen and archers had stood, now a series of solid structures had formed, with shields forming both wall and roof. Peppered like a cur that had attacked a porcupine, yet the shield formation prevented most serious casualties.

Finally the enemy blew their own signal horns, and the mounted archers withdrew.

Polonius ordered a single note on the Slav signal horns. The formation rippled fluidly and the 'Turtles' were replaced by the former continuous ranks of infantry. There was a difference, however. Each man in the first three rows thrust forward a huge spear.

The heavily armored lancers advanced next. A sigh went through the Slav ranks. These riders were what the Slavs feared above all else.

Phillip casually strode along the edge of the spear wall. "Dress this line! Get those spearheads up, lads! I want to see a wall of spears that a sparrow couldn't make it through! First rank! Plant the butts firmly. Let the horse do all the work when it hits your spearheads."

The heavy cavalry was on its way, but instead of a skjaldborg, they now faced an impenetrable wall of steel spearheads.

On the left stood the Varangians, arrogant in their strength and bravery. Few Pechenegs rode willingly against them. To the right was the Slav wing. It was the wing the khan had chosen as the weak link. As the khan watched, however, the space between the trees and the dressed ranks suddenly filled with running archers. Hundreds more bowmen raced into the spaces behind the phalanx. Without hesitation, the archers proceeded to loose volleys of arrows high into the air. Their quivers were full, as they had lain hidden in the forest while the nomad riders had emptied theirs.

The Khan raised his arm to prevent the charge, but it was too late. The massed regiments had already started forward at a trot that quickly escalated into a thundering gallop.

The sky was dark from sling stones and arrows. Many Pechenegs never lived to reach the enemy lines, yet their horses, excited by the mad charge, followed the others; never slackening their pace even after their masters tumbled from their backs.

With a tremendous crash, loud enough that the entire earth trembled, the two lines met. Railing at the triple line of extraordinarily long spears that met them, the Pecheneg riders were quite unable to reach the Slavs.

Because of their speed and fantastic mass, the leading riders were unable to turn aside. Those not struck down by the hail of missiles died on the spears. Hundreds of Pechenegs died within a minute, but in their death they weighted down the spears with their dead bodies. Stubborn cavalrymen scrambled over the dead bodies of their own horses and men and found that the Slav defense had been seriously compromised. Their officers, seeing the opportunity, signaled for reinforcements. Hundreds more spurred forward.

Ambrose watched from his position in the line while he hacked at stubborn Pecheneg warriors who crawled over their own dead horses and men to attack the weakening Slav line. The Slavs were fighting heroically, but many in the three lines were down. They were close to being unable to fill the lines and Ambrose knew that when they couldn't, then the horsemen inevitably won. He looked involuntarily towards the fleet that floated on the river nearby. Askold had told the men that the fleet was ready to rescue them if necessary. What he hadn't told them was that the river, a thousand feet away, might as well have been a hundred miles away. Between them and the water was open ground; prime Pecheneg cavalry killing ground.

Finally they stopped coming. The surviving lancers limped back to their own ranks.

Ambrose stepped back out of the front rank and approached the thin Byzantine. "Polonius, there are not enough men left uninjured to do that again. If our line breaks, then we are all dead. What are we waiting for?"

Polonius looked at Phillip. "Weapons-master?"

"I don't think they will hold next time. It is time."

"Then order it."

The Saxon thane turned to the line of men behind him. "Signalers! Sound the retreat."

As the strident new signal reverberated across the battlefield, the archers turned and ran back fifty feet. The phalanx spearmen marched slowly backwards. Once the remaining spearmen had dressed their lines, another signal blared out. The second rank of spearmen pulled on ropes that snaked back towards the ground they had just retreated across. As the wooden planks were withdrawn, a long pit lined with sharpened stakes appeared. The pit was wide enough to prevent a horse from jumping it, and deep enough that a cavalryman would have great difficulty in getting his horse to climb back out . . . and that was if they missed the stakes.

The fresh line of advancing Pecheneg lancers skewered any Slavs who had been slow to retreat, but suddenly the front rank of horsemen found itself pushed into the deep trench. Spears and arrows were rained down on them from the embankment, and many more brave Pecheneg horsemen died.

A messenger, exhausted, ran to stand beside Polonius.

He tried to stand at attention. "Commander!"

Polonius replied. "Speak. What is your report?"

"You were right, Commander. They sent several hundred lancers into the forest behind us in a flanking movement."

"And what happened?"

The messenger grinned. "Great man-traps opened in the forest floor. They fell into the deep pits lined with sharpened stakes, riders and horses both. Bent boughs with spears attached swung at others. Our archers stood in the open and shot at them, but when the riders gave chase, they just found more pits and many, many sharpened stakes. We broke the bastards, Commander! They lost half their number before they broke, but break they did!"

As the Pechenegs attempted to withdraw, Slav skirmishers climbed through the protective ditch and moved forward. They ruthlessly cut down wounded and any others too slow to escape the vengeful axes and swords. They watched the cavalry carefully, however, and were prepared to run at a moment's notice.

The battered Pechenegs reformed in their regiments and squads and Ambrose wondered what he would do next if he were the Khan. He realized that if it was not for the forest, the rear would have been all but defenseless. The cavalry could take care of the foot archers, who needed a skjaldborg for protection, yet the skjaldborg could not defend all sides, at least not with such unwieldy spears. And yet . . . And yet . . . But Polonius had chosen the site carefully, and the Khan, in his arrogance, had not disputed the choice. The forest WAS there, and the archers and spearmen could destroy any cavalry who dared enter where cavalry mass-tactics couldn't be applied.

With no way to flank the enemy, the battle was lost for the Pechenegs. The Pecheneg hope for success would have been to make use of their great mobility, but Polonius had countered that brilliantly.

Now the Khan had a dilemma. Could he leave such a strong force not far from the Pecheneg women and children?

Polonius wouldn't dare advance much further south onto the open steppes in the face of a large army. Flat land favored the integrity of the phalanx, but open land gave the ferocious Pecheneg cavalry much needed mobility. Yet if the khan sent his main force across the river and back to threaten Kiev, then the horde's dependents were in considerable danger.

His train-of-thought was broken when Phillip put a heavy hand on his shoulder.

"You fought well, today, Prince. It may not be over yet, however. Here comes more cavalry - no, it's just a squadron, and it is approaching the Rus wing."

Seeing the horsemen coming, the Slavs retreated to their ditch while hundreds of archers lined up behind the spearmen. The Viking wing, having been ignored all day, just held their ground. Finally one Rus warrior, carrying a white shield and no weapons, left Askold's side and stepped forth alone to parley.

"Pechenegs!' he yelled, 'Askold, leader of our army, wishes to know if you want to remove your dead and wounded. If you wish to so signify, send forth small groups of unarmed men and we will make no further hostile moves."

As one, the squadron of horsemen, driven into a fury by their frustration, spurred their horses into a gallop towards the envoy. At last, here was an enemy that they could touch! The ten lances hit in rapid succession, and the envoy's body was driven back many foot lengths. Ten lances grew out of his supine body.

A great cheer went up from the other mounted warriors. Even the cheers, however, could not hide the commotion that occurred in the combined Varangian and Slav ranks. Within a hundred heart-beats, a blond warrior, naked except for a huge two-handed axe he swung about his head in dizzying circles, climbed through the ditch and stepped forward, alone.

"Odin! Odin!" shouted the warrior, with the madness of the berserker coursing through his veins. Frothing and spitting in his insanity, he yet yelled wildly at the advance squad of horsemen who were retrieving their lances from the corpse of the emissary.

"My brother, an honorable man, lies at your bloody feet! Come then, and meet a warrior, you bloody scum of the earth! Come you ten! See how a man fights! Odin, I come to you!"

The ten warriors, taken aback, bemusedly watched the weird apparition advance upon them. Too late for the front two, they discovered that he was a fanatical fighting machine.

The berserker fought naked only to prove his courage, for he felt armored by his anger and his beliefs. His terrible weapon loped the two from their horses in a single stroke. Scattering then, and swerving, the survivors surrounded the warrior. His long axe, almost the length of their lances, carved great glittering arcs in the air, and cut down a third lancer who ventured too near and whose metal helmet, far from stopping the axe blow, merely slowed it slightly as it smote his helmet. The man's head was crushed like an eggshell.

At last, at a safe distance, a warrior threw his lance so that it transfixed the naked northerner. Without hesitation, the berserker leapt at the man. He struck the amazed horseman right out of his saddle. The remaining horsemen, seeing the transfixed dead man charging next in their direction, forgot their military discipline and fled towards the main horde. The naked berserker lurched after them. He continued to yell in his native tongue as long as he was able to draw breath.

"Come and fight, you cowardly bastards! Odin receive me! Odin! Odin!"

Finally he came to a halt, close to the main body of the horde formation. There he slid slowly to his knees. Even as he fell, a dreadful apparition bathed in his own blood, he held his great axe over his head, and called out to Odin a last time.

The defeated Pecheneg army turned south and abandoned the field. The Slavs and Varangian warriors had won!

CHAPTER 29.

The Varangians Fight at the Ford.

The messenger could be heard long before he could be seen. "Can anyone tell me where Polonius, Canuteson, and Phillip are camped? I am looking for the foreigner Polonius, and his companions Canuteson and Phillip."

The three friends looked at each other. Polonius smiled at his two companions. "I wonder what trouble we are in this time?"

Ambrose responded. "I guess there is only one way to find out.' He raised his voice. 'Polonius and his faithful companions are here!"

Soon the messenger stood over their little fire. "Sirs, Jarl Askold has requested your immediate presence."

The three friends followed the messenger into Askold's makeshift tent. The Rus jarl rose when he saw the men enter. He hugged each man in turn.

"Welcome, Canuteson. Welcome, Polonius and Phillip. Our new empire owes all three of you a great debt. Polonius, without your ideas and your training, the Slavs would never have held. You gave them the tools, and the confidence, to hold against the worst that the Khan could throw against them.

Ambrose and Phillip, you were the voice of Polonius, and it was you two that translated Polonius' brilliant ideas into sound tactics. We are truly in your debt. Please, sit down. I would talk with all three of you."

Askold smiled at the three foreigners from across the little room. "Good news, my friends!"

Polonius spoke for his companions. "We are all ears, Jarl."

"Our scout ships have traveled down-river as far as the ford, and it is clear that the Pechenegs are retreating to there. This little expedition has, in one fell swoop, managed to siphon off enough enemy warriors from the siege of Kiev that the Pechenegs have had to cease offensive operations, and also managed to protect our northern settlements on the eastern bank. Finally, and perhaps most important, we have unequivocally defeated the Pecheneg in open battle.

News of what we have done here will be recorded in song and story, and will entertain Slavs and Varangians for generations to come. We have stood up to the toughest there is, and we have won!

I tell you, my friends, this victory will allow us to dramatically expand both our influence and our borders. Mark my words. Kiev will one day become the hub of a great empire.' Askold grinned. 'And the Rus will be the masters!

I have an offer to make you. Tomorrow I intend to sail south; to join Dir at the next great battle site. We have almost closed the fords to the Pechenegs, and I intend that we hurt them a lot more before we are finished. I would be honored if you would join me there as guests."

Polonius looked worried. "Jarl, surely we are not leaving the army here, leaderless. The Great Khan has lost the battle, but he is not done yet. His army could return to the attack at any time. I do not feel that I can abandon my regiment so far from safety."

Askold smiled. "You, who expressed no interest in being an officer, are one of the greatest, my Byzantine friend. It is right that you think first of your men. Safety, however is not as far away as you think. Before I so much as put one foot on a ship, I will see each and every man of this army embarked and safely on the waters."

"Jarl, with so many of our trader vessels trapped far to the south, we simply do not have enough ships to embark the entire army."

"Quite true, Polonius. But there is an island within sight, that is quite safe from any force without ships. The army can camp there until sufficient ships can be sent to transport them."

"Forgive me for asking, Jarl, but after the island, where are we transporting them to?"

"You see, Polonius, you are a good commander. You think first of your troops . . . even if you never wanted a command in the first place. The answer to your question, however, is simple.

The Slavs will be sent north to strengthen Kiev's defenses. Once the Pechenegs withdraw completely, we will send the villagers home to guard their own lands. There are rumors of other hordes crossing farther north, and I took a calculated risk in moving the army away from its home territory.

As to the Varangians, they will be sent south as reinforcements. The battle there is just warming up.

ᛝ

The karve was anchored north of the deepest channel of the river ford, and just out of arrow range. It floated, one of a line of six. Dir stood in the bow, along with Askold, Ambrose, Polonius, and Phillip. Dir pointed to the two massive wagons now half way across the river.

"Here they come! The fools are going to try again. Signaler, sound the call for logs!

Now watch, lads. First they will send the archers to hold us off."

Even as Dir spoke, more than two hundred riders raced across the sandbar and plunged as deep into the waters as they could. The sky filled with arrows, but all fell short of the waiting karves, though some by less than a hundred feet. One karve, with its sides raised by planking, slid into arrow range. The frustrated Pecheneg archers peppered it, but at some cost. From carefully prepared arrow slits, arrows flew back. Several mounted archers fell, and the riders were forced to retreat a little.

In turn, new Pecheneg crews ran forward with massive wooden beams. In a remarkably short time, several portable catapults were put together. As large rocks started to hurtle into the air, the ship was forced to retreat northward.

Dir grinned again. "They keep trying the same tactic. We know just how close we can get, and the armored ship kills a few of them each time we use it. Then they chase us off."

Polonius looked puzzled. "Jarl, why do they not build permanent catapult emplacements on the sandbars?"

"A good question, Polonius. And the answer is, they did. We landed a couple of hundred warriors late one night, and bad things happened to their precious catapults. Now they dismantle them before dark each day.

But where are our logs? The timing of the next part is tricky."

As he spoke, teams of hard-rowing men in dugouts approached. Behind them, attached with ropes, were massive logs. Dir pointed.

"Gentlemen! Here comes Polonius' 'warriors'. They are even bigger than a Varangian warrior, and a lot dumber, but by all the gods, they can fight! Watch now."

As the front wheels of the first of the massive wagons slipped into the raging water, the first of the logs were pushed into the current and released. Ambrose and his companions watched with interest. The massive log moved only sullenly and slowly, until the main current gripped it. The channel was narrow and relatively shallow, but the constricted water rushed south and took the ponderous log with it. The next crew readied their log, waiting for Dir's command before releasing it.

Dir watched attentively. "Here is where we play a game. When they first started this, we just used Polonius' giant crossbows to kill a couple of the horses. Once the wagons were stopped, it took the very devil to get them moving again. If the archers aren't around, the men take the dugouts and pepper the stupid bastards. If they are, we release the logs. The wagons became perfect targets, and if we get it right, the wagon is either knocked over or pushed into the deeper waters just south. Either way, it's finished."

As Dir spoke, crewmen on each of the half-dozen anchored ships ran to the ballistae mounted in their bows. Several men cranked the metal arms back, while another carefully laid a giant arrow in the trough.

"Here we go, lads!"

The thrum of powerful ballistae filled the air. The darts, really spears with feathers, flew in a low, flat trajectory. Of six shot, two struck. The two horses screamed, kicked a few times, and then died.

Dir spoke again. "Unfortunately they have learned a few new tricks, too."

Teams of Pechenegs on either side of the channel strained on massive ropes, and suddenly a rope barrier emerged from the water. The first log pressed against it and applied enormous force, but several hundred men strained, and the log was brought to a halt.

At the same time, men ran along the wagon hitch. With sharp knives, they cut loose the dead animals. Another team of men, on the western bank, pulled on a massive cable that was attached to the wagon. In spite of the loss of the two horses, the wagon grudgingly moved forward.

Dir turned to his companions. "I must admit, the bastards are good. With that rope in place, we can't stop the wagon even if we kill all of the horses. When the wagon is across, they will pull on a thinner one, retrieve the thick one, and be ready for the next wagon."

Polonius turned to Dir. "Jarl, do you have rags, some oil, and a flint?"

"What are you thinking, Polonius?"

"My people use a substance that burns even under water. It is their greatest weapon. The wagons are wooden. Just regular fire should at least do some damage, and the ballistae give you the perfect vehicle to deliver the fire to the targets."

"By Odin's balls! You are right, Polonius.' His eyes swept the deck, and fell on a warrior working in a wool shirt. 'You!"

"Aye, Jarl?"

"Strip off your shirt, man! I need it. Captain, find me some cooking oil. And I need a fire. Have the cook start one up, immediately!"

The first wagon was now half-way across the channel. Three of its draft-horses were dead, but the cable to shore still stretched taut, and the wagon crept inexorably forward. Four logs pressed against the rope barrier, but it continued to hold.

The powerful ballista on Dir's karve thrummed twice, and the huge darts struck the wagon both times. Sullen flame crept upward and the warriors on the wagon stripped off their shirts, dunked them in the river, and beat madly at the fire.

Dir turned to Polonius. "Well, my friend, it caused trouble, but it looks like they can get it under control. And you can be sure the next wagon will have buckets."

"The problem is not the concept, Jarl. We just have to get more flammable liquid to the target."

"Polonius, tell me you have an idea!"

"Well, Jarl. What about if we removed the spearheads and mounted a bottle instead."

"A bottle filled with flammable fluids! Captain, we return to the island. Polonius has to search through our supplies. We are not done destroying Pecheneg wagons yet!"

"And, Jarl, do you have a really good swimmer in your ranks?"

"Why do you need a swimmer?"

"That rope barrier has to go. I was thinking that a midnight swim might help solve the problem."

On the third day after the Varangians started using Polonius' incendiary spears on the wagons, a Pecheneg envoy stepped out onto the sandbar, carrying a freshly painted white shield.

Dir watched idly from the deck of his command ship, and turned to Askold. "I do believe I recognize that man. Isn't he the one who told us we had to surrender or face having our town brought down around our ears?"

Askold smiled. "I do believe it is. Do we want to talk with him?"

"Sure. Why not?"

"Captain, send a boat for that Pecheneg officer. Bring him aboard."

"Aye, Jarl."

Dir smiled at the envoy as he clambered up the side of the sleek vessel. "I remember you. Have you come to threaten us some more?"

"If I had my way, your town would have been leveled by now, but my master is generous. He is still prepared to negotiate."

"Negotiate. I do not know what we have to negotiate about. Some weeks ago I told you that you had five days to clear out of our territory or we would close the river to you. You besieged our town, and we held you off. You attacked our army in open combat, and we decimated your men. Now we are destroying your wagons one by one, and there is not a damn thing you can do about it. What, exactly, do we have to negotiate?"

"Make no mistake, Rus. Our men are still camped around Kiev, and the Great Khan has more than enough men to send north to overrun your puny walls."

"Of course you do . . . if you wish to abandon your women and children to the tender mercies of the Ghuz and the Khazars . . . and us! We both know that the two armies will be arriving soon. And I have enough men here to keep the ford closed for as long as I wish."

"We cross when we want. You cannot stop us, Rus."

"You may be right, Pecheneg, but we can destroy perhaps half of the wagons when you do, and each crossing costs you more dead warriors. Without the wagons, how will you get the women and children across?"

"Khans of the Rus, I have not come to argue with you. I have come to speak my Khan's words to you."

"Then speak, Pecheneg, and be brief. We have more wagons to destroy today."

"My Great Khan, in his infinite wisdom, has agreed to withdraw the men from Kiev if you, in turn, will withdraw your forces to Kiev. We will cross in peace, and be out of your country in less than a week."

"The Khan is surely generous. Kiev is quite safe from you. It may be that you should worry about the men you left there. The paths through the forest are long and narrow. There is much to fear in the forest, where your gods cannot see you."

"The Great Khan will agree to a peace treaty, guaranteeing that we will not again invade your country."

"Pecheneg, you tried. You couldn't take our main towns. You couldn't defeat us in open battle, and now you can't even get across the damned river! Give me one good reason why we should agree to a treaty."

"Khan, we still have over twenty thousand warriors! If the Great Khan wills it, we have the means to devastate your land."

"Then try it. Burn our towns while the Khazars and Ghuz are raping your women and killing your children. In a few weeks we will be buying your women and children in wholesale lots, for shipment to Byzantium."

"My master told me to tell you that we must cross the river."

"We know that. We also know that you are running out of time."

"Name your price, Khans. If it is reasonable, we will consider it."

"Pecheneg, you are asking us to betray our allies the Khazars. They are good friends to us, even now protecting our fleet of ships south of here. They would be very angry if we let you escape."

The Pecheneg officer took a deep breath. "The Great Khan is aware of all that you have said. What is your price?"

Dir turned to Askold. "Cousin, could we even consider betraying our own overlords?"

"It would be a foolish thing to do, Askold. Only a very large quantity of gold would even make me consider it for a moment."

"And jewels, cousin. My wives love jewels. Very large jewels."

The grizzled warrior looked from one to the other. "Have the two khans yet agreed to a price?"

"What you ask is foolish for us even to consider. The Khazars would punish us severely if we let you go. Perhaps with enough gold we could dissipate some of their anger. We would thus need enough to placate them, to compensate the thousands of widows you have made, and, last, but far from least, to make it worthwhile for us. The Khazars would be very generous if they had found that we had prevented your crossing. And they would sell us the women and children cheap."

"The Ghuz, cousin. You forgot the Ghuz!"

"We dare not forget them, cousin. They have not been civilized by Jehovah yet. They are a savage tribe who would definitely wish to punish us for letting the Pechenegs escape. It would take much gold to placate them."

The envoy gritted his teeth. "I await your answer, Khans."

Askold smiled. "Then let it be this. We trust in the Great Khan's generosity. Any of our people who are held as captives or slaves are to be freed. Have your khan gather what he thinks is sufficient gold to pacify the Khazars, the Ghuz, us, and to compensate us for the deaths and damage our empire has suffered. If the pile is sufficient, then we will cease hostilities . . . oh yes, remind him of our rapacious women.

We will need to see many fine jewels."

"And the peace treaty between our two nations?"

"We do not need one. If you return to the land of the Dnieper, we will finish the job we started in the last few weeks. Do I make myself clear?"

The envoy sighed. "Perfectly. I will carry your words to my master."

ϼ

Ambrose watched the small boat return the envoy to the sandbank. He turned to Dir. "You expect a lot of gold, Jarl. Do you really think the Khan will pay a vast sum?"

Dir shrugged. The Khan can give us half of his treasury and escape, or watch the Khazars and Ghuz take it all, along with the women and children. I think we offer him a bargain."

"What will it take to placate the Khazar and Ghuz leaders?"

Dir grinned at Ambrose. "You are an excellent warrior, Canuteson, and a better-than-average-officer . But your grasp of politics is still a little naive. Polonius, what is the answer to Canuteson's question?"

"It is my guess that not so much as a single copper coin will be paid to either the Ghuz or the Khazars. If the Jarls pull this off, they will probably never again be in a position to have to pay tribute to anyone. Kiev will be feared and respected the length of the Dnieper, and even more men will flock to its banners. It will also, not incidentally, have a large enough treasury to buy men and weapons in time of need."

"Well put, Polonius. I couldn't have said it any better myself. And, knowing that, would you pay any tribute to our Khazar overlords?"

Polonius nodded. "I might consider a generous present to the Khazars."

"Why so?"

"They protect the steppes with the blood of their young men, and could easily cut off the vital river trade if they so wished. It might be expedient to placate the Khagan with a gift, but it would be a gift from equals, not from a vassal."

Dir smiled. "Truly it is said, even in the far north, that the wily Byzantines are the masters of intrigue."

CHAPTER 30.

Kuralla.

The remaining Pecheneg forces around Kiev abandoned their positions and rode south. Dir and Askold, after filling ships almost to overfilling with gold and precious stones, ordered the southern army to return to the city on the bluffs.

The fearsome nomads disappeared as if they had never been. Only the gold, the jewels, the widows and the ashes reminded the Rus and Slav allies that Kiev had faced a mighty nomad horde.

Hard riding scouts returned from the southern steppe country west of the river to report that the Pechenegs were now far to the southwest and attempting to settle on open steppes claimed by the Magyars.

The Rus and Slav allies spent the rest of the fall rebuilding ruined villages and strengthening fortifications. In spite of the rampaging Pecheneg hordes, more Rus families had slipped down the river from the north. As well, boats from other Viking tribes had sailed south on the spring crest. On their return north, seeing that the nomad menace had ended and that Kiev was securely in Varangian hands, some of the adventurer traders chose to winter there.

Kiev's location was extremely fortuitous. It was both an easily defended point just north of the grasslands, and near the point where the Slavs and Varangians traditionally gathered in spring for the dangerous run south through the rapids and across the open steppes. Further, trails from the Far East brought laden caravans to the river bank.

As the newcomers arrived, the Viking warriors and their families were assigned villages to watch over, and billet with for the winter. After the departure of the Pechenegs, there was little excitement. Most of the Slavs in the area submitted with no further resistance. In spite of their sometimes harsh rule, the northerners had proven that they were capable of defending their new subjects.

Ambrose had become concerned about Polonius. He seemed morose and stared at nothing for hours at a time. The prince poured both him and Phillip a horn of ale and sat down beside him.

"Here you are, scholar . . . I must tell you that I am worried about you. You are not yourself. What is wrong?"

Polonius sighed. "You are right, Master."

"Then out with it! We are your friends."

Polonius mumbled. "There has been something much on my mind."

"Then spit it out."

"I had meant to talk to you about it . . .It is just . . .'

He took a deep breath. 'Prince, I would like to discuss a boon with you that has great importance to me."

Ambrose stared at him, surprised at the almost shy quality of speech emanating from this normally silver-tongued mouth.

Bemused, he yet responded. "Speak on, my friend, and if the boon is in my power to grant, consider it given."

Polonius plunged on. "I would ask of you, if you could find it in your heart . . . to sell me the lady Kuralla . . . whom I crave to take as my wife."

Ambrose looked at him very solemnly. Ambrose spoke softly.

"My good and faithful friend, it is with great anguish that I tell you that I cannot accede to your request.

Nay!' he said, for he saw Polonius preparing to grovel at his feet. 'Do not kneel to me, but let me tell you why I say what I do."

Ambrose spoke on. "The cost of Kuralla is not relevant between you and me. I would in any case make that a wedding present to you, yet there is another, more severe problem here."

Suddenly Ambrose swivelled on his bench and turned to face Kuralla. "Kuralla, would you please come and stand before me?"

Ambrose looked into the beautiful woman's eyes. "Kuralla, do you wish to marry Polonius?"

"My lord!' she uttered softly. 'A slave girl has no feelings save that of her master."

"Then let me rephrase my question. Kuralla, if you were allowed to marry, would you marry Polonius?"

"If that could ever be, my lord, I would be honored beyond my imagination."

"Kuralla, what did I tell you the morning after I bought you?"

"That I was free, but I replied that I could not stay in the village."

"And what did I tell you just before we left Novgorod?"

"That I was free, but I chose to follow you here."

Ambrose took her hands in his. "Kuralla you have been both faithful and obedient, yet you have not been a slave since the morning after your father was killed. You may do as you please! I will give you both a dowry and my blessing if you wish it, but you do not need my permission to marry my best friend in the world!"

☞

Polonius explained to Ambrose how he felt about marrying Kuralla. "I am a Christian, Prince, but there are no Greek priests in Kiev. I do not really understand much of Kuralla's beliefs. She mentioned the need to revere her ancestors, as well as various animals, yet she in the same breath mentioned Perun, the god of thunder and lightning."

"Polonius, you could always ask Askold if he would, in his capacity of priest, perform the marriage."

"Yes. I will then pray that the One True God will understand that it could not be a priest of His that said the magic words. I want someone official to say the words, however, so that we can be committed to each other for ever. I have to tell you, Master, it is a strange feeling, for I have never before voluntarily taken on such a commitment, and yet I feel only joy."

As Ambrose and Polonius were walking to the trading factory, Polonius turned again to his friend. "Once, Ambrose, a wise man of the Franks told me that the attraction between a man and a woman is an instinctual one. He said that it provided the woman and her offspring with a life-long willing slave who provides food and security in return for the occasional grudging use of her body. I can only say now that the wise man had obviously never known such a woman as Kuralla!

While I know it to be true that marriage provides benefits for the woman that she otherwise might not have, yet the man is in turn provided a willing servant, who, after a long day of laboring on his behalf, then keeps him warm at night. Nay, more! A wife is a friend and companion, to share all of one's life with."

Polonius and Kuralla had a simple marriage ceremony, and Ambrose was more pleased than words can say that most of the settlement came to see them wed. As Kuralla was now considered the free daughter of a Slav chief, even the local Slavs paid her the compliment of coming. Some even came from a considerable distance to pay their respects.

After the ceremony, Polonius and Kuralla spent some time alone in a little house that Ambrose, Phillip, Polonius and some hired hands had built in haste. Several days passed after their marriage before the happy couple stepped forth.

Polonius sat at a table in a shop which sold mead to the merchants and soldiers of Kiev. The three had put in a long day at the trading factory, and were taking a well-deserved rest before heading home; Ambrose and Phillip to their shared quarters, and Polonius to the little house he shared with Kuralla. The thin Byzantine looked across at the Saxon prince.

"Ambrose, now that the Pechenegs have fled and the trading factory is functioning, what are our plans?"

Though they could not be seen from where they sat, Ambrose knew that several of Gunnar's river karves floated at anchor off their private dock located directly below the bluff. It was less than a year since the Pechenegs had attacked, but the town, and the trade, had grown enormously.

The Novgorod post had sent several ship-cargoes south on the spring floods, and two more arrived shortly after, having come directly from Gunnar and the Rus tribal lands. Ambrose was hard-pressed to contract adequate crews to deliver the cargoes to the waiting merchants in Constantinople. The river settlements absorbed more and more Vikings. The empire of Kiev grew daily. Settlement after settlement of Slavs bowed to the fierce Varangian warriors, and Varangian traders were quickly becoming masters of immense territories.

Ambrose thought about Polonius' question. "Polonius, the weakest link in Gunnar's trading chain that stretches from the Varangian to the Black Sea is the Constantinople link. There, wily Greek merchants take delivery of the northern goods, and sell the goods on consignment for Gunnar. In return, they buy for us the commodities eagerly sought after in the north.

The ship captains then bring the payment, or cargoes that Gunnar has in turn contracted for, across the Black Sea and back up the Dnieper River. Now that we have established a permanent trading post in Kiev, it is this trading factory that receives the cargo or payments from the south.'

Ambrose looked across at Polonius and Phillip. 'I feel, my friends, that altogether too much of the profit doesn't make it back up-river. I know that the Khazar and the Byzantine authorities take their prescribed amount, but they are generally scrupulous in their taxation."

Polonius smiled. "I suspect, Prince, that they have no wish to kill a goose that lays golden eggs for them."

Ambrose replied. "It seems to me that the Greek merchants are taking altogether too big a cut. Still, Kiev is the key to the trade. Someone has to stay here and ensure that the ships of Gunnar are able to sail north or south, as needed. Someone has to ensure that provisions and funds are available."

Polonius sipped on his horn of mead. "I think, Master, that you are telling me that Kiev is going to be our base of operations, at least for the next little while."

"Polonius, I think that this post is the key to the river trade. If Kiev falls, the already dangerous run across the steppes would be far harder. We promised Gunnar that we would take care of his merchant house on the southern rivers. I can see no better place to do this from than right here. This is a growing town, and I think we are in an exceptional position to grow with it.

Are you thinking that we should head south to Constantinople? It is true that we need to eventually do something about our dishonest agents there. Far too much of the profits seems to stick to their greedy fingers."

"No, Master. At the moment I prefer the rustic serenity of Kiev to the excitement of Constantinople. Perhaps one day it would be nice to visit . . . but not now. I am well content here.

Ambrose turned to Phillip. "What say you, Sword--master? What are your thoughts?"

"To honor our commitment to Gunnar of the Rus, to try and keep you out of trouble . . .And to see you safely home one day."

Ambrose looked at his two companions fondly. They were an odd trio, yet each complemented the other. Together, he felt that they were an unbeatable team!

"Well then, my friends. Let us toast to our future in Kiev. One day I must return to my brother's land . . . but that's in the future sometime. Let us settle here a while, and make Gunnar proud! My friends, a toast! To the traders of Kiev!"

APPENDIX I

CHARACTERS

ALDRICH: (Fictitious) is one of the Saxon officers killed when Ambrose is captured by Viking raiders.

AMBROSE: (Fictitious) Anglo-Saxon bastard prince of Wessex, he is but a youngster when a Viking raid makes him captive. In turn, he was slave to Canute the Dane, and then trader for Gunnar of the Rus. After considerable adventures, Ambrose becomes a trader of Kiev, helping to organize the river trade from Gunnar's domains in the north to the city of Constantinople in the south.

ANNA: (Fictitious) A young Saxon slave of Canute's, she is Ambrose's first lover. As she is pregnant, Ambrose must leave her behind to save Phillip's life.

ASKOLD: He, with his cousin Dir, are the Rus leaders who left Novgorod to settle at Kiev, a city they feel will be best able to control the Russian-Byzantine river trade. Under their leadership the Dnieper River region comes under Varangian control.

BJOURN: (Fictitious) A drunken lout who challenges Ambrose to combat at the gathering at Lake Ladoga.

BOSK: (Fictitious) A servant of Gunnar.

BOTHI: (Fictitious) A cousin of Rurik, he holds a fief near Novgorod, and rules with unnecessary cruelty. Ambrose buys Kuralla from him to save her life.

CANUTE: (Fictitious) Ambrose's Danish master, he treats Ambrose as an adopted son, and arranges that Ambrose and his party will be given refuge in Sweden.

CARL THE BRAVE: (Fictitious) Father of Gunnar of the Rus.

DAEL: (Fictitious) is Ambrose's aged tutor, who is killed by the Vikings when Ambrose is captured.

DIR: See ASKOLD.

EADWARD: (Fictitious) He is one of the Saxon officers under Phillip who are killed when Ambrose is captured.

ERIC THE ROUND: (Fictitious) He is the chief of the isolated Norwegian village where Ambrose, Polonius and Phillip land after fleeing Denmark.

ETHELBALD: Eldest son of Ethelwulf. He seized the throne in his father's absence, but agreed to let Ethelwulf rule the kingdoms of Kent, Essex, Surrey, and Sussex. He ruled from 858 to 860, when he died suddenly.

ETHELBERT: He was crowned king of Wessex upon the death of his brother Ethelbald (860). He re-united the subject kingdoms with Wessex. He died in 865, and was succeeded on the throne by ETHELRED.

GUNNAR: (Fictitious) Head of a great Swedish trading House, he owed a debt to Ambrose's former master, and paid it by allowing Ambrose, Phillip and Polonius to act as traders for him on the Russian River systems.

HAMMAR: (Fictitious) One of Gunnar's karve captains.

HANS: (Fictitious) He is the steward of Gunnar of the Rus.

IVAN: (Fictitious) A Slav peasant who was declared outlaw by Bothi. He wounded Phillip, but Ambrose spared his life.

JORN: (Fictitious) The son of Canute, who was some years earlier killed in a skirmish in Frankland.

KELL: (Fictitious) Is the Norse blacksmith.

KATARZ: (Fictitious) Is the Pecheneg prisoner captured just after the siege of Kiev.

KIARR: (Fictitious) The eldest of the village youths in the Danish town where Ambrose is held captive.

KURALLA: (Fictitious) She is a Slav chieftain's daughter whose village defies Bothi. Her father is tortured and killed, and she is about to be given to the warriors when Ambrose purchases her to save her life. After Ambrose abuses her, she marries Polonius.

LATHAM: (Fictitious) He is the Norse bowyer.

LARS: (Fictitious) He is the son of LIEF THE DRUNKARD. It is he who beat Philip almost to death.

LIEF THE DRUNKARD: (Fictitious) The cruel Danish master of Phillip. It was he who offered Phillip up as a sacrifice to Odin.

OLAF: (Fictitious) He is the portly and influential Slav at who grudgingly agreed to share power with Dir, Askold and the other colonists when they arrived at Kiev.

PHILLIP: (Fictitious) A giant of a man, he is a thane and has appointed himself guardian of Ambrose. Where-ever Ambrose goes, there will be Phillip. His great goal in life is to protect his prince and get him home.

POLONIUS: (Fictitious) He is born to noble Byzantine parents, and given an excellent education. When his family has financial reverses, he and his sisters are sold into slavery. He is taken to Lombardy, France, and eventually Frisia. There, he chances to meet Ambrose and Phillip, and has adventures with them that take him to Norway, Sweden, and the Ukraine.

RAGNAR: (Fictitious) He is one of Bothi's lieutenants.

RURIK: He is the Rus chieftain that led the expedition to Novgorod. Once settled there, he becomes ruler.

UIGBIORN: (Fictitious) He is the veteran warrior who undertakes the training of the village boys in the town where Ambrose is held captive.

APPENDIX II

Glossary

A-Viking: Go raiding.

AEGIR: Was the god of the sea. He was a personification of the ocean. He caused storms with his anger and it was said a ship went into "Aegir's wide jaws" when it sank.

ANGLELAND: For my purposes, it's England.

ATHELING:: An ATHELING was a royal prince. The Saxon kings were chosen from amongst their ranks by the WITAN, or council.

BALLISTA: Sometimes called a bolt thrower, it was an ancient military engine for throwing stones or a large dart, using torsion springs made of rope.

BONDI: Was a truly free and land-holding farmer. From this class came many of the traders and hunters, sailors and raiders.

BRETWALDA: or over-king, was one of the kings of the various Angle, Saxon, or Jute kingdoms who was so much more powerful than the others that he was officially recognized as being the 'chief' king of the entire island.

A **BUCKLER** is a shield.

BURH: A Saxon fortified Great Hall, which belonged to an Ealdorman or the king.

CALTROP: A sharp metal object made up of two or more sharp nails or spines arranged in such a manner that one of them always points upward. It was used to impede horses or infantry.

COMITATUS: An armed escort or retinue serving a leader.

CHURL: A peasant. His property was guaranteed, but he had to farm and provide military service.

CONSTANTINOPLE: The capital and chief city of the Byzantine Empire. A city of possibly half a million people, it was heavily fortified. It was also a very important trading center. The Vikings just called it 'big city, or Miklagard.

DRAGON SHIP: The largest Viking warship, it was up to 160 feet in length, and had up to 72 oars. It could carry a crew of up to 300.

EALDORMAN: A nobleman next in power to the royal princes. The Saxon kingdom of WESSEX was divided into shires, and an Ealdorman was in charge of each SHIRE. It was the Ealdorman who called out the FYRD, or local militia.

FIDLA: A Viking fiddle.

FRANKLAND: The land of the Franks. Under Charlemagne, this included modern France, and Germany, and a good portion of the rest of Western Europe.

FREEDMAN: Generally a THRALL who had bought his freedom, he was still somewhat dependent on his former owner to champion him.

FYRD: Militias made up of THANES and churls. For every five hides of land, one fyrdman, mounted and armed, was obliged to answer the call-to-arms.

HOLMGARD: Viking name for Novgorod.

HOLMGANG: A ritualized duel.

JARL: Important Viking land-owners, they acted as priests and judges.

KARVE: Viking utility craft with a draft of less than three feet.

KHAGAN: Khazar King.

KHAN: Leader.

KHAZARS: A strong nomad tribe that was quite supportive of trade, and controlled the territory where the Dnieper River enters the Black Sea.

KIEV: was a town just north of the open steppes on the Dnieper River. It was apparently seized by Dir and Askold sometime soon after 860 A.D.; after the death of three brothers who had ruled there.

KNARR: is a short, deep-keeled and beamy vessel that could carry up to 15 tons of cargo. Unlike most Viking vessels, it relied mainly on sails rather than oars.

LOKI: He is the god of mischief, who liked to play tricks.

A **LONG-SHIP** was a Viking sea-going vessel somewhat smaller than the dragon ship. It was up to a hundred feet in length, and carried up to 200 crewmen.

MARCH: A MARCH is a border region; one that may need to be defended.

MIKLAGARD: or NEW ROME is the Byzantine capital of Constantinople.

MJOLLNIR: Thor's hammer.

NARVESUND: The Viking name for the Straits of Gibraltar.

NIGHT: The Saxons counted days by referring to the 'nights'. Thus a 'week ago' was a 'seven night'.

NORN: Supernatural beings who were often represented as three maidens who wove the fate of men.

NORSE: Norwegian.

NOVGOROD: A town where legend has it that Rus settlers were invited (circa 860 A.D.) to come and rule, in return for their military protection.

ODIN: Viking god of wisdom and war.

ONAGER: A Roman-style rock-throwing catapult that uses the tension of twisted rope to hurl a single beam against a padded cross-beam.

PERUN: The Slavic god of thunder and lightening.

PONTUS EUXINUS: Is the Black Sea.

RAGNAROK: In Norse mythology, the time when the giants were supposed to come and destroy the world as men knew it.

RUS: I am presuming that Dir, Askold, and the majority of the warriors were Rus. When I am sure that I am referring specifically to a Rus warrior, migration or leader, I will use 'Rus'. I use the word 'Varangian' to refer to any combined forces, even if the majority of them is composed of the Rus tribesmen.

SAX: A Viking or Saxon long knife.

The **SEVEN CATARACTS** were on the Dnieper River, and they were a major problem for boats going up or down river.

SHIELDBURG: Turtle formation.

SKAGERRAK: The narrow area between the coasts of Denmark and Sweden.

SKJALDBORG: Viking shield-wall.

THANE: A Saxon nobleman.

THING: The Viking assembly of free men that acted as a council.

THRALL: A Viking slave.

ULL: The Norse god of archery and the hunt. He was called upon for help in duels.

VARANGIAN: I use it to mean the various Viking tribes that traveled the Russian rivers. The Rus were but one of the Varangian tribes.

VIKING SEA: Baltic Sea.

WERGELD: Money paid as compensation for injury inflicted on another.

Royal Seat at WINCHESTER: Ethelwulf's (839-858) capital was at Winchester, though the royal court customarily traveled throughout the kingdom, staying at various royal estates for carefully circumscribed periods of time.

The **WITAN**, or Council, had the right to choose the next king from amongst any of the royal ATHELINGS, or princes. The usual tradition, however, was for the council to choose the eldest son.

WYK TE DUURSTEDE: A major port of the Frisians. While conquered by the Franks and then attacked by the Vikings, it was still considered to be a major port in Alfred's time. It was also involved in the slave trade.

APPENDIX III

The History of Wessex, of Russia, and of Ambrose and his Son and Friends in the Ninth and Tenth Century AD.

Historical facts are in plain text.
Fictional stories in this series and comments are in italics.
Parts specific to this story are in bold.

793: First recorded attack by (Norwegian) Vikings on England.

832-865 AD.: Danish Vikings attack East Anglia, Wessex, and Kent.

838: Cornwall surrenders to Wessex.

845: The king's mistress gives birth to AMBROSE.

849: Alfred the Great is born.

850: Vikings winter in Kent for the first time.

853: Alfred is sent to Rome where he is made a Consul by the Pope.

855: Ethelwulf, king of Wessex, takes his son Alfred to Rome again.

856: Ivar the Boneless and Olaf the White take Dublin.

858: Ethelwulf dies. Ethelbald becomes king.

(Trader of Kiev)
860: *Ethelbert becomes king. Vikings sack Winchester before being driven out of Wessex.* Ambrose and Phillip are enslaved in a raid on the coast of Wessex.

861: *Pope Nicholas sends envoys to Constantinople to investigate Photius' ascension as patriarch.*

862: Rurik, a leader of Varangian Rus Vikings, is invited to rule at Novgorod.

Ambrose, Polonius and Phillip arrive in Sweden after escaping from Denmark. Pursued by their former captors, they hurriedly agree to go south with Rurik and his Rus tribesmen.

863: Dir and Askold, Rus jarls, take over the Slavic town of Kiev. Nb. There seems to be considerable debate about both this date and whether Dir and Askold actually really existed. After setting up a trading post in Novgorod, the friends join Dir and Askold's force going south to Kiev.

864: The Pechenegs, a savage steppes tribe, attacks Kiev. Only with Polonius' expert help, and the fanatical fighting bravery of the Vikings, do they survive. An attack on the Pechenegs at their most vulnerable point not only ends the siege, but forces the Pechenegs to pay to cross the Dnieper River.

(Emissary to Byzantium)
865: Kent is invaded by a Viking force and Danegeld is paid for the first time to stop the destruction. The Great Army (Danish Vikings) arrives in East Anglia from France.

Dir and Askold lead a combined Slav and Varangian force against Constantinople because of a perceived injustice. With both the Byzantine fleet and army away, they manage to do considerable damage, although they never seriously threaten the city. On the way home, a savage storm sinks many of the Viking and Slav ships. Meantime, Kuralla is kidnaped in Kiev. That there was an attack by Varangians, and a storm, within a few years of this date seems inconvertible. Since the Russian Primary Chronicles set the date somewhere between 863 to 867, I arbitrarily assigned it to 865.

866: Reign of Ethelred in Wessex. The Great Army seizes York. Ambrose and Polonius are sent by Dir and Askold as official envoys to Constantinople. They return north to find word from Kuralla waiting for them. The friends rush north, free Kuralla, turn around, and travel again to Constantinople.

After attempts by Basil to involve them in a plot against the emperor, Ambrose, Kuralla, Polonius and Phillip sail for Wessex. Basil, aware they know altogether too much, sends agents after them.

(Southern Journey)

Basil is told by the Byzantine emperor, Michael III, to divorce his wife so he may marry Michael's mistress.

Bardas plans a sea campaign to retake Crete. Michael has Basil kill Bardas.
Michael adopts Basil and makes him junior emperor.
Ambrose and his friends are captured and enslaved by Muslim pirates operating out of Crete. Polonius' skills allow them to break out of their prison, and they escape to the dubious safety of a Byzantine Fleet. When they realize one of Basil's agents recognizes them and intends to kill them, they flee to Egypt, where they join a caravan heading west.
The Byzantine admiral harries them across North Africa, but Ambrose and his friends do manage to strike back and damage the Byzantine ships. Ambrose then finds a Muslim slaver to transport them to Calabria. Attacked and hunted, the friends finally cross the border from Calabria to Benevento.
Ambrose feels that they are finally safe.

(Journey Home)

The friends start north. Ambrose and his friends pay a visit to Admiral Demetrious in Naples. They escape and make it back across the frontier just ahead of vengeful Byzantine soldiers.

Ambrose makes it to Rome, where he meets Pope Nicholas. He and his friends then head north for the mountain pass to France. They arrive after the pass is closed for the winter, and must spend the winter in Aosta.

867: Aelle, king of Northumbria, is killed trying to retake York.

Basil 'the Macedonian' kills his own sponsor, Michael III, emperor of Byzantium. (September)
Ambrose and his friends survive an attack by assassins, and in the spring they head north into the mountains where they

are captured and enslaved. After Kuralla rescues them, they reach France and relative safety. They reach Paris and meet the king. Then they head for Calais and a ship to England. The Vikings, however, are raiding along the coast. Finally, after many adventures, they reach Calais and Phillip finds a captain willing to risk the dangerous crossing.

867: Finally, Ambrose and his friends arrive in England, where Ambrose is welcomed back to the court. Ambrose meets a beautiful girl and falls in love.

(Warrior of the King)
868: The Great Army occupies Mercia. King Ethelred and his brother, Alfred, ride north to support Burgred of Mercia. The Vikings are besieged at Nottingham, but Burgred decides to pay Danegeld. The West Saxons go home.

Alfred marries a Mercian noblewoman - Ealhswith. Ambrose and his companions return north and join the Great Army as spies. After finding out the Vikings are going north, they flee. Ambrose is wounded and nursed by his loved one. The Great Army pursues, and catches up. Strangely, the attack is called off.
Ahmad ibn Tulun, a Turk, is appointed by the Caliph to rule Egypt.
Pope Nicholas the Great dies.

(Gretchen; Future Princess)
Gretchen and her father head south for Wessex and her marriage. She is kidnaped and taken to Wales.
In Wales, Vikings attack the group, and Gretchen is taken to the Viking stronghold of Wexford in Ireland. Ambrose visits Wexford, but is unable to free Gretchen.

869: The Great Army returns to York in the north for a year. Ambrose attacks the Viking ship carrying his beloved north. They are finally re-united.

870: Danes kill King Edmund of East Anglia, then invade Wessex under the Danish leader Halfdan.

871: Alfred becomes king. After fighting nine battles, Alfred pays
　　　 Danegeld to buy peace for five years.

873: Ivar the Boneless, 'king of Dublin and York', dies in Ireland.
　　　 His brother, Halfdan Ragnarsson, becomes king in his place.

874: Edward, son of King Alfred and future king, is born.

(Alfred the Great; Viking Invasion)
875: Alfred takes out a small fleet and routs seven Viking ships.
　　　 (Nb. For dramatic purposes, I arbitrarily moved this event to
　　　 the following year, where I tied it in with Guthrum's
　　　 invasion.)

876: Danes under Guthrum break their word, slip past Alfred and
　　　 seize Wareham.

877: Guthrum agrees to a truce, but slips away to Exeter, which the
　　　 Danes fortify.
　　　 After a Viking fleet is dashed on the rocks in a storm, the
　　　 Danes agree to withdraw.
　　　 Halfdan Ragnarsson is killed in Ireland fighting Norwegian
　　　 Vikings.

878: Guthrum, a Danish chief, rides south across the Wessex border
　　　 in winter.
　　　 Alfred at first hides in the forest of Selwood.
　　　 A second Viking army, led by Ubbi Ragnarsson and
　　　 invading from Wales, is defeated in Devon.
　　　 As spring approaches, Alfred builds a military camp on the
　　　 island of Athelney.

　　　 Battle of Edington: Alfred's forces meet the Vikings here in
　　　 May. The Danes break and run to Chippenham.
　　　 The Saxons blockade the Danes within their fortress of
　　　 Chippenham for 14 days.
　　　 At last Guthrum surrenders and agrees to be baptized.

879: Guthrum takes his retreating army to East Anglia, where the men eventually settle down.

882: Alfred fights a battle against four Danish ships.

883: Halfdan dies. Guthred is recognized as king of Jorvik.

884: Ethelflaed, daughter of Alfred, marries Ethelred of Mercia.

(Alfred the Great: King's Revenge)
885: A Danish army crosses to England and besieges Rochester.
Alfred relieves the city before it falls.

885: Later that summer Alfred fights a naval battle at the mouth of
the Stour River. He takes all 16 enemy warships.
Guthrum breaks his treaty. He gathers every Viking vessel
and attacks Alfred's laden fleet. He wins.
Alfred calls up his entire force and marches on London. He
takes it and garrisons the city.

886: Alfred signs another treaty with Guthrum, where he gets
London and control over part of Mercia.

889: Edgar, son of Ambrose and Gretchen, is born.

891: Danes in France suffer two serious defeats.

(Alfred the Great; Young Edward)
892: Five thousand Danes land in Kent and seize an unfinished fort
at Appledore. A second fleet follows, led by Haesten, and
lands at Milton Royal. Alfred arrives with his army, drives
Haesten away, and then moves against the Danes at
Appledore.

893: Haesten's fleet sails away, to Benfleet, and is eventually joined
by the second, larger fleet. The Danes then raid deep into
Hampshire and Berkshire. Edward, son of Alfred, inflicts a
major defeat, and then chases the Danes across the Thames.
After being forced to surrender, the Danes give hostages and
depart. The Danes of Northumbria and East Anglia send two
fleets to Dorset as a diversion. Alfred rushes to the west,
while Edward marches on Benfleet. Edward wins a great

victory.

The Danes gather all their forces and march along the Thames again. They are besieged, break out, gather fresh forces, and try again. Besieged at Chester, the Danes break out yet again and flee to Wales.

Late summer, 893: Edward, Ethelred, volunteers from the London garrison, along with reinforcements from the West Country, gather and march on Benfleet. The Viking army is away raiding, and the Saxons take the town.

All Danes now gather at Shoebury in Essex. They march west to the Severn River. They build a camp at Buttington, in Montgomeryshire. Though besieged, the Danes break out and make it back to Essex.

Early autumn 893: The Danes in Essex march without pausing along the old Roman Watling Road, into Cheshire, where they seize the tun of Chester. Besieged, the Vikings break out yet again, though they suffer heavy losses. They flee to Wales.

Spring 894: The Danes split up and flee back to Essex via different roads.

Winter 894: The Danes sail up the Lea River and build a fort. London men attack, but are repulsed. Alfred arrives and guards the peasants who harvest the local crops. Alfred then moves his army to the mouth of the river, where he builds twin forts to blockade the Viking fleet. The Danes abandon their ships and ride north and west, to Bridgnorth in Shropshire.
Athelstan, future king and son of King Edward, is born.

895: In the spring the Vikings sneak back to Essex or move to Northumbria or East Anglia.
Guthfrith, king of Northumbria, dies on August 24.

896: *Sitric Ivarsson dies.*

(Edward the King)

899: King Alfred dies. Ethelwold seizes two royal estates and
kidnaps a nun. Faced with an army under Edward, he flees
northward. The Danes of Jorvik (Northumbria) accept him as
king.

902: Ethelwold arrives in Essex with a Northumbrian fleet, and the
Danes there submit to him.
The Norse are expelled from Dublin. Ingimund attacks
Wales. Driven out, he settles on the Wirral Peninsula with the
permission of Ethelflaed, since Ethelred is sick. (While the
exact date is in doubt, the most likely year of this event was
in 902.)
Elfweard, second son of King Edward, is born.

(Introduction to 'Ethelflaed, 'Lady of the Mercians')

903: Ethelwold convinces Eohric of East Anglia to join him, and
together they raid Mercia and Wessex as far as Cricklade and
Braydon before retreating. In retaliation, Edward gathers his
fyrdmen and ravages the Viking lands as far north as the
northern fens. He then orders a retreat, but the Kentish
fyrdmen are slow to obey and the Danes catch up with them
on December 13. Ethelwold and Eohric are killed on the
Danish side, while Sigehelm, the Ealdorman of Kent, falls on
the other side. Both sides suffer serious losses. This is known
as the Battle of the Holme.

(Ethelflaed, 'Lady of the Mercians')   (902 to 919)

905: The Norse under Ingimund demand land and the old fortress of
Chester. When their demand is rejected, they revolt and
besiege Chester. Ethelflaed provides extra fyrdmen and the
garrison is able to hold the Norse off.
Edgar is Kidnaped by Ingimund and Ambrose goes after his
family in Hitchingford.

906: King Edward concludes a truce with East Anglia and
Northumbria, and probably pays Danegeld.

907: Ethelflaed refortifies Chester.

909: Ethelflaed & Edward raid Danish East Anglia and bring back the body of St. Oswald.

910: The Saxons and Mercians defeat and kill joint Jorvik kings
Eowils and Halfdan II at the Battle of Tetenhall. Ethelflaed
builds the fortress at Bramsbury.

911: Ethelred dies.
Ethelflaed is chosen by the Witan as 'Lady of the Mercians'.
Edward annexes London and Oxfordshire.

912: Ethelflaed builds two more burhs along the Welsh border - along
the Severn River.
1. Bridgnorth - main crossing point to Wales.
2. Scargeat- location is unknown. Probably upriver north and
west from Bridgnorth.
Edward takes his army to Essex, builds a fortress at Witham,
and receives submission from Essex.
Some of Edward's supporters moves to the burh of Hertford
and work on it.

913: Danish forces at Leicester look west and see two new burhs:
Tamworth and Stafford.
Danes march south to the village of Banbury, joining forces
with Danes from Northampton for a coordinated attack. The
Angles meet them in battle and defeat the Vikings.

914: Ethelflaed fortifies the largest town south of Danish
Northampton - Buckingham.
She builds a fort on either side of the River Ouse.
Danish armies of Northampton and Bedford submit to
Ethelflaed's army at Buckingham. Jarl Thurcetel submits.
A Viking army arrives from Brittany, led by Ohter and
Hroald. They land in the Severn estuary. They go inland, but
the men of Hereford & Gloucester meet them and put them to
flight.
The Vikings finally leave in the autumn.
A Danish Viking, Ragnald, seizes power in Northumbria after
Tetenhall, and defeats the Scots in the First Battle of
Corbridge in 914.

915: This allows Edward to establish a fort at Bedford, directly

across the Ouse from the former Danish camp.
Ethelflaed now had a nearly straight line of forts from
Chester to Hertford.
There are two gaps. Ethelflaed closes the Mersey gap with
several more burhs.
914 - Eddesbury. Warwick.
915 - Runcorn.

916: Edward builds a fort at Maldon.
Ethelflaed sends her army into Wales. An abbot had been
killed. The army destroys a town and captures a Welsh king's
wife.

917: Ethelflaed signs a treaty with two Scottish kings, both called
Constantine, insuring their alliance against Jorvik.
Ragnald is unwilling to face Ethelflaed. He fights the Scots
and Picts again at the Second battle of Corbridge. He wins
again but the numbers of his army is cut in half.
Edward fights the Danes in the east - Towcester, Bedford,
Wigingamere, Tempsford. He kills King Guthrum II at
Tempsford and all resistance in East Anglia collapses.
Ethelflaed's troops march into the Danish center at Derby and
take it.
All Danish leaders now submit to Edward and accept him as
their protector.
They are granted their estates and allowed to live according
to their Danish customs.

918: Edward builds a burh at Stamford. The Danes there submit
without a fight.
To the west, Ethelflaed marches into Leicester, where Danes
surrender without bloodshed, probably led by Danes seeking
support against the Norse threat from the west.
The last two Danish enclaves, Nottingham and Lincoln, fall
to the West Saxons by the end of summer, but Ethelflaed dies
on June 12, 918.

(Elfwynn, Traitor Queen)
The Mercian Witan gives the title of queen to the twenty year
old daughter of Ethelflaed - Elfwynn. Ambrose and Polonius
kidnap her during the winter. They return to rescue the boys
of the Royal School in the spring of 919.

919: Edward calls Elfwynn to his court and officially annexes
Mercia.

Edward moves his army to Gloucester and Betlic flees.
Ambrose and Polonius chase him northward. They fight on
the way, and Elfwynn finally kills Betlic.

Norse adventurer Ragnald storms York and establishes a line
of Norse kings.

During his reign he gives nominal allegiance to Edward, who
recognizes his new kingdom.

921: Edmund, son of King Edward, is born.

(Athelstan, First King of England)
924: There is a Mercian revolt in Chester. King Edward is killed at
Fardon-on-Dee. Mercia supports Athelstan as king. Wessex
supports Elfweard, his half-brother. Elfweard suddenly dies a
few months after his father.

925: Athelstan is finally crowned as king. He is crowned at Kingston-
upon-Thames, by Ayhelm, Archbishop of Canterbury. This is
the first time a Saxon king is crowned with a crown instead
of a helmet.

926: Athelstan arranges for his sister Edith to marry Sihtric of York.
They agree not to invade each other's territory and not to
support the other's enemies.

927: Sihtric dies. Cousin Guthfrith leads a fleet from Dublin to try
and take the throne. Athelstan captures York and receives the
submission of the Danes. (It is not known if he fought
Guthfrith). The Northumbrians are outraged at this
usurpation.

July, 927: at Eamont, King Constantine of Scotland (Alba), King
Hywel Ddn of Deheubarth, Ealdred of Bamburgh and King
Owain of Strathclyde accept Athelstan's overlordship, which
leads to seven years of peace. Athelstan is now the first king
of all the Anglo-Saxon people.

933: Prince Edwin drowns, possibly after a rebellion where someone
called Alfred attempts to blind Athelstan.

934: Athelstan invades Scotland, though the reasons are unclear. Sometime thereafter, Constantine of Scotland marries his daughter to the Norse king of Dublin.

937: The Norse king of Dublin, Olaf Guthfrithson, joins with the Scots and Strathclyde Britons under Owain to invade England in the fall. Ambrose meets with the Scottish king. The opposing armies meet at the Battle of Brunanburh. Athelstan wins an overwhelming victory, though he also takes heavy losses. Ambrose and Polonius die protecting the king.

939: (October) Athelstan dies.

(Edmund, King of England)
939: Edmund is proclaimed king. Crowned in November.

939-940: King Olaf III Guthfrithson conquers Northumbria and invades the Midlands. Conquers as far south as Watling Street.
Olaf marches south from York to Northampton. When that siege fails, he goes on to Tamworth, which he takes by storm. King Edmund besieges King Olaf and Archbishop Wulfstan at Leicester, but they escape by night. Battle is averted when Archbishops Oda and Wulfstan reconcile the two kings and a truce is concluded. Watling Street becomes the new boundary.

941: Olaf Guthfrithson raids Bernicia and dies shortly thereafter. Olaf Sihtricson succeeds him on the Northumbrian throne. He has his cousin Ragnall as co-ruler.

942: Edmund defeats Idwal of Gwynedd.
Edmund reconquers the Midlands.

943: Edmund becomes godfather of King Olaf Sihtricson of York.

944: Edmund reconquers Northumbria.
Edmund drives out of Northumbria both Olaf Sihtricson and Ragnall Guthfrithson.
Congalach Cnogba, High King of Ireland, sacks Dublin.

945: Edmund conquers Strathclyde, but cedes the territory to King Malcolm I of Scotland in exchange for a treaty of mutual support.
Blacaire of Dublin driven out by Olaf.

946: Edmund is killed in a brawl by an exiled thief named Leofa. Eadred, Edmund's brother, succeeds to the throne.

APPENDIX IV

A Map of Ambrose's Travels

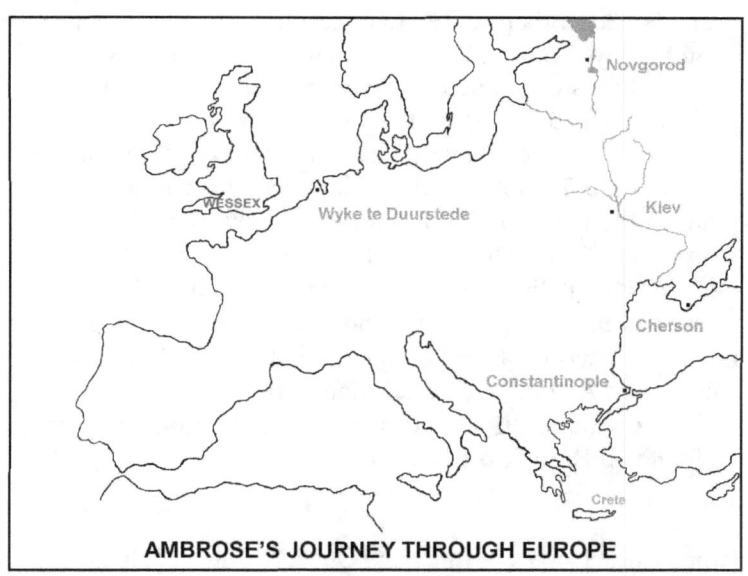

AMBROSE'S JOURNEY THROUGH EUROPE

APPENDIX V

About the Author

After counseling teenagers and adults for more than forty years, Bruce Corbett retired to concentrate on his writing and photography. To date, he has written a collection of Science Fiction short stories and two Science Fiction novels. The project closest to his heart, however, is his series of well-researched historical novels based on a family of fictional heroes, set in the time of Alfred the Great, his children and grandchildren. **Ambrose, Prince of Wessex, Trader of Kiev**, is the first in this series. This particular story borrows much of its timeline from **The Russian Primary Chronicles**. These novels are arguably the most comprehensive series of novels ever written based on the time of the Anglo-Saxon Chronicles. A complete description of the various novels, including samples, links and supplementary information, may be found on Bruce Corbett's web site:

Bruce Corbett lives in Pincourt, Quebec, Canada. He is an avid landscape and wildlife photographer, and is generally found reading anything historic. For more information, please go to

www.brucecorbett.com

APPENDIX VI

Other Fiction Books from the author.

In chronological order

HISTORICAL

The Ambrose Sagas
1. *Ambrose, Prince of Wessex; Trader of Kiev*
2. Ambrose, Prince of Wessex; Emissary to Byzantium
3. Ambrose, Prince of Wessex; Southern Journey
4. Ambrose, Prince of Wessex; Journey Home
5. Ambrose, Prince of Wessex; Warrior of the King
6. Ambrose, Prince of Wessex; Gretchen, Future Princess

The King Alfred Sagas
1. Alfred the Great; Viking Invasion
2. Alfred the Great; King's Revenge
3. Alfred the Great; Young Edward

The King Edward Sagas
1. Alfred the Great; Edward the King
2. Queen Ethelflaed; 'Lady of the Mercians' **2023 release**
3. Elfwynn, Traitor Queen of Mercia **2023 release**

The Anglo-Saxon Kings of all England
1. Athelstan, First King of England **2023 release**
2. Edmund, King of England. **2023 release**
3. King Edred of England **2024 release**

SCIENCE FICTION

Bruce Corbett's Speculative Short Stories
The Goldmines of Alpha Centauri **2023 release**
The Vuorran Pogrom **2023 release**

The complete Prince of Wessex Sagas are available as e-books or paperbacks from your favorite bookstore or worldwide from Amazon.

www.ingramcontent.com/pod-product-compliance
Lightning Source LLC
Chambersburg PA
CBHW071235250626
47163CB00001B/185